with ♡
Kate Spencer
x

Twelve Lessons Later

By Kate Spencer

Published by Katherine Spencer Publishing

ISBN: 978-0-9934416-2-2

Acknowledgements

This book was written during a house move and then what seemed like endless building work. The chaos around me reflected the chaos within me as I battled to get over the fear that Twelve Lessons Later might not be as good as Twelve Lessons.

I know how my first book changed lives all over the world, and a part of me was really worried about you not loving what happened next to Stephanie. For many of you she is the mirror in your life, and the hope and inspiration that things will come good, especially when you don't believe it yourself.

With a deep breath and a whole load of encouragement from the people around me, I rolled up my sleeves and got on with it. One day I will look back and wonder how I did it, I'm sure. Once I started it was like connecting with an old friend I hadn't seen in a long while, I hope you feel the same. Thank you for supporting me to support you. And thank you once again Stephanie for making me laugh, cry and want to write more.

Thank you to my husband Darren for sharing the journey, especially the detours, roundabouts and the bloody dead ends! I know I can count on you to always be there to support me, whatever that looks like in a given moment, and that means everything.

Thank you to my parents Pam & Graham for keeping me grounded and loving me through all of my human moments.

Thank you to my sister Emma who started this whole Twelve Lessons thing, you are the most inspiring person I know, fact.

To the two little ladies in my life that are growing so fast, Amy and Anna. One day you will read this book I hope and see why I was relentless about getting these lessons out there to the people that need them.

Love and gratitude to the friends that surround me and keep me sane (my version of sane). Amanda Fletcher, Jill Newton, Nicola Oliver, Rachel Noble, Jane Turner, Carrie Craig Gilby, Jennie Harrison, Sheena Waters, Anna Pereira, Anne Strojny, Margery Gledson and Jane Bland. You all know why you are mentioned and the part you play in my life, thank you for showing up and helping me.

Thank you again to Michelle Emerson the lovely lady that edits my books and puts up with my constant chopping and changing.

Thank you to Emma Holmes for your unwavering belief, tough love and constant cheerleading, and to Claire Mitchell for a dose of the same.

And thank you again to life for all of your lessons. It is because of you that I can write for others. **Love Kate x**

Chapter 1

"You're blooming!" said Sue as she threw her arms around me.

I hugged her momentarily before she stepped back and held both my hands at arm's length, fixing her gaze on my enormous bump.

"Blooming big you mean!" I puffed, getting my breath back from the stairs.

We both laughed and Sue led the way to the small and familiar room. The traffic noise wafted through the window, along with a slight breeze that I was grateful for, and the floral curtains brushed against the windowsill.

We small talked for a while, filling in some of life's blanks, until the conversation naturally turned to what the future may hold. Sue pulled up a chair opposite me, reaching for her well-worn cards.

"I won't say parenting is easy, Steph, but it's worth every second."

"I can't wait. But I do wish I could jump straight to the umbilical cord being cut," I said.

"It's natural for you to feel a little nervous the first time." Sue shuffled the cards as she spoke and I slipped my pumps off under the table, airing my feet and ankles.

"I just can't stop myself from watching those programmes on the television about childbirth. It's ridiculous when I know about Law of Attraction! I should be focussed on everything going smoothly instead of panicking along with the rest of them and stuffing in even more biscuits." I shook my head.

"As long as you remember that they choose the dramatic births that will pull in viewing figures, and in real life it's hardly ever like that," said Sue, still shuffling. "Have you started nesting yet? I had a friend that felt compelled to have such a clear out that her poor husband came home from work and had hardly any clothes left!"

"Crikey, I don't think Damien would be impressed with that!"

"Neither was Barry," laughed Sue and handed me the deck.

"Just focus on receiving what is right for you right now," Sue said and sat back in her chair. "And no, I'm not telling you if it's a girl or a boy!"

I closed my eyes and shuffled for a moment or two, remembering how anxious I was the first time I'd sat in this seat. So much had changed since then, and it was all going to change again any day now. The baby started to turn inside of me, new life that I would be bringing into the world. I placed a hand on my bump and smiled to myself. Not long now. Sue had entered *The Zone* as I was shuffling, and when I placed the cards on the table her eyelids fluttered.

"The first thing I get through for you is that you need to do all you can to stop being afraid."

I kept quiet as she drew a breath and exhaled slowly, fighting back the urge to giggle, which was better that the urge I had last time to shit myself or run.

"Afraid that is of things going wrong. Not during childbirth, although you are worried about that and every first-time mum is, but things going wrong in general. It seems that a part of you feels that this life you are living is too good to be true, that you maybe don't entirely deserve it, and that it could be taken away from you in any moment." She opened her eyes and stared right at me. "I call it The Push Away, others would say resistance."

I didn't know if I should speak or not, so I nodded.

"This happens when you ask for something from the universe and it's either manifesting in your experience or just about to, and the human part of you starts to go into fear."

"So you block it?" I asked.

"Yes. The fear creates an opposite vibration to the one that you were sending out, the one that has drawn the experience in," said Sue.

"But I love the life I have now," I said and shrugged my shoulders slightly.

"Yes, but there are aspects of it that you are fearful of losing. Remember that the universe responds to how you are *feeling*, it's the emotions and the feelings that set up the vibration and frequency that attract in a match."

"I'm not sure I get it," I said and shook my head.

"I know you love your life and you are grateful Steph, and that's all good. Don't go into fear of losing it, there is no reason why this is not the way things are now."

"Ah, ok. That's a relief."

"See?" said Sue. "You feel relief when I confirm that because it calms the part of you down that is in fear."

"Ah, right," I said as the penny dropped.

"And so it is," Sue replied and dealt six cards face-down in front of me. She turned the first card and the image was one of a large old book and a quill writing the word

Lessons across an open page. "I thought this one would come up for you," she said.

"This card has two messages for you, Stephanie. The first one is that there is going to be a lesson coming up for you soon…"

"I figured."

"BUT the lesson in your case is about knowing when a lesson is happening. You are at a point on your journey now where you need to be able to recognize the difference between random life events and lessons." Sue raised her eyebrows and waited for my confirmation.

"So how do you know?" I asked.

"Well, how can I put this… lessons feel different. They are often uncomfortable for a start, and there is often some kind of challenge or struggle involved."

"I thought I'd been through all of this, Sue. Can't I just have the good stuff now?" I said, somewhat deflated.

"Lessons are inevitable I'm afraid, as long as we are human. And when you are on a path of growth and enlightenment the universe keeps sending them to help you on your way."

"I don't think I can take anymore after the last twelve."

"But the gift in the lesson is always worth the lesson itself, that's the point of going through them," Sue reassured me. "Just look at the gifts you received last time."

I thought for a moment and felt my baby move again, right on cue. "Yes, of course you're right," I sighed. "I couldn't have the life I live now if I hadn't been through the learning."

"Exactly. So don't fear what's coming up, just know that you are now at the stage where you need to be able to recognize your own lessons as they appear in your life. You need to be able to step back from them and know that they hold the key to your growth and evolution, and that you're being sent what you need in any given moment."

"Even if it's really tough?"

"Those are the lessons that will accelerate you like nothing else. The bigger the lesson, the bigger the gift."

"Ok, I'll try to remember that when it's hitting the fan."

"That's why it is so important that you know it's a lesson coming up, you need to be able to detach yourself and not get sucked into any drama that is playing out around you. Look at the experience from a higher-self perspective and see past the behaviour and the human moments that we all love to whip up with our ego. You are more evolved than that now."

"I'll do my best," I said in a less-than-confident tone.

"It's going to take a while to master this one, and the rest actually," said Sue and continued quickly before I could object. "But don't worry about that, you need to have an overall intention that everything is happening perfectly, Stephanie, that it's all unfolding the way that it should be."

"So you mean these cards aren't for the next six months?" I asked.

"No, not this reading. There is no timeline here. It's about you learning what you need to at the right time for you, and that will vary depending on what you have going on in your life in that moment."

"So lesson one is about lessons, right?" I checked before I reached into my bag for a notebook and pen.

"Yes, but it's actually lesson thirteen," Sue corrected me.

"Ah yes! I've learned twelve so far." I opened the notebook at a clean page and started to write.

"You have, but you need to be mindful as well that lessons can come back again." Sue sat back in her chair and I looked up.

"You mean if you don't learn them?" I asked.

"Yes, if you don't learn them or work with them in your life then you can find that they come back up, and sometimes it's tricky to see them. Usually because the human side of us and our ego thinks that we have done this before and learned what we need to, so we become closed to learning anything else."

"Lesson One – Be Open to Possibility."

"Correct. And lessons sometimes have different layers to them Stephanie, different facets or aspects if you like."

"This is getting really complicated." I absent-mindedly tapped the pen on my teeth.

"It can be, but remember that you get what you believe, so thinking that it's going to be complicated will only make it so."

"You Are a Creator – Lesson Five."

"Yes, now see what just happened there?" Sue asked but continued before I could answer. "You are seeing the different lessons that are playing out at given times and how they overlap with each other to create a whole fabric of learning."

"Ok, I think I'm starting to understand," I said.

"You will, at the perfect time." Sue said as she reached for the second card.

"Be Present," she said.

"That doesn't sound so bad," I said scribbling it down.

"Well it's something that a lot of people struggle with Steph, it's actually quite a skill."

"How so?" I asked "I mean how hard can it be to show up and be present?"

"It's not just about showing up, it's about being really present in the now time, in *that* moment and all of you being there to experience it," Sue said.

"Like being fully in the moment?" I asked.

"Yes, and making sure that you are not allowing your mind or your consciousness to wander back into the past, into worry and old situations, and equally not spending time in the future, worrying about what may or may not happen or always wanting things to be ok one day."

"Ah right, I think I get it," I said "So wherever you are, make sure that you are there altogether and not distracted."

"Yes, but it's more than that. Have you had that experience where you are speaking to someone and you know that they are not really hearing what you are saying? I mean they might be listening but they are not *hearing.*"

I thought for a moment and recalled a conversation I'd had with Damien just before we left home, about dropping me off here and then picking me up again after his meeting, and how he'd spoken in all of the right places, but I knew his mind was on the agenda with the recruitment agency he had an appointment with.

"Yes, I get it now. And you've told me a bit about that before, about the present moment being where your power is and that it's important for attracting in what you want in your life."

"That's right, you need to be present when you work with Law of Attraction in order to create the frequency in the now time of what you want to draw into your experience. It's no good sending a message to the universe that says it's going to be ok in the future, or you will never experience the good stuff in the now." Sue looked at me and I confirmed my understanding with a nod as she turned the next card.

"Discernment," she said as I looked at the picture in her hand, showing someone waving to someone else. "This card is about discernment and being selective in relationships, and knowing that sometimes people move in and out of our lives for good reason."

"Is that the whole reason, season, lifetime thing?" I asked.

"Yes, in a nutshell I suppose it is. But it's also about being selective in the first place about who you allow into your energy, and about being ok about letting things drift when they need to." She continued, "And that is sometimes not so easy, when it involves friends or even family members."

"Oh?" I commented.

"When feelings and expectations are involved it's sometimes hard to detach, even though it is in your best interests. The thing to remember is that the more you evolve and heal and grow, the less resonance you might have with people that are not on that path. This can lead to you feeling that you don't have much in common anymore, or interactions can become uncomfortable."

As I scribbled in my notebook, Sue continued.

"Heal Yourself," she said as the next card showed a picture of a beautiful woman sitting peacefully and surrounded by a golden glow. "This card shows that you still have work to do to heal your old wounds."

Jay crossed my mind and I surprised myself with a shudder and a flashback to being on my knees in front of him in a nightclub toilet - my lowest point for sure.

Sue sensed this and reassured me "You have come such a long way Steph, in a really short time, and you should be really proud of yourself."

I suddenly felt teary, I had been on quite a journey for sure and maybe I didn't give myself the credit I ought to for getting this far. "I know you're right Sue. I still have moments where I don't feel worthy of Damien and I know it's a hangover from my past. It just sneaks up on me every now and then and I'm back there feeling needy and desperate and not good enough."

Sue passed me a tissue and I dabbed at my cheeks, not knowing why I had suddenly felt so overwhelmed, and putting it down to pregnancy hormones.

"This stuff can take a long time to heal Stephanie, and some people never do. Some people live their whole lives playing small and not feeling good enough because of something that has scarred them and made them feel unworthy." Her tone was compassionate and I felt her hand reach out for mine.

"You can do this, Steph," she said and I raised my chin. As my eyes met hers I felt that she could see into the depths of my soul.

"That means such a lot coming from you," I whispered.

"I believe in you." Sue smiled and I smiled back weakly. "Now you need to work on believing in yourself and healing those old wounds. Because as long as they are with you, Steph, they are active in your vibration and your energy field."

"And good old Law of Attraction will deliver me a version of what I am sending out there?"

"Exactly."

"There is no way I want to go through any of that again," I said shaking my head. "I'm going to work on that for sure." Sue smiled and although she didn't say it, I knew she felt proud of me for starting to bring it all together.

"Drama Queen," she said as the next card showed a theatrical set with someone in an over-the-top costume, in front of an audience. "Don't be dragged into the drama of what is playing out in human or earthly terms if you can help it. Step back, take a breath and look at the situation from a more evolved perspective. That goes for your own drama or someone else's, because other people's dramas can suck you in."

"I know people like that!" I commented as my mother entered my mind, and Sue turned over the next card which would represent lesson eighteen.

Sue laughed as she explained the meaning of the next card which showed a picture of someone dragging a heavy load up a hill and the description said Burden.

"I like to call this one The Shit Cart." I laughed too and wondered what on earth she could mean. "This card is about you dragging someone else's shit cart. Honestly, there is just no other way to put it, really, Steph!"

"Well you certainly don't need to explain that in detail, I definitely get the idea!"

"I'm glad you do, sometimes when it comes out it's for someone all serious and I'm dying to laugh! Anyway it's got two meanings really, and I like to think of it this way. Everyone has a cart that they drag up the hill called life, and as we go through our stuff we tend to fill it up with all kinds of stuff that we are not ready to get rid of or process, and it slows down our progress hugely..."

"With all of the shit that we can't resolve?" I asked and laughed.

"Yes!" Sue snorted. "Exactly that!"

"So it's a bit like Lesson Four, Old Stuff Keeps You Stuck?"

"Yes, because whatever is in that cart is also in your vibration and you will attract more in, or a version of that stuff in..."

"More shit?" I asked and we both knew that we had lost all chance of this being serious as we laughed and laughed.

Sue eventually composed herself and took a breath. "When this card comes up in a reading it's about you sorting out your own stuff, releasing what you don't need, healing your wounds and cleaning up your vibration but it's also about other people as well..."

"Other people's shit cart?" I asked in a mock serious tone and we both collapsed in giggles again.

"Yes actually, other people's burdens are not for you to carry. When you take on other people's stuff and try to resolve it for them, you are actually being unkind to them and yourself."

"Unkind?" I asked, surely it was selfless to help people with their shit?

"Yes. Think of it this way, everyone comes here to earth as a soul with their own stuff to experience and learn whilst they are here in human form. So that means that everyone has unique lessons that they are going through in their life in order to evolve, and if someone steps in and shortcuts this lesson, or stops you from learning it, then it's not learned and experienced for you."

"So it comes back?" I asked.

"Yes, often it will, or an aspect of it will come back, or maybe that person will just stay stuck in their own stuff and be disempowered because they don't know how to move forward themselves," Sue said.

"But is it not mean to see someone struggle and not help them, though? I mean that's not exactly spiritual?" I asked.

"You are right, Steph, and there is a very subtle difference here. When this lesson comes up for you it's important to know that you can support someone and give them guidance and signposting, but always do this in a way that you feel will empower them and help them to sort out their own stuff. It's the difference between buying a man a fish and showing him how to make a net, see?"

"I think so. It's a bit like lesson nine, You Can't Fix Other People."

"A little like that, yes. That's also about allowing people to take responsibility for themselves, without you judging the outcome or taking any ownership of what they do or don't do… knowing that it's their stuff really. This lesson is more about you not taking other people's stuff on and sorting it out for them."

"Ok, so what do you mean by signposting?" I asked.

"Showing them the way to be able to sort it out for themselves. This could be giving them good advice, connecting them with a service they need or a professional person, buying them a book you know will help, or making suggestions and being supportive. You can do all of those things without actually getting involved in their stuff and doing it for them."

"Right, and dragging their shit around." I laughed again.

"Exactly!" laughed Sue "We all need to sort our own shit cart out and let other people sort theirs."

"And I need to get Jay out of mine," I said.

"You do, and once you have you will feel so much lighter and life will flow better for you, Steph. But don't beat yourself up, it's a journey and it is going to happen when the time is right. Big stuff is never easy to move on from, and that goes for us all. This lesson will go hand in glove for you with healing those old wounds."

"You're right," I sighed, knowing that even when the healing was done there would likely be battle scars that would always be a weak spot. "I have to go easy on myself."

"Yes, because if you start to beat yourself up about it then you will create more resistance. Remember Lesson Eight, Compassion and Forgiveness. You need to apply this to yourself as well as others." Sue smiled and concluded the reading by saying, "We all do the best we can, Steph."

"And when we know better we do better," I added. "And hopefully I know better now."

Sue returned the cards to the deck and folded them back into the silk patterned scarf I knew kept them safe.

"Thank you. That's plenty to be going on with," I said and closed the notebook. "How long will it take me to get through them?"

"That's unwritten as yet," said Sue. "It depends on different factors, it could be months or it could even be years."

"Years?"

"Well maybe a couple. You've got to get through them so that you can include them in your book."

"Oh yes, the book," I said tentatively, although it sounded like a great idea in principle I had no idea where the time to write it was going to come from, especially with more lessons and a baby due any day.

"How long is it going to take me to write a book and get it published?" I sighed. "Are you sure it's me that's meant to be sharing them?"

"All I get through is that it's going to happen at the perfect time Steph, and that being impatient will delay things."

"That's a lesson in itself right there."

"Maybe there are things that have to happen before you get lined up with the right people?"

"Like what?"

"That's for you to find out!" laughed Sue. "Remember, this next chapter is all about you recognizing the lessons and going through them yourself. It's about you being more empowered and applying what you have learned so far."

"I might not like flying solo!" I objected.

"You won't be, but the message is loud and clear from your guides, the universe or whomever you believe in. This is time for you to be more tuned into your own journey. I'll be your safety net and if anything doesn't make sense or you find yourself in a pickle you can come back, but this next step is for you to take."

I sighed and patted my bump. "Next time I see you I might not be alone."

"I'm sure you won't be," said Sue and I heard a car honking from the street below.

"That might be Damien," I said, using the edge of the table to heave myself up before looking at my watch.

"Good luck, Steph. It's all going to be fine with the birth so you don't need to worry," Sue hugged me tight.

"Really?" I asked.

"Really," she said. "It's going to happen perfectly, although at the time it might not be *your* version of perfect, just know that it's all fine. And before you leave I'm being asked to tell you that no matter what anyone else says it *is* going to be fine. You have to remember that everyone has had a different experience and they don't necessarily know about the way energy works, so they go into the situation in fear and expecting the worst."

"And then they draw it in?" I asked.

"Yes, but you know better so you can do better. Get aligned with the experience that you want and don't let other unconscious people knock you off your perch. It really is going to be fine, I promise you."

"Thank you Sue, I have been worried," I admitted.

"I know you have, love, that's why this is coming through for you." Sue squeezed my hand and then allowed her palm to float above my bump for a second.

"Can't wait to be here, this little soul is really excited about coming to earth." She smiled and closed her eyes. "You've been chosen and so has Damien, just like all babies choose their parents… but this little one is going to be different to others, in ways that you will find out when they get here. They had to come to someone *awake* they are saying, because they will need to be raised consciously." She paused and took a deep breath. "And you need to go home and pack your hospital bag, they'll be here sooner than you think… and no they won't say whether they are a girl or a boy!" Sue snapped back to reality as the car horn sounded again.

"I should go," I said. "I'll let you know when the baby comes, and I'll pack my bag this afternoon."

"Yes, I would if I were you," said Sue as I stuffed my notebook into my handbag and turned to waddle towards the door.

Chapter 2

"Well?" Damien asked as I opened the car door.

"Not that much really. More lessons and knowing when lessons come up really." I pulled out as much seatbelt as I could to get over my bump.

"But nothing bad though?" he asked distractedly as he indicated to get back into the traffic flow.

"No, nothing bad. But apparently I do need to pack my hospital bag soon. Baby is going to come earlier than expected."

"We've got four weeks yet!" He waved to the bus driver that had flashed him out.

"Not according to Sue, and she's never been wrong yet."

"Well you'd better get packing after this midwife thing then."

"I will, maybe after a lie down, I'm so tired. Sue said that the birth was all going to go well by the way and that I shouldn't worry."

"And she's never been wrong yet." Damien reached over and patted my bump.

"You can never get a space round here."

"Just pull in and drop me off, it's fine," I said, reaching over to unfasten my seatbelt.

"Are you sure?"

"Of course I'm sure, it's only going to be ten minutes on panting, pushing and gas and air."

Damien indicated left and kissed my cheek when the car came to a stop. "OK then, I'll get parked down the road, ring me when you are done and I'll come back up."

"Just have a coffee at the café on Bridge Street while I'm going through the gory details."

"Thank God for that, do you need a push to get out?" he sniggered.

"I'll get you back for that! I'll have you know I am blooming."

"I agree, blooming big."

The automatic door swooshed open for me and warm air mixed with piped music wafted in my direction. I approached the reception desk and checked in for the midwife, she tapped my details on the keyboard and told me to take a seat.

The waiting room was standard magnolia, with a rack full of leaflets ranging from athlete's foot to dementia and everything in between. I reached for a magazine and started thumbing through it, wondering how on earth celebrities managed to look so groomed and slim during pregnancy? I felt like a house end and with only a few weeks to go, the fear that I was going to have to push this baby out was looming. No matter how many times I heard it was the most natural process in the world, the only comment that stuck was Asha telling me it's like shitting a melon.

Stop thinking that! I said to myself. *It's all going to happen perfectly, it IS happening perfectly.*

"Is it your first?" a stranger spoke.

"Oh, erm yes… and you?"

"Not likely she's been round the block more times than you've had hot dinners!" a woman snorted next to her.

"Shut it, Sylvia, or we'll talk about why you're here!" she retorted.

"I was only joking, there's no need for that," Sylvia mumbled.

"And there's no need for you to be here if you'd used that cream and kept yourself to yourself," the first lady stage whispered and her friend glared.

She turned back to me. "Anyway love, is that your birth plan?"

I had an envelope folder on my knee containing all of the forms that I'd filled out since my first appointment. Damien and I had gone over the birth plan last night and I'd tucked it into the front, ready to discuss.

"Yes, today's the day to go through it all before the big push!" I laughed nervously and thought about the melon again.

"Water birth is it?" she asked and her friend sniggered.

I had no idea what could be funny about that. "Yes actually, how did you know?"

"It's the in thing now, everyone seems to want a water birth for their first one, along with the mood music, reflexology and nothing else but gas and air…"

"I must be so predictable, that's exactly what I've written down." I felt a bit embarrassed and really wanted my name to be called. These two might be from the school of hard knocks but I wasn't. I wanted it to be a wonderful experience and so did Damien. They could mind their own business. Sue had told me to ignore other people's opinions, and that advice couldn't have been more timely or relevant right now.

"Well pet, it usually starts all hearts and flowers and before you know it it's backside over elbow, and your legs up in stirrups while you're shouting at him for getting you into this mess." They both cackled at their hilarious comment, and I gulped.

"They still have stirrups?" I asked in a quiet voice.

"Don't worry. If they aren't quick enough to get you tied in they'll just get a couple of doctors to hold your legs and look up your flue while you push," said Sylvia, and her friend agreed.

"There's no dignity in having a baby."

"You're right, Denise."

"I mean look at that girl up your street, what was her name again…? We used to call her Shrek, no one knew how on earth she'd fallen pregnant…" Sylvia was on a roll now and the room seemed to be getting hotter.

"Or who he was," Denise chipped in to fill in the blanks.

"She had a rough time of it mind, what with the escalator and all that, and once they'd managed to stop it they still couldn't get that smocky dress pulled out of the teeth so they had to rip it, and by then there was a crowd."

"Well what do you expect? No one goes on like that shouting and wailing when their waters break. If she hadn't been so dramatic and leaned over the side she wouldn't have got tangled up." Sylvia shook her head at the ridiculousness.

"Still, it's not right having to walk the length of the shopping centre with your backside hanging out of maternity knickers just because there was no wheelchair… and it's not like things looked up much." Denise let the statement hang in the air for a few moments as her and Sylvia exchanged a knowing look.

"What happened?" I asked quietly.

"Well, she'd been going on about a water birth," Denise continued.

"You could say she nearly got one," Sylvia said.

"More like 'over the water birth' really."

"The traffic was gridlocked because of the football and the roadworks. They couldn't get her to hospital in time, so she had him in the ambulance."

"On the city bypass, on the bridge over the river."

I could feel myself getting a little dizzy, the air felt thick and hot and stale and I clutched my birth plan tighter. "Really?" I asked wide-eyed and worried.

"And they had nothing to give her for the pain, which must have been awful. Quite honestly that kid's got the biggest head I've ever seen…" As Sylvia spoke I started to fan myself with the folder and unfastened the top button of my linen maternity shirt.

"Twenty-eight stiches she needed and that cognitive behavioural therapy for the trauma. I heard she's got a claim in."

"What the hell for?" asked Denise.

Sylvia lowered her voice, which was ironic since there was only the three of us there. "Well, she must have, you know *followed through* shall we say and apparently the ambulance driver opened the back door and chucked it out! White van man and his pals behind started honking the horn and cheering her on when he saw her flat on her back with her legs in the air, and nothing left to the imagination…..apparently that's post-traumatic stress nowadays… and she can't get over it."

"*She* can't get over it, poor bloke if you ask me he should be claiming against her," Denise said as I felt myself digging my nails into my palms.

She looked at me and registered my horror. Her tone changed and became far more upbeat as she patted my knee. "Don't look scared love, things like that don't happen very often. Usually it's all straightforward. Having a baby is the most natural thing in the world."

An uncomfortable silence descended apart from generic panpipe music in the background. I tried to relax and focus on my breathing, reflecting on what Sue had said about being present and not going back over old stuff or forwards into fear. I was allowing other people to drag me into an energy that I didn't want, and I needed to bring myself back to the present moment and get aligned with the outcome that I wanted once more.

I was abruptly brought back to reality, as in an effort to change the subject Sylvia asked,

"Have you got your bag packed yet, love?"

Signs & Serendipity.

"I'm doing that this afternoon," I mumbled. I really didn't want to talk to them anymore and I fiddled with my sleeve trying to see my watch. How much bloody longer was this going to take? I seriously might have to go and stand outside and get some air. The receptionist could shout out of the door when my turn arrived. I could be present on the road side a whole lot easier than in here. I just wanted to talk about my fabulous birth plan with my lovely midwife and get back to Damien, who probably thought I had eloped by now. This had to be a lesson coming up. It certainly ticked the box labelled extremely uncomfortable. I tried to sit back and breathe, to work out what the universe was trying to show me, but all I could think of was 'avoid idiots.'

"Well, you want to hurry up, how many weeks are you now?" Denise just wouldn't let it go.

"Thirty-two."

"Well, don't forget to pack some food. Not for him for you, you look like you like your food," Sylvia chipped in.

"Right," I said through my teeth and forced smile.

"You'll need some calories if you're in labour for a couple of days, love. I mean I've always been lucky. It's like shelling peas and they said this time I'll have to call the ambulance as soon as I get a twinge, but some people are at it for days." Denise really should approach the charm school for a refund.

"Slow labour they call it."

Shut up Sylvia ran through my head as I tried desperately to remember what had Sue said about discernment. I could feel myself starting to choke back tears, my mood had been all over the place this last two weeks and it took nothing to set me off. I'd been fine when I left Sue, and she had promised everything would be ok, so I just needed to believe that.

I took a deep breath and said, "Well, it'll probably all be straightforward," hoping that was an end to the conversation.

"That's what they all say, then the pain starts and you've got no idea what's going to happen next."

Seriously Sylvia could you piss off?

"They don't feed you once you're in there, in case you need an emergency caesarean. You'll be Hank Marvin if you've been struggling on for 72 hours, nil by mouth," she said trying to be helpful.

A welcome break in the conversation opened and I sighed, shifting position in the chair to see if I could relieve the dull ache in my back. I closed my eyes and tried to relax into the plinky plonky piano that was tinkling quietly through the speakers now.

"It's no wonder they used to eat the afterbirth." The voice cut through the momentary peace like a rat up a spout.

I couldn't help the vomit suddenly rising in my throat, or the accompanying retching sound.

"I know, I don't even think Jamie Oliver could do much with that, have you seen the size of it? You could feed a family of four for a week. Apparently it's just like liver," Sylvia's voice announced loud and clear from behind *Woman's Own*.

I retched again and started looking around for the toilets, or a wastepaper bin, anything really.

"You alright, love? You look a bit pale now, maybe you need some air," Denise asked and started fanning me with a leaflet about verrucas.

"No, honestly I'm fine it's just the thought of…" I retched again.

"Oh, I know it's awful, but I mean people eat those donner kebabs you know, and who knows what's in them." Denise wouldn't let it go, and in an effort to make things better, made them a whole lot worse.

"I think I'm going to faint." I could feel my face draining and the room started to spin a little.

"Hang on, I think I've got some chocolate, it's your blood sugar. You need to be a grazer when you're on the hefty side like you. *You've* got a high metabolism. Have they checked your thyroid?" She started rummaging in an oversized leather handbag; it boasted Gucci on the tag but looked anything but.

"No, honestly I couldn't eat anything, I feel sick…" I objected and wondered if the receptionist would come through if I shouted for help.

"I don't believe it," Sylvia said with conviction.

"What's wrong with you?" Denise said, getting annoyed now.

"I recognise that mullet."

"What are you on about, Sylvia?"

"That's him!" Sylvia said.

"No, not Peter the Pole? Oh, Sylvia, I think he might be here for the same thing as you… I mean he looks… itchy, unless he's just really embarrassed and that's why he's squirming all over the place…"

In a blink, Sylvia stood up and darted behind the information leaflets, there was the sound of a door slamming.

"I'm going to be sick…" I said, cupping my hand under my chin and gagging again.

"You'll have to hang on, love she's locked herself in the loo. There's no way she could face him after last Friday. Hang on I'll see if I've got a carrier bag." Her hand went back into the depths of her bag and started rooting around for a something plastic that crinkled.

I took another deep breath and fanned my face again, blinking back tears now. How could this have gone so horribly wrong? Maybe I should just go now and re-arrange the appointment on the phone. Yes that's what I should do, once I was outside in the air I could phone Damien and he would come and collect me. I could have a lie down and pull myself together.

"No bag, but I've got a pork pie if that's any good? Sometimes a lining on your stomach helps with sickness, the date's not up until tomorrow." She used her fingernail to pick at the thin plastic covering with a 69p price mark. She peeled back the wrapper to expose the brown pastry crust and a waft of its warm contents caught in my nostrils.

"It smells fine," she said taking a sniff herself. "There you go, that'll sort you out."

Before the sentence had finished, it had finished me off. I couldn't hold back any more and as the door opened and a friendly round face looked out and called for "Stephanie Anderson", I had puked.

"Too late, what a shame it looks like an expensive top. Is it dry clean only?" Denise asked as she shuffled along a seat.

The midwife looked at me covered in vomit and crying, her sympathetic tone made me feel even worse. "Oh dear, what's happened to you?"

"I just came over a bit funny." I managed to sob.

"Don't mind if I open a window do you it's a bit whiffy." Denise stood up and started eating the pork pie whilst reaching up and opening the window behind us.

Oh, God No! I thought as I retched again, watching her stuff more or less the whole thing in at once.

"I don't even like pork pies, all I wanted was a chat about my birth plan and now you can hardly read it, it's all smudged," I cried as the midwife led me into her consultation room.

"It's your hormones, love. We all feel a bit teary when we're expecting, would you like a glass of water?" she said and I nodded. "It can be overwhelming, let's get you cleaned up and settled down. It's normal to overreact when you're pregnant."

"All I wanted was a water birth and some reflexology," I stammered through tears.

"Good luck, love!" shouted Denise and then said to the midwife. "She's a bit highly strung, I had one like that in the bed next to me last time, you know the type… nothing but gas and air."

The midwife nodded her head and agreed, "First timers can be a bit flaky. I'll keep an eye on her."
Then she spoke to me in an overly cheery voice, "Come on, love, pull yourself together and let's go through this plan of yours. Water birth you said?" and pulled the door shut.

Stephanie's Journal ~ Lesson 13
Life & Soul Lessons

Knowing that something is a lesson, is a lesson in itself. I need to be able to feel the difference in my life when things play out that are coming my way to help me to grow, learn and expand. They will have a different energy about them, and I need to be open to signs that the universe wants me to see, in order to recognize what I need to do. Getting sucked into the human drama of a situation will not serve me, I need to step back and breathe, connect with a higher-self perspective and then look for the essence of the lesson. Lessons can often be shared with other people and there may be a soul contract in place for this, as you help each other to grow... but the chances are it won't feel like it at the time! The trick is to remember that it's a lesson, and ultimately it will work in your favour. The greater the lesson, the greater the gift.

"Some people come in our life as blessings, some people come in as lessons." Mother Teresa

Chapter 3

"I'm sorry Steph, I know I shouldn't laugh but you have to admit that it is hilarious," Damien chuckled as he handed me a cup of tea.

"It might be funny for you, but I was the one sitting there puking on myself." I blew away some of the steam and took a sip. "God knows what the midwife will think now."

"She'll think you are going to be a nightmare." He laughed again and I shook my head.

"I know! I hope I she isn't on duty when I get booked in."

"I'm sure she's quite used to handling difficult patients." Damien raised one eyebrow and waited for me to react.

"I'm not difficult!" I shouted, throwing a cushion in his direction and laughing too. "I was bloody well organized and fine until Sylvia and her friend started. I mean for God's sake who wouldn't feel sick talking about cooking a placenta while she was wafting a warm pork pie in your face?"

"I take your point," said Damien, shaking his head. "But they were right about one thing, you have to pack your hospital bag."

"I will! But I really could do with a lie down first."

I stopped on the landing to catch my breath before the next short flight of stairs to our bedroom.

"Are you ok?" asked Damien carrying a mug of tea in each hand as I cradled my bump and sighed.

"Yes, I think so, I'm just exhausted. It's tiring growing a baby, you know."

"It's going to be even more tiring in a couple of weeks." He walked behind me as I heaved one leg and then the other up the remaining steps, whilst leaning on the bannister.

"For both of us that is, not just me!" I sat on the bed and Damien put my tea beside me, but I wasn't going to finish it, I'd come over quite nauseous.

"You know that's what I meant. I can't wait for this baby and I'm going to be as hands on as possible," he said as he lay down beside me and spooned into my back. I felt his hands span over my bump and the baby inside me kicked. We both laughed and Damien nuzzled the back of my neck. You know those perfect moments you see in movies that you think are totally unrealistic for regular people? Well they're not. I know because this was one, and as I allowed myself to drift off to sleep in the arms of the man I loved and I felt my baby move, I knew that things couldn't really get much better. Maybe I could master being present after all if this is what it could feel like.

I don't know what time it was when I felt Damien stir, but the light had changed in the room and the sun had moved around to the front of the house. It cast orange stripes on the white walls through the wooden blinds, and the first thing I felt was a dull pain in my lower back.

"Steph, Steph, wake up!" I heard in a loud whisper and felt Damien gently shake my shoulder.

"What? What is it?" I asked trying to turn onto my side.

"Either you've pissed the bed or your waters have broken."

Just then the pain in my back worsened and I felt what I guessed was a contraction, I drew a sharp breath and opened my eyes wide.

"Oh, bloody hell I think it's started!" I said with fear rising in my tone.

"Don't panic!" said Damien and promptly started panicking.

"Where's that bloody hospital bag anyway?" he said and started to open drawers and cupboard doors. "And where's that list of stuff we need to take? We should have done this weeks ago now. You're going to end up having it in a bloody layby!"

"Calm down, we'll get there on time, it's just the start." I groaned as I tried to sit up and realised that I was, in fact, soaking wet from the waist down.

Damien had found the small black suitcase on wheels and was throwing in random items.

"I need a bath or something…" I said as Damien ran past me with my hairdryer.

"A bath? Have we got time for that?" he stopped and held it arm's length looking like a police speed trap.

"I'll have to Damien, I'm soaking!" I made to stand up and fell back onto the bed with a whimper. I closed my eyes and heard the hairdryer hit the polished wood floor.

"Steph, are you ok? Should I call an ambulance?" Damien kneeled at the bedside and squeezed my hand.

"I'm ok, I'm just having a baby." I said and as the pain rippled through my abdomen and I breathed out slowly. I opened my eyes and Damien looked like a deer in headlights.

"I'm fine!" I laughed, nervously. "This is what's meant to happen, remember what they said at the class?"

"I only came to the one where they talked about breast feeding! I missed this bit!"

"You're talking through your teeth, Damien. Relax, I went to this one and this is perfectly normal I promise." I cupped his face in my hands and kissed his forehead. "We're having a baby!"

He relaxed his shoulders a little and placed both hands on my bump.

"Dad to bump, dad to bump, come in bump…" he pressed his lips on my stretchmarked belly and chuckled nervously.

"The list for the hospital bag is stapled to the birth plan." I said.

"The one you puked on?"

"The very same."

"Right, I'll just be a minute, are you ok?" I nodded and he got to his feet, I heard the sound of water running in the bathroom and footsteps on the stairs. Damien came back and folded over the damp front page at arm's length, and then set about gathering tiny vests and first size nappies, muttering under his breath about muslin cloths. I managed to stand up and start to peel off the linen trousers that were sticking to my thighs, and with a wriggle and a jiggle they fell to my feet and I stepped out. I started to waddle to the bathroom.

"Will you help me get this top off please?" I asked and Damien slipped his hands under the hem and undressed me.

"Are you sure a bath is a good idea?" he asked, stuffing my slippers into the case.

"It's what they tell you to do, remember I was at the class!" I continued down the landing towards the bathroom.

"It's just that you haven't had a bath for a couple of weeks and you're much bigger now." He shouted from the bedroom "I'm just concerned that I might not be able to lift you out."

"Thanks a bunch." I snapped back. "I'm pregnant, not morbidly obese you know!"

"I didn't mean it like that, Steph, you know that. I'm just saying that the baby puts on a lot of weight towards the birth and you've got much bigger in the last fortnight, and you struggled to get out of the bath two weeks ago, didn't you?"

I gripped the roll top of the cast iron bath tightly as pain shot across my back, and hoped that the sound of the cascading water would drown out the whimper that escaped from my lips. This was only the beginning of labour, and it was going to get a whole lot worse. After the pain had passed I swished the water around with my hand and unfastened my bra, then rolled down my sopping wet knickers, flicking them into the corner of the room with my foot.

I carefully supported myself with one hand on the tiled wall and gently lowered myself into heaven.

"Too late, I'm in now," I shouted and turned on the hot tap again with my big toe. The relief was immediate, and I knew that when the next contraction came in a few minutes time that it wouldn't feel so bad. I felt my baby move and looked down at my huge belly, feeling panic rise a little.

"It's all going to be perfect," I said out loud to myself and The Universe, although there was a part of me that didn't feel it. I knew that giving birth was the most natural thing in the world, but right now I wished I hadn't watched so many reality shows where it had all gone horribly wrong. Sue had told me it was going to be fine and she had been bang on with everything else, so I just needed to relax and enjoy the experience…

"I'll put the bags in the car," Damien said as he passed the bathroom door and made his way downstairs. "Then I'll help you out and we'll get to hospital."

"Ok, I'm fine in here, take your time." I winced a little and formed an O shape with my mouth to breathe more slowly. "I wonder if you are a girl or a boy?" I whispered as I closed my eyes and relaxed into the steaming water. The silence was shattered by the heavy old Victorian front door slamming hard and I jumped. As the worst case scenario ran through my head, I heard the letterbox flapping insanely and Damien's voice shouting up the stairs.

"Steph! Steph! Are you ok? I'm bloody well locked out!"

"Damien? What's happened? Are you there?" I shouted back and my voice echoed around me.

"I'm bloody well locked out Steph, the wind caught the door and my keys are inside on the table, I can see the bastards from here!"

"Locked out?" I shrieked "What the hell are we going to do now?"

"I don't know, will your mother be in? She's got a spare."

"How will you get there you moron your car keys are inside!"

"I'll ring a taxi!"

"Have you got your phone?"

"Erm… no actually."

"For Christ's sake, Damien!" I could feel tears welling up of both anger and fear and I tried to sit up. I heaved myself into something near a sitting position and a tsunami of water poured onto the tiled floor.

"I'll get in, don't panic!" He yelled in the most panicked tone I had ever heard and then the letterbox flapped shut.

"Damien? Damien? Don't leave me!" I wailed and had to grab both sides of the bath as the next contraction started. As lessons go this was becoming rather a worry. The longest two minutes passed as I sat nipple deep in hot water, crying my eyes out and praying that he would come back. Then I couldn't help but bursting out laughing, probably hysteria, and there was no one around to slap me. I'd wanted a water birth and it looked like I was going to get one after all, that sure is a lesson in being specific when it comes to Law of Attraction.

"Steph! I'm back! Are you alright?"

"Damien, what do you think? I'm going to give birth to our child on my own in the bath! Do you think I'm alright with that?"

"It's going to be ok. I went into Mrs. Dawson's next door and rang for an ambulance."

"I don't need an ambulance I need you to get me out of the bath!"

"It's ok I explained you are stuck and they are sending the fire brigade as well."

"The fire brigade?" I shrieked.

"Yes they'll be here soon. Oh, and an ambulance."

"What about the coast guard?" I yelled back.

"I don't know what to say about that really, I hope you're being sarcastic because you're angry. Look try to relax if you can and I'll see if I can get in anywhere."

"Don't go, Damien!" I sobbed.

"I'm not going, I'm just looking to see if I can get in anywhere!" his voice softened. "I'll smash a window if they're more than five minutes, ok?"

"Ok," I said half-heartedly, knowing full well that there was no way he'd be able to wedge open the double-glazed sash windows and climb through. The place was like a fortress since Mrs Dawson had been burgled and the neighbourhood watch had recommended upping security.

I tried to focus on my breathing and everything unfolding perfectly, but the more I tried the more the voices from earlier in the day came back to me, laughing about the poor woman that had her baby in the ambulance, oh and shat herself…

"Why am I focussing on that for God's sake?" I shouted to no one in particular. "I believe in the bloody Law of Attraction! I don't want to shit myself in the back of an ambulance!"

What on earth could the lesson be in this situation? I had absolutely no idea, but I did know that the contractions seemed to be getting closer together and the bath water was now lukewarm. I turned on the hot tap again and closed my eyes tight.

"All is unfolding perfectly," I started to affirm and tried to align with the feeling of holding my new-born baby in my arms and shift my focus from the horrendous thought of having him or her on my own, in the bath.

"I'm back, Steph, are you there?" I heard Damien yelling on the doorstep again.

"Erm, let me see… of course I am still bloody here!" I shouted back. "How long will they be Damien? I need to get to hospital…"

"Are you having contractions?" he asked.

"Yes of course I am! And they are bloody painful as well, I need to get to hospital!"

"They won't be long, I'm sure they'll be here any minute..." his voice trailed off and I felt everything around my belly button clench.

"Agggggghhhh!" I shouted. "They're getting worse, I don't know how much more I can take here!"

"Is it meant to happen this fast?" Damien shouted. "Did they mention this in the class?"

"Never mind the class, Damien! They didn't have a week on getting trapped in your bath and your husband locking his bloody self out, you know. This is not exactly happening the way I thought it would!" The phone started to ring out shrill and loud in the hallway, after four rings I heard my own voice telling the caller that we were unavailable and they could leave a message after the tone.

I heard my mother asking me if there was anything I wanted from Sainsbury's and the lunatic in me started shouting, "Mum! Mum! Help! I'm stuck in the bath!"

"She can't hear you!" said Damien.

"Thank you, Captain Obvious shouting through the bloody letterbox!" I screeched.

Then in the distance I heard the wailing of a siren.

"Steph, I think they're coming… hold on..." the letterbox snapped shut and I imagined that Damien was running to the end of the terrace to flag down the emergency services. Sure enough a different voice came onto the letterbox line and started to ask me if I was ok.

"No I'm not!" I shouted back.

"They know that love, they mean are you ok?" said Damien in the background.

"I'm still bloody not ok! I'm trapped in a roll top bath, like a beached whale, in labour with what feels like the biggest baby in the world who's desperate to make an appearance!"

"How far apart are your contractions, Stephanie?" Voice number one was back.

"I don't know, there's no clock in here but they feel like they are getting closer," I yelled.

"How long has she been in there?" I overheard a woman.

"I don't know exactly, maybe about half an hour, or maybe longer?" said Damien.

"I've topped it up with hot water three times," I shouted, but I was starting to feel faint, I hadn't eaten since the vomiting incident.

"We're going to break in Stephanie, there's going to be a loud noise, ok?" voice one said.

I heard a collective mumbling and then a series of loud thuds as they broke down the door, the finale was one loud bang as it swung open and hit the wall. Footsteps rushed towards me and Damien threw a towel over me before the midwife and two men in uniform bustled in.

"Ok, ok." said the woman who I seemed to remember from antenatal class "Can you two just wait out there on the landing please, I'll shout if I need you." They nodded and moved out of the room as Damien knelt beside me and cradled my head.

"I'm feeling faint," I said.

"I'm Carrie," said the woman. "One of the community midwives. We need to get you out of there."

No shit. I said to myself and wondered if I had enough strength left to haul myself out if Damien helped me.

"I want to see how dilated you are first, if you don't mind?" said Carrie snapping on white latex gloves and indicating to Damien that he might want to leave the room.

"Oh, right," he said and blushed a little.

I heard Damien's weak attempt at small talk with the paramedics in the background as the midwife rolled up her sleeve and water sloshed up to her elbow.

"Just try to relax," she said as I gritted my teeth and let out a moan.

"That's good," she said standing up from a crouch. "You're doing well, about two centimetres I'd estimate."

"Only two?" I shrieked. "I'm going to need an epidural!"

"Was that in your birth plan?" asked Carrie, in a tone that said she knew fine well it wasn't.

"No, but I didn't know it would hurt this much," I whimpered, hoping for the sympathy vote.

She crouched down again, and touched my arm. "You're going to be fine, love. We'll get you some gas and air in the ambulance and that will really take the edge off it. Have you been to the antenatal classes at the community centre?"

"Yes, a couple of them."

"Good, well you'll know what to expect and how to breathe through the contractions? You've had a fright and you probably aren't as far on as you thought so we've got plenty of time."

"Yes I remember the breathing."

"And I bet you've been watching everything you can about childbirth on the television?" she smiled and I smiled back, my fear started to dissolve.

"Yes." I laughed.

"Well no wonder you're scared witless! They only show the ones on there that go wrong, you know!" She squeezed my arm and as the next contraction started I held eye contact and she repeated the word, "Breathe..." until I was drawing in long slow breaths with both fists clenched.

"Now listen love, ninety nine percent of births happen like clockwork, there's nothing for you to be scared of at all. I'll stay with you in the ambulance and help to book you in when we get to hospital, but we need to get you there first." I nodded and she stood up to open the door. "I'm going to need a hand here," I heard her say to Damien, "and possibly a stretcher, guys" to the paramedics.

Damien reached for my hand as soon as he could. He bent over and swept my fringe away from my clammy forehead. "Steph, are you ok? I'm so sorry that it's gone so tits up, I really am." He looked worried and glanced at Carrie for reassurance.

"She's fine. Damien, isn't it?" she asked whilst strapping a Velcro cuff around the top of my arm and inflating it with a balloon pump.

"Yes, that's right," he answered and stepped back as she read the dial and listened for my pulse.

I smiled weakly.

"Ok, that's a bit high but that's to be expected, you've had a shock." She turned to Damien and asked if he could get some big towels. He disappeared for a moment and came back with his dressing gown, 2 bath sheets and a maternity night shirt.

"How are we going to do this?" he asked.

Carrie was thinking the same thing, and for a moment they both stepped back to survey the scene. Initially I had been really embarrassed that a complete stranger had found me trapped in a bath tub, in labour, completely naked. That had passed quickly and any scrap of dignity I was hanging on to had dissolved in the lukewarm water along with a pee.

"Ok, Stephanie, if you sit up, love," she said and Damien reached into the water to support my back.

"Good. Now we need to get you on your feet. Can you lift her slowly onto the edge of the bath?" Damien slipped his arms under my armpits, and with an under the breasts and over the bump heave, he started to lift. I pushed the best I could with my arms and then legs, and thanks to the lavender and rose scented bath oil, I slid into a sitting position on the edge, with my feet still in the water.

Carrie threw a towel around my shoulders as Damien held me steady.

"Catch your breath, love, and we'll swing your legs round," she said. "We need to do it before the next contraction."

"Ok," I said. "I think it's coming."

"Right, here goes then. You keep tight a hold now…" Carrie grabbed my ankles and as Damien manoeuvred me around in a semi-circle, it was only seconds before my feet felt the fluffy bathmat and the pain ripped through me again. I grabbed hard onto Damien and was aware of Carrie telling me to breathe through it, and a trickle of warm fluid running down my legs.

Once it had passed I managed to stand and hang on to the wash basin whilst Damien slid one arm and then the other into his bath robe, he tied the cord around my enormous bump and asked me if I wanted anything on underneath.

"No, it's fine. Every man and his dog's going to see what I've got south of the equator anyway." I managed a chuckle and the paramedics asked if I could walk to the ambulance.

I managed the stairs with Damien walking in front of me, backwards, ready to break a fall, and Carrie behind me as backup.

"Don't forget the bag and the keys," I said to Damien as one of the paramedics opened the door.

"Christ no, I'm not going through this again," he said, and although I was still angry with him I did chuckle to myself at the thought of him flapping on the other side of the locked door.

"Should I ring your parents?" he asked.

"Not yet, I've had enough drama for now." I turned to Carrie, "How long will I be in labour for?"

"I couldn't say, love. If you keep progressing like this it might be tonight but everyone is different."

I must have looked a picture in a man's tartan dressing gown when I stepped out of the door, as a cheer and applause broke out from the people that were crowded on the pavement. I smiled weakly and wished I had put some knickers on as I drew the robe around me tightly.

"What the bloody hell is going on?" I heard Damien say to no one specific.

"I think it must be a slow news week," said one of the paramedics, "the local television station is here."

I looked up with horror and saw the familiar groomed appearance of Beth Sharp talking to camera about the "Bath Tub Baby" story that had gripped the local area. She swung on her heel and flung the microphone into my embarrassed, chubby face with traces of makeup that had been all but sweated off due to the combination of steam and terror.

"Stephanie, how are you feeling?" she smiled fake and wide.

"Erm, I'm ok now… glad to be out really. I just want to get to hospital…"

Damien snatched the microphone out of my hand and started to say things about the paparazzi being bloody parasites, and plenty of words they would have to bleep out including a very clear F OFF straight to camera.

Beth continued talking about the stressful situation and the impact it could have on mother and baby, her words became muffled when they closed the ambulance doors and the sirens started to wail.

"Christ I can't believe that, who do these people think they are?" Damien looked like he needed his blood pressure taking instead of me.

"Nosey bastards, they can't be left out of anything. If I find out who called the press…"

I had been given a tube to breathe gas and air mixture through and it was making me feel all floaty and nice.

"Oh, just leave it Damien, nothing ever happens on our road so an ambulance, the fire brigade and a police car would have caused quite a stir. People are bound to want to know what's going on," I sniggered.

"What's so funny?" he said and I passed him the tube.

"This stuff is amazeballs…" I laughed. "Try some!"

"I can't Steph, it's medical..." he objected.

"The vein is throbbing in your head," I laughed again. "Have a big gulp."

Damien tentatively brought the tube to his lips and took a deep breath.

"Nothing." he said, and then a smirk.

"You haven't had enough then!" I laughed and thought that this felt like I'd had almost a whole bottle of wine. "Have shum more."

"Shum more?" he laughed. "You're pissed!"

"Pished wet through in your dressing gown!" I laughed harder but stopped as a contraction began to niggle. I grabbed the tube from him and started puffing in as much as I could.

"Slow down, Steph, you'll be on the ceiling!" Damien chuckled and as my breathing slowed down and my hand relaxed, he took the tube back.

"Hey!" I said. "That's mine."

"It's calming me down a treat thanks, great idea you had there, one of your better ones in fact…"

By the time we arrived at the hospital and the paramedics opened the doors Damien looked shitfaced with a dopey grin from ear to ear.

"Alright in here?"

"Yes, yes all good, great, super, it's been great," He garbled.

"You haven't tried any of that gas and air, have you sir?"

"No, no sir, not me sir, definitely not me sir. It was her."

The paramedic shook his head as he wheeled me out of the double doors.

"It's every bloody time," he muttered to his colleague who agreed and shrugged, resigned to standard husband idiocy.

Chapter 4

It all seemed to happen really quickly.

The pain escalated and peaked, but then quickly waned after a shot of morphine made me feel woozy, and I found I could even doze a little between the contractions.

It wasn't long before I was ready for the big push. After about twenty minutes of gritting my teeth and bearing down when the pain prompted me to, I felt a momentary hot, excruciating, stinging and burning feeling as our baby entered the world. I collapsed into the bed, panting with exhaustion and covered in beads of sweat. A final tremor shook my exerted muscles and I heard Damien's voice asking the midwife if everything was alright. My heart jumped and I raised my head from the pillow, my words, laced with opiates, sounded sleepy and didn't reflect the panic that was rising within me.

"Damien, what's wrong?" I asked.

"Nothing's wrong love, you just relax you've done well…" the midwife's voice didn't sound as calm as it had done when she was telling me to push a moment ago.

"It's fine, Steph. She's perfect..." Damien's voice cracked with emotion but in a drug-induced haze I couldn't gain context.

"Why can't I hear her crying?" I unexpectedly started to cry myself. I felt like a beached whale lying here in the near darkness of the delivery room covered in sweat, blood and amniotic fluid with the aftershocks of contractions still grumbling through my womb. The elation of knowing that I had a daughter was eclipsed by the fear that something was terribly wrong, and as Damien took the few steps to the head of the bed and grabbed my hand I saw concern etch itself across his face in a way that I'd never seen before.

And then as her cry rang out around the room, I saw his brow relax and tears spill over his cheeks. I draped my arm around his neck and pulled him in close as he nuzzled me and whispered through the tears that he loved me, and I said it back through what felt like a veil of exhaustion and relief.

Chapter 5

Nothing could have ever prepared me for motherhood.

The practical stuff, yes. I was expecting sleep deprivation and the cycle of feeding, winding and changing. I knew that nothing much would get done in the way of housework or shopping, and that I would rarely get to drink a whole cup of coffee while it was still hot, or blow-dry my hair.

But the emotional side of being a mother was unknown territory for me. I wondered if every new mother felt the same. If we all spent hours looking at our newborn and wondering if they were really here? I couldn't remember what it was like without her, but I did know for sure that I must have been walking around incomplete and not even known.

Everyone with a new baby had always talked about formula milk and nappy rash, weaning and baby massage. But no one had ever told me that I would never be able to hear her cry and not feel my own heart breaking with every sob. No one said that when she curled her tiny fingers around one of mine that tears of gratitude would catch in my throat, and I'd want to freeze frame the moment to keep with me forever. I'd never heard anyone say that once you are a mother you can never again read a paper or see a news story about child abuse and not feel a rising anger and fear bubble within you like an emotional volcano. If I had ever wondered about my life purpose before, I didn't have to now. Here she was. Choosing a name felt like the biggest responsibility ever. Nothing we had initially liked felt right, and I toiled about how she would be as a teenager and an adult and eventually a mother herself. It was on the third day that I sat in my new mum uniform of pyjamas and bed head, that I caught a sound bite on the television that inspired me. I was sipping the second half of a barely warm cup of tea and half watching morning television, when a celebrity said she had called her baby Mia.

"Mia," I said out loud, and then reached for my phone to google the meaning.

Apparently it meant 'mine' in Italian, and as I looked down on her in the wicker Moses basket with her tiny fingers, and the gentle rise and fall of her chest, I felt blessed beyond belief. She really was mine, and Mia suited her perfectly.

Stephanie's Journal ~ Lesson 14
Be Here Now

Being Present means more than just showing up. It's about bringing all of you into the now time, and not allowing your energy or mind to wander into the past or the future, it's about being here and totally immersing yourself in the moment. This helps you to experience the joy of the now time, and also to manifest what it is you want in your life using Law of Attraction, you need to be in the present moment and generate the frequency that you want the universe to match, in order to bring it into your current experience.

"For the present is the point at which time touches eternity." CS Lewis

Chapter 6

"Maybe we should try to go out today?" said Damien at 3:30am on day eleven.

"Where do you want to go?" I stage whispered as I gently lowered Mia back into the crib next to my bed and rearranged my maternity bra. I wondered if every nursing mum felt like she was wearing air bags instead of breast pads.

"Anywhere, I just thought it would be nice to get out and about a bit." Damien whispered back and I yawned.

"We need some food shopping," I said.

"Christ we are so rock and roll now. Let's live it up between the pulses and the pasta sauces." I elbowed him in fun, I knew he was joking.

"We need somewhere with baby changing and breast feeding," I said as he turned over and slid an arm around my waist.

"Where did we used to go when we had a day off together?" he said.

"Things have changed now Damien…"

"I can see that!" he said as the fingertips that I once relished caressing my body poked out of the top of the duvet waving a breast pad.

"Piss off!" I said and grabbed it back in the darkness, stuffing it back under my pyjama top.

"You know I'm joking don't you?" He pulled me close again and kissed the patch of skin behind my ear. "I love you, and I love it that I am sharing this whole parenting thing with you. I couldn't ask for a better mother for my baby girl."

"I love you too," I whispered and rolled onto my back as his lips brushed mine, and as I kissed him back I felt my heart open with gratitude and connection. It was far too soon to think about making love but that didn't mean that we couldn't still be close. I could feel Damien's erection pressing onto my thigh.

"Sorry" he mumbled "I know we can't and I would never pressure you."

"Don't be sorry, I can still do something for you…" I wrapped my fingers around him and heard him sigh as my grip tightened. I could tell that this wouldn't take long and God knows we hadn't gone there for a good few weeks, no wonder he was horny. Any man that could overlook a baby belly and breast pads must be! Moments before the finale, which was only a few minutes into the first act, I felt his thigh muscles start to twitch and his breathing changed. Then a murmuring in the crib and a wriggling sound made me stop.

"Don't stop, Steph!" he panted.

"Hold on, I think she's waking up…" I sat up and forced Damien to roll away onto his side of the bed whilst I peered in the darkness waiting for her to wake up or settle.

"Steph…" he said shakily. "I'm nearly there…"

"I'll just be a second," I said, as Mia started to whimper more. I got out of bed and picked her up as I perched on the edge of the mattress and rubbed her back in gentle circles.

"Can you do that in a minute, Steph, I'm going to explode!"

"We shouldn't be doing this kind of thing in front of our child anyway!" I said.

"She was asleep when we started!"

"You'll have to erm… you know… finish it off yourself. You do it in the shower, anyway."

"You know about that?" he said and I was so glad my back was turned as he was discreetly trying not to miss a beat, but the chiropractic mattress wasn't soft enough to absorb much in the way of bouncing.

"Of course I bloody know! Maybe you could go now and *have a shower*?" I suggested. "I don't want to have to change the sheets!"

"Christ this is so romantic…" he said pulling the duvet back with one hand and tugging with the other.

"I can't help it. I can't ignore her when she's crying!"

Just before he had time to get to his feet Mia burped from her boots and a jet of warm half-digested breast milk fountained over my shoulder and splattered across Damien's back. A couple of seconds passed as I held my breath and waited for his response.

"I'll just go and have a shower then," he said as I stifled a giggle.

"Don't be long. I might need a hand changing the sheets after all," I chuckled as he walked past me, naked, flaccid and covered in puke.

"Welcome to parenthood," I said to myself and sniffed in the scent of love as I nuzzled Mia's velvety scalp.

I'd changed the sheets and bundled up the soiled ones in the laundry basket by the time Damien slid back into bed beside me. He pulled me close and told me he loved me, and I said it back.

"I really, *really* love you and Mia. You know that, don't you?" He sounded emotional and I felt his arms tighten around me.

"Of course I know, Damien. Is something wrong?" I whispered in the darkness. "You're not upset about what just happened are you? We'll get our sex life back on track you know…"

"No! Of course I'm not upset about that, it's never been about that for me, you know that. What we've got Steph runs a lot deeper than a fumble in the dark. I want you to know that you and Mia literally are my world. I mean that." He sounded choked but I felt like whatever had bothered him was not open for discussion. I let him hold me tight until I felt his arms relax and his breathing deepen. As he rolled away from he and onto his own side of the bed I told myself that he was tired and overwhelmed like me, and I eventually managed to switch off the niggle that there was something wrong.

Chapter 7

The days soon merged into weeks, which then spanned into months and it felt like we had always been parents. Our lives revolved around feeding, changing and nap time, then weaning and more interaction as Mia grew and became more interested in the world around her.

"What's the plan for today then?" asked Damien one Monday morning as he sat giving Mia her bottle and I came downstairs from the shower.

"I think we might try something totally new today," I said dragging a wide-toothed comb through my wet hair. "We might try a toddler group."

"Isn't she a bit young for that yet?" said Damien "How old is toddler exactly? Isn't it about two?"

"I don't know exactly, but apparently they can go to the group at the church hall from six months." I dropped two slices of bread into the toaster and flicked the kettle on.

"Ah right, sounds like fun." He sat Mia up in her highchair and kissed the top of her head and then came to me to kiss me.

"Have a good day," I said. "I love you."

"I love you too," he replied and held my gaze a split second too long.

"Are you ok?" I asked, thinking *weird.*

"Of course I'm ok," he answered and spun me around to kiss me again full on the lips. "I'm married to the most gorgeous woman on the planet."

"I wouldn't go that far..." I objected. "I've still got a whole load of baby weight to shift and I look like I've started getting dressed from a lost property box in a dark cupboard with no mirror…"

"I'll be the judge of that," he said and playfully slapped my buttocks before he made his way down the hallway to the front door.

I felt myself blush a little as the door closed. Would it really be such a big deal to fire up some of the old bedroom magic again? We hadn't tried anything since the ultimate passion killer night of the aborted hand job, but I really wasn't joking when I said that I didn't feel gorgeous. I'd never exactly been a goddess anyway. But right now the thought of prancing around in sexy lingerie and staging a night of adult fun seemed like another world. I'd read in women's magazines about the top twenty things that you could do to get your sex life back on line after the birth of your baby, but it was far easier and safer for my feelings to have an early night on my own.

We'd fallen into a routine where I went straight to bed once Mia was settled, because I knew I'd be up at some ungodly hour heating milk and winding – at least once a night. A couple of nights a week Damien opted to sleep in the guest room, and although I missed him initially, I also relished the chance to starfish in the bed, and to know that if anything woke me up it would be Mia and not his snoring. Sleep had suddenly become a really precious commodity.

It wasn't that things weren't good between us, it just felt that being a mother had eclipsed being a wife for the moment. I knew that other couples' evolution into parents moved them further away from being lovers, I'd read about it in the hairdressers when they gave you the packet of biscuits and the stack of magazines whilst your colour developed.

I blamed EL James for the last one I'd read. The columnist had called it 'Fifty Shades of Surrey' and it went on to talk about how a mummy that felt far less than yummy, vamped herself up and surprised her husband by meeting him after work in a bar, wearing a full-length black trench mac and high-heeled boots, with nothing much underneath. Apparently they'd ended up getting a taxi home early and having the night of her life, with things definitely back on track in the bedroom department.

I couldn't imagine going that far, but I could make some kind of effort and at least shave my legs. Mia broke my train of thought by starting to murmur.

"Come on baby girl." I lifted her out of her high chair and into her car seat, and gave her a soft toy to look at while I looked for my trainers.

"Let's go and see what toddler group is all about."

She gurgled in response and we made our way into the car and then towards the town centre to find a parking space, which I had already asked the universe for and imagined myself driving into with plenty of room.

I walked down a ramp and into the church hall, which smelt like old ladies and stewed tea. There was a corkboard to the left covered in sales and wants cards, as well as a Jesus Saves leaflet and a list of church services. On the right was a small table with a doily and a basket for donations, a copy of the bible and a notice about the church roof fund. Someone had made a thermometer type poster with a financial target of £15,000 and it was coloured in to the level that said £8,200. I could hear the noise coming from further in that sounded like feeding time at the zoo.

"That's where we need to be I think," I said to Mia and made my way into the main hall. To begin with I stood with my back to the door I'd just come through and surveyed the scene, wondering if this really was for us. Women sat in little cluster groups around the edge of the vast hall and the high ceiling had perfect acoustics to really amplify the sound of the hard plastic wheels on a toy tractor, a child screaming at the top of her lungs and general noise. I looked at Mia after I'd put her car seat down momentarily, and she didn't seem phased. Maybe if I turned around now and back through the doors no one would be any the wiser and we'd be able to sneak away.

"Morning!" shouted an overly cheery voice above the furore.

"Morning!" I said back.

"You must be new, I haven't seen your face here before," said the rotund lady with sensible shoes and a brown Purdy style square cut. "I'm Jean." She waited for me to respond.

"I'm Stephanie," I replied. "We just dropped in. We can't stay for too long today."

"Stay as long as you want love, and who is this little treasure?" She bent down and Mia looked up at her and gurgled.

"Mia," I said. "I'm not sure if she's old enough to be here yet."

"She'll love it, and so will you once you get to know a few folks. Are you new to the area love?" I'd been rumbled. There was a concern in Jean's voice that told me that she knew I was feeling overwhelmed and that it would be much easier to turn around and get back home with the door shut and *Loose Women* on the box.

"Not totally, I moved around the time I fell pregnant," I said, keeping upbeat but feeling like I wanted to bolt.

"It's really important to get to know other mums in the community you know, we all need a support network. Can I get you a cup of tea and then after that you can see if you've got time to stay?" Jean had a careworn face but, based on her choice of haircut, took no crap.

"Ok then, yes please. Tea would be lovely thanks." God I was trapped now for at least half an hour.

"Let's get you a seat and I can introduce you to a couple of mums…" Jean looked into the hall and her eagle eyes caught a seat in the far right corner near the fire exit and underneath a wall hanging about Easter. "Follow me love!" I did as I was told, as she carefully picked a path through kids and toys I tailed her closely dodging building bricks, a toy garage and a sandpit filled with plastic balls.

"This is Stephanie," she said and the two ladies that had looked deep in conversation looked up and smiled.

"Hi Stephanie!" they both said and one of them pulled the vacant brown classroom style plastic chair out for me.

"I'm Rosie," said the one with the glasses and gingery hair tied back in a messy bun.

"I'm Mel," said the blonde with skinny jeans and full makeup.

"I'll just get that cuppa," said Jean. "These two lovely ladies will make you feel at home."

I shifted awkwardly in the seat and unfastened my coat then hung it on the back of the seat as I had noticed others had.

"Are you from round here then?" asked Rosie.

"Yes, just five minutes in the car, what about you?" I had to speak above the racket.

"I'm from the next village along, but Mel's from here," said Rosie.

"Right, it's my first time at this kind of thing…" I said. "Is it always so noisy?" they both laughed.

"Yes!" said Mel as a child ran up to her crying and she swooped him onto her knee. "What's the matter, George?" she said in a kind tone. He snuggled into her and she stroked his fair wispy hair.

"He's just tired I think, he didn't have a great night last night. I think he's got some more teeth coming through."

"I've got all of that to look forward to," I said, looking down at Mia and wondering how on earth she could manage to fall asleep in her car seat with such a racket going on. She wouldn't settle at home sometimes in the stillness of the night.

"Are you going to play for ten more minutes George while mummy has her tea?" Mel asked.

He shook his head and said, "No!"

"Have your tea, Mel! You're in charge, not him!" said Rosie in a mock school teacher tone.

"You know what he's like Rosie, there's no point when he's tired and he's in one," Mel sighed.

"He's like that because you let him be like that! I've told you, it's about tough love, lady."

It may have just been me, but I felt Mel shrink a little at her comment, and I wondered how close they were as friends. Perhaps they just saw one another here, but Rosie seemed to be more inner circle than that.

"Maybe so, but I'm too tired to be tough with anyone today." Mel passed a wriggling George to Rosie and stood up to pull on her coat.

"George, now stop that!" said Rosie in a voice that she would have probably called 'firm but fair'.

Mel slung her navy tote over her shoulder which I guessed doubled up as a nappy bag, and reached for George. He buried his ruddy cheeks under her chin and Mel turned to leave. "Nice to meet you Steph, I'll no doubt see you on the circuit."

"Yes, nice to meet you too," I said and her eyes flashed what felt like an apology in my direction for a split second. I was left wondering if this was meant to say sorry for George, for which there was no need, or for Rosie being so outspoken.

"She lets him rule the roost, that's the problem there," Rosie shook her head. "Once they think they are the boss that's it, you've made a rod for your own back."

I half smiled in agreement but started to feel like the spotlight was being shone on my parenting as well. I didn't let Mia rule the roost, but I did feed her on demand and couldn't for the life of me get away with controlled crying. Rosie was probably the kind of mother that sat at the top of the stairs with a timer and a glass of sauvignon blanc after 6:30pm, letting her kids scream themselves to sleep rather than disturb 'adult time.' I was being judgemental, I needed to step back and know that people are all different and we are all doing our best.

"Christ, here she is, Ugly Betty," Rosie hissed under her breath as Jean approached with a tray balancing three steaming cups and a stack of custard creams.

I didn't respond outwardly, but I knew that this had to be a lesson coming up and I had everything clenched.

"Has Mel gone?" asked Jean as she passed us a cup each and I took two biscuits, noticing the subtle stare from Rosie that linked my biscuit intake to the size of my thighs.

"Yes, his highness started kicking off and she caved," Rosie shrugged.

"They're all different, and mum knows best," commented Jean, taking the neutral standpoint although her words felt loaded. "Biscuit?"

"No, thank you," replied Rosie in a blunt manner. "A moment on the lips, forever on the hips…"

Meow! I took that to be directed towards Jean, but perhaps a side order of it was meant for me too? As Jean walked away, Rosie leaned in with her head cocked to one side.

"She's a bitch really that Jean, so watch yourself. She struts around the place thinking that she knows best looking down her nose at all of us childminders because she's in charge. She thinks she's a cut above if you ask me, knows everything apparently."

"Oh, you're a childminder?" I asked huddling my cup close to protect it from any low flying toys.

"Yeah, I have been for fifteen years now, so I guess I know what I'm doing." Rosie sat back now that Jean was out of earshot and became more aloof.

"Just because I haven't had any kids of my own doesn't mean I don't know about them. In fact, it makes you much better at raising them in my opinion." She didn't wait for me to comment as she continued with her campaign. "And when I say raising them that's what I mean, I get people *desperate* to go back to work, because they thought having a kid would be a walk in the park, but a few months in they are begging me for a place."

"Wow, well I guess some people have to go back to work…" I dared to interject.

"They should have thought about that before they started having kids then, shouldn't they? Honestly I get them dropped off at 8 am and picked up at 6pm. All the parents have to do is give them a bath and read them a story, then they open the wine that they got with their Marks and Spencer meal deal and get quietly pissed in front of the soaps." The look on her face was indignant and she smirked. It ran through my head that she had no idea about my life and that I could have been here as a one-off and be returning to work next week.

"So it's me that they've got to thank when their kid turns out ok, it's me that's putting in the hours with them and raising them, not the bloody parents. They might get them all fancied up and take them to birthday parties at a weekend, or take them on all-inclusive holidays once a year, but they always end up in the kids club! Why? Because they can't cope with their own kids, that's why."

A welcome reprieve while she sipped her tea and I tentatively tried to give the other side of the story.

"I'm sure they are really grateful to you for all the good you do."

"So grateful that they have another kid and bring that one a couple of years later, then get straight back in their company cars and leave me to it," she said, shrugging.

"It must be something that you enjoy if you've done it for this long, I mean you must love children?" I was thankfully nearly finished my tea now and busy fabricating an excuse about somewhere I had to be and just popping in for half an hour.

"I dunno, it's what I've done for so long that I wouldn't change now."

"But don't you love it?" I asked. "Isn't it some kind of calling to you, like teaching or nursing? I mean raising children is one of the most important things you can ever do, you're actually shaping lives and the fabric of humanity with the next generation."

Conversation Fail.

For a moment you'd think that I suggested that she buy a pet unicorn. Then she laughed. Really laughed, and I strangely found myself laughing along too, although I didn't know why.

"You are so funny!" she said.

"Am I?" I laughed back.

"And you don't even know it Steph. We're going to get along so well… I just know it."

She must know something I seriously don't then.

Mia started to stir right on cue and I drained the cup in my hand as I leaned over for her to see my face as her eyes opened.

"Well we have to go now, but it's been nice meeting you Rosie." I stood up and put on my coat.

"Here's my card" said Rosie and passed me her details. "You have to keep in touch! And if you want a childminder you know who I am now. I don't know how people leave them with strangers…"

"Thanks." I tried to look genuine as I smiled through the thought that there was no way on earth Mia would be left with Rosie. She might be doing the best that she could do and I wished her well on her journey, but I didn't have to befriend her.

Mel, on the other hand, had seemed lovely. I wondered if I'd bump into her again.

"Thanks for keeping me company," I said over my shoulder as I made my way out of the hall with Mia's car seat handle looped over my arm like a shopping basket. I couldn't see Jean to thank, and I was doubtful that I'd be back anyway, but it had been really worthwhile. As I made my way up the ramp back to the main street and onwards to the car park, the lesson that had presented itself came together in my consciousness.

"So how was toddler group?" asked Damien as he picked Mia up from her play mat and she squealed with delight.

"We only stayed half an hour," I said.

"That good then?" he asked me by asking Mia and she grabbed his nose and squealed again.

"No wonder you didn't make lots of friends if you go round doing that!" He pulled up her t-shirt and blew a raspberry on her bare belly and she laughed and wriggled.

I love you so much, I thought, and the gratitude of having a man in my life that loved my child so completely. It felt in that moment more precious than the love he had for me.

"And what did mummy think?" he asked me and I sighed.

"It was ok I guess, it might not be for us."

"It's the first thing you've been to Steph, give it a chance."

"I got trapped with some girl who did nothing but moan and slag other people off, it was really uncomfortable."

"Don't let her spoil it for you, you meet moaners in every walk of life not just toddler group. There were probably loads of nice people there that you didn't get the chance to talk to."

I knew he was right, and now I knew that this was a lesson in discernment I could step back and not get sucked in. Tomorrow was a new day and I'd seen an advert for mum and baby aqua aerobics, hopefully it was going to be worth shaving my legs for.

Stephanie's Journal ~ Lesson 15
Discernment

Discernment is the power to choose. It's not judging someone or something as negative, or less important than you - that comes from ego. Discernment is about being empowered and knowing when there is alignment or not, and then choosing your actions based on this. Think of this as Divine Guidance or a cosmic heads up.

Discernment is an act of great self-love, it is telling the universe that this does not feel right for you at this time and that you honour that feeling. Putting yourself into situations that feel wrong or uncomfortable will lower your vibration and make you feel bad, which in turn will lead to you attracting things you don't want. It is not only ok to have good personal boundaries, it's necessary for your own self-care.

"You cannot change the people around you, but you can choose the people that you choose to be around." Unknown

Chapter 8

I felt super organized and proud of myself when I arrived at Water Splash between feeds with my maternity costume underneath my joggers, shaved legs, breast pads in place and a happy baby.

You can do this. People bring babies swimming all of the time.

I paid the smiley lady at reception who clearly had no small children, as she was in full make-up this early. Yes, I had a pound coin for the locker, that's because I am super organized sporty mummy who brings her child swimming. Didn't she recognise me? I laughed to myself and made my way into a family cubicle. I was ready in minutes, thanks to my pre-swimming preparations.

This was better than toddler group already, I had this nailed. Swimming was going to be our thing, I just knew it. I took Mia's coat off and she gurgled at me.

"Today Mia, we are swimmers." I told her and she laughed. "Thanks for the vote of confidence," I said, as I wriggled her out of her clothes and held her on my hip as I started to delve into the bag and find the special regulation swimming nappies that all serious swimming mums with babies considered a must have. As my fingers touched the coloured plastic, my leg grew warm. Mia giggled as she peed freely and a dark patch spread across my Lycra-clad waist and the 'support panel' that promised to lift and sculpt. "Mia!" I held her at arm's length and the flow stopped as she laughed again. "That had better be all there is!"

I quickly pulled on the Little Swimmers nappy and thought that it would probably be a good idea to have a shower before I went into the water, and should I tell someone we'd had an accident? I could hear more mums and babies around us now, some sounded less than happy, but Mia thankfully was still giggling.

"Ok kid, here we go," I said as I slung the bag over my shoulder and carried her on the dry hip towards the locker. Why did my swimming costume feel so snug? I'd worn it when I was pregnant and surely I wasn't that big now. It was mainly over the breasts that I was having trouble. I'd literally had to put my hand up one of the leg holes to try to get the breast pads in properly, doing some funny kind of crouching contortionist moves with my hand up my own gusset was not flattering at all and made me glad I'd had the foresight to get sorted at home.

I shoved the bag and our clothes into the locker and turned the key as the pound coin clinked into the mechanism. All good! I bounced my happy child, who could be a future Olympic swimmer, on my knee as I fastened the blue plastic bangle around my wrist and swivelled the key into the indentation. I pulled up the front of my costume just as the top of one of my nips peeked out with a white frill of paper, mentally noting that dry jiggling was going to lead to Embarrassed mummy rather than Swimming Mummy.

I could hear music starting, and I made my way to the poolside telling myself that once I was wet the fabric would stick to my body better and there wouldn't be a problem. You always had to peel a swimming costume off once you got out of the water didn't you? I mean it's not like you could just slip it off like a cotton t-shirt! And it was snug. That's what I was focused on. Snug. Which of course means that everything is in its place.

This could be just what I needed to help me to lose my baby weight and get back into shape, well the old shape anyway. It would be like the good old days and Damien wouldn't be able to keep his hands off me, and with Mia sleeping better now once I'd started weaning and stopped lactating, there was a glimmer of hope that something of a sex life could be back on the cards. Swimming Mummy was going to save me, I knew it. I loved her, she was so organized and fabulous, she really had her shit together!

And the funny thing is – it's me!

Could everyone make themselves laugh? Maybe Damien was right and I needed to get out a whole lot more. I chuckled my way to the water's edge and congregated with the other mums and babies, I dipped my toes in and it felt a lot colder than the 21 degrees it said on the wall.

"Stephanie!" I heard a voice behind me and turned to see Mel's smiling face.

"Mel! Hi! It's so good to see you, do you come every week?"

"We try to, George loves it. We're in the toddler group with Melinda, you'll be in the baby group with Luke… he's a bit of a hunk, it's a good job I moved up a group I couldn't concentrate on the moves!" She had to speak above the music, which was nothing at all I recognized, but I'd been in baby land for the last few months where cartoons reigned supreme. Even the radio in the car had been replaced with a Favourite Nursery Rhymes CD, I had no idea what was in the music charts.

"It's a shame we're not in the same group," I said over the sound of a girl singing about giving a boy her number.

"We could have a coffee afterwards in the café if the kids are settled?" suggested Mel as a spray tanned, blonde young instructor rounded the corner carrying a net full of balls.

"Great, I'll see you there," I said as she followed who I presumed was Melinda, and I scanned the poolside for Luke.

There was only one hunk in the building and Mel had been right, I could feel my face flush slightly and I automatically sucked in my stomach (for all the good it did) as I set eyes on him. The mums with babies all looked thinner than me. Two of the small group stood preening and speaking a little too loudly, about the fact that they thought the red room in *Fifty* was tame.

Luke busied himself with a clipboard, giving me the chance to stare openly at his amazing physique. I guessed he was in his late twenties, with thick dark hair and blue eyes that nearly matched the azure blue of the pool. His biceps bulged from underneath his white polo shirt and his thighs were perfectly sculpted under his (thankfully) very short navy shorts. He was the first man in my life I had ever seen look sexy in flip flops, and as he licked his lips to blow on his whistle, I licked mine too.

"Ok, yummy mummies! Let's get you gorgeous girls in the water and see your moves!"

There was a collective girly giggle as we all waded in to waist deep, and then I dangled Mia's legs into the water. She took a sharp breath in and looked shocked, but her expression soon changed to one of glee when she realized that she could kick and splash at the same time.

"That's right, just ease yourself in…" said Luke, in a voice that in a totally different context would have had me close to an orgasm.

"Come a bit closer ladies, I'll be gentle with you…"

More giggling and preening, and for the life of me I knew I was joining in but I couldn't help it.

The first routine was mainly bobbing up and down and some stretches where we held our babies out at arm's length and moved around the pool. As the music changed and became more up tempo, Luke shouted above it to be careful if we had any back injuries or history of back pain.

"Work at your own pace ladies" was the message here as he demonstrated two ways to do the following exercises, one was to lift your baby out of the water a little and use them as a weight to work on your arms. The more advanced technique for mummies that really wanted a great workout, or were fitter, involved lifting your child as high as you could.

I knew which one Swimming Mummy was ready for, and with strict instruction to hold baby around the waist and breathe out on the effort, I started to go for it.

Mia squealed with excitement as I lifted her high and her tiny feet kicked in the air. I stole a glance to either side and saw that I probably had the lightest baby. So what if this was an unfair advantage and none of the other mums were lifting nearly as high as me.

Luke had started at one end of the line and was encouraging us to keep a straight back and suck in our tummies, by the time he got to me Swimming Mummy was going to amaze him. The track he was playing morphed into a remix of *Flashdance* at the same time and I hit my stride with gusto. Panting on the outbreath and practically throwing Mia into the air with buttocks clenched, I saw Luke's face. As predicted he looked amazed at Swimming Mummy's technique. And then he started moving his hands up from his waist to his chin and looking a little frantic. I tried to copy but this move was impossible with a baby, what on earth was he thinking? I looked around and saw confused expressions, and my eye caught something lilting on the top of the water that looked like a jelly fish.

Breast pad... it's a bloody breast pad.

Swimming Mummy's udders were on display for all to see. Thanks to overenthusiastic exercise and overinflated breasts, my swimming costume was now sporting a deeply scooped neckline around my waist. I was dressed like a wrestler from the eighties with my tits out in a pool in front of a gorgeous man and the general public. Mia was no help and just kept laughing as I furiously tugged the costume into some kind of cover up, and Luke used a nearby net to catch the floater.

"Maybe you need a better fitting costume for exercise?" he said, diplomatically.

My face burned crimson and I mumbled in agreement.

"Or perhaps go for a bit less impact to start with..." He was trying to make me feel better but that was clearly impossible.

"I think I'll call it a day," I said and started to wade my way towards the shallow end, which was like wading through treacle and seemed to take forever. I couldn't bear to look back over my shoulder but could hear him starting to demonstrate the next exercise.

"Everything alright?" Mel mouthed as I passed the toddler class with a baby over my shoulder and a hand clenched like a vice at the cleavage of my swimming costume.

"Kind of, I'll see you in the café." I said, desperate to get back in to the cubicle and lock myself away, possibly forever.

The door creaked shut and I sat on the plastic bench not knowing whether to laugh or cry. I wasn't sure if I could face anyone in the café after that, for God's-Actual-Sake I had my mammaries out for all to see whilst jumping up and down to an eighties classic, and swinging my kid around like a lunatic. Nice one Swimming Mummy, or should I say Swimming Moron.

I dried Mia and got her dressed as fast as I could and propped her up between bags and towels, whilst I peeled off my wrestling suit and flicked it into the opposite corner with my big toe with hatred. "You twat!" I said under my breath and then thought how awful it would be if that was her first word due to one unfortunate day at the pool.

I pulled on my clothes, clipped up my hair and pulled up the hood on my hoody before I made my way out. I looked left and right and the coast seemed clear, anyway I could still hear Luke shouting about keeping your heart rate up and arms high, as well as Katy Perry belting out *Firework.*

I had to go to the café. Mel would think I'd dodged her if I didn't, even though the walk between the reception desk and the table tucked away in the corner felt like miles away, I had to take that walk of shame. I took a deep breath and began to walk purposefully towards the counter, ordered a latte and a large piece of cake then scuttled off to take a seat.

Ten long minutes later after I had flicked through the *Go Local* magazine twice, which was really for me to hide behind as the café filled up, Mel and George appeared.

“Didn’t she like it?” Mel asked breezily and dragged over a second high chair for George.

“Oh yes, she loved it, it’s just that I had a bit of an incident…” I mumbled.

“Oh?” Mel waited for me to elaborate and I coughed and quickly looked around.

“I had a bit of a wardrobe malfunction,” I said as Mel pressed her lips together and tried hard not to smirk.

“Oh right. Someone was talking about that in the changing room…”

“Christ, what did they say?” I asked, and Mel couldn’t contain it any longer.

“I’m really sorry for laughing,” she said, “but it’s the kind of thing that would usually happen to me!”

I relaxed a little and cracked an embarrassed smile.

“I literally feel like a massive tit, actually two massive tits,” I said and she snorted.

“Steph, you are so funny, honestly I am laughing with you not at you!” Mel was officially helpless and I wondered if her pelvic floor was up to this, not sure mine was.

“I would like to say I have never been so embarrassed in my life, but the bloody fire brigade had to rescue me from the bath when I went into labour.”

Tears were running down her face and there was no point in hiding behind *Go Local* any more. I may as well Go Public. So I put the magazine down and pulled down the ridiculous hoody disguise.

"Sorry anyone who saw more than they'd bargained for earlier," I announced with a bright red face and a couple of mums shouted messages of support.

"If you've got it flaunt it!" rang out, along with, "We've all got them love!"

"Exactly," said Mel in solidarity, once she'd caught her breath and possibly pissed her pants.

"I don't really know what the hell to say next," I said.

"I think we are going to get along famously, Steph." Mel chuckled, and ordered two coffees.

Chapter 9

The next morning felt like it started in the middle of the night as usual, and even though the sun was barely peeping over the horizon, Mia was wide awake.

"Guess who is coming to see you today?" I said as she looked at me all smiley and gurgling, with a mass of blonde curls. Sometimes the love I felt for her was so overwhelming I could have burst into tears for what seemed like nothing, but was really everything. Her smile, her fingers curling around mine, her laugh. The everyday things that make up the whole precious experience of life, the things that we take for granted as the minutes and hours of each day tick past are the parts that we would want to relive in a heartbeat if they were taken from us.

A sunbeam shone through the window and rainbows scattered around the walls. Mia pointed at them as I lifted her up and I breathed in her baby smell. I felt my heart expand and she opened her tiny fist to catch the colours and then looked at me, laughing and instead tugged at my hair.

"Granny is coming today, Mia, so we've got to get tidied up."

It was too early to wake Damien so I would have to wait for a shower. It had crossed my mind one day last week when Mia had gone back to sleep after her breakfast, that I could have sneaked into bed with him and maybe begun the campaign to reignite our sex life. Nothing much had happened on that front since the vomiting incident, which to be fair must have been pretty off putting. I did find myself feeling confused though. It wasn't like we weren't close, it just felt like there was something not quite connecting the way that it used to. I couldn't put my finger on it and convinced myself that maybe this is just the way that having a child changed a relationship. Maybe I was putting too much onus on the physical side of things. I knew he loved me and that he would never think of being with anyone else. As that thought crossed my mind I felt an echo of the old me ripple through my awareness.

Don't be ridiculous, Steph, he would never, ever cheat on you. I told myself and shook my head, and even though I believed it, an unsettling emotional undercurrent stirred somewhere deep within me.

It's old stuff, I need to move on from that.

Although I had done my best to heal and release my past, there were still some wounds that had been etched so deep that they would take longer to close and I might always bear emotional scars. This was one of them rearing its head, the fear that I'd be betrayed again and that a man I love would choose someone over me.

Step back and breathe.

I knew that this was my past reality and not my life with Damien, and I didn't want him to have to pick up the tab for the way Jay had treated me. But a part of me was scared and unhealed and stuck in the past. Time is a great healer people say, and I intuitively knew that the many years it had taken to reduce me to my lowest point couldn't be erased in just two.

Mia started to cry a little, I needed to warm her bottle before she woke Damien. I bounced her up and down on my hip and made my way onto the landing.

"Shush, shush, shush..." I whispered and made my way downstairs. Once she was winded and settled in the baby bouncer I surveyed the scene and regretted not keeping on top of the housework. I probably had about three hours before my parents arrived, but I doubted even three hours was long enough to get me and the house in any kind of order. Maybe half of each would be ok?

I started by hiding the ironing pile in the understairs cupboard, followed by a swift pick up of toys and stacking the dishwasher. It didn't look too bad now and would be improved further by a quick hoover and a squirt of air freshener just before they arrived. I heard the radio alarm start upstairs and Damien stir. I scooped Mia up and snuggled her close while I carried her upstairs and bundled her into bed beside him.

"Morning, Daddy!" I said cheerily and Mia started to chew the corner of the duvet.

"Already?" said Damien and opened one eye.

"I'm going in the shower," I said and pulled the pillow from under his head, using it to barricade Mia into the confines of the mattress. I hadn't even turned on the water when I heard Damien's raspy morning voice making baby talk, and Mia gurgling in response. I smiled and shook my head at my own silliness, how could I ever doubt that man? I stood below the torrent of steaming water and imagined that my old fears were being washed down the plug hole along with the soapsuds, and by the time I was done I felt a whole lot better.

"Are your parents coming over today?" Damien asked as I squirted around furniture polish and flicked a duster.

"Yes, they should be here in about half an hour," I said.

"Well I'll bail out now then." He smiled and kissed my cheek before he turned to Mia and ruffled her curls. "Be good for mummy."

"Have a good day," I said absently, fussing around with curtain tie backs.

"Relax, Steph it's only your parents." He kissed me again and I turned my cheek so that his lips brushed mine. I caught his gaze for a second and he looked back at me, a sadness from somewhere made me catch my breath.

"I love you," he said.

I paused before I returned the sentiment which was usually automatic.

What's wrong?

The unspoken question hung in the air between us for a split second too long before he broke into a smile.

"I'm the luckiest man alive." He kissed me full on the lips and turned to leave.

So why does it not feel like it?

"See you tonight," I shouted down the hallway as his footsteps created distance between us that suddenly felt like a canyon.

Chapter 10

"We've brought some cakes darling, and milk and tea bags," my mother said as soon as I opened the door.

"Thanks, Mum, but I do have stuff in you know," I said as she passed me a carrier bag and took Mia.

"Come to Granny!" she cooed as her face lit up and her granddaughter nuzzled into the collar of her coat.

"She's tired, Mum. She might go to sleep if you cuddle her in." I made my way to the kitchen and reappeared a few minutes later with a tea tray.

My mum was nestled in the corner of the couch with Mia in the crook of her elbow, talking quietly and hypnotically to her as she started to drift off to sleep.

"Do you want her in her crib, Mum?" I whispered. "Then you can have your tea?"

"Definitely not, Stephanie," she whispered back through a contented smile. "I'm not missing a moment of this."

I poured the tea, leaving Mum's in the pot, and as Mia's breathing turned into the softest of snores we started to speak nearer normal volume. Dad told me all about the new shed he had his eye on and Mum chipped in with a couple of comments about the back garden and her washing line. The conversation turned to Mia and what proud grandparents they were, and how someone in their cul-de-sac had a grandson that slept right through from the day he was brought home from hospital, and he was about the same age as Mia, and his christening was this weekend. I knew what was coming next before my mother had finished her sentence, and I knew why. She was thinking about how she could one up the neighbours in the christening stakes.

"Have you and Damien discussed that yet?" she said and dad said he'd have another cup. He had obviously had this conversation already, probably several times.

"No, Mum, we haven't really," I said stuffing in an éclair.

"Well, you really should darling, I mean time is ticking on you know…" she continued, the floodgates were open. "I know people get christened as adults but I mean how ridiculous is that? And I think at some churches you have to go right into the water or something, don't you? In a white dress? It would go all see-through if you ask me, and that's hardly very holy is it?"

I choked back a giggle as I had a flashback to Swimming Mummy.

"Anne, it's up to them," my dad said firmly, I imagined that this was after weeks of ear bashing.

"I'm not saying it's not up to them! I'm just saying that Mia would look adorable in a christening gown, and it's about time they thought about it!"

"It's not something we've really thought about," I said, which might have been the wrong thing to come out with.

"Exactly," said Mum, from the moral high ground. "That's my point exactly. You haven't even thought about it. Isn't it a good job I'm here bringing it up then?"

I sighed. "Yes, Mum, it's a good job. I'll speak to Damien and see what he thinks."

"Does it really matter what he thinks, darling? I mean I would help you to organize it you know, there would be nothing for him to do apart from show up really."

"Of course it matters, Mum!" I laughed in disbelief.

"Well I don't see how Stephanie, I mean it's just a bit of a get-together."

"Mum!" I nearly spat out my tea.

"Shush, Stephanie! You'll wake the baby!"

"How can you say that?" I hissed.

"Because that's what it is, it's a lovely celebration of the birth of a child." She looked down at Mia and smiled. "Our little angel."

"And speaking of angels and God and c*hurch...*" I raised my eyebrow.

"Well, yes. Of course it's about all of that, darling."

"All of that?" I said and laughed again.

"Well, you were christened and you've grown up alright haven't you?" Mum's tone had a bit of an edge on it now.

"What's that got to do with how I've grown up? It's not like you made me go to Sunday School or bible class, is it? I'm not a good human because I got christened, Mum!"

"How do you know?" she tried to defend herself. "You might have had some kind of epiphany or something that's made you who you are!"

"For God's sake Anne, she was only six months old." Dad spoke via the voice of reason.

"Well, why *wouldn't* you get her christened, Stephanie? It's harmless and it would be a lovely day. We could get her a lovely gown…"

"I can't believe you're suggesting it because it would be a lovely day Mum, and because she might have some kind of epiphany and she'll be frilled up to her neck in white. You can't have a christening because of that!"

"Well what else is there, darling? I mean seriously. Who on earth is really going to take their child to church every weekend? People have better things to do on a Sunday like washing the car and making the dinner, no one's got time for that in real life."

"Mum! That's outrageous!" I said, laughing again.

"It's not funny darling, I mean it. Religion is old fashioned, unless you're Amish, that seems to be on the television all of the time at the moment."

"Amish? Where on earth is this coming from?"

"Channel 4," said Dad.

"Christ on a bike." I muttered and shook my head.

"Don't take his name in vain darling, not with your morals…" Mum said sarcastically, and before I had a chance to respond, Mia started to stir and we were back to baby talk.

The rest of their visit revolved around safer topics of conversation such as what they were having for tea and how they had changed electricity provider. I waved them off just before lunchtime, hoping Mia might go down for a nap and maybe I could join her. Of course I wanted to celebrate the birth of my child, but I didn't want to sell out on myself either. Religion was something that Damien and I had never really discussed and I didn't know how I felt about it anyway.

What about integrity? I couldn't go through a religious ceremony if I didn't believe it.

I did believe in a higher power, I knew that we were all made from creative consciousness and that people had different names for this, including Source and God, but I wasn't sure how I felt about tying Mia to a specific religion when I felt so ignorant about it myself. Who knew what she'd believe when she got older? She might want to renounce God altogether, and that would be her right. Or she could choose a religion or a belief system that was totally different to Christianity, it would be up to her. I didn't want to judge anyone that had decided to have their baby christened, but I did feel that maybe it's an empty promise to make if, in that moment, you have no intention of raising them in alignment with the teachings of the church. Perhaps in the past it had been different, but it seemed to me that a christening in many ways was more of a cultural expectation and event than a religious one, and it didn't sit right with me to get swept along without really considering what it meant.

"What about a naming day?" said Damien after I'd bent his ear throughout the whole of dinner about the christening dilemma.

"Ooooooo! That could be the answer!" I said and clapped my hands together. "You're so clever!"

"I know, it's my cross to bear in life…" he sighed sarcastically.

"Well, that and being handsome of course…" I joined in.

"Of course." He played along and I opened my laptop.

"Here we go… naming day ceremony" I muttered and started to scroll through the first page of links.

"This is going to be perfect Damien, we'll be able to get everyone together and have a lovely day."

"And show off to everyone that we have the best child and the most money." He rolled his eyes and I knew that this was a dig at my mother.

"It's not about that!" I said and elbowed him in the ribs.

"It is to your mother," he said and I couldn't disagree, but at least this way we could have something special to welcome Mia into the world, without me feeling like I was selling out or being dishonest.

"It's going to be perfect," I said and wondered if Josie would let us have a garden party at The Haven. It seemed fitting to have Mia's naming day in the same place that we married. I phoned mum and told her that this was the case.

"So really, darling, it's a christening but not in a church," she said.

"Yes and no, Mum…" I tried to launch into a second explanation but could hear the theme tune for *EastEnders* in the background, all bets were off.

"Great, that's what I'll say to the neighbours then. I'm so glad you came round to my way of thinking!" I was shaking my head as the call disconnected.

Chapter 11

I phoned Josie the following day and asked if we could use The Haven for Mia's naming day. She was delighted and said she would help to organize it.

"We could get a marquee!" she said on the other end of the phone. "How many are you inviting?"

"I don't think I could fill a marquee, Josie. I was just thinking of a similar number of people that we had at the wedding really, in fact the more I think about it, the people that we had at the wedding would be more or less the guest list with perhaps another couple added in." I wondered if Mel and her husband would like to come with little George and if I could get away with inviting them and not Rosie.

"Yes of course, you're right. You had your nearest and dearest at the wedding so it's more or less the same people. So how many was that? About thirty?"

"Yes, so if we say between thirty and forty and I'll ask Damien if he has a burning desire to invite any colleagues or friends I don't know about..."

"Sounds like a plan, do let me know when you settle on a date and we can work towards that. I only have two ladies here at the moment, but that can change any time, so if I get new arrivals I will be able to tell them it's happening. How are things anyway Steph, it seems like forever since we talked? Maybe you could drop in for a cuppa and we could go through the arrangements, and you could bring Mia. She must have changed so much since I saw her as a new-born."

"Things are great for me Josie, and yes I would love that," I said hoping that she didn't pick up on the slight sadness that edged my tone. After years of helping women in crisis you couldn't usually escape her honed intuition.

"And you and Damien?" There it was, the scab that I didn't want picking off.

"We're fine." I tried to brush over it. We were fine, I was just tired and hormonal and a bit chubby.

There was a telling pause on the end of the line. "Ok, well you can tell me all about it when you come for that cuppa, how fine things are and all that," she said with the end of the sentence rising to frame the statement as a question.

I sighed and suddenly felt little crying. "I think I'm probably just tired Josie, and hormonal as well. I'm probably just looking for things that aren't there and overreacting." I tried to sound convincing, I wanted to convince myself, never mind anyone else.

"Steph, what's wrong love?" she said in a sympathetic tone and the floodgates opened.

"It's me Josie, I'm being ridiculous, that's what's wrong," I sobbed. "I'm just being silly."

"About what love?" She tried to coax it out of me but it felt like the truth was stuck in my throat. I tried to swallow it down with my tears.

"It's you know… bedroom stuff," I whispered.

Josie matched my whispery tone, "What kind of bedroom stuff?"

"Well, no bedroom stuff," I sniffed.

"Oh right," said Josie and paused. "And how old is Mia now?"

"Six and a half months!" I said and I could tell as Josie spoke she was smiling.

"Stephanie, that's nothing love. I honestly don't want to minimize your feelings at all, but I don't know any couples who get their sex life back on line within the first year or so of having a new baby. It's a massive adjustment love, and you're both worn out." She spoke with empathy and I thought of the experience that she must have with the hundreds, if not thousands, of women she had helped and supported. She was telling me the truth, so why did it not make me feel any better?

"I just feel so unattractive." I caught a glimpse of myself in the mirror in the hallway which confirmed that as truth. The bags under my eyes were now highlighted with the red rims and ruddy cheeks that crying brought in a side order, as well as a snotty nose, bed head and a patch of sick on my right shoulder.

"Most new mums feel like this Steph, like a nappy bag on legs. Like a milking machine. Like you don't recognise the body that you are walking around in, with your new stretch marks and wobbly bits," she chuckled. "What was a nice, big, round baby bump that everyone wanted to pat and comment on, is now a muffin pelmet that you want to hide behind control knickers. The highlight of your week used to be date night and now it's the night before the bin goes out so you can fly tip an extra bag of nappies in your neighbour's in the dark, if you can stay up that late."

"Really?" I asked "Everyone feels like this?"

"Really, Steph. Your whole world has changed now, and that includes your relationship. You just need to give it time and find a new level that's all."

"Do you think I've got postnatal depression?" I asked.

"No. I think you are totally normal and that you've just had your first baby and you are adjusting to being a wife and mother, and not just a wife anymore, and that takes a little bit of getting used to."

"Really?"

"Really. I hear so many women's stories and I know that it's what happens the world over. I think you need to give it time and make sure that you express your love for each other in different ways and stay connected, and that things will unfold in the right direction soon."

"Ok, I told you I was being silly." I shook my head.

"You're not being silly Steph at all, you're just finding your way love. We're all different and having a baby is the biggest change in anyone's life. Some people can get right back to a physical relationship and some take more time, it's literally a very personal journey. And it doesn't mean that he loves you any less, or doesn't find you attractive you know, it can be a whole raft of other stuff. Is he stressed at work?"

"I don't really know." I hadn't asked. I'd been all wrapped up in poor me.

"Well sometimes that can have an influence. I just think that you need to not put pressure on yourselves, relax and let things happen naturally. Maybe you could ask your mum to have Mia for a weekend and get yourselves away somewhere nice, just the two of you," Josie suggested.

"Maybe," I said in a non-committal tone.

"Just a thought anyway. Now make sure you come for that cuppa soon I want to know all about how your book is going."

"That's easy to answer, it's not," I sighed again. "In fact I'd forgotten all about it these last few months."

"Hmmmm," said Josie and paused long enough for the penny to drop.

"Ok, ok I get it," I said. "I need to stop fixating on problems and do something that will help me to get back into The Flow!"

"You once explained to me that whatever I give my energy and attention to would grow, and at the moment it feels like you are giving a whole load of energy and attention to things *not* being great. I can also remember how excited and happy you were when you talked to me about the idea of taking your journal and sharing the lessons that you'd learned with the world."

"Ok, you got me." I managed a smile.

"Don't worry I won't tell anyone when you're famous," Josie laughed.

"Thanks Josie, I really mean that. You're a great friend."

"And so are you Stephanie, so are you."

Chapter 12

It seemed like such a long time ago that I'd written my journal, even though it was just over a year that I finished the final entry.

Mia was sleeping, but wouldn't be for long. Perhaps just long enough for me to find it and have a quick flick through. That one comment from Josie had opened up a whole stream of thoughts that washed over me now, as I made my way upstairs I thought about how much my life had changed in such a short space of time.

I had to kneel on the floor to reach right to the back of the bedside cupboard, and underneath a stack of old magazines and some foot lotion. My fingers brushed the leather cover of the book that held the message that I needed to get out there to the world. Although I hadn't looked at it, the thought of getting it published had been on my mind on and off since the wedding, but becoming a parent had taken over. I smiled to myself and thought of lesson ten, signs and serendipity. Josie had gently nudged me in the right direction at probably the perfect time to open the pages of my past.

I slid the book out carefully and sat on the edge of the bed with it on my lap. I traced the word Journal with my index finger. A mixture of nerves and excitement started to dance in my stomach and I hugged the book to me and closed my eyes.

"Whatever happens next is for the greatest and highest good of all concerned," I said out loud, then I took a deep breath and turned the first page.

The lessons weren't what made me cry.

It was the story behind them, and only I knew the truth that made me shrink back into my former self and feel some of the pain that I had back then. We are all a product of where we have been and what we have been through. The book that I held in my hands right now documented *Twelve Lessons* that would help others in their lives, but it was underpinned with my own transformation and struggle. Without me going through life's assault course and waking up to the knowing that I was worth so much more, these lessons would never have been learned for me.

Although they had been my lessons this time around, I knew that they were far bigger than me. Religious and spiritual texts the world over cited similar concepts and ideas about loving yourself, forgiveness and being a good human. But how many people right now in the real world, the crazy busy world that we live in would reach for one of these texts in order to change their lives and gain some wisdom and insight? I knew that a part of my calling was to package up these timeless lessons in a way that would appeal to the world now, to bring forward some kind of spiritual manifesto that would inspire people and help them to see that they could apply this to their own lives.

Maybe I needed to tell my own story, and maybe that's why I was scared of starting. I didn't want to lose my privacy or to open up old wounds. But I wanted to reach people and be real and show them that they could change their lives in amazing ways. I had a lot of thinking to do, and a lot of reading. I closed my eyes and tears dropped onto the first page as I saw my own handwriting.

Happy New Year you washed up silly cow. You have made a complete mess of things. You are a fat failure with no money and no prospects, a failing marriage and you're about to be unemployed imminently. No wonder your husband is probably going to leave you for someone better and your life is going down the toilet. You never deserved to be happy anyway, you have been fooling yourself all of this time, you stupid, silly cow.

The words on the page made me cringe. How could I have thought so little of myself? And how many other people felt that way because of the journey life had taken them through? I knew that this was the old version of me and when you know better you do better. But I felt like a part of me was back there, being sucked into the ocean of sadness again, and trying desperately to swim for the shore.

That's why people will relate to it, because it's real. It's how you're going to reach them.

I knew my intuition was right as its whispers sounded deep in my soul, but I also wondered if I was strong enough to do this. If this was my reaction with the first page, then how on earth could I go through the twelve months that brought me to my knees without folding in the short term? I had a lovely life now, one that I could have only dreamed of back then, and I didn't want to contaminate it by raking up the past and bringing up all of the pain and trauma that I had already endured once for real, and relived many times in nightmares.

Old Wounds.

Sue had mentioned healing old wounds, and how when things are unresolved for you that they are still active in your vibrational escrow or resonance. My reaction must be based on the fact that I haven't fully healed and processed the old stuff, and although I've moved on in my life and I'm happy now, there is still some old pain lingering in my heart and soul from what happened before.

I wondered how long it would take to be able to really release the past.

Damien's love had been a band aid. It had stopped the emotional bleeding and protected my vulnerability, cocooned me as I started the healing process. He'd held me in a safe space and surrounded me with love as I gradually started to believe that I was worthy. As my heart healed, so did my life and I was not a living testament to how you could turn things around with a willing spirit. So why did my past still haunt me?

As soon as I asked the question I knew the answer.

Because I am human.

The human condition is a paradox. People ask how we are and our default answer is 'fine' even when we aren't. Maybe a part of me thought that if I mentioned my past or reflected on it in any way, that I was being ungrateful for the life I had now. And anyway in terms of Law of Attraction we need to focus our energy in what we want to create, don't we? Why should I wallow in the past and focus on the misery I experienced there? I don't want another helping of that, thank you.

I reasoned with myself for another moment or two, but I knew that deep down there was work to be done here. I wouldn't have reacted this way if I didn't still have unresolved feelings, and this was the time to step back and try to be honest and objective with my own emotions, so that I could get to the bottom of them and heal.

Part of what Sue had asked me to consider was that a lesson will come up at the perfect time for you to learn it and make progress in your life. This is why it is important to have a belief that the universe is sending you what you need all of the time, even when your conscious mind disagrees.

Why would this be coming up for me now? I was generally in a good place with myself, apart from feeling a bit wobbly with Damien and our sex life. I stopped the next automatic thought that would have usually jumped in about me being fat and frumpy and him not being attracted to me anymore… That's why this was coming up right now, it was a lesson in healing my old wounds from the past because they were unresolved and affecting me in the now time, even though I hadn't seen it before now. The whole experience with my ex-husband, Jay, was about me feeling like I wasn't good enough. I was unattractive, unworthy of him, unloved and in fear of him betraying me with someone else. As I stepped back from my own mind and really looked at the thoughts objectively that surrounded this whole historical experience, I could see aspects of them in my consciousness now in relation to Damien and I.

The essence was the same, even though the detail was different. An old pattern was playing out in my vibration and it was drawing in matching experiences from the outside world, or life as we like to call it.

"You can pixie and unicorn it up all you like, Steph," I said out loud. "You need to sort your shit out from the past or you're going to have to pick up the tab in the now."

I heard Mia stir and closed the journal.

Heal Your Old Wounds was the lesson, and although I didn't truly know how I was going to do it, I did feel that recognizing the lesson was of course the first step.

Stephanie's Journal ~ Lesson 16
Heal Your Wounds

As we experience life in human form, some of what comes our way leaves us bruised and battle scarred. Trauma and challenging experiences thankfully do not usually last forever, but their resonance and energy will if we don't do our own inner healing word.

The wounds that we still carry keep us stuck in the past and keep us tied into that experience energetically, as the energy frequencies still play out loud and clear to the universe. This means that we can't be free emotionally or otherwise, and we also run the risk of attracting in people and situations that are in alignment with that old pain and circumstance. Healing your old wounds is so important in order to create the life you want to live now, and attract in what you are so worthy of.

"Although the world is full of suffering, it is full also of overcoming it." Helen Keller

Chapter 13

I really had to make a big effort to be present for the rest of the afternoon.

My mind was whirling with ideas about my book, and I could hardly wait for Mia's bed time to get started. After the dishes were done and Damien was reclined in his favourite chair with a cup of tea and the television on quietly, I made my way to our bedroom and slid the journal from under my pillow.

"You can do this," I told myself and started again with lesson 1, Be Open to Possibility. As I read the words I had written over two years ago now, I found that I felt detached. This seemed to me like someone else's words on a page, someone else's insights and observations. Maybe the distance that time had created between the now and then had given me a different perspective, or maybe the lesson was different for me now?

I lifted my eyes from the page and gazed out of the bedroom window. The wind was making the tops of the trees sway against the sky, and my mind drifted.

Be Open to Possibility.

The statement settled into my awareness and I thought about my own life. Sue was right that lessons were never 'done'. We learned them and then took that experience with us into the next chapter of our lives, sometimes applying it and sometimes not, depending on where we are on our journey and what is unfolding. Sometimes aspects or echoes of lessons might come back around to us, or we may be able to observe other people going through their learning and take the lessons as reflections of where we need to heal, evolve or make progress.

In that case, lesson one was always evident. The moment we stopped being open to possibility in any area of our life was the moment that we closed the door on our own progress and life's opportunities. Perhaps you didn't need to *learn* lessons again, maybe we just needed to be mindful of them and their application in our lives?

I sighed and closed the journal. Such a lot to think about and if I was going to be bringing this concept to the masses then hadn't I better make sure that I understood it all first?

Be Open to Possibility.

And there it was again! I laughed at myself and opened up the journal again. Maybe some questions would help people to really get into the way that a lesson could occur in their life?

What are you closed to? I wrote in pencil beneath the biro from two years ago. I knew that the answer for me at the moment was twofold. I was closing down to the fact that Damien might ever fancy me again and also to getting my book published.

The common theme here was the fear of rejection, and that fear was firmly rooted in my past and my experiences with Jay. So really I had both lesson one coming up for me again, along with a side order of *Heal Your Wounds.* This did feel like an overwhelm but the fact was, that without lesson one, it was unlikely that I would have been open enough to see where I had closed the door on the possibility of positive change.

"Lessons are layered in our lives," I said absently and wondered why I hadn't seen this before. Maybe I wasn't ready for it. Sue had said that recognizing lessons as they come up was a step forward in my own evolution. I guess I just need to trust that the timing was perfect. I made a note to include the observation in the introduction, and leaned over to switch on the bedside lamp. I could hear a spoon clinking on the side of a mug and I looked at the clock. Damien would be making a cup of tea to bring to bed, as was the night time routine after he'd locked up.

He padded up the stairs and appeared in the doorway. "I made you some tea," he said placing the cup beside the lamp and then making his way around to his side.

"Are you sleeping in here tonight?" I asked.

"I was going to, if that's ok with you?" he sounded somewhat apologetic and I quickly reviewed the tone I had used, had I sounded like I didn't want him here?

"Of course it's alright with me," I tried to lighten the atmosphere. "I won't need bed socks if you're here."

"You might need earplugs though," he said slipping his t-shirt over his head and unfastening his jeans. He slipped between the sheets with nothing but his boxer shorts on, naked sleeping had stopped being on the agenda these past months.

I get the hint.

I thought and felt my heart sink a little.

At least he's here in bed with you, that's a start.

"I'll just elbow you if you start snorting like a pig," I said and stood up to get some pyjamas out of the top drawer. "I'm going to have a quick shower," I said, when the truth of it was that I just couldn't bear to get undressed in front of him.

I wanted to believe that this was my old stuff that was unresolved, and that Damien did still love me and want me, but as I stripped off in the bathroom and caught a glimpse of my super-sized stretchmarked backside I couldn't stop thinking that this was my fault.

He must have sensed that something was wrong as I hung my wet towel over the radiator and pulled back the duvet on my side.

"Are you ready for lights out?" he said, closing the latest murder mystery from his favourite writer.

"Yes, I'm shattered," I said and switched off my lamp and so did he.

"I know how you feel," he said, slipping an arm around my waist. Usually this comment would have been loaded with a totally different inference.

"I love you," he said as he pulled me into him and kissed the back of my neck.

I felt emotion rise in my throat and I didn't trust myself to answer straight away without crying.

"Steph? We're ok right?" he whispered in the dark.

I composed myself for a moment and then answered.

"I love you too, Damien, and yes we're ok." He squeezed me again and I felt a tear run down one cheek and onto the pillow, I hoped with everything I had, that we would be soon.

Stephanie's Journal ~ Lesson 17
Ditch the Drama

Drama is a drain on your time and energy. It usually occurs when you place your focus on something that does not serve you, and you feed it by keeping the story active in your vibration. Where attention goes, energy will flow. Talking about something incessantly, posting on social media, texting friends and getting generally sucked in, will not only perpetuate the drama, it will make it grow. Stop feeding the drama by being conscious of your thoughts and actions and shifting your focus. If someone is stuck in Drama, they are dedicated to their story and their pain. You can have compassion, but you cannot save them, we all wake up when we are ready.

"Pour yourself a drink, put on some lipstick and pull yourself together."   Liz Taylor

Chapter 14

As I immersed myself in my journal and re-read the lessons I had lived and in most part learned, I found that a strange thing happened. I was able to step back more easily from my own life and my own experiences and be more objective. At times it felt like I was observing rather than participating. When I asked Sue about it she said that this was good, it was looking at life from a Higher Self perspective rather than being in the 'stuff' or the drama of life as it unfolded. Once she had explained this I was also able to see when other people were not doing this, and I found myself noticing that drama seems to feed people in some way, perhaps feeding their inner victim or the parts of them that were still in pain from their past experiences or sabotaging beliefs.

I did what I could to stay present, not judge and look for reflections in my own life, which Sue explained could also be contrast. In other words, life could be showing you what you don't want to be, do or experience in order for you to align to something different and create a new outcome. I wasn't sure if I'd ever fully understand. Just when something started to make sense it seemed like another concept needed to be considered as part of the journey and the big picture.

I was finding that it was so hard to heal your old wounds from the past without giving them attention. How could I know what I needed to work on if I couldn't think about it? And how would I know if I was making any progress if I couldn't reflect on how I used to feel? I'd once heard someone talking about how your story affects you, and that you need to focus on the story that you want your life to be like in order to create it. I could agree with that, this was good old Law of Attraction in action, focus on what you want and you will get more of it or draw it to you. But how could you focus on what you wanted when you were picking over the scabs of your past?

I decided in a flash of inspiration, in between changing a nappy and boiling the kettle, that what I needed was a brain dump. I needed to allow myself to go there once, to dig through yesterday's trash with my bare hands and bare soul and write down everything that I felt. Then I could look at the parts of my story that were pointing me towards the lessons I needed to learn. I wanted to be able to see what mattered, without getting sucked in to a poor me feeling and allowing my inner victim to stage a pity party.

As Mia nodded off in her baby bouncer, I reached for paper and a pen.

I didn't give myself a chance to back out, this was the difference between ripping off the band aid and it hurting once or peeling it off over time and hurting yourself on an ongoing basis. I started to scribble furiously, feelings, names, places and even doodles of a broken heart, a smiley face and a baby. I kept going until the page was nearly full, and that included tiny scrolling sentences jammed into horizontal and diagonal white strips of space. There were several F words and a couple of Twats. After about ten minutes I sat back and put the pen down. I flicked my fingers in and out on my right hand, I didn't realize how hard I had been gripping the pen.

"And that's that," I said and puffed out my cheeks, then exhaled slowly.

I did feel relieved, but maybe a little overwhelmed as well.

I sure had a lot of shit.

Luckily the pen I had used was one of those biros that you can click to write in a different colour, and I changed from black to red. I started to circle all of the issues that were connected to the fear that I wasn't good enough, since this seemed to be what was coming up for me at the moment.

There was quite a lot, which initially felt like a bad thing, but then I felt quite positive when I saw that by resolving one pattern in my life, I could help myself in lots of different ways.

I changed the colour to blue and wrote underneath each issue what my common thoughts and feelings were about each. I remembered from lesson four that I was drawing in matching frequencies to my thoughts and therefore creating my experience. Another layer onto being open to possibility and healing old wounds, but all coming back to the same thing in essence. If I could get to the core of why I felt like I did and change that, then I would feel better and attract a better experience… the penny was finally dropping.

Sort out your shit cart! I wrote and underlined it twice. That sums it up quite nicely.

It was becoming obvious that although I knew about The Law of Attraction that I had perhaps overlooked its implications in my current situation. When I looked at what I had been thinking about - my relationship with

Damien, my weight, my book and other situations in my life - it was no wonder that I'd been stuck.

It just goes to show that even when you think you know everything, you really don't.

The things that I was saying to myself were totally reflective of the experiences that I was drawing in, and it was only through changing this and my perception of it that I could change my life.

I knew this stuff!

Why was it tripping me up now?

I needed to remember to Be Present and to step back from the experience of life as it unfolded and be conscious of what I was thinking and feeling and therefore creating. The journey to enlightenment meant that I was always going to be a work in progress, and I guessed that accepting this and not beating myself up, was going to be involved as well.

This was the journey, and there was value in that. Instead of rushing ahead to the destination that I wanted, I needed to slow down and be in the here and now more, not only to help me to manifest what I wanted, but to process and grow and evolve as a human.

I hadn't given much thought to that recently, I'd just been coasting along and letting life happen, and the irony in the situation was that I didn't even know that whilst it was happening! It's in the stepping back and being conscious that you can see where you were unconscious, which is the cosmic way of saying 'you don't know what you don't know'.

So now I had a page full of my stuff and some ideas about what was keeping me stuck, but before I could bring these lessons to the world I had to find my own way. I knew enough about Law of Attraction to know that if I was in fear and generally stuck that there was no way I could draw in the outcome that I wanted.

I heard Mia stir and I paused to see if she was waking fully. The sound of gurgling was confirmation and I folded away the paper for now. I'd go back to it later, but for now I had a date at soft play.

Stephanie's Journal ~ Lesson 18
Put Down What is Heavy

When you drag your old stuff around with you it's going to weigh you down. It's time to stop and have a really good look at what is burdening you. What are you carrying that needs to be dumped from your psyche or your story? The past is just that, past. You can't create the future you want until you are ready to sort through your shit cart and lighten the load. And for goodness sake don't drag other people's cart up the hill called life! It feels like the kind thing to do but it's robbing them of an opportunity to grow and learn. Support them from the side lines, but allow them to live through the lessons that are in their soul curriculum, and get on with yours.

"Let go or be dragged." Zen Proverb

Chapter 15

Mel was camped in the corner when I arrived, barricaded in with the pushchair and nappy bag, sipping a latte with one eye on George in the ball pool.

"Sorry I'm a bit late," I said bustling in and steering around the assault course of shoes and toddlers.

"It's totally fine, when you are on baby time there's nothing you can do about it!" She smiled at Mia, I knew she was trying for another baby and wanted a little girl this time.

"I'll just grab a cuppa," I said lowering Mia into the ball pool, sitting her right in the corner within grabbing distance of Mel. Mia picked up a red ball straight away and started to dribble all over it, does it really build up their immune system to be exposed to other children's snot and spit? Who knows, but I was here now and gasping for a coffee.

"So what's going on in your world?" I asked as I eventually got back to the small round table with a coffee and two doughnuts.

"Just the usual I guess. I'm not pregnant yet which is just as well because there is a mums night out happening at the end of the month and we are going!" She grinned like a crazy mother who had not been out in months.

"We are?" I asked with trepidation. I could vaguely remember going out with the girls and there were times it had not ended well, usually in fact. There was no way I could manage being a mum with a hangover, and even though a night on the town would have appealed to me back in the day, I didn't want to leave Mia to be honest.

"Yes Steph we are!" Mel said with gusto. "When was the last time you went out, and I mean *out*?"

"Erm, before I had Mia obviously," I mumbled.

"And I bet you didn't go out much when you were pregnant either...?" Mel quizzed me and I squirmed.

"No I guess I didn't," I mumbled again and used my index finger to press on to the small white plate to make sure no doughnut sugar was wasted.

"Well you *deserve* it then Steph! We both do!" She became more animated and I wondered if it was partly a sugar rush, maybe I should have gone for the diabetic friendly brownies.

"We can get our hair done and our nails and find something really lovely to wear. We've got three weeks to get sorted. It will do us the world of good to dress up and not feel like just a mummy for a few hours, please say you'll come?" Eventually she paused for breath and looked at me with puppy dog eyes and a mock pet lip.

"I'll think about it, ok?" I said, lying through my teeth.

"Yay!" Mel clapped her hands. "I knew you would!"

"I said I'll think about it!" I reinforced and sighed. If I did go it would be through obligation and to not let Mel down, but was that good enough reason?

"Well don't think too long, we have to get a taxi booked!"

"Mel, it's three weeks away yet!" I laughed at her enthusiasm and realized how much I had grown to like her in the past few weeks.

Friendships change when you have a child, and although I was still in contact with my good friend Lizzie, her life was very different to mine. She loved Mia and she always asked about her when we talked, but there was not only very little common ground there. The subject also exposed the scar that we shared about the past, and that threatened to open a chapter of our lives that we had both moved on from and didn't care to revisit. I didn't think Lizzie would have any children now, she'd said as much anyway. She was happy with Matt and the lifestyle that they had, and when I really thought about it, cream carpets and designer bags weren't a good match to chocolate buttons and nappies.

There was a little sadness when I thought about her situation, although having children is an entirely personal choice, I knew how much being a mother had filled me up. I had always presumed that I would have a child or maybe even more than one. It had never been part of my reality to not procreate, but I appreciated that other people felt differently. I looked at Mia giggling and throwing balls into the air and I felt every part of me radiate with love. This was different to any other feeling I'd had, so much more intense and precious, so much more all-encompassing and even overwhelming at times. When people used to say that their child was their world I thought I understood that, but I know now that this understanding was from a very superficial standpoint. You have to experience this to really know it, and I wondered if people that chose not to have children knew what they were giving up.

"Let me talk to Damien and see what he thinks," I said, as possibly the most feeble half excuse I could come up with.

"Ok, he'll be fine with it I'm sure. He'll want you to go out and have a great time!" Damien was now Mel's ally.

"So when and where is it, Mel? And I'm not saying that I'm coming, I'm just finding out," I asked and Mel started to gush details.

Apparently it was something that happened a couple of times a year and the mums from the toddler group all got together and had a night out somewhere in town, usually with food and some kind of entertainment. There had once been a nightclub involved but I made it very clear that wasn't for me, not now anyway. It seems that the venue of choice was a lovely big country pub that had been bought by a chain and gutted inside and out, and that part of the refurbishment had included a dance floor, a mezzanine floored restaurant and themed party nights.

"And what's the theme this time?" I asked whilst I reached down to sit Mia back as she had slowly slid underneath the multi-coloured plastic sea.

"It's eighties!" Mel squealed. "Can you believe it? We could be Bananarama!"

"But there were three," I said wondering if she'd had another bad night with George.

"Oh yes, well Rosie is definitely going, in fact she's the organizer." Mel grinned.

We hadn't had the talk about my opinion of Rosie yet, but it could be pending.

"Great," I said trying not to sound sarcastic. "Do you want another coffee?"

Chapter 16

As soon as Mia had settled for her afternoon nap I reached for the journal and the folded up brain dump of a spider chart.

If I could sort out my own stuff then maybe I could include it in the completed book and help people with their stuff as well. I needed a new story, and I needed to get rid of some of the beliefs that were underpinning the feelings that I still had to some degree about my past.

"That's it, I'll write a new story," I said out loud and reached for a new sheet of paper.

Stephanie's Story became the title and was underlined twice.

I'm crazy doing this, I thought as I started to scribble notes about the way that I wanted my life to look. A part of me felt guilty that I had been blessed with so much that other people wanted, could I not just get my shit together and be happy? If only it were that easy. I knew in my heart that the scars ran deep and that I would never be truly free to love the life I lived now unless I cleared up my past, and that at some level the pain that I still felt was contaminating the now. I am sure there would be plenty of people that would have looked in on my situation and thought I was being ridiculous, but was this not the whole point of being here? Surely, as humans, we needed to understand that everyone's stuff is big stuff to them, and no matter what is holding them back, it's relevant in their lives and therefore a problem?

I didn't know why I had to keep justifying it to myself, I was here at my kitchen table all alone and no one would ever have to read this apart from me. There was no reason to be bothered or worried, even though a part of me was.

Fear of Judgement I wrote on the brain dump sheet and then continued with my new story, which was one of being connected and happy with Damien, being my ideal weight, a really good parent to a happy and healthy child and no longer dragging around the past that was holding me prisoner.

I stopped and puffed out a deep breath.

I crossed out the part about dragging around my past and being held prisoner, everything else in the new story was really positive and this was a reminder that I was still wounded. It felt wrong to not include it though, maybe I could find a positive spin on it.

I am free to experience the joy of the moment, I am present in the wonder and happiness of each day as it unfolds for me. I live in the now.

That felt better, and it meant the same thing really.

My mind wandered to publishing and how on earth I was going to get the lessons in the journal out there into the world. I didn't know the first thing about publishing, and truth be told I was an accidental writer when it came down to it.

I started a google search and quickly realized that publishing was a minefield.

There was so much information it was scary, and it seemed as well that there were different ways to go about it. There were blogs about self-publishing, agents, big publishing houses, foreign rights, movie rights and more. This was far more involved that I had first naively thought and I would have to get to grips with more than I had bargained for.

I skimmed a couple of the first websites and saw that they both had something in common that struck fear in me, social media. I'd seen Facebook on my friends' phones but I'd always been of the opinion that my private life was just that, and I didn't want it plastered all over the internet.

'You're so old fashioned,' was something Hannah said to me a lot. "It's just a way of keeping in touch with people."

"Why not just keep in touch with people then?" I answered sarcastically.

"Steph you need to drag yourself into this century," she laughed.

I knew she was right, and I'd used her profile before to have a nose at what people were up to, and even browsed a couple of pages that I'd kind of liked. But I couldn't bring myself to get on the social media bus. According to what I was seeing from agents, writers and publishers worldwide this was something I was going to have to review if I wanted to be a success though.

What's stopping you, I asked myself, and no sooner was the thought formed a familiar feeling washed over me of regret and sadness and Jay. I didn't want to know what he was doing with his life because I *did* want to know. I wasn't quite done with it yet, and I knew myself well enough to be certain that I would not be able to help myself when it came to spying on him. I couldn't trust myself to not be curious, and I was worried that it would contaminate my life now. Then that first thought unlocked a whole stream of questions about his life right now. Had he met anyone? Did he think about me? Was he happy? Did he have any children? I found myself being sucked further and further into the pit of 'what if' with every thought that formed in my mind.

That's exactly why I should never join Facebook, I thought, and a part of me whispered, *that's exactly why you need to sort your shit out*. And I knew that they were both right.

Chapter 17

"Of course you should go, we'll be fine won't we baby?" said Damien that night as he played with Mia and her bath toys.

"I don't know," I said. "I'm not sure I want to go but I don't want to let Mel down."

"It's just one night, Steph, and it will do you good to let your hair down and have a giggle with the girls." Mia was laughing and splashing water in his face and he was pulling faces at her.

"I'll think about it," I sighed. "I just like being a home bird now I guess. Speaking of which I'll go and put our pasta on, and warm a bottle, everything's out that you'll need."

I made my way downstairs and thought about going out. Was it really such a big deal? Maybe Damien was right I should just get over myself. After all it's what normal people do. Maybe having a baby had made me a bit of a hermit, but other mums were going so maybe I should make the effort.

If it feels wrong it usually is, sounded through my mind and although I heard it, I made a mental note to come back to that later.

The half hour before Mia's bedtime was one of my favourite parts of the day, second only to the moment when she woke up with bed head and out stretched arms for me to lift her out of her cot. I snuggled her in close and breathed in the warm baby smell from the top of her soft scalp, wisps of hair tickled my nose as she sucked greedily on the bottle in my hand. After a few moments her eyelids started to close and as her belly filled with warm milk she started to breathe a little deeper. I sat her up gently, lifted her onto my shoulder and rubbed her back as I made my way up the stairs to put her down for the night.

"Sleep tight," I whispered and kissed her brow before I switched on the baby monitor and made my way downstairs.

Damien had opened a bottle of wine to have with dinner which was unusual but tasted delicious with the pasta.

"From a client?" I asked as I refilled my glass, feeling slightly giddy I was well out of practice.

"No not this time, I just fancied a glass and stopped at the garage on the way home."

"That's not like you," I said "Is everything ok?"

"Yes, of course it is, just work stuff you know how it is..." his voice drifted into a tone that probably meant *don't ask* but I couldn't help it.

"Maybe you should leave Damien, sell up or whatever?" I said for at least the hundredth time.

"I know, I'll think about it, Steph. But you know I love what I do and I've built it up from very little." He swirled the wine in his glass.

"I know you do, but there must be other things you'd enjoy doing and we'd see loads more of you." I reached out my hand to touch his. "It's not like we need the money."

I knew that it wasn't about the money for Damien, his business had been a labour of love and he'd steered the estate agency through the boom and near bust of the late nineties and early noughties, clawing his way to success and still managing to create a nice portfolio for himself before we had been reunited. For him it was about the people. He felt invested in helping the people that worked for him and also the people that came to him to sell their houses, and although as a couple we were financially sound, we had invested some of our own money into expanding the business and opened up more branches in the past year.

I often thought that this might be about Damien proving himself. He hadn't done as well in school as both of his parents had hoped, and the feeling of parental disappointment had weighed heavy on him ever since. He had worked relentlessly before I met him, first of all on his own and then with a part-time assistant to help him by answering the phone and some admin. Then gradually he was able to employ someone to help with valuations and expanded from just selling houses to letting them as well. By the time we got together he'd had a good few years under his belt and wisely invested in small properties that he knew would let easily and instead of using the whole of the rental to overpay a monthly mortgage, he had saved alongside an additional deposit and bought another. They were all paid for now and his company managed them, and to be honest I didn't know much about it as I didn't have to be involved.

I did hope that sooner rather than later he'd take his foot off the gas and look at being at home more. But I understood that the new branches needed attention at the moment to get up and running and into profit before he could even think of doing that. I had suggested a few months ago that he employed someone to manage the whole group, but he had resisted, saying that a manager in each branch was good enough and that he was in charge of overseeing everything. I just wondered what the cost would be for that, and if the stress was contributing to the distance I felt between us more and more. There had still been nothing on the cards in bed and I didn't want to push for fear of rejection, but that was something I had to work on and my new story would hopefully help with that.

"I've thought about what you said, you know," he sighed.

"Oh?"

"About an operations manager, I've got someone to interview this week as it happens." He refilled his own glass and took a sip.

"Damien, that's great news!" I was genuinely pleased that he was considering letting someone else take the strain, and perhaps this would lead to him handing over the reins altogether.

"We'll see, it's early days and it might take me a while to get the right person but this girl comes with great references and a few years' experience as well."

That took the wind out of my sails. Why had I presumed that he would be interviewing a man for the job? I could feel anxiety starting to build a little, as I drained my second glass of wine and decided to have no more. "That sounds good," I said trying to sound genuinely pleased. "So she's worked in another estate agents then?"

"Yes, she managed a couple of branches in town so she's got good people skills and she started off as a negotiator so she knows the business from the bottom up. Although she's quite young she seems to have a good head on her shoulders."

"Right. So how young is young then?" I asked trying to sound interested and not panic stricken. This reaction was ridiculous, it was just fear coming up from my past but even though I knew that alarm bells were sounding in my head and I felt like I was back there with Jay cheating on me and lying.

"About your age, I think."

"Twenty-one, then!" I blurted out and laughed.

"You're pissed."

I couldn't really defend that statement so I ignored it instead.

"So when are you seeing her?" I asked.

"On Friday afternoon."

"Well let's hope it goes really well," I said swallowing the trepidation I was feeling - that was no doubt alcohol and history induced. "I'd love to have you around more."

"I'd love that too, Steph, I really would," he said and smiled at me. "I've missed you." From nowhere tears pricked my eyes and my voice was caught in my throat, I wanted to say it back but I knew that if I spoke I'd be sobbing. "Come here you," he said, putting his wine glass down, opened his arms and I fell into them. "I know I've been a bit distant recently, but it's just work stuff and I love you." I squeezed my eyes tight shut and felt tears on my cheeks momentarily before they slightly darkened the fabric of Damien's shirt.

"I love you, Damien and I have missed you so much," I sniffed.

"I'm sorry, I'll make it up to you. I just need to get this sorted and then I'll be back." He stroked my hair and kissed the top of my head.

"And it's just work stuff, right?" I asked in a muffled voice, I didn't want to leave his embrace.

"Of course. What else could it be?" He released his hold and I sat up straight next to him, with my eyes cast down to my hands in my lap.

"I just thought that maybe I was a bit…" I could hardly bring myself to say it out loud.

"A bit what?" he asked and I took a deep breath.

"A bit fat."

Damien burst out laughing and his arms were around me again. "I'm sorry Steph, I'm not laughing at you…"

"It feels like you are!" I snivelled.

"Of course you aren't fat, and even if you were fat, which you're bloody not, I would never stop loving you."

"What about fancying me, though?" I dared to whisper.

"Of course I still fancy you. I just haven't felt like it that's all."

"Really?" I asked as I felt his thumb beneath my chin as he gently raised my head so that his eyes met mine.

"Really," he said and kissed my lips. "I'll be a whole new man once I'm not working so hard, I promise."

"Ok then, as long as you promise." I smiled weakly and kissed him back.

"What's her name?" I asked and Damien looked confused.

"Who?"

"The girl you are interviewing on Friday," I said, trying to sound like I wasn't bothered and secretly pleased that he'd moved on from her in his mind so quickly even if I hadn't.

"Oh her, Louisa. But she gets Lou."

Of course she does, how cute. Mia started crying on the baby monitor and I stood up. "Can I leave you with the dishes she's probably not got all of her wind up from that last bottle?" I said as I walked out of the room and towards the foot of the stairs thinking about what Lou might look like, and hoping - yet knowing it was very unlikely - that she was at least a good size 18 with a top lip that desperately needed waxing and BO.

Chapter 18

I rang Lizzie's office the following day and caught her between appointments.

"I've phoned to pick your brains, and invite you to Mia's naming day which my mother is insisting is a christening but not in church..."

She laughed and I knew that on the other end of the phone line she'd be shaking her head at my mother's attitude.

"Pick away!" Lizzie said. "But I'm no good on christenings or naming days. Divorces, wills and fraud I'm good at but hopefully you don't need any of the above!"

"God no, well not yet anyway. I want to know where you and Matt would go for a weekend away? I'm going to ask mum to have Mia and I wanted to book somewhere really nice for us both, you're always jet-setting around the place and I thought I'd shortcut the process and give you a call."

"So I am Trip Advisor, am I?" Lizzie asked and I told her to bugger off and spill the beans on her list of romantic hideaways.

"It depends what you want Steph, in this country or abroad?"

"Here really, I don't want too far to travel or the hassle of flights, and anyway I think my mum would really freak out if I left the country."

"Let's think then, what's on your wish list?" asked Lizzie and started reeling off a whole load of things I hadn't considered. In between the suggestions of a hot tub and a Michelin Star restaurant I knew I'd so come to the right girl.

"I know the perfect place!" she said after a couple of minutes of tossing ideas around. "It has to be Eskdale Hall. I'll email you the link later, I think you'll love it."

"Great thank you, I knew you'd be the person to ask."

"Let me know what you decide. Oh, and what do you buy as a gift for a naming day?"

"The same sort of thing as a christening, I suppose."

"So your mother is right then, it's a christening but not in a church."

"Well, maybe but we're not telling her that!" I chuckled and finished the call.

I googled Eskdale Hall and immediately agreed with Lizzie that it was the perfect place. I scrolled through the gallery of pictures and swooned at the Bridal Suite with its private terrace and hot tub, champagne on arrival and four poster bed. That was definitely the room for us, and if we couldn't reconnect there then I'd have to give up hope altogether! There was a drop down calendar that showed availability and prices, and according to that in a fortnight's time my dreams would be coming true and my sex life well and truly back on track. With a couple of clicks and an upgrade to an all-inclusive fine dining package, I'd saved the day. If my mother agreed to have Mia that is, which she kept pestering me about, so I didn't think it would be an issue.

I sat back and scanned the emailed booking confirmation, wondering if I should tell Damien about it or surprise him. I was rubbish at keeping secrets and really excited about going, which didn't bode well for this being a revelation the day before we left. I'd try to keep it in for as long as I could, however long that was, but for now I could tell mum and she could be my accomplice.

I had two weeks to get fabulous, and mum could have Mia for a couple of afternoons while I worked on releasing my inner goddess. I started to scribble a list including nails, hair, and possibly a spray tan. Underwear! I needed underwear and maybe even outer wear as well, my mummy uniform would be no good and I doubted I could squeeze into anything pre-baby.

I dialled mum's number and told her my plan.

"That's great, darling, we'd love to have Mia!" she said and I knew that she'd be planning who she could invite over to see her granddaughter as soon as we had finished on the phone.

"Thanks Mum, maybe I should bring her over a couple of times for the afternoon and leave her with you, just so she gets used to it," I suggested.

"Oh yes! I'd love that Steph I really would, just let me know when and I'll keep it clear." By that she meant work it around my coffee morning and voluntary shift in the charity shop once a week, which I was sure she only offered to do so that she could get first shout on anything decent that came through the door.

"Most days are good for us, Mum, so just work it round you." I said looking in the mirror and finger combing my hair to expose months of root growth.

"Well, why don't you bring her today then?" Mum asked and I paused for a moment.

"Erm, today?"

"Yes Stephanie as in TODAY!" Mum replied indignantly, but softened a little and said, "the days merge a bit when you're tired, don't they."

"Yes, they do. Sorry, Mum, I just didn't expect you to say today! That would be great, I'll get sorted and then head over in about an hour is that ok?"

"Of course, darling, I'll make you a sandwich."

I felt a sudden gush of love for my mum that she wanted to look after me, being a mother myself had made me realize what she must have sacrificed of herself to have a child and this was now a membership club I had lifetime access to. The feeling soon passed when she commented that she had Weight Watchers bread. I shook my head as I ended the call.

Chapter 19

"So she'll be ready for a nap in about an hour and a half, but she did have a snooze in the car so that might be later than usual." I was in the middle of giving Mum final instructions and pulling my coat on as she ushered me to the door.

"And make sure you really get her wind up, Mum, or she'll be sick and you don't want that on the new carpet." I picked up my handbag and stepped further towards the door.

"She'll be fine, darling. We have actually done this before you know." I knew that she knew this was a wrench for me. Properly leaving Mia for the first time wasn't easy, even if she was with my own mum.

"Now go and have a lovely afternoon and we'll see you at tea time. I'll make you something healthy." I knew that was code for low calorie. I kissed her cheek and made my way to the car, when I looked back I could see Dad with Mia in his arms waving her hand like a puppet at me out of the window. I waved back and swallowed the lump in my throat as I reversed onto the street and made my way into town.

By the time I had parked, Mum had sent me a picture message of Mia on dad's lap covered in chocolate. *She's never going to sleep now,* I thought, but still smiled at her dirty little face.

"Right, Steph, it's time to get your glam on," I said to myself as I made my way to the high street. I walked purposefully towards my favourite clothes shop and stood in front of the window display. There were some gorgeous outfits displayed on mannequins that looked perfect for a weekend away. I hadn't been in here for a good few months. I'd been in maternity clothes from being three months pregnant.

I walked in and started to browse through the tops first, I flicked to the back of the rail where the bigger sizes were, although I had no idea what size I was now. I guessed I was bigger than I used to be still so I picked the next size up and made my way to the jeans.

A sales assistant looked up, smiled at me and mouthed "hello" and I smiled back. She probably remembered me as we'd had a long discussion about her wanting to become pregnant as well one day, when I was explaining why I needed an elasticated waist band moving forward.

I chose some jeans and made my way to the changing room, she followed me and after counting my five items passed me a plastic disc that confirmed the amount.

"So how's child birth?" she asked and I noticed that she looked as stick thin as the last time I had seen her.

"Well they don't call it labour for nothing!" I laughed. "But it's worth every second."

"Did you have a boy or a girl?" she asked me and I went into my bag to pull out my phone.

"A little girl, Mia." I showed her one of the new-born pictures and then the one my mum had just sent as well.

"She's perfect," said the sales assistant who, according to her name badge, was Vicky.

"And what about you?" I lowered my tone and waited for her to compose herself a little.

"Nothing yet," she said stoically, then she sighed and lowered her own tone to match mine. "I've lost two since I saw you last." She closed her eyes and shook her head a little.

I reached out my hand to touch her arm and she looked at me with tears making her eyes glisten and threatening to spill over onto her cheeks.

"I'm fine," she said. "Really I am, it's just a bit overwhelming sometimes. I don't begrudge people that have children, but I do wonder why it's not me. What have I done?"

"I really can't answer that, I wish I could but there is nothing that I can say that will make that feel any different. It's awful for you." I was trying hard not to feel guilty that I had a healthy baby at home.

"It's no one's fault, really. I'm sorry if I upset you. I'm going through another IVF cycle at the moment and my hormones are all over the place!" she smiled weakly. "My husband says he can't take much more of this permanent PMT!"

I smiled back and said genuinely, "I really hope this is the time that it works for you. And who knows you might even have twins. That's common with IVF, isn't it?"

"Yes, multiple births are quite common because they put more than one egg back in sometimes." Vicky nodded and looked over my shoulder as another customer approached with an armful of clothes to try. "I don't know how people cope with having more than one at a time though, can you imagine? You must find it easy though or you wouldn't be having another one."

I sidestepped to the right as Vicky smiled full on at the next customer and held out her arms for the stack of colourful fabric that needed to be counted as items.

"Let me know how it goes, maybe you'll have a boy this time, a little brother for Mia."

Oh, God she thinks I am pregnant again.

I smiled back through gritted teeth and managed to say the word, "Maybe," before I made my way to cubicle three and locked the door. I stood shell-shocked looking at myself in probably the world's most unflattering full-length mirror, under a flickering strip light, holding an armful of beautiful clothes that I knew for sure I wasn't going to try on now.

I dropped them to my feet and leaned my back against the door as tears stung my eyes.

Did I look that big? I'd read in load of magazines that it can take a long time to lose baby weight, and I was still breastfeeding. No matter what I said to myself, the reflection glaring back at me was a bit less goddess and a bit more fuller-figure to say the least. How on earth was I going to be able to speak to Vicky on the way out? And how long was I going to have to stay in here, like a bloody prisoner? I looked at myself in the mirror one more time, maybe the weekend away was not such a great idea after all. I could reschedule for about two months' time, that would give me four weeks to shed shed-loads. No wonder Damien didn't fancy me, I had let myself go.

"I'll take my break now," I heard Vicky say and I sighed. Here comes my moment, the moment when I give an armful of stuff to some size ten Barbie doll and say that none of it was any good. I slid the lock open and stuck my head out, looking both ways and then made my way to the rail. I was grateful there was no one around and I could hang the items up as fast as humanly possible and slink out of the shop, if fat people could slink that is.

I made my way back down the high street towards the car park, I'd had my fill of shopping for one day. Maybe I'd drop in on Damien at the office on the way back to mum's, I'd only been away an hour. I drove out of town and towards the next village where Damien worked, maybe he'd have time for a coffee and I could tell him that I'd booked a weekend away for us both and his happy reaction would make me feel better.

I pulled into the last space in the tiny carpark that the estate agents shared with the solicitors upstairs. I dabbed a little bit of concealer under my eyes and glossed my lips, then coughed my guts up when I sprayed a mist of perfume all over my chest. I was still sounding like a little like an asthmatic dog when I stepped out of the car and reached onto the back seat for the box of doughnuts I'd stopped for en-route. The last ever doughnuts I was going to eat because as from tomorrow, I was a Slimmer. I bustled into the shop shouting, "Hello!" just as a gust of wind caught my hair and blew it into my mouth. I spluttered it out and tucked it behind my ear, dragging lip gloss across my cheek like a pink slugs trail.

"Christ it's windy out there…" I looked up at the office and Helen the girl I had known for ages smiled.

"Hi Steph," she said, "where's the little one?"

I was aware that I had mumbled back something about her being with my mum, but my eyes were fixed on the beautiful young woman that was now getting to her feet and approaching me. She outstretched her beautifully manicured hand and stood, taller than me, in red stilettos.

With a hint of cleavage and draped in a beautifully tailored suit, she spoke in a voice like honey.

"I am so pleased to meet you Stephanie, Damien has told me so much about you and baby Mia."

I shook her hand although it was against my instinct and for some reason, I found that I didn't want her to say Mia's name. I didn't want her to know anything about me and I wanted to ask just what Damien had said exactly.

"You must be Louisa." I forced a smile.

"Oh call me Lou, everyone does." She held my gaze and my hand for a moment too long and I felt myself stand up straighter in my boots.

"Where's Damien?" I turned and asked Helen.

"He's in a meeting." replied Lou, before Helen had time to answer. "Do you want to leave a message for him?" She reached for a notepad and pen.

"No, it's fine." I said and put the box of doughnuts down on top of her desk.

"Oh, they look yummy, but I couldn't possibly eat any," Lou chuckled. "A moment on the lips, forever on the hips!" I looked at Helen and she busied herself with some paperwork, probably feeling as awkward as me.

"Right, well I'll just leave them in case anyone comes in and you can offer them around," I said through my teeth.

"I'll just put them in the kitchen for now and see what Damien thinks," smiled Louisa and walked like a catwalk model across the floor, with the cake box in one hand and a flick of her hair. I glared at Helen and raised my eyebrows in a questioning expression. She shrugged and shut her eyes tight, shaking her head. So it wasn't just me then. Louisa's stilettos announced her return and she walked past me back to the desk.

"Was there anything else, Stephanie?" she smiled, wide and fake.

"No, not really," I said but thinking a whole lot more than that. An awkward silence descended and when the phone rang out I nearly jumped out of my skin. Louisa was on it before the second ring and after the generic introduction her demeanour changed along with her tone.

"Hi Damien, yes that's no problem, of course I can just leave it with me. I'll see you when you get back for our meeting." I looked at Helen again who was like a rabbit in headlights, and clearly squirming with embarrassment, as I stepped towards Louisa's desk and waited to be passed the receiver. "Ok, toodles!" she said and finished the call.

Really?

"Oh sorry, Stephanie, did you want a word?" She looked at me through fluttering fake lashes and waited for me to respond.

Two actually, starting with F and ending in off.

"No, that's fine I'd hate to bother him when he's so busy," I said in a tone that was loaded.

"Yes, well he does work sooooo hard, I was telling him just the other day that he really should have some down time and go away with the boys golfing or something, maybe Spain?"

"Right, well I have to go and pick Mia up from mum's." I knew I had to get out before I lost my temper with her, who the hell did she think she was? For a start Damien hated golf and secondly he was coming away with me and thirdly he was my bloody husband so hands off.

"Nice to meet you, Steph. Do you get Steph or Stephanie? I wouldn't want to get off on the wrong foot." Louisa asked and it took all of my strength not to tell her that she had, for sure.

"I get Steph, yes. But that's from friends and we don't really know each other yet," I said with dignity and turned towards the door. "See you soon, Helen." I said over my shoulder as I opened the door and made my way back to the car with the wind whipping my hair back from my burning cheeks.

Chapter 20

I didn't stay long at mum's. She wanted to talk about the 'Christening' but I just wasn't in the mood.

Mia slept in the car whilst the songs on the radio fuelled a torrent of emotions. I cried as beautiful melodies and lyrics about being in love filled my ears and hopelessness filled my heart. What on earth was I going to say to Damien? He'd employed her because he was stressed and needed help, and I didn't want to add to that load, and probably push him further away in the process. And what was there to say anyway? It's all subjective, and could well be me overreacting again because I'm fat and frumpy and my mojo has done a hike.

I don't like her. I could start by saying that, but so what? I don't have to like her, she's an employee not my new best friend. But there's more to it than that, a whole lot more, but in real terms can it be justified? My intuition was doing cartwheels about what a bitch she was, and I couldn't understand why Damien wouldn't have been the same. He was usually such a good judge of character, but he had been overworked and stressed out recently and perhaps her CV really had been as stunning as her cleavage.

I really needed to get a grip, he would be home soon and tired and not wanting an interrogation about Louisa. I had to play this carefully or I would end up looking like some crazy jealous stay-at- home mum and he would be working with a groomed and accommodating professional young lady.

I'd text Helen when I got the chance and see if I could get any dirt on her, and for now I'd work on raising my game. I had red high heels, even if my ankles meant they would never again be worn with anything less than full floor length, I had them. I also had an M&S meal deal for two which I was saving for Friday night, but that would be perfect with its main, side, dessert and wine. I could do mid-week fabulous for sure.

By the time I heard the front door, the lasagne was nearly ready and the salad tossed with balsamic dressing. I kissed Damien on the cheek and handed him a glass of Rioja.

"How was your day?" I smiled, fighting the urge to throw questions his way like a verbal firing squad.

"Tiring," he answered and took off his tie. "I'm pleased to be home."

Of course you are because we are fine and I am fabulous.

"I called to see you today." That just slipped out and should not be elaborated on at all.

"Did you? The girls didn't say, Helen was just leaving by the time I got back. Dinner smells lovely, Steph, but can we eat a bit later? Lou bought some amazing doughnuts and we had them with coffee this afternoon, I'm still stuffed," he said.

I turned away so that Damien couldn't see the look on my face, now was not the time to address what a lying bitch she was.

"No worries, it's ready so I'll eat now if you don't mind and you can reheat yours later." I walked away from him as I spoke and hoped he'd collapse in front of the television and give me some space. I stood in the kitchen with both of my hands balled into fists on the counter top, tears of anger blurred my vision. Who the hell did she think she was? And what the hell was I going to do about it? Maybe I should say something right now about her, but as I rehearsed it in my mind it all sounded so petty. She hadn't passed the phone to me when you were on the line, she had let you believe that the doughnuts were from her, everything could be explained away as pretty much nothing, but I knew different. Call it intuition or a woman's sixth sense, whatever it was this girl was trouble and I had sniffed it out straight away, but convincing Damien of that and not making myself look like an insecure fruitcake might be a tall order. I swilled back the wine in my glass and poured another, I ate a little lasagne but pushed more than half around my plate with a fork before giving up and scraping it into the bin.

This was going to have to be something that I thought about and didn't rush into, otherwise I'd end up creating such a contrast between me and her that Damien would think I had lost the plot. Maybe I had, but the plot that I was seeing unfold before me involved a villain and a hero and I knew which one I needed to portray.

Mia gurgled on the baby monitor and I flicked the kettle on to warm her night-time bottle and I wondered what on earth the lesson could be in this one.

Chapter 21

"What do you think?" I asked Mel over the background noise of kids at the soft play.

"I think I'd probably be the same as you, but can I be honest Steph?" she asked sipping coffee and keeping one eye on George.

"Yes of course, I don't mind a shit sandwich. I'll have to stop saying that, it's going to be her first word." I bounced Mia on my knee.

"Well, I totally get where you are coming from and I would feel exactly the same, but you need to step back and think. Could you be reading her wrong? I'm not saying you are, mind, I'm just saying it's all kind of based on your perception of her and sometimes we meet people we don't like."

"There's more than that Mel, I just know it." I pushed my chair away from the table and leaned over to put Mia in the ball pool.

"I'm not saying there isn't, I'm just saying that so far there's no proof of anything. You think she's a bitch, end of."

I sighed. "I know you're right, but I know I'm right too, does that make sense?"

"Yes of course it does, and I'm just saying that at the minute this looks like it's your stuff, and maybe even a little bit of sour grapes," Mel said and then quickly continued. "Not in my opinion of course, but I think it could come over that way to Damien if you mention it without getting any evidence."

"I know what you're saying. I'll leave it until after the weekend away or maybe even mention it while we are there?"

"No! Don't do that! You'll ruin it!" Mel said shaking her head.

"Right, I wasn't thinking. This Lou thing has got me round the twist at the moment."

"You want to be the perfect, easy-going, funny, happy and attentive wife." Mel counted the attributes off on her fingers.

"Yes, yes I do and yes I am. Fabulous that is," I said with gusto but not really believing it.

"You are Steph, and this will blow over, you know. From what you've told me about Damien he loves you so much and I'm pretty sure this is just a blip."

Don't be a Drama Queen.

"A blonde blip in red high heels." I sighed.

Mel chuckled and changed the subject. "Yes. Now tell me about the christening that isn't a christening."

We spent the next half an hour talking about my experience in Prospect House and the friends I'd made, as I explained to Mel that there would be an eclectic group of guests. She listened with interest and laughed genuinely at some of the stories from the past. When I had finished she said "You should write a book, Steph, that's an amazing story."

Signs & Serendipity.

"Well, now you come to mention it..." I smiled and told her about the concept I had for the *Twelve Lessons* Journal.

"That's amazing! I can't believe you didn't tell me all of this sooner!" Mel was wide-eyed.

"I don't know why I didn't mention it to be honest, maybe I thought you'd find it a bit boring."

"Steph, how many people can say they are friends with a writer? You should be shouting it from the rooftops lady, it's a great achievement!"

"Well, it's not published yet, I still have loads to do and to be honest I have no idea how you go about finding a publisher or an agent or whatever people do."

"But you said it's all in draft form, ready to tidy up and submit?" Mel asked.

"Yes, well the first twelve lessons are, but there are more to add. I guess it won't take long to pull together in real terms, the beginning anyway," I agreed. I could feel excitement stirring at the thought of getting the project going which had to be a good sign.

"So what's stopping you?" Mel asked and I shrugged.

"I don't know, maybe the fear of getting it out there?" I answered. "Or not getting it out there and being rejected by everyone, or maybe I'm just worried in case it's shite and no one gets it?"

"What on earth do you mean, no one gets it?" Mel asked.

"The lessons I mean, what if people think it's a stupid idea?"

This is a lesson in itself.

"Well, you've told me and I don't think it's a stupid idea, last time I looked I was a part of the human race."

"But you might be being kind to me because you don't want to hurt my feelings."

Mel laughed. “Yes I might be, but I’m not. I want to see it.”

“It’s not ready yet, I’ve told you!”

“Well get it ready, Steph, because that’s the only way it’s going to get out into the world and help all of the people that you want to reach. I saw your face light up when you said that, and I believe in you.”

“Really?”

“Yes, really. And as your friend I am going to kick your backside to get this done.” She smiled and took my hand. From nowhere I felt a lump in my throat.

“You’ve got this,” She said, looking me straight in the eyes.

“Thanks,” I spoke through the emotion that I felt, maybe I could do it after all.

“Just imagine how proud of you Mia will be when she grows up and sees what you have achieved,” said Mel. “I know we feel like nappy bags on legs at the moment but that’s going to pass and we’ll be back in the real world again once they start school.”

“You’re right, Mel, I know you are,” I smiled and knew that this was a sign for sure that I had to get my act together and start thinking about how I was going to get *Twelve Lessons* out there to the people that needed it, and maybe a second edition could contain the lessons I was learning now. Or, perhaps I could call it something funky and appealing like *Twelve Lessons Later*? I was turning into quite the savvy marketer. Sue had said there was no timeframe applicable, and I was relieved to know that they weren’t going to come as thick and fast as the last twelve. That meant also that there was no point in waiting for them all to unfold to include them in the book at this stage, I could use it as an excuse but I might be waiting years to get going.

"So when are you going to get started?" she asked.

"This week for sure, I'll have to make progress before the christening, I mean Naming Day!" I laughed, my mother had me confused as well.

"And before our big night out," said Mel.

"Oh yes, that." I said less than enthusiastically.

"Steph! Come on, stop being such a moan about it. You'll have a great time, it's going to do us both the world of good to let our hair down and have a proper night out."

"Ok, sorry. I'll come then." I had hardly finished the sentence and Mel shrieked with excitement and grabbed my hands.

"I knew you'd come! I'm super excited now! We'll have to get our hair done and nails and things, and get something to wear. We have to have a shopping day!"

The thought of clothes shopping on my own again made me feel sick, maybe it was perfect to have someone with me that was also not a stick thin waif. Mel thankfully looked about the same size as me I had noticed, maybe she was pregnant again? I laughed and then had to explain the total calamity that had happened the day before. Halfway through I thought, between this and Swimming Mummy, she is going to think I need to be sectioned. It turned out that Mel had experienced something similar when she'd tried on a summer maxi dress that was all floaty and full-lined for a wedding last year. She'd been slightly optimistic about the size she had taken into the changing room and said that trying to get into the bloody thing was like trying to get a sausage back in its skin. The zip was certainly not going to go up past her bra line, despite enthusiastic tugging, and by the time she'd got the underneath right she looked like she'd survived a Zumba class.

"I was all red in the face and hot and bothered," she laughed, "and my hair was sticking to my sweaty face."

"It's not just me then!" I laughed back and nearly spat the remainder of my coffee out as she went on to tell me what happened next. Apparently she'd tried to get the dress off, over her head and succeeded in part. The floaty lilac fabric wasn't an issue and if it had been in the right size, may have hidden a multitude of sins… it was the lining that was the spoiler here. It was made from a fabric that was tight, but with little stretch or give in it, and try as she might Mel couldn't get it up past her torso.

"It was like a band around my chest and face Steph, and the more I tried to get out the more I panicked. I was waving this purple chiffon stuff around in the air, like one of those sea anemones that you see on the nature programmes, and suffocating to death inside the lining."

"What on earth did you do?" I managed to say through the laughter.

"Well I was obviously blind as well, I had to feel around the cubicle and find that thing you pull for assistance. It seemed like an age before someone came and then when they opened the door I had to back right up into the corner so they could get in with me. She was really nice and said it had happened once before with a zip malfunction and a onesie, someone had tried it on over their regular clothes and fainted with the heat when they couldn't get it off."

"So how did they get you out?"

"First of all she pulled all the floaty stuff back down and the lining kind of peeled down at the same time so at least it wasn't over my face anymore. Then she sat me on the little bench thing and had to go for some scissors."

"They cut you out?"

"Yes."

"Right." I said "Did you have to pay for the dress?"

"Luckily no. I said something about it being the wrong size and trading standards so they let me off with it."

"You sound like the perfect shopping buddy for me then."

"If we go next week you'll be able to get something for your weekend away, girls' night out is the following week."

"Sounds like a plan."

"Let me know when, and remember that I want to see the book!" said Mel picking up George and the nappy bag.

"Yes I will, you're not going to let me off the hook with that, are you?"

"No I'm not. Because I'm your friend," said Mel and turned to make her way to the toilet, by the whiff of things George needed a change.

Chapter 22

My mail order underwear for our weekend away was fabulous, and trying it on at home was far less traumatic. I'd also ordered a gorgeous black dress, and to my surprise with a well-fitting but still sexy black lace bra and 'full' panties, it looked beautiful. I could wear this for the mums' night out as well the following Saturday.

Mum had agreed to have Mia on Wednesday afternoon and I had booked myself into the salon. If I was honest I was as excited as I was nervous about going away for the weekend. It felt like a first date all over again. Damien didn't know yet, there were a couple of occasions where it nearly slipped out but I managed to keep it in. I'd called Helen and let her in on the secret, she said she would make sure that there were no appointments put in to the diary for Friday afternoon.

We chatted a little about Helen's love life which had apparently experienced an unexpected upturn recently, thanks to a website she had taken on a thirty day free trial with. Apparently she had been inundated with messages from prospective partners, most of them had profile pictures that suggested that they were only allowed out on day release – but it had done wonders for her confidence and there were two front runners. As she told me about the businessman from South America my heart sank for her, lovely naïve Plain-Jane Helen, who until recently lived with her parents but now lived in a one- bedroomed flat with a rescue cat called Marley.

"Just be careful." I said as softly as I could, not wanting to burst her bubble, but recalling the stories I'd heard of vulnerable women being ripped off by fraudsters.

"I'll tell Louisa that Damien is leaving at lunchtime," she said, brushing off my concern. "And we won't breathe a word to him so he'll know nothing about it until you show up with the suitcases."

I didn't like it that I thought about Louisa's reaction. A part of me wanted to show her that he was mine and that she could back off, but when I stepped back from this and observed myself – I could tell that this was coming from fear. In truth I had nothing to prove. I knew that on a rational level, but there was still a part of me that wanted to show her 'He's Mine'. *What's that all about,* I asked myself, and the answer came to me as a heavy feeling in my heart. It's because I still don't feel good enough, and that's probably why I'd attracted the horrendous shopping experience. If I was thinking and feeling like I was fat and unattractive, the universe was sending me experiences that matched up with that and made me feel more so. I needed to change my thoughts on that and also on Louisa, who I was thinking of as the enemy and potential marriage wrecker.

This all seemed so easy in theory, but actually making the changes was a challenge to say the least. It is both a gift and a curse knowing that you need to stop your limiting thinking to create the life you want. A gift because this is the start and without that self-awareness no change can happen, a curse because the knowing that you are sabotaging yourself leads to self-reproach and frustration when it can't be changed in a blink.

I had to get myself together, I didn't want to contaminate the weekend by dragging my fully loaded shit cart into the situation. I'd hopefully feel loads better after going to the salon and being pampered, doing something nice for myself was going to send a message to the universe that I was worthy of being looked after and treated well, and this was a good start. I would do my best to stay conscious about what I was thinking and knock out some affirmations that would help me, about feeling fabulous and beautiful and loving and accepting myself for who I was.

I dropped Mia off and made my way to Serenity Spa and Salon, telling myself that I was awesome and hoping any minute that I would start to believe that.

"What are we having today then?" asked Debbie.

"Just a good tidy up and the usual colour please." I spoke into the mirror in front of me as she stood behind be and finger combed my hair, fanning it out over my shoulders.

"Perfect. I'll get you a cuppa and some magazines and Hayley will find your client card." She smiled and I started to relax. This was the beginning of feeling awesome.

"So how are you?" Debbie asked as she started to separate off layers of hair and hold them in bunches with crocodile clips.

"I'm great," I lied.

"Good and the little one?"

She probably couldn't remember her name, so I helped her out. "Mia's perfect thank you, it's tiring but I just love being a mum." Now that *was* the truth.

We small talked a bit more about where she was going on holiday with her boyfriend this year, and the fact that they wanted to buy a house but he had to pay child support to an ex that was so unreasonable, and that Debbie had been through a really hard time recovering from an abusive relationship before this one. I had mostly zoned out the conversation until she started to talk about therapy, which sounded very American to me but was also something I was curious about.

"I just couldn't get over it, no matter what I did," she said.

"I'm not surprised though after what you went through." She had shared some of the details with me a couple of appointments ago, and I remembered thinking that she was stuck in the story and that she needed to work on changing what she felt or she would never create a life she truly deserved. Easier said than done though when you have lived through years of someone making you feel horrendous about yourself and controlling your every move, not to mention the odd back hander.

"I know, it was pretty bad."

"That's an understatement, Debbie," I said. "When you've been treated so badly for so many years it's going to leave some wounds that will take a long time to heal, and even then you might wear the scars for a lifetime." My words hung around me with the sound of blow dryers and snipping, and as Debbie folded foil strips as close to my scalp as she could, a moment of realization dawned. I may as well have been talking to myself, I'd lived through something so similar and I needed to walk out of my history as soon as I could. It made no difference that I had

Mia and Damien, until I could stop living in my past and stop feeling not good enough, then I would never be truly happy, and it was no good beating myself up about not getting there sooner. As I'd just so rightly said to Debbie, the wounds run deep and you might bear the scars forever. I so badly wanted the scars to fade, I thought I had done so well and almost left this in the past, Sue was right calling it a shit cart – I'd been dragging this shit around for far too long, but it seemed that I was no different to most. When you know better, you do better, rang through my mind, and I knew that was true. Perhaps this was the perfect time for me to finally heal and release Jay.

A strange kind of sadness washed over me with that thought, what would finally letting go feel like? Maybe the process wasn't like erasing what had happened, but being able to look back at the memories without the heartache. I know that I needed to forgive my former self as well as Jay, we were both doing the best that we could at that time, based on the people that we were then.

I felt guilty thinking about Jay when I knew how much Damien loved me. I wouldn't ever want to admit to him that a part of me was hanging on to the pain perhaps because it was better than feeling nothing. I really needed to resolve this, I knew it was coming up as another lesson or layer of my old self that I needed to process and move on from, but how on earth was that possible?

"So what kind of therapy did you have in the end?" I asked as Debbie removed another clip and started to comb long strands of wet hair ready to divide.

"I tried counselling first, that was what the doctor said and it was good to start with." She said whilst reaching for a black brush with a long skinny plastic handle and the smell of ammonia wafted past my nostrils. "But after a while it just felt like I was going over and over the same stuff, and once I'd got it all out I wanted to move forwards instead of dredging through it every week."

"I've read some stuff about that," I said.

Lesson 4 – Old Stuff Keeps You Stuck.

"So I didn't go back for any more of that. Don't get me wrong, the six sessions that I had were a great chance to get everything off my chest and not feel judged about it. It was a helpful process and I was glad for it at the time, but as I started to get stronger I knew I needed something else." She moved from the back of my hair to my left and kept talking. "Then came the support group." She'd put down the brush and made quotation marks with her fingers and spoke in a sarcastic tone.

"Not for you I take it?" I laughed.

"God, no! I only went once." Debbie shook her head. "It might have just been the group that I was in, but it was so depressing!"

"That bad?" I asked, imagining a group of people that had been battered by the storms of life all sitting around with cups of tea in a community centre sharing their stories. "I guess it helps some people sometimes."

"Yeah, but not me. The thing is that some of the people that were there had been going for ages, and they had never moved on. I wanted to meet inspiring people that had come through it and out of the other side, people that life had kicked when they were down but they still got back up and made it happen… you know… the survivors."

"Yes, I've met people like that," I said as my mind drifted back to Prospect House.

"Had they been through big stuff?" Debbie asked, tearing off more foil strips and hanging them over the handle of a black trolley like metallic tagliatelle.

"Yes, some had a similar story to you and some different, but all of the women I met had survived a life that had nearly broken them and found a way to get through it and shine again."

"Wow, now that's what I'm talking about. That's inspiring." She folded the last foil strip into the long layers that framed my face and stood behind me with a hand on each shoulder.

"Tea or coffee?" she smiled.

"Tea, thanks." I answered her but my mind was wandering back to Sheila, Jude, Asha and Josie and how they all were now. I would hopefully see them all at the christening that was really a naming day - once I'd set a date and started to organize it that was. I opened a magazine and started to flick through glossy pages and Debbie soon appeared with my cuppa. "That's what I had!" she pointed over my shoulder to an article about EFT or Emotional Freedom Technique. "It's amazing, and it works really fast."

Signs and Serendipity.

I sat back with my brew and educated myself on how tapping meridian points and saying affirmations at the same time could help me to take the handbrake off my shit cart and let it roll away for good.

Chapter 23

"You look lovely, darling." Mum said as she opened the front door.

I caught a glimpse of myself in the mirror in the hallway and smiled, I felt a whole lot better, especially since I'd had a preliminary chat with a lovely lady called Robin that I'd found when I googled for therapists.

The only appointment she had available was late Friday morning, which as it happened was perfect for me. I could drop Mia off with Mum and then make my way over to my life-changing appointment, en-route to Damien's office for my surprise weekend of passion. Things were going well at last!

She sounded lovely on the phone, at least when I let her get a word in edgeways. Actually most of the fifteen minute complimentary call was taken up with me beating myself up and admitting that I really had a perfect life but couldn't get over my past to fully enjoy it in the now. That about summed things up, and Robin ended the call saying that she was confident she could help me. I didn't tell her that I needed a one appointment wonder to reinstall my mojo ready for the weekend that would save my sex life, but I could always mention it later.

I had even braved a spray tan, in preparation for standing in a pop-up tent in paper knickers and a hair net I had taken care of deforestation and moisturised as instructed, so hopefully it would 'develop' nicely. I was going to be fabulous, a bit chunky still, but definitely fabulous and no one was going to take the wind out of my sails.

If any sabotaging thoughts came up between now and my appointment with Robin, I was allowed to acknowledge them and then let them go. She'd said so on the phone, so I didn't need to feel guilty about the odd Jay memory that crept in, because as from Friday they would have less of a hold on me. Even just being told that had felt like a huge weight being lifted from me emotionally, and the confirmation from Robin that relationship wounds run deep. So I wasn't cracking up then, not yet anyway.

Mum had Mia sitting up in a high chair wearing a bib. There was an empty yogurt pot and a plastic spoon on the tray and milky white streaks in Mia's hair that smelled peachy.

"She's been lovely, Steph," she said to me and then turned to Mia and continued in baby talk. "Haven't you been good for Granny? Haven't you?"

Mia gurgled and lifted her chubby little arms up high, then slapped them down onto the white plastic try making the spoon and the yogurt pot bounce.

"Come to Granny, then," said mum and lifted her out, Mia's little legs dangled and kicked in mid-air for a moment and I had a flash back to the horrendous swimming experience.

Stop beating yourself up.

"I'll just check her nappy before you go, Steph. Do you want a cup of tea?" she asked whilst sniffing the backside of Mia's babygro, the way only a close family member ever would with a baby.

"No thanks, Mum, I'm going to get back and get dinner on for Damien coming in."

"You should be going out somewhere Stephanie, you've just had your hair done and you rarely get the chance when you have a baby." She had Mia on a changing mat on the floor and started blowing raspberries on her stomach, Mia was squealing with delight and it was obvious that she was perfectly at home here.

"I'm away all weekend, Mum," I half-heartedly objected. "I don't want to take advantage, you've had her all afternoon."

"Stephanie, you're not taking advantage, she's our granddaughter and we love having her."

Just then, Dad tapped on the window and waved from the back garden, then gave Mum a thumbs-up. Mum hurried with the three poppers, fastening them quickly, and not nipping baby's skin was a skill in itself, and then she lifted Mia up and walked to the window.

"Look what your grandad's done for you!" To my amazement she let Mia lean forward and press her face and hand on the glass, leaving three tiny imprints. Mia was quiet, whatever she could see was of great interest, and then she squealed with delight and started clapping her hands. I walked to the window and saw my dad surrounded by windmills, multi coloured plastic windmills that were in every plant pot and border, spinning furiously in the breeze. Becoming grandparents had certainly had an effect on them.

"You want to see? Does Mia want to see?" Mum started dressing Mia in some trousers and a fluffy cardigan and took her to the back door to get a better view, and Dad handed her a windmill that he'd saved. It spun in Mia's chubby fist as Mum made sure she held it at arm's length, and Mia's face lit up. It's amazing to see a child's reaction when they experience something for the first time, their world is ever expanding and the surprise and elation they show is a joy to see. I saw my parents in a different light in that moment.

Be Present.

I thought about the way that they must have connected with me when I was a baby. The love and the care they had for Mia, must have been a version of the love they had for me as a child. It would have been different for them then, of course, they had little income and were definitely from the 'make do and mend' mindset, necessity driven though, not chosen. I imagined that being a grandparent must in many ways be easier than being a parent, the love and the joy must be the same, but the pressure is off in terms of going to work and making ends meet. Maybe it was the fact that they were much more financially stable now, who knows. I did know that I could have burst into tears as I stood in that kitchen and watched my mum with my child in her arms, kissing Mia's tufty crown and breathing in her baby smell just the way I did – and my dad out in the garden planting windmills, just to make my little girl smile. I was blessed, in so many ways, and I said thank you in that moment from the bottom of my heart for the goodness that flowed through my life.

Still feeling loved up I reached into my handbag and found my phone. Maybe we could go for an early dinner at the Italian in the village and then head home in separate cars, I could come back and pick up Mia and Damien could get home and run her bath.

Damien picked up after a couple of rings and sounded a little stressy, which was the norm these days.

"Steph, I'd have loved that but I had a late lunch meeting with Lou and I've only eaten an hour ago," he said, and I could tell I'd caught him in the middle of something.

"It's ok, I know I've dropped it on you a bit, don't worry." I tried to hide my disappointment as well as turning down the voices in my head that were calling Louisa all kinds of nasty.

"Ok, I'll just see you at home, then." He was trying to get off the phone, probably because he was with a client or bollocking a member of staff or rushing to catch a solicitor before close of business. Nothing to do with her, seriously, nothing. So why was I thinking that? Because I needed some help to get rid of the old wounds that I was dragging around that were making me look at my life through a filter of insecurity and betrayal. If I knew that consciously, why wouldn't I back off about Louisa?

Intuition.

Chapter 24

I heard the key turn in the door as I was lifting Mia out of the bath, followed by Damien's footsteps making his way up the hallway and the familiar thud of his briefcase as it was slung into a corner.

"Where are my two favourite girls?" he called up the stairs and I checked myself before I answered. The last thing he wanted was to come home to a nagging wife after a long day at work.

"Just coming," I shouted back and snuggled Mia in her white fluffy hooded towel before I opened the door. "Can you warm a bottle for her please?" I called over the bannister from the landing and made my way to the nursery to dress her for bed.

Just as I was fastening the last press stud and Mia was rubbing her eyes, Damien appeared in the doorway with her milk. He paused for a moment and looked at us both, an expression that I read as love but found hard to accept with reference to me after the doubts that were racing through my mind. He walked over to us and slid his arm around my waist, kissing me behind my ear.

"Good day?" he asked and then went on to swoop Mia up high, making her squeal with delight.

"Yes, all good here, just been to mum's and what not," I said in a non-comital tone.

"I'm really sorry we couldn't go out for dinner, Steph, were you calling from your mum's?" he asked, cradling Mia into one elbow and gently rocking back and forth in the wooden feeding chair.

"Oh, it's fine," I lied. "It was just a thought, that's all. No big deal, she was settled and Mum suggested that we go out for a change." I fussed around him with a muslin cloth so that the milk didn't spill onto his suit. Mia started guzzling as soon as she could, and I felt glad that I'd moved her onto formula a couple of weeks ago, I don't think my nipples could have taken much more.

"I would have loved that, it just seemed pointless when I'd eaten but as soon as you put the phone down I thought about how selfish I'd been. I could have had a starter or even just a drink and let you have something." He looked at me with his head on one side, "Steph?"

I could feel tears starting to well up and busied myself with generally tidying around. I couldn't look him in the eye and guarantee that I'd remain composed. "Yes?" I asked, trying to retain a neutral tone.

"What's wrong, my love?" he spoke quietly, Mia's eyelids were starting to close and she'd stopped sucking. There was only about a teaspoon of milk left in the bottle.

"Nothing," I replied, the default answer.

Damien got to his feet and gently laid Mia over one shoulder so that he could rub her back. "I know that's not true," he said and came closer. I held my breath and closed my eyes as he reached out and touched me and spoke again. "Tell me Steph, what's wrong – you've been off for weeks."

"I'm fine, Damien, really, I think I'm just tired." I couldn't possible tell him the truth, that I hated Louisa for no legitimate reason, I felt desperately disconnected from him and had been reflecting on the failure of a relationship that was my first marriage. Oh, and I was booked in for therapy tomorrow. I couldn't possibly rock the boat now, we were literally hours away from the marriage-saving weekend away, complete with hot tub. Once we had reconnected we could talk, and things would feel a million percent better. I gathered my strength and turned towards him. He pulled me in with his free arm and the three of us stood in an embrace. He kissed the top of my head and I gulped back tears.

"I have everything I need as long as I have you two," he whispered. I tried to answer but the words caught in my throat and emotion threatened to make my voice crack. Instead I tightened my hold on him and breathed him in.

Mia burped from her boots, and we both laughed and said, "Good girl!" as she sleepily dosed over Damien's shoulder. I was grateful for the change in atmosphere as I lifted her into her cot and kissed her goodnight. Things were going to be ok, somehow.

Chapter 25

"I'm so jealous!" Mel said on the phone. "A whole child-free weekend, you'll be able to have a lie in, Steph and do stuff that we used to do before we had kids."

"Like what?" I asked cradling the receiver between my ear and shoulder whilst trying to fold a shirt of Damien's to pack.

"Coffee shops, mooching, long lazy lunches, maybe a movie..." her voice trailed off in a way that told me she was reminiscing.

"It's only two nights, I think you were right with the lie in, that's the ultimate luxury." I was in the bathroom now looking for new toiletries, I didn't want to take the half full bottles we had in the shower and raise suspicion.

"Are you excited?" Mel asked.

"Yes, excited about telling Damien, I really think he has no idea."

"It's so romantic, Steph! Have the best time and when you get back I want all of the details over coffee and then we need to get planning for our big night out," she said and I could feel my expression change. I must have delayed my response a fraction of a second longer than the flow of natural conversation and she picked it up straightaway.

"Steph, you are still coming aren't you?" she asked in a stern tone.

"Yes, yes, of course I am." I fluffed over the fact that I still wasn't on board with the idea, maybe I would feel more like it next week.

"Good. Now have a great time and text me when you get back," said Mel.

"I will, just need to get Mia to mum's and then it's grown up time! I've phoned ahead and ordered champagne for the room," I said as I stuffed some tea lights into the front pocket of the suitcase.

"Enjoy!" said Mel and I hung up the receiver.

I hadn't told her that I was dropping Mia off as soon as possible so that I could fit in a quick therapy session with Robin before the off. What the hell do you wear for therapy? I was in my mummy's uniform of tracksuit bottoms and crocs, with a washed out long sleeved tee and my hair bobbled up into a messy bun. If I showed up like this she might have me sectioned straightaway.

I could change at my parent's house, I wasn't sure if Mia would sit for much longer in front of the television and I needed to hit the road shortly. I think I had everything I needed, including butterflies that were making me feel a bit giddy.

"I hope Daddy's pleased," I said to Mia as I wiped around her mouth and lifted her out of her high chair. She gurgled at me and I wondered if I really could leave her for a whole weekend.

"I'll be back before you know it," I told her, "and your granny will have you spoiled rotten."

She gurgled again and stuffed her fist in her mouth. I must remember to tell mum she's teething.

"Where's my baby?" Mum shouted up the drive as soon as the engine had stopped. Before I had time to get out, she was in the back, unfastening the straps on Mia's car seat and talking about what they were going to do today, which involved a run out in the car and a picnic lunch at Auntie Sheila's. Sheila wasn't a real auntie, but had been a longstanding friend of my mum's, so I'd always called her that, it looked like the tradition would continue.

"Can I have a shower here please, Mum?" I asked hauling Mia's bag out of the boot, and my own change of clothes too.

"Yes darling, you know where everything is." She was already on her way down the drive with Mia, who looked over mum's shoulder at me. A long hot shower was a luxury that I didn't often get now, and it felt great. As my hands lathered soap suds onto my skin I thought about Damien's touch and how I'd missed it, this weekend couldn't come soon enough.

Wrapped up in a towel and my hair in one of those quick dry turban things Mum had bought mail order, I reached for a pair of nail scissors to snip the price tag off the first set of new underwear. Ivory lace skimmed my cleavage beautifully, and gave me a great shape under the gorgeous classic white shirt I'd brought to wear with new jeans and high heeled boots. I was hoping this would be 'smart casual' or 'weekender' attire. I didn't want to show up done up to the nines, especially if Louisa was there, but who knows what I'd look like in actual fact – I had therapy first.

Once my hair was blow dried and make-up applied, I stood back from the full-length mirror in Mum's spare room. I ruffled up my hair a little and sprayed a fine mist to hold it. I looked good, and I felt good. Result. I made my way downstairs for a quick cuppa and goodbye, narrowly avoiding getting my shirt covered in tiny jammy handprints. I swallowed back a lump in my throat as I reiterated information to mum about teething gel, bedtime routine and more. She listened graciously which was unusual, and then she hugged me tight.

"She'll be fine, Stephanie. I have done this before remember."

"I know, Mum, it's just…"

"I know, love, it's the first time you've been away but you need couple time as well. Me and your dad never had that and God knows we could have done with it. Now don't ruin your make-up." She pulled a clean tissue from up her sleeve and handed it to me to save my mascara.

"I'll send you a text with an update later on, and you're only going to be an hour way."

"Yes, you're right, Mum."

"Now go and surprise that gorgeous man of yours and have a fabulous time."

"Thank you so much."

"It's us that should be thanking you. We are having the best weekend ever with our granddaughter," said Mum and I felt the tears well up again. "Now go!"

I smiled through the mixed emotion and got into the driver's seat, grateful that my sunglasses were inside the door, so Mum couldn't see me bawling as I reversed into the cul-de-sac and waved one more time before I left my baby for whole two days, with someone that no doubt loved her just as much as me.

I found the address easily that Robin had given me on the phone, and I made my way up the path and rang the doorbell. The house looked like any other and as the wind made the hanging chimes tinkle gently that were tied to a tree in the garden, I heard footsteps coming up the hallway and the door swung open.

"Stephanie?" she smiled a warm welcome and I liked her immediately.

"Hi," I smiled back, thinking that therapy felt good already!

Robin showed me into a downstairs room that was painted in a neutral palette with wooden flooring and a subtle floral roman blind. It was light and airy, with two welcoming brown leather armchairs and a therapy couch against one wall. She gestured for me to take a seat and offered to take my jacket and handbag to hang on a hook on the back of the door. There was a small round coffee table to my side with a glass of water and a box of tissues. I relaxed, thinking that if I did have a meltdown it would be ok.

I would have said Robin was in her early forties, with dark hair tied back, minimal make up and a professional yet friendly approach. She wore smart jeans and a black long sleeved tee, with a long silver chain with what looked like a quartz crystal wrapped in silver wire. She wore glasses and was about my height.

"Let's start by taking some details," she said and produced a clipboard with a Client Information sheet clipped to the top. My name was already printed in the right place, as was my phone number and date of birth. Robin then asked me about my medical history, prescribed medication and allergies, and then we got down to the nitty gritty of presenting symptoms.

"So what is it you need support with at the minute, Stephanie?" she asked with a gentle tone.

"It's kind of hard to explain," I started, finding it a struggle to put Help Me Empty My Shit Cart into something polite and less psycho sounding. "I guess I need some help with some stuff in the past maybe?"

"Ok," said Robin "Was this the recent past?"

"Well, a couple of years ago, three years maybe… but then there was stuff before that too, for a long time…" I squirmed in my seat, this had felt like such a great idea at the outset, but now I wasn't sure that I could open up and spill my darkest secrets to someone I didn't know. That could be a good thing though, I didn't know Robin. *That's why therapy works*! I told myself.

"Do you want to give me some context Stephanie, was this an ongoing situation?" she asked, pen poised ready to write down the gory details of my failed marriage, driving ban and general screw up of a life that I couldn't quite get over… before I became fabulous of course.

"Yes, sorry, erm, it's difficult to explain this to someone else, I guess I'm a bit embarrassed." I admitted and immediately wished I hadn't. I wondered if Debbie the hairdresser had just blurted it out in the first five minutes.

"That's ok, lots of people feel like that to begin with, it's totally normal, especially when you have not been through a process like this before," Robin said and I took a deep breath in and exhaled slowly.

"When we spoke on the phone you said that you wanted some help to heal your past and clear up some of the stuff that had happened before, that was contaminating now. Is that right?" she asked, flipping pages on the clipboard to look at notes she'd made during my free call, I presumed.

"Yes, that's right." I was relieved that the ball was now rolling.

"Do you want to tell me what kind of stuff happened before and how you feel about it now?"

I looked down at my hands on my lap and sighed, it's now or never.

"I feel like a bit of a fraud, I guess." I imagined this is what confession must feel like, thank God I wasn't Catholic. "Everything in my life is perfect, I have a beautiful baby and a fantastic husband, I'm healthy and I have no money worries… but I just can't shake what happened years ago and I don't know why."

Robin paused and I found that I couldn't make eye contact as the tears started to flow and my lip started to tremble. "I love Damien, I really do and I want to get over the shit that happened to me in my first marriage, and I was doing so well with that, but recently it's like someone has pulled the rug from under me and I'm right back to the quivering wreck I used to be." I looked up and made eye contact to emphasis the next statement, "This is SO not me!"

Robin looked empathic, and nodded in the right places as I continued to explain that Damien was the love of my life, and that he was totally different to Jay who had treated me so badly for so many years. I told her about the subtle emotional abuse, the betrayal and the debt, and then sobbed the hardest when I spoke about him leaving me for Lizzie.

"And now Damien has got this dolly bird working for him called Louisa who's all high heels and hips. She's got no children obviously and a side order of fabulous and I just feel like I might be losing someone again that I love." I dabbed at my eyes with a tissue and then gave up trying to look dignified when I trumpeted into it loudly. "It doesn't help that we have had one aborted attempt at a shag since Mia was born, which ended in disaster and now he would rather sleep in the spare room, probably because I'm still hauling around baby weight and I can't compete with the new girl in the office..." I eventually felt like I was running out of steam and sat back in my seat, looking at Robin with mascara running down my face and a screwed up handkerchief in my hands. "I'm a mess, right?" I managed a weak smile.

"You're human, Stephanie, that's all," she said back and smiled genuinely. "You've been through some massive stuff, it's no wonder you feel overwhelmed."

"Really?" I asked. "It's not just me being ridiculous?"

"Of course not, and anyway, everyone's stuff is big stuff to them. However, I do think you have been through some really big changes and experiences, and that it's no wonder you need some support at the moment."

"Do you think you can help me?" I asked hopefully, but with everything clenched in case she said no.

"I think we can make some great progress together for sure," Robin said and I wanted to believe her.

"Thank God for that!" I managed a chuckle and so did she.

Robin spent the next few minutes explaining about how energy therapy worked, and that trauma could get stuck in our energy system, and keep playing out in our vibration.

"Ah, that makes sense to me, I know a bit about that stuff," I said. "I learned about Law of Attraction last year."

"Great!" Robin's face lit up. "Then this will be so much easier for you to understand. You'll know that we are all made up of energy and that we have a core signature vibration?"

"Yes, that's like your energy fingerprint, it's unique to you." I confirmed that we were on the same page.

"Exactly," Robin continued, "and that is made up of everything that is us, in essence it's a combination of all of who you are, and it's sending out a signal all of the time to the universe…"

"….that matches it up with an experience," I finished the sentence for her.

"Correct. And when you have old stuff in your energy system that is unhealed, unresolved or generally hanging around…"

"It keeps you stuck and attracts more of the same," I said.

"You've got it," agreed Robin.

"So how come I know this stuff and I'm still stuck?" I asked. "I know the theory, I say the affirmations and I think I have forgiven the people I need to, including myself – why am I holding on to this?"

"Because it was so traumatic for you, that the feelings of hurt and betrayal and insecurity are coded into your energy system at a really deep level, Stephanie. And you need more than an awareness and a bunch of affirmations to change that. Don't get me wrong, being aware and conscious of what is going on in your own thought patterns and your energy is always the first step to healing something, you haven't got a hope in hell of changing something that you are not aware of."

"What do you mean, coded into my energy though?" I asked.

"Think of it as an energetic imprint, or a cell memory. Something that runs so deep it's become ingrained, a bit like a very deep wound that you can't completely heal because it was so painful for you. Even though you want to heal it and sometimes you think you have, a song will play on the radio or something will happen to trigger that old feeling, and all of the associated feelings start to pour out," said Robin. "And apart from that, having a baby is a life-changing event in itself, not to mention the hardest work ever. Relationships change when you are juggling sleepless nights and nappies."

"So it's not just me then?" I asked, relaxing more into the fact that I was maybe not going crazy after all.

"Definitely not," Robin said. "And the good news is that we can work on all of the above and really help you to feel a whole lot better."

"That would be amazing, Robin. I would be so grateful if you could help me to get past this." I was starting to believe that this could be a real turning point. "Especially if you could do something today, I've booked a weekend away you see, it's a surprise. I'm going to spring it on Damien after I've been here."

"We'll do our best to clear what we can, but you'll only be able to let go of what you're ready to release," she said.

"You mean if I've learned the lessons attached to the issue?" I asked.

"Yes, that's right and if you've been able to truly move on as well. It's not just about learning the lessons, it's the practical application of what you have learned in your life. Practising things like forgiveness and compassion for example, and not just knowing on an intellectual level that you ought to be, but never putting it into action."

"Walking my talk then?" I asked.

"Yes, and being congruent and authentic," said Robin.

"Sounds like a plan to me." I wanted to get started straightaway.

"Great. If you could slip your shoes off and get onto the couch that would be great." Robin stood up and gestured to the other side of the room, as I took off the black patent ankle boots I was wearing. I had no idea what was going to happen next, but felt excited just the same. Robin held my right arm in a funny position and gently moved it up and down. She was muttering to herself as she did so.

"Right, we need to do a couple of kinesiology corrections this time," she said and started reaching for bits and pieces nearby, whilst moving my arm up and down at the same time. "Ok, ok," she muttered and I heard a clink of what sounded like glass. "It's like a recipe, your body chooses what you need and the combination of everything makes the vibration that you need in order to re-pattern the old trauma."

"Oh right, that sounds perfect." I closed my eyes and relaxed, after a moment I felt Robin placing things on my body and she asked me to think specific affirmations.

After a couple of moments I felt a subtle energy current moving through me, and I couldn't stop yawning. Robin changed a few things and asked me to think a different affirmation, and then repeated the sequence one more time.

I opened my eyes after a few moments and it felt different, it was subtle, but it was definitely different. Everything Robin had asked me to think was about me loving and forgiving myself, exactly the opposite to how I'd felt before we started. Things looked and felt different around me, it was hard to describe but I felt in some way lighter and less burdened.

"What just happened?" I asked.

"We've re-patterned some of the old stuff that you were carrying around, so that you can heal and release it," Robin explained. "The affirmations were an energetic ingredient we needed along with the crystals and essences I used.

Before today I might have laughed out loud at the thought of some rocks and gems stones and little glass bottles being placed on my torso, and me lying with my eyes shut thinking different phrases over and over in my head. There was no denying that I felt different though, and as each minute passed it was getting more obvious.

"I can't believe how different I feel," I said, sitting up as Robin passed me my water.

"You need to go easy on yourself the next couple of days," she said, "there is sometimes an integration phase where you assimilate the new frequencies. You can use the affirmations from the session to help you with this. I can write them down for you."

"Sounds like the perfect time for a weekend away then," I said and slowly swung my legs over the bed and my feet dangled just above the floor.

"I completely agree," said Robin. "But be aware that sometimes deep seated issues have many layers to them. Not wanting to sound all doom and gloom, and sometimes one session is just what someone needs and they feel loads better – for good - but sometimes it's like peeling back layers to get to the core issues and that can take more time."

"Ok, I understand," I said, hoping that I would be a one hit wonder. "Would it be ok to use the bathroom before I go please?" I asked. I might feel a lot better but chances were, after crying through the first quarter of an hour, I didn't look a million dollars.

I emerged looking a whole lot better than when I'd gone in, and as I handed Robin her fee I asked her if I would have to come back.

"It's entirely up to you really, you'll know if you need to come back," she said and folded the notes into a red tin with a silver handle and a tiny padlock.

"Well, right now I feel great, like a weight has been lifted," I smiled.

"And so it has been Stephanie, the weight of your past. See how you get on and I am only a phone call away if you want to come back. Trust yourself, you'll know."

Trust your intuition.

"It's amazing how this stuff works!" I said and stepped towards Robin to hug her. "Thank you so much, I feel so much better."

"My pleasure, I hope you have a wonderful weekend," she said and hugged me back. "Oh and speaking of weight, you will probably find it easier to lose those few pounds that you said were bothering you after today."

I looked at her with a questioning expression.

"Weight gain is usually emotional padding that we attract, when we feel wounded and vulnerable. Once we start healing and we feel less this way, it's easier to let it go." She smiled and opened the front door for me.

The nerves I had been feeling about surprising Damien had made room for excitement. I felt like the cork in a champagne bottle - I was sure that if I hadn't been wearing heels I might have skipped to my car.

I was singing along to the radio as I pulled into the tiny carpark, feeling better than I had in months. This weekend was going to be amazing, I could feel it. I imagined Damien's face when I walked in, looking gorgeous, and announcing that he has the afternoon off to be whisked away to our country hotel hideaway. He would be elated, and blown away by his beautiful wife and her amazing idea. This was just what we needed. I could barely contain my excitement as I checked my appearance in the mirror and sprayed myself once more with his favourite perfume. I loved this man and he loved me, there was nothing to fear.

I walked confidently into the office and smiled widely at Helen, who looked back at me and squirmed in her seat. She had no need to feel uncomfortable, I know I am the boss' wife but we had known each other for two years now.

"Hi, Helen," I whispered. "Is he in there?" I gestured to the tea room over my shoulder.

"Hi, Steph, erm… no he's not here I'm afraid." She started to shuffle random items on her desk and wouldn't look at me.

"But he'll be here soon, right? You blocked this afternoon off as a half-day holiday, didn't you?" I asked trying to remain in my happy place.

"Yes I did, but something came up apparently," Helen mumbled.

"What could have come up Helen? I told you that I had us booked in somewhere for this weekend surprise!" I was starting to lose it with her, but my voice softened when I saw that she was fighting back tears.

"I'm sorry, Steph, he's gone out with Louisa and they didn't say where but they did say they would be all afternoon."

Before Helen had time to elaborate I had spun on my heel and marched back to the car in full Drama Queen mode.

Chapter 26

I called Damien's mobile and it went straight to voicemail, I didn't leave a message.

What on earth was I going to do now? I started the car and reversed out of my space and then on to the main road. I'd go to Eskdale Hall myself, and work it out from there. I didn't know if the tears I was fighting back were in anger or disappointment, or why I was shaking slightly by the time I drove into the long gravelled drive. It was lined by mature Canadian Redwood trees that stood tall and majestic, gracefully announcing the curve that opened up into a car park in front of the old restored building.

I'd wanted us to drive up here together and see the beauty, and I shook my head wondering again how this could have gone so terribly wrong. I would check us in and leave the bags in the room, maybe even unpack, and then I could pull myself together and go back for Damien. There, that's a plan. And he'll tell me that he couldn't avoid this super important meeting and that he is really sorry, and had he known about my surprise he would have met with the client or bank or whoever in the morning. All good.

I reached for my mobile again and tried his number on the off chance that I'd get him, but straight to voicemail again. He must be doing something really important, he usually had it set to vibrate in case I phoned and I needed him. I could understand that he didn't want it buzzing in his pocket at a crucial moment.

It's fine Steph, he is just at work and he'll be here soon.

I lifted the case out of the car and wheeled it towards the entrance, where I was greeted and checked into the suite I had booked.

"I'll take your case up, madam," said a handsome young man in a navy blue suit. "Would you like to follow me?" as we walked to the lift we skirted the library to our right, which was set with opulent furnishings. Heavy cream brocade curtains framed the large Victorian windows, through which I could see the gardens, and from the ceiling hung a spectacular chandelier. Lizzie had been right, this place was really special – I just wished I'd been experiencing the grandeur with Damien.

I couldn't see the whole room as we sauntered past, but I could hear classical music drifting towards me and the sound of voices. One of the tables had a fancy cake stand on it of three floral bone china plates stacked in size order, and a teapot. A girl in a white apron appeared with a silver tray and cleared them away as the lift door came into view.

Lizzie had told me that the food was delicious, but there was no way I could eat before I went back for Damien, my stomach was doing somersaults.

It was right then that I heard something that made me freeze. I had to be imagining it.

"Just a moment please," I said softly, and took two steps back.

I walked into the grand room and looked into the alcoves that had not been in my line of sight previously. There they were, with a fancy cake stand and a silver bucket where a half empty bottle of champagne bobbed in icy water. I stood statue still with my heart racing and my mouth agape, as the scene before me matched what I had heard, but hadn't been able to believe.

Damien and Louisa sat intimately and deep in conversation, and I had no idea what to do. Damien was sitting with his back to me and Louisa faced him, twirling her hair around her finger and leaning over the table to make her presence felt in his personal space and give him an eyeful of her bust line. I could have sworn she flicked her eyes in my direction, as I stared at them. She could have been nominated for an Oscar with the performance she gave as I approached the table and placed my hand on Damien's shoulder. I had no idea what I was going to say or do, but I was dizzy with adrenalin.

"Steph!" Damien exclaimed and looked genuinely surprised. He stood up and put his arms around me and I got the chance to look over his shoulder at Louisa, she half smiled at me and shrugged. "What are you doing here?"

"I could ask you the same thing!" I said trying to stay calm and remembering that I was not going to let her make me look like the crazy one.

"Lou thought it was a good idea to get me out of the office for a while, so we've had an extended lunch and business meeting combined." Damien looked me up and down then leaned in to whisper "You look bloody amazing." I smiled at Louisa and was glad that I'd blushed slightly. My anger was starting to dissolve as I gained the moral high ground.

"And you've been drinking through the day." I whispered back, smiling at him coyly. "You need a lie down." Damien held my gaze, and raised one eyebrow, and I leaned in to whisper again, "I've got us a room."

Louisa coughed.

"Oh sorry Louisa, we are probably making you really uncomfortable – how rude," I said in a sickly sweet tone.

"No, its fine, Steph, I'm glad we pulled it off between us." She threw back at me, with a cherry on top. "He had no idea that you were planning a secret weekend away here until you walked in…"

You Bitch I could have leapt the two steps between her and I in a split second and slapped her over-made-up face.

"A weekend? What about Mia?" Damien asked.

She had stolen my surprise, my moment of glory, but she wasn't going to ruin this for us and I needed to retain the upper hand.

"She's with Mum until Sunday night," I said and although I was ready to burst with anger, somehow I managed to step out of myself and act the part of the seductress. My body language said it all and Damien leaned in to kiss me. What was probably meant as a sexy brushing of his lips against mine turned into a full on snog when I ran my fingers through his hair and opened my mouth.

He pulled away and looked around, "Not here, Steph…"

"It's ok there's no one around," I said then casually glanced at Louisa, finishing the sentence under my breath and firmly in her direction, "that matters…"

"I can see you two are dying to get your hands on each other," she said and got to her feet, smoothing down the front of her dress.

"I'm sorry, Louisa, we are being really naughty here, thank you so much for playing along with my little scenario today and getting Damien here in time for me." I smiled at her and thought that two could play this game rather nicely. "It's great to have someone to rely on that can do as I ask, someone that understands a husband and wife need time together… alone."

She looked a little flustered and angry as she gathered up her designer handbag and started to make her way out. I could see that she had worn her red killer heels for the occasion, shame they were wasted when she didn't manage to upstage me at all.

"And thank you for suggesting all of the other places that you've stayed before with different men, but I knew straightaway that this place was perfect when I found it." I was perhaps going a little too far now, she couldn't wait to get out.

"I'll keep hold of your car until Monday," she said to Damien. I hadn't even noticed it in the carpark when I drove in.

"I'll have the keys now thanks Louisa, I'm busy on Monday morning so I won't be able to take Damien into work," I said and held out my hand.

"How will I get home?" she asked, looking bewildered and directing the question at Damien.

"A taxi?" I answered before he could. "You can put it on the company account."

I turned and fluttered my eyelids at Damien, "If that's ok with you, darling?"

"Of course," he answered.

Louisa forced a fake smile and handed me the keys. "Have a lovely weekend," she muttered and walked towards reception.

"We will!" I called after her.

Chapter 27

Our room was beautiful, with all of the grandeur you would expect in a Victorian Manor House, but with a clean and modern twist on the décor that made the room feel light and airy, and of course romantic. There was a bottle of champagne on ice and two crystal glasses on the table waiting for us, fresh flowers and gorgeous Egyptian cotton bed linen. French doors opened up on to a private patio where the hot tub was steaming and his and hers white bathrobes hung on wooden hangers in the tall fitted wardrobes. Lizzie was right, it was perfect here and I was so pleased I had taken her advice to upgrade to this room.

"This is fabulous," said Damien. "I can't believe that you and Lou organized this for me."

I took a breath and was pleased that I had my back to him, as I took in the view from a large sash window. Should I make a big deal of the fact that she was a complete bitch and deliberately stole my surprise? I would risk contaminating the two days we had together, but I was on to her and Damien should be too. "It was Lizzie that recommended this place, actually." I skirted around the Louisa issue, hoping that she wouldn't be mentioned again after this conversation and I could keep a lid on my irritation and anger with her.

"She's probably been with Matt," Damien said, sinking onto the plush grey chaise longue.

"Yes, I think so." My ego was screaming that this was my idea and that Louisa was a fake and trying to get her claws into Damien.

"Are you ok, Steph?" he asked and I snapped back into the present.

"Yes, I'm fine just wondering how Mia is at mum's." That was nearly true, she'd been on my mind as well.

"Why don't you give her a ring?" Damien suggested. "Then we can go in the hot tub."

"Good idea, once I know things are ok I can relax. I'll go down to reception to ring, the signal is better there. If you get in before me don't lock the door," I said hooking my handbag over my arm.

"I'll wait for you, but don't be long." He kissed me on the forehead and I made my way to the door, on the other side of which I sighed with relief that I'd been able to contain myself.

As I walked towards reception and back into range, a text message from Lizzie pinged its way into my inbox wishing me a lovely weekend and that she hoped I loved it. My instinct was to call her and rant about Louisa, but this was probably the one subject that was out of bounds between us. Whenever anything came up in conversation or on the television about betrayal, it was quickly fluffed over when we were together. A shared wound that we both knew might never heal fully, but there was no point in picking at the emotional scab. We'd moved on since her fling with Jay, and I totally understood how he had manipulated her, but there was a part of me that was still bruised from the fact that my friend could do that to me.

I know she felt terrible about the whole thing, and that she had felt like losing their baby was karma. I wouldn't have gone that far but I was certainly relieved that things had turned out the way that they had, there was no way I could have stayed friends and watched my ex-husband's baby grow up. Least said, soonest mended on that front. There he was again in my mind, Jay. But perhaps the work I had done with Robin was starting to 'integrate', as she had said it would, I could think about him and feel less of the raw emotion of the event. A subtle sadness framed the memory in my mind, but none of the gut-wrenching pain I had been carrying these last weeks.

I ordered a large glass of wine and took a seat at the bar. How was I going to play this one? Damien liked Louisa and needed her in the business at the moment, he said she was helping him out and taking a lot of the stress on board that he had previously had to endure. I didn't want to undo that for him, although I hadn't seen the benefit at home yet of him being less stressed, him telling me that this was the case was a good start. Nothing she had done so far was obvious. It could all be written off as me being insecure, or getting the wrong end of the stick, but I knew that she was playing a game and the best possible thing for her would be for me to have a meltdown. Then she could 'support' Damien with the issues at home. I could just see her asking him if I had postnatal depression. I knew he wouldn't betray me, we'd talked so much about Jay and what the whole experience had done to me and I had every faith that he would never cross the line and sleep with another woman, especially a colleague. If she was after that she was barking up the wrong tree. I did however feel horribly insecure, and like I needed to give him the shag of his life this weekend in order to seal the deal that he was a one woman man.

I had tonight and tomorrow to hopefully reignite the spark, and I planned to fan it into a flame of passion on Saturday night. There was nothing I could do about what Louisa had done, it was how I handled it that mattered. I finished my wine, touched up my lip gloss and made my way back to our room.

Chapter 28

Damien was dozing on the bed when I walked in. I slipped off my heels and curled up next to him.

"Hi," he said. "Everything ok?"

"Yes, all good," I said and spooned into his back.

"I love you," he said and a near silent sigh emerged from his lips.

"I love you too, Damien, so much. We're good aren't we?" There it was, the question that hinted at the torrent of feelings that I'd been swimming against for a while now. Although Robin had helped to calm the waters, it felt that there was emotional riptide ready to pull me under after the afternoon's events.

"Of course we are," Damien spoke softly, and my first thought was that he was holding something back. "You know I have no interest at all in Louisa, don't you?"

"Well, I had thought that maybe you liked her," I confessed quietly.

Damien rolled over to face me and spoke with conviction that made my heart want to burst with love for him. "Stephanie, you're my missing piece, my soft place to fall, you're my world." He tucked my hair behind my ear and leaned in for the tenderest kiss as I closed my eyes and allowed my arms to slide around his waist. The kiss was long and slow and as we found the familiar landscape of each other's bodies, my leg naturally swept over the curve of his hip and we entwined in an embrace that I had missed for what felt like forever.

Damien cupped my face in his palms and kissed me deeper. I ran my fingers through his hair and felt my cheeks start to blush with passion and lust. I'd wanted to wait for Saturday night but the way that this was going, it seemed that we'd be naked any moment. I could feel a bulge in his trousers and I gasped as he started to kiss my neck and skim my bra line with his fingers, I could feel my back arching as I threw back my head to expose more skin for him to stroke. I began to fumble with his belt and he gently moved my hand away from his groin.

"This one is for you," he breathed into my cleavage and I didn't want to argue.

I unfastened a button on my shirt to reveal plunging black lace, and I closed my eyes and surrendered to the lover that I knew would take me to the edge of ecstasy. I had forgotten how erotic it felt to keep most of your clothes on, as my toes curled and I panted softly.

Damien's fingers slid down the front of my jeans and his lips scattered hot kisses all over my breasts and it wasn't long before I was gasping with the onset of orgasm. He held me tight as I shuddered, releasing his hold slightly when I'd caught my breath and he felt my body relax in his arms. He kissed my face and spooned me as I basked in the afterglow.

"That was amazing," I whispered.

"I know," he said coyly and although I could not see his face I could hear him smiling. "And now we get to drink champagne in the hot tub."

"Don't you want me to reciprocate?" I asked, remembering that he had been turned on, too.

"Maybe later, my love," he said and made his way over to the table where the glasses had been left.

"I feel a bit selfish," I said half-heartedly as the cork popped out of the bottle and I heard Damien pour.

"It's my pleasure," he said and handed me a glass of bubbles. "To us." The glasses clinked together and the cool, crisp taste filled my mouth. Things were going to be just fine, I was sure of it.

"Shall we go in naked?" I giggled.

"Erm… no thanks. What if there's a fire?" Damien said refilling his glass.

"A fire?" I laughed. "Well, we'll be in the safest place then."

"I think I'd feel a bit vulnerable, if you know what I mean, it's outside, you know."

"I know! On a *private* patio, Damien. Are you worried that you'll get your bits caught up in the jets?" I laughed again. "It's not that big you know..."

"Hey! It filled a bloody pram!" he said in mock defence. "I'm leaving my shorts on if it's all the same to you."

"Suit yourself," I replied, holding my glass out for more champagne. "I could get used to this."

Damien turned his back to me and the buckle on his belt jangled as he unfastened his jeans and let them fall to the floor. His black Calvin Klein's hugged his buttocks, and as he unfastened his shirt I noticed he looked slimmer. He's lost weight and I'd found it, maybe I'd wear a swimsuit after all.

Chapter 29

To wake up naturally the next morning was more luxurious than the three hundred thread count bedding. I drifted into wakefulness from a deep champagne-induced sleep, and as my eyes blinked open I saw the room service tray from last night. Damien snored lightly and the clock said 7:52am.

Please let things go well tonight – I thought to no one especially, and feeling more excited than nervous at least. Maybe I was overthinking this? Things were certainly back on track based on last night, perhaps I could just suspend my own neurosis and actually get on with the day.

I had to relax and know that Damien loved me, wobbly bits and all. And I had to get back to loving me too. After all, it was one of the lessons that I'd learned in order to draw the relationship in to begin with, I knew that I could only attract what I was able to feel – so for now I was going to focus on feeling loved.

Sue had been right that lessons end up being repeated and layered in our lives as different facets and aspects of the old blend with the new. The path to self-mastery was certainly not for the faint- hearted, or for those who couldn't be honest with themselves. I wondered how on earth the Dalai Lama did it, perhaps it was a whole lot easier on a mountain top away from the real world stuff.

And what about the book I was supposed to be writing? I still hadn't worked out how that was going to happen, or when. Surely it couldn't be that hard to write, I had my journal notes to build on. I just didn't have the time, did I? After all I had a baby and a house to look after and a husband, how was I going to be able to fit in writing a book? I could have smirked at the absurdity of such an idea.

I gently pulled back the covers and tiptoed to the bathroom, I didn't want to miss breakfast.

Damien was sitting up in bed flicking through the television channels when I emerged in a complimentary bathrobe and my hair wound up in a bath towel turban.

"Morning," he said and stretched, "did you sleep well?"

"Yes, and to wake up at 7:52 without having to rush and warm up a bottle straightaway while you're dying for a pee was great!" I untied the towel and dragged a wide toothed comb through my hair, wondering if I would be able to get naked in front of him in the cold light of day. I didn't want to put him off the main event later that night, when lighting would be subdued and a couple of glasses of wine had softened the edges. This was 8:16 am in a hotel suite that was mainly cream décor and it didn't take a genius to work out that bending over to pull up my underwear was not going to be a flattering move in the cold light of day. It felt ridiculous to go into the bathroom with my clothes, we were married for god's sake and he'd seen the sights loads of times and actually just a few hours ago.

The next thing I was going to work on with Robin was my weight and my self-confidence.

I gulped back my nerves and turned my back to the bed, allowing the robe to drop to the floor. I sat on the edge of the bed, and feeling my cheeks start to blush I bent down to step into my underwear as Damien asked,

"What shall we do today?"

I stood up and slipped the gorgeous full lace briefs over my hips and felt relieved, whilst wondering if he was looking at me or still watching the news. I reached to pick up my bra and just before I looped it around my back to fasten at the front, I caught his reflection in the mirror that hung on the back of the door. He was watching me, and the expression on his face was hard to read but in that snapshot there was definitely an undercurrent of lust.

"I haven't really thought about it," I muttered and shook my head back so that my long dark locks fell further down my back. My cold hair made me shiver slightly, this was actually a bonus as my nipples shrank to a normal size rather than their newly found post-breastfeeding diameter. I fastened my bra at the front and slid the cups around to the front, as seductively as an amply proportioned, slightly hungover girl with damp skin can, and I pulled a strap over each shoulder. I knew this underwear worked miracles, so I had nothing to be worried about, I just needed to turn around and give him a full on trailer of tonight's feature presentation – or matinee if things happened earlier. I licked my lips and turned around slowly.

The bed was empty and I heard Damien shout from the bathroom, "We can decide after breakfast."

"We sure can," I shouted back above the television, sighing with what may have been relief and disappointment in the same breath.

Chapter 30

After breakfast we walked into the local village and spent time shopping and holding hands. I saw glimpses of who we were when we first met in our reflections in window panes and felt it in my heart. I loved this man so very much, and I knew by the way he was with me that he loved me too. Whatever awkwardness or distance I had been feeling was being dissolved now, as we talked about everything and nothing and sat on a bench overlooking the village green sipping coffee from Styrofoam cups. The conversation naturally evolved to parenthood and then to the naming day that I was planning for Mia.

"Do you believe in God, Damien?" I asked.

"Hmmmmm." He rolled his eyes up towards the tree tops and the sky beyond before he answered in a considered tone, "I don't know, Steph. I believe in something."

"Me too," I said. "I don't believe that this is it."

"It can't be," said Damien. "But I don't believe that I need some bloke wearing a frock in a church to save my soul."

I laughed. "I'm with you on that. The more I think about religion and what's going on in the world, the more I lose faith in any kind of institution."

"I think if you step back and really look at it, Steph, religion is mainly about controlling people and instilling fear into them if they don't tow the line. I mean look at the Catholic church for example, you've got to confess every little thing you do that isn't holy, to get forgiveness, in a little cupboard with a bloke behind a screen who could well be a pervert."

"You can't say that!" I laughed again.

"I bloody well can, don't you watch the news? It's not natural for a bloke to wear a dress and be told he shouldn't be interested in women, or men for that matter, and there are plenty of them that like that, you know."

"Damien!" I said sharply and was just about to launch into a whole telling off about being judgemental and stereotypical when I saw him smirk.

"Got you," he elbowed me and laughed.

"I am so going to get you back for that," I laughed back. "Anyway I knew you were just kidding."

"That's why you nearly lost it," he said.

"Shut up," I replied.

"One nil," he said under his breath and looked around with a smug expression.

"Seriously though, I do believe in something," I said. "But I don't really know what, and for that reason I'm not having a christening in a church when I have no intention of tying Mia to that religion for the rest of her life."

"I totally agree," said Damien taking the lid off his coffee to drink the last mouthful. "It would make us hypocrites, Steph, and that's not who we are."

"That's quite a thing to say!" I replied. "So are you saying that everyone that gets their child christened in a church and then does badly on the lifetime follow through is a hypocrite?"

"No, I'm saying that we would be, not everyone."

"I don't get it."

"Because when you know better you do better, Steph." He stretched out his legs and crossed his ankles. "I don't mean we are better than other people; that's not my point here. I'm saying that when you are aware of something you act differently, and that's across the board. Look at you and the way that you believe in the Law of Attraction, you live differently because of that, don't you?"

"Yes, because I know that what I give out comes back."

"That's my point. Once you had that realization or epiphany, if you want to call it that, you started to look at your life in a completely different way."

"You're right."

"And what I am saying is that this is the case with just about everything in our lives that we learn and experience. When we know better, we do better – or another way of looking at it is that we are evolving all of the time and we apply what we learn."

"But it's not the same for everyone, some people go through live oblivious to all of this stuff and never seem to do any better."

"But perhaps they can't do better because they don't know any better." Damien's words hung in the air around us and I felt them make perfect sense. He wasn't talking from ego or judgement; he was observing the human condition.

"That's like one of the lessons – You Can't Fix Other People," I said. "Based on the fact that everyone wakes up and evolves at the perfect time for them."

"Exactly right. And we can't judge others or make them see things in a different way, just as we wouldn't allow other people to do that to us. It's all happening at the right time and pace for each one of us, I guess."

"And people are doing their best."

"I agree with that to a certain extent."

"What do you mean?"

"I mean, generally I agree with that. People are doing the best they can even when it's utterly shite. You can usually look at someone's life and their upbringing and all of the different influences that are going on with them, then you can kind of understand when they act in a way that's moronic."

"But?"

"But I don't get it when people do far out crazy, horrible things. Things that really shock you when you see them on the news."

"I know what you mean, but isn't that just another level of doing what they can do based on who they are? We never know what's happened in their lives and how their beliefs have been programmed into them through parenting or brainwashing or mental illness or whatever."

"You're probably right, Steph. I just struggle with that. I think basically people know right from wrong, and there's a lot of wrong in the world sometimes. I guess you see it more when you're a parent." He reached for my hand.

"I know what you mean, I can't even watch the news now – it terrifies me."

"We are so fortunate having the life that we live." Damien's voice was loaded with emotion "People around the world pray for what we have, Steph."

I squeezed his hand and thanked God or whoever may be out there for the blessings I'd been given.

"Are you ok?" I asked and he turned to face me.
"I think so," he replied and reached out to touch my cheek.
"You know I love you and Mia more than life itself, don't you?" he said, and as the words hung between us the intensity of his tone made me catch my breath.
"Of course I do, and I love you too." I threw my arms around his neck, not only because I wanted to pull him close but because I couldn't hold his gaze any longer. Why did I feel like crying?

Chapter 31

If I could have scripted a perfect day this would have been it. It felt like the invisible barriers that had been between us had dissolved into thin air, and being together was easy once again. Maybe this is why people talk about having time as couples in women's magazines, or perhaps it was our combined intention to reconnect this weekend and the universe heard. It felt like we were back in our own bubble, our own intimate space where it was natural for Damien to walk with his arm around me and kiss my neck as I looked into shop windows.

"I've missed you," I had the courage to whisper and he cupped my face between his palms and kissed my forehead.

"I've missed you too," he said and drew me into a bear hug.

"We're alright, aren't we?" I asked in a voice that was slightly muffled by his jacket. I felt him sigh and I pulled back slightly. "Hey!" I looked up into his eyes and saw a sadness that caught me off guard. "Damien, what's wrong?"

"Nothing Steph, really. I'm just feeling overwhelmed and emotional." He snapped back to reality and his expression changed, a smile that felt forced lit up his face but not his eyes. "I'm a big softie, you know that."

"I do know that, but it feels like something else Damien, like something's bothering you?" My intuition started nagging behind the scenes.

"It's nothing, my love, really. I've been working too hard and I've been an arse, I feel bad for not being around more for you and Mia." He tucked my hair behind my ear.

"Don't feel bad," I reassured him. "We're fine, and you wouldn't really like toddler group anyway." I tried to lighten the conversation, but part of me was in resonance with what he said. He had been away from us for too long, and not only that he had become disconnected, as had I.

"Mia's growing so fast, Steph. Every time I look at her she's changing, and I don't want to miss any of that." He drew a breath. "And I want to share it all with you."

And there he was, my Damien. He was back, and I was back and we were together again. He gently lifted my chin and his lips found mine in the softest of kisses. I closed my eyes and melted into him, wanting the world to stand still so that this could last forever.

When we arrived back at the hotel, Damien ran me a hot bath full of heady scents and bubbles. He brought me a glass of champagne and I sank a little deeper into the water when I heard the door handle, allowing the bubbles to cover a little more of me than before. The flames of the tea lights flickered as he left the room and I thought about the fire of passion that I hoped we would ignite later. It was going to be the sweetest and most intense lovemaking that he could imagine, a true reconnection of us in the physical intimacy that we would never share with anyone else. I had butterflies of anticipation dancing in my belly. Although we knew each other's bodies really well, in some ways this felt like the first time.

I sat up and drained my champagne glass, then pulled the silver chained plug from the plug hole.
The water level began to drop slowly, leaving a rim of bubbles around the outside of the bath. I stepped out of the ankle-deep water and onto the sumptuous fluffy bath mat. I could get dressed while Damien was in the shower, I didn't want him to catch a glimpse of my underwear before the big reveal later.

He was watching television and drinking a second glass of champagne when I came into the bedroom.

"All yours," I said.

"What time is dinner?" he asked, swinging his legs over the side of the bed that he had been lounging on.

"I reserved a table for 7:30," I said. "I thought we could have a drink in the bar first?"

"I'd love that," he said and kissed my neck as he passed alongside me.

"Good, now go and shower!" I smiled and felt a little giddy.

When Damien came back into the room with a white towel slung low over his hips and wet hair, I wondered how fast I could eat. Maybe it was my hormones, whatever it was I could have sworn I felt my temperature and heart rate rise at the same time. My lingerie hugged me in all of the right places, and my make-up was subtle but sexy with lashings of his favourite perfume. I had untied the bun that I had my hair pinned up in and my long locks tumbled over my shoulders, down to my cleavage which was rather spectacular thanks to my new black lace "push up and plunge" bra.

"Wow, Steph, you look amazing!" he said, and I tried to look nonchalant.

"This old thing?" I said whilst fluttering my eyelashes, and then I giggled.

"You look absolutely beautiful," he said and walked towards me. I cast my eyes down to my painted toenails and the diamantes sparkling on my black high heeled sandals. As he slid his arm around my waist I lifted my head and my lips met his, as he pulled me in closer I felt my back arch and my hips level with his. As our lips parted he held my gaze and he reached out his hand so that his fingers could brush my cheek.

"I love you," he whispered, and I could have melted.

"I love you, too," I said back and lifted my arms up to lock around his neck.

"Are you sure we shouldn't just stay here and get room service?" he said and raised an eyebrow.

"If you really want to," I said and leaned in for another champagne flavoured kiss.

"I'm tempted."

"Me too, but it's only just after six and we have all night," I heard myself say. I hadn't got all dressed up like this for nothing. But surely the point was that Damien thought I looked amazing and wanted to undress me, and that box was ticked.

"You're right," he said reluctantly and kissed my neck just behind my earlobe, giving me goosebumps.

"As always," I said. "Now where did we put the room key?"

Three delicious courses and a bottle of Shiraz later, and we were heading back to our weekend love nest.

"What about a dip in the hot tub in the dark?" I suggested as we walked back.

"If you like," said Damien. "We can do whatever you like afterwards…"

"After what, exactly?" I chuckled and felt the wine-induced heat in my checks flare a little more.

"I want to make you feel every inch of the gorgeous woman that you are," Damien said, slipping his arm around my shoulder and stroking the side of my breast.

I wasn't used to being seduced, I felt like an imposter – a mummy disguised as a hottie for the night. I took the key card from my clutch bag and opened the door. A soft, flattering candlelight surrounded me, and I remembered Damien having a word with one of the waitresses out of earshot of me and wondering what he was saying. As the door clicked shut again behind us, Damien raised my chin with his index finger and looked deeply into my eyes. His lips brushed mine seductively and my mouth opened as his arms found my waist and his hands found my buttocks.

Everything felt so slow, deliberate and intense and I wondered how long I could contain myself for, I could already feel my body responding and I was still fully clothed. His fingers found the zip at the back of my dress and he slowly pulled it downwards, as I reached up and scooped up my hair momentarily. My dress fell to the floor. My first instinct would have been to cover myself up, perhaps the wine had given me some Dutch courage or maybe I had super faith in my control panel full lace briefs and knock out cleavage support. Regardless of the reason I managed to maintain my posture and step out of it gracefully, then I slipped out of my shoes and reached up to unfasten Damien's shirt.

He watched me as I slid each button through its hole, deliberately drawing out the process and building up the tension between us. I ran my fingers over his bare chest and gently used my nails to scratch over each nipple and heard him moan. He unfastened his belt and his trousers fell next to my dress, he stepped out of them along with his socks and shoes and he started kissing me full on the mouth. I could feel his fingertips sliding down each bra strap, and the across my back looking for the fastener. I gasped as he found it and undid it in one smooth pincer movement, then ran his thumbs over each of my shoulders as the straps fell into the creases of my elbows, and my breasts fell into his palms.

I hooked my thumbs in to the waistband of his underwear, and he gently moved my hands up to his chest.

"Tonight is about you, not me," he said.

"It's about both of us," I objected breathlessly. "I want it to be for us both."

"I want to love you, Steph. Let me love you." He guided me the few steps to the king size bed and threw back the cover, climbing between white cotton sheets and gently pulling me in too.

I closed my eyes and bit my bottom lip in surrender as Damien started kissing my neck and slowly worked his way downwards. His feather light touch was tantalizingly gentle at times, but pressured where he knew I wanted it most. By the time he had reached my stomach, both of my fists were full of the white cotton bedding and my back was arching to meet his lips with my skin. I moved my right hand and dug my nails into his shoulder, my breathing and heart rate quickened and I threw my head back and murmured that I wanted him to make love to me now, that I wanted him inside of me.

"I want to do this for you, Steph, let me please," he spoke as his fingers found me and I gasped with pleasure, knowing that I'd be in ecstasy any moment now. I was literally in no position to argue. I was about to explode with passion and I could feel the waves of excitement that had been building were about to crash over into a tsunami of a climax.

"Please Damien," my words were breathy and my eyes closed as my body writhed in his hands. "Make love to me, I want us to do this together."

"Come on Steph, let go… come on…." and as his words rang out in the darkness with the soft panting and moaning that escaped my lips, I couldn't hold back any more. I'd never felt such intense physical pleasure before. As soon as the waves turned to a sea of calm, I felt his mouth on my breasts and he rocked me back to ecstasy again. I cried out this time as the pleasure rippled through me again, and I felt my thighs quiver and my back arch away from the mattress. Damien spooned into me and held me as my breathing slowed, and I felt him pressing hard into my back.

I reached behind me for him and whispered "Let's make love."

"I can do you again if you want me to," he whispered back.

"I want to make love with you Damien…" a couple of the candles had burnt out and the reduction in light had given me the confidence to sit up in bed with the intention of seductively pulling down his shorts and then straddling him.

"Steph, please." He held my shoulders and half turned me back onto the mattress.

He kissed me hard, and I reached down to pull him out of his shorts.

"No," he said and pinned my arms to my sides.

"What's wrong with you?" I chuckled "You certainly haven't got stage fright."

"I want tonight to be about you, that's all, and if you're not done yet I can help you out there." Damien said as his fingers traced a line between my breasts and towards my navel. Surely he wasn't being body shy? I know it had been a while since we had seen each other naked but he certainly had nothing to worry about.

"I want you Damien, please," I said again. "I've gone back on the pill you don't need to worry about that." I tried again to pull his shorts down, and again he moved my hand.

"What's wrong with you?" I asked. "For God's sake Damien, screw me!"

I put my hand behind his head and in the throes of passion grabbed a fistful of hair, I kissed him hard and deep and he kissed me back. He was lying on top of me with nothing but Calvin Klein separating us from the shag of our lives, any moment now we'd be connected fully. My pelvis was grinding against his and my hands were down the back of his shorts, pushing his buttocks towards me.

"Damien!" I asked him again and moved my hands around to the side of his hips where I could have pushed down his shorts in one swift move.

"Stephanie, no I can't," I thought I heard him say.

"Come on, Damien, please take me to heaven again, please," I whispered, pushing the elasticated waistband downwards.

"Steph, please, no..." he was objecting, and this time I heard it.

"What? Why not? What's wrong?" I asked, still engrossed in the physical.

"Nothing's wrong I just don't feel like it tonight," he mumbled, "but you can go again."

"Damien!" I said and put my hand on his chest, pushing him away slightly. "What's wrong with you? Of course you feel like it, what's going on?"

He rolled onto his side and mumbled again about nothing being wrong and he just didn't feel like it.

"I've told you, I've gone back on the pill so if that's what you're worried about…" I was totally confused, from fifty shades to twenty questions and nothing was making sense. I suddenly felt emotionally and physically vulnerable, and I pulled the top sheet over my naked body. The nearest emotion I could draw on felt like shame. How on earth could this have changed so quickly from feeling wanted and connected to feeling dumped and exposed? I started to cry. I didn't want Damien to hear my sobs, but I couldn't stop them escaping and he sounded like he wanted to cry too when he reached out for me in the darkness and said my name.

"Steph, it's not you."

"Well it certainly bloody feels like it's me, Damien. All night we've been leading up to this and you've been stringing me along for the big moment when you actually can't bear to take your pants off and give me one." I turned away from him and swung my legs over the side of the bed. I didn't want him to see my naked body, if he couldn't bear to be with me. I blew out the final candle on the bedside table and felt him reach for me. His touch brushed my back as I stood up and made for the bathroom, I could hear him calling my name again as I closed the door and turned the lock. I saw my reflection in the mirror briefly, and then reached for one of the white towelling robes hung on the brass hooks.

No wonder he doesn't want to screw you, you look a bloody mess, I said to myself through tears and toilet paper. But he had been so lovely all day, I really felt like we had connected again in so many ways. He had kept telling me how much he loved me, and I knew in my heart that he had meant it. The way that he had looked at me before dinner, and the kisses; there was an intensity and passion there that had been gone for so long I knew it was real because I had not only felt it before, I had craved it.

How could this have gone so wrong? I hugged my knees up to my chest and cried hard. I didn't care if he heard me, and part of me hoped that he did. I had flashbacks of being on my hands and knees in the nightclub toilet at Jay's feet with his forcing me to pleasure him. Why the hell was that coming up now? Because the feeling was similar I supposed. It was the nearest experience that I'd had that felt like this, and I hated myself for thinking of Damien in the same context as Jay. But there was no denying that I felt like some silly fat tarted up cow that my husband literally could not give a fuck about.

The rest of my crying happened in the shower, I supposed metaphorically I wanted to wash away the experience in the moment, even though memory would be ingrained forever. When I crept back into the bedroom with the robe fastened tight around me, I could see around the edge of the roman blinds that the light was starting to change outside. Damien was lying on his side facing away from me and as I lowered myself into the bed he didn't move. I didn't know if he was asleep or not, but I wished that I'd been able to retreat somewhere on my own and not face him, which I would have to, regardless, in a few hours' time. I closed my eyes and willed sleep to come, knowing that it was unlikely and wondering how this could have unravelled so spectacularly and what the hell was going to happen next.

Chapter 32

I must have dozed off eventually. The sound of running water made me stir as Damien took a shower and the first moment of wakefulness was blissful before I recalled the happenings of the night before. I pulled the duvet over my face and closed my puffy eyes again as humiliation covered me in a blanket of shame and heartbreak.

I had no idea what I was going to say to Damien, no idea if I could even face talking about this in the cold light of day. What I had planned as a dream weekend had turned into a nightmare and I had no idea why or how, but the only thing I could grasp at by way of an explanation, was that for some reason he couldn't bring himself to make love to me. All kinds of self-pitying excuses were running through my mind by the time he came back into the bedroom, and I wondered if I should lie still and pretend that I was still asleep. A few more minutes of solace before the awkwardness of having to speak to each other.

Damien had opened one of the blinds a little so that he could navigate his way around the room. The light streamed in and illuminated my discarded underwear, the burnt out candles and two champagne flutes. All of the indicators that this room had been the venue for a night of passion.

I tried to lie as still as I could as he pulled on his clothes, thinking about how ridiculous I was being but with no other idea of how I was going to play this.

Just before he left the room Damien, I felt him pause and although my eyes were tight shut I was sure he must be looking at me. The door closed and I exhaled loudly.

"Please God don't let him come back until I'm dressed," I said to myself and scanned the room for the suitcase. There was no way he was coming back in here and seeing me anything less than fully clothed, I threw back the covers and made a dash for it. I dressed as quickly as I could underneath the robe, but had no choice in exposing myself as I wrestled with a pointlessly pretty bra – fastening the hooks and then swivelling it around to stuff myself into. The arms of the robe were flapping around my waist but at least my tits weren't on show when the door opened and I flew around in a semi-circular motion to see Damien standing there. Instinctively I turned my back and then tugged my arms back into the towelling sleeves, pulling the fabric around me protectively.

"Oh you're awake," he said timidly.

"Yes, I was just getting dressed." I stated the obvious awkwardly.

"I got you some coffee," he said and I turned to see the two cardboard cups he was carrying.

"Thanks," I replied. There was nothing else I could bring myself to say, the paradox of wanting to say everything and wanting to say nothing had reduced me to the safety of one word answers. I couldn't look him in the eye, so I busied myself opening the blinds fully and packing bits and pieces into the case I'd just ransacked.

"Steph?" he spoke quietly.

"I can't talk about this now, Damien," I replied without looking in his direction.

"I just wanted to say," he started to speak again and I knew that no matter what he said there was no way back from this right now.

"Say what you like." I spun on my heel and spat the words at him with what started as hatred and then melted into pain as the tears spilled freely and my voice cracked with emotion. "You'll never fix this, and don't think I wasn't desperately trying to, Damien." He walked the two steps between us that felt like a void and came into my personal space. I stepped away from him and shrugged off his hand when he reached out to touch me. "Don't," I said. "Just don't."

And with that I zipped up the case and pulled out the handle so I could wheel it to the door.

The journey to my parents was beyond excruciating. Every song on the radio was about love, sex or breaking up and it took all of my strength to contain the tears of temper and sadness that were threatening to fall. Whatever the lesson was here, it felt like it was killing me. I had no idea how Damien was feeling, and I didn't have the emotional or physical energy to wonder. I had locked down, and this would be the way of things until I felt that I could cope. The tiny reserve of strength that I had left would be sucked out of me by my parents as I had to put my game face on and duck in for Mia, who hopefully would sleep in her car seat as we headed home.

Luckily my mum was worn out with the two day child care marathon, and the house looked like a bomb site. Although she had clearly loved having Mia, I could tell that she wanted to get her feet up and the handover was thankfully brief. I declined a cup of tea and scooped Mia up into a jammy embrace and her little legs dangled as she shrieked with excitement.

"Hello, baby!" I said and snuggled her in tight. "I have missed you so much!"

Mum was giving me final instructions as I stepped over the threshold about what time she had eaten, when she'd had her nappy changed and did I know that she quite liked white chocolate buttons – just a half a one snapped up and put it on her tongue.

"Thanks, Mum." I leaned back into the doorway to kiss her cheek. "Say goodbye to Granny." I took Mia's hand and waved it in Mum's direction and she waved back.

"Ring me when you get home, love, and I know you're all back safely," she shouted as I fastened Mia into her car seat. Damien had turned around to see her and she was giggling and gurgling something in his general direction. I wanted him to turn around again so that he wasn't invading my space. I couldn't bear the thought of him touching me, accidently or otherwise, it would have been torture in that moment.

"I'll get in the back," I said in a tone that could only be described as informative.

I took my seat beside Mia and waved at Mum through gritted teeth. It wasn't long before the sound of the tyres on the motorway and the motion of the car rocked Mia to sleep and I found myself staring out of the window at passing cars, wondering how many other people were living a lie.

Chapter 33

Damien and I had hardly spoken a word. I'd taken up residence in the spare bedroom for the last two nights. The distance between us felt like a canyon, and there was no way I had anything left within me to fuel a reconnaissance mission for my broken heart. I focussed on practical things like the washing and housework, looking after Mia and a half-arsed attempt at making an evening meal.

Mel sent me a text on day three when I wasn't at toddler group, asking how things had gone and reminding me that the taxi was booked for 7pm on Friday night. If my heart could have sunken any lower it would have at the thought of getting dressed up and painting on a smile. To be honest I had forgotten about it, what with my marriage hanging in the balance and my husband having such a horrendous reaction to me suggesting we get laid.

I sent her a vague text about everything being fine apart from Mia having a temperature, and perhaps it was chickenpox because I had heard it was going around. At least I could build a tenuous excuse on that fib of a foundation if I had to come Friday. *Do you need anything picking up? I will drop in later* – she sent back, followed by - *George hasn't had chickenpox and I want him to catch it.*

Any and all excuses left my mind for the moment and I text back a lame - *OK* x

There was no chickenpox and nowhere to hide. I'd bottled up the feelings that the weekend had stirred up altogether, apart from a brief chat to Robin about weight loss and feeling fat and unattractive, which we were going to work on next. I just knew that Mel would be able to tell something was wrong, and perhaps if I was honest with her then she would see that I was clearly in no fit state to drag myself through Friday night.

By the time she bustled in with George he was nodding off in his car seat, which was perfect as I'd put Mia down five minutes earlier. Mel tiptoed into the vestibule as I held open the big wooden Victorian front door and gestured for her to follow me into the kitchen.

"I'll put him here," she mouthed and gently put the car seat down in a corner.

"Do you want tea or coffee?" I asked quietly.

"Tea thanks, there's no need to whisper, he'll be sound in a moment he had an awful night," she said. "But never mind that, how was your weekend?"

I stirred in milk and the half a sugar I knew Mel liked, then opened the cupboard door to reach the cookie jar. "Well, it didn't exactly go as planned," I said placing the steaming tea onto a wooden coaster.

"What do you mean?" Mel asked reaching for a Kit Kat.

"Oh, God," I sighed and with my elbows on the kitchen table and my head in my hands I started the abridged version from the moment I'd arrived at the estate agents.

Mel listened, wide-eyed and nodding in all of the right places, until I got to the bedroom scene at the end and the abrupt ending. Her hand flew over her mouth and she spoke through her fingers as she stared in disbelief.

"What the hell?"

I sighed again and cast my eyes down to my hands in my lap, still feeling the weight of the shame that has engulfed me since that moment. "I have no idea Mel, none."

"What did he say the next day?" she asked.

"Nothing, we haven't spoken since, well not really," I answered, still unable to make eye contact.

"Steph, that's terrible." Her tone was kind and her hand reached out for mine, which was enough for me to let down the emotional walls and the tears started to flow.

"I just don't have any idea why he would do that to me, Mel. I mean we'd had such a lovely day and such a lovely night, he'd literally been all over me moments earlier, and then when it came to taking off his pants and actually doing it – it was game over."

Like all good mums Mel had a tissue up her sleeve, which I used to dab at the mascara tracks on my face.

"I just can't work it out, Steph. It seems so bizarre for a bloke to do that. I mean I'm not defending him, but I can't imagine why he would want to get off before the last stop if you see what I mean."

"I know, it's crazy," I agreed. "The only thing that I can think of is that there's something about me that he doesn't fancy anymore. I know I've put on weight but I wasn't exactly size zero when we met, and I've got stretch marks now…"

Mel interrupted me, "Steph, it's not you."

"What else could it be, Mel? I mean seriously what else?"

"I don't know but I know from what you've told me about Damien that it can't be that. He loves you, and whatever this turns out to be it's not you. Perhaps he was having a bit of performance anxiety? It's not easy getting things back on line after you've had child, I blame that fifty shades – no man is ever going to feel like he measures up now we've all read that!" she said and I forced a smile.

"Really? Do guys get that?" I asked. "Damien has always been so confident in bed. That would definitely be a first."

"Yes, some of them do, of course," she said and although I nodded, it didn't feel right to me. "You need to make friends again, Steph. He'll be feeling the same way you are, you know."

"I don't know if I can, I feel so fragile, like one look from him would break me," I mumbled.

"Someone has to make the first move, and it might have to be you." Mel squeezed my hand.

"Why can't it be him?" I asked.

"And what would you do if he came home tonight with a bunch of roses and a bottle of champagne?" she chuckled. "You would tell him where he could shove them and sleep in the spare room again anyway, wouldn't you?"

"Yes I bloody well would!" I said and chuckled a little myself.

"Well there you go then, he's got no chance unless you make the first move. Alternatively you can retain your position on the moral high ground, but you're going to get very lonely."

"You're right. I just don't know how to do it."

"You'll figure it out Steph, but the first thing that you have to do is be open."

Back to lesson one then, no matter how hard it was.

"You know what you need?" Mel asked

"Prozac?"

"No silly, a night out!" she enthused and I rolled my eyes.

"I'm not up to it Mel, really," I objected, clearly to no avail.

"Steph, we've been through this, and now you need a girly night out more than ever," Mel said with conviction. "Please say you'll come. I promise you'll have fun."

"I don't know if I can, I feel like I have had the shit kicked out of me," I said.

"And that is exactly why you have to come," said Mel. "This thing with Damien will be ok, Steph, really. It's going to turn out to be a mid-life crisis or something, but whatever it is, it's still going to sort itself out whether or not you come out on Friday."

I looked at her face and saw the expression of anticipation and I couldn't find it within me to let her down.

"Ok then, I'll come," I said under my breath and she clapped her hands.

"Yay! We are going to have the best time ever," Mel said and I smiled tentatively, hoping that she was right on all counts.

After Mel had left I did feel a bit better and mulled over what she'd said about the weekend disaster. Maybe she was right, and Damien was having some kind of 'issue'. If he was then perhaps I was being the least supportive wife in the world by camping out in the spare room and giving him the cold shoulder. Maybe I could do something to instigate a thaw, after all, this situation was no good for either of us. I didn't want another evening like the last two where we had barely uttered a word to each other, with an atmosphere that made me want to burst into tears.

I could be the hero here, the brave one that put their heart on the line, even though I felt like I'd been mangled and I wasn't sure that I could take anymore. If he had a problem then that would be different, right? Then maybe it wouldn't be about me or my weight. Then it would be about him getting some help and us working together to haul him through a mid-life blip and he could retire early and play golf.

"It starts here," I told myself and picked up the phone. I was just going to say that I loved him and I would see him tonight, nothing else. He would know what my intention was and he would be relieved, and then maybe if he did stop for flowers I would be looking for a vase and not an orifice to shove them up.

I dialled his line and waited as it rang out, and just before I disconnected, Helen answered.

"Hi, Steph, you've just missed him but you'll get him on his mobile. Do you want me to take a message?"

"No thanks, I'll give him a call it's not urgent," I said my goodbyes and downed the receiver.

Damien's mobile went straight to voicemail, I didn't bother leaving a message, instead I dropped him a text with a silent prayer to the universe that he would feel the intention behind the words. As I heard his key turn in the lock I smoothed down my hair and busied myself with pots and pans on top of the stove. I had made a subtle effort, nothing over the top and blatantly obvious, but I had made up my face a little and changed into something without baby sick on the shoulder.

He didn't speak as he walked up the hallway, and I heard his footsteps along with the familiarity of him shoving his laptop bag into the cloakroom. I took a breath, forced a smile and tried talk myself into calming down. Any minute now he was going to turn the corner and this would mark the beginning of the healing, I had to believe that or we were dead in the water and I needed a lawyer. I turned around expecting to see his arms full of flowers and his face full of apology. He looked dishevelled and tired, stressed and about ten years older. Maybe this wasn't the time to try to paper over cracks after all. His greeting was polite and distant, and so was my reply. I tried to expand a little on the conversation in a safe way and ventured into asking him what he'd done today.

"Nothing unusual, I've just been in the office all day pushing paper around," he replied and took off his tie, oblivious to the olive branch I was clinging onto with both hands.

"Oh, your office?" I asked, slightly perplexed.

"Yes my office, that's what I said, Steph," he snapped.

"Right, well it's pasta for tea and it's going to be about half an hour," I answered, not sure if he'd heard as his back was turned and he was making his way out of the kitchen, presumably to the lounge so that he could zone out in front of the television.

"That went well then," I said to myself, wondering why he would lie about where he's been. He must be getting confused, after all there were different sites and they probably all feel the same when you're in there picking through profit and loss forecasts or signing off expenses. Maybe he was even more stressed out than I had realized?

One thing was for sure, I would be spending night number three in the spare room and I certainly wasn't going to mention that I'd called work that afternoon. Damien may well be a man on the edge, the edge of what I had no idea.

After dinner and more stilted conversation, thankfully in front of the television, I cleared away the plates. I was carrying them into the kitchen when Damien's phone lit up on the hall table, and caught my eye. It had been turned to silent and I noticed that my message from earlier that day remained unread, and another had dropped in. One line of text from Louisa that had the power to make me crumble as I read the words a part of me had been dreading now for months.

Same time, same place again tomorrow? Lou x

Chapter 34

I was surprised how good I looked when I stared at my reflection in the mirror. The last three days had been a blur. I must have been through the whole spectrum of human emotions since I had read the text from Louisa, but no matter which one was most prominent in a given moment, fear and panic were ever present. I had tried to look at the scenario from every possible angle, yet I just kept coming back to the obvious answer, that they were having an affair.

Damien had sent me a text late on Wednesday night saying that he loved me too, and there had been some slight bridge building attempts by him I supposed, but none of them would be able to come close to patching things up now. Mum had been asking me when she could have Mia overnight and I had arranged Saturday with her, for two reasons. Firstly I was now really looking forward to going out on Friday night and letting my hair down, and I saw no reason why Damien shouldn't get used to having Mia on his own. As a single parent he was going to have to step up, and that was in fact pending. Secondly, I wanted to gather a little more information myself in order to be fully prepared for Saturday night's showdown.

I'd asked him again on Thursday evening if he'd had a busy day at the office and he had confirmed that he was there all afternoon again. I lied right back to him when he asked me about my day, saying that I'd had Mia at the park when in fact I'd been with Lizzie talking about the big D. Naturally she was shocked to hear that Damien was cheating on me, and told me that she would of course navigate me through the legal minefield that was ahead. It would be different this time, because I had instructed her first so there was no way Damien could trump me by using someone from the same firm – which was of course renowned to be the best.

"Are you sure you want to do this, Steph? I mean there's no going back for you or counselling or anything?" Lizzie asked. "Speaking as your friend and not just your divorce lawyer, you need to know that you've tried everything to make this work. You want to be able to tell Mia when she is older that you exhausted every single avenue to save it."

"I've been here before remember." I didn't have to remind her, although it was water under the bridge and she had been heavily manipulated at the time, Lizzie had been caught up in the crossfire when it came to my first philandering husband. "And papering over the cracks just doesn't work. Trust takes a lifetime to build and a moment to break Lizzie."

She looked away from me for a moment and I regretted the words that had left my lips.

"I don't mean us," I said.

"I didn't think you did," she replied. "And although I'll be sad to represent you against Damien, you're my priority, well, you and Mia."

"And I don't want to fight over the money or business or anything, I just want what's fair and enough for us both. He is still her father even though he is a cheating bastard," I said.

"As we know there is more than enough money, Steph, it's not going to be about that. It's going to be about custody of Mia and access and such like." Lizzie looked serious "You need to be really sure that this is what you want before we start, these things can get nasty very quickly."

"Lizzie, he is having an affair with a bimbo from his office and going God knows where with her in an afternoon, then lying to me about it! What more is there to think about?" I shook my head in disbelief.

"I know, I know," said Lizzie in a calm tone. "I mean I know that's what it looks like…"

"Well what the hell else could it be?" I asked impatiently.

"I don't know, Steph. I just don't feel like Damien is the bastard that you think he is. I've got nothing at all to base that on. By the way, it's just a niggle that I have – I just don't see it."

"I know what you mean, Lizzie, and I would never have believed it either, if it weren't for all of the stuff I've told you and the weirdness when we went away for the weekend."

"You didn't tell me about that," Lizzie leaned in as I explained how Louisa and Damien had been together all cosied up when I arrived, and then the whole horrendous bedroom fiasco.

"What the hell?" she said. "And have you talked about this, after the event I mean?"

"No. Then I found the text on his phone and found out he was lying about where he had been all afternoon," I replied. "How can I possibly think anything other than the glaringly obvious here?"

"Well, it does look that way," she agreed and shrugged. "I'll draft up a petition and cite the reason as adultery. We don't need to be hasty and serve anything yet but we'll have it in hand ready for the shit hitting the fan."

"Hearing it said like that makes it sound very real," I said and I thought I might cry again - if there were any tears left. "I'm going to give him a chance to come clean about it on Saturday night and if he lies to me then I really can't see an alternative."

"I'm so sorry that this is happening Steph, I honestly am shocked that Damien would do such a thing. You guys always look so in love," Lizzie said.

"I can't believe it either," I replied. "I think I'm just numb with the shock of it all, I never thought I would be going through this again."

"Well this time I am with you," she said and reached out to hold my hand. "And you'll get Mia, I promise."

I gulped. Maybe this was all moving far too fast for me, I hadn't really thought that there was a chance I wouldn't have custody of her. On the other hand I couldn't imagine her being away from Damien either, her tiny hand in his and her face lighting up when he swooped her up in his arms. Maybe we could get through this, with some professional help and a P45 for Louisa. Maybe he was having a mid-life meltdown and she'd offered it to him on a plate, he was a red blooded male after all.

My head was spinning with possible outcomes, and I felt sick.

"Steph?" I heard Lizzie's voice and came back to reality. "Steph, are you ok?"

"Yes, well a version of ok anyway."

"You've had a massive shock, you need to process this and see how you want to move forwards," she said. "I'll get ready this end so that you know it's all in order if you need me to step in at a moment's notice. And if it comes to nothing, no one need ever know. We're just two friends having a catch up, right?"

I looked at her through my tears and mouthed the words, "Thank you."

I wondered if Damien recognized the dress and shoes that I was wearing as he walked through the door and I handed him Mia. I thought I looked better than the night he'd rejected me, the worry of the situation had made me feel sick and I must have lost nearly half a stone in the last week.

"Taxi's coming," I said kissing Mia's cheek, stepping into his personal space briefly.

"Steph," he said and the sound of my name from his lips made me want to stay so badly. I turned to look at him and he looked so, so sad. I let my hand release the door handle and drop to my side, and holding his gaze I took a step closer to him. Without saying a word, he seemed to say everything. My whole world stood before me, the love of my life looking lost and afraid and my baby in his arms.

"I love you," he said and he looked as if he was going to cry.

"Damien, I…" there was a loud toot from the street as my taxi pulled into the kerb and the intensity of the moment was shattered. "I have to go. Can we talk later?"

"Wave to Mummy, Mia," he said and raised her chubby arm in my direction. "We hope Mummy has a lovely night, don't we?"

Another honking of the horn and I walked out of the door wishing that I'd found a reason to stay, and knowing that perhaps the irony was that I had – but I'd chosen to go anyway.

Chapter 35

We were meeting for cocktails around the corner from the restaurant first, and although I had the urge to ask the taxi driver to take me home several times, I arrived in time to see Mel walking in with another couple of faces I recognised. One of them was Rosie, whom I deliberately avoided where possible, as I found her too harsh and overly critical. I certainly didn't want to get stuck sitting next to her for dinner.

I had started off by thinking I would be out until the early hours, after I'd danced on the tables and snogged a load of strangers, but that was before I saw the sadness that was written all over Damien's face. I wanted to go home and ask him what was going on, and if there was anything left between us. I wanted to look into his eyes and see if there was any depth to his explanation, or if he was covering up the sordid truth. Was the worry that I saw etched into his brow a fear of getting caught? Or maybe a fear of losing me after making a silly error of judgement? Whatever it was he looked like death warmed up and I didn't want to be out too long.

"Steph!" said Mel above the sound of the loud music, and threw her arms around me. "I think you know everyone, you look fabulous by the way."

"You do too," I spoke loudly as well and smiled awkwardly.

"Go and get a drink!" said Mel and offered me a sip of hers. "See what you think of this mojito, it's divine."

I made my way through a sea of people and ordered a large glass of white wine. By the time I had navigated my way back to Mel and the others I'd gulped at least half. It was hard to have a conversation over the music so small talk was the order of the day, but I didn't mind, I was pretty sure that discussing your husband's affair and pending divorce proceedings would have dampened the atmosphere anyway.

"Shall we have one more here?" Mel said and I nodded, following her to the bar and feeling that warm fuzzy change in my body and mind that starts to creep up on you as the alcohol starts to have an effect. "Same again for you, Steph?" she asked over her shoulder and I mouthed back, "Yes please."

"Are you having a good time?" Mel asked as she passed me my glass.

"Yes, all good here," I faked and raised my glass to chink against hers. "Here's to a great girl's night out."

She smiled back "I know you aren't, but I'll make sure I am sitting next to you when we eat and you can give me an update. It's impossible to talk in here."

Was it that obvious that I didn't want to be here? I handed my glass to Mel and made my way to the ladies'. I needed to pull myself together or go home. I looked at myself in the mirror and brushed on some bronzer, slicked on some lip gloss and sprayed myself liberally with perfume. I was here and I may as well make the most of it, nothing had changed. I had no further evidence that Damien was knobbing Louisa and nothing to refute it either. The only thing that had de-railed me was the way that he had looked when I left, and so what. It's Friday and he has been at work all week and he could well be hiding a deep dark secret from his wife, of course he looked wrecked. Whatever was coming my way or not I could handle it tomorrow, this was a one off and I never got the chance to go out like this. I would be home in a few hours' time and if I was really desperate to talk about it then I could ask him then. There was no point in spoiling the evening, no point at all. We could go through the details of his bloody mid-life crisis later on and I could confront him with the evidence I had that he hadn't been in the office when I'd called, and that he had been with her, doing God knows what.

And then she would get sacked and he would say it was only a couple of times and he loved me and that he would spend the rest of his life showing me.

Fine.

I sighed and closed my eyes. The only part of that whole rant that I'd had in my own head that was fine, was that I was out and I would be home soon. I was all over the place, confused, angry, upset and pissed. Not the best combination for me, and one that had never ended well. I nipped to the toilet before I went back to the bar and noticed that I had started my period, great. Luckily I had an emergency tampon in my purse, the possibility of a full on reunion tomorrow night whilst Mia was at my mum's and Damien was begging for forgiveness, seemed very optimistic.

As I re-joined the others Mel passed me two glasses of wine. "You missed a round so I got you wine, is that ok?"

"Yes thanks," I drank from one glass to make room and then combined the two, making a mental note that I really should go onto soft drinks next. The bar was getting busier and someone said it was nearly time to go. I drank most of what was in my glass and started to head for the door, where the cold air nearly knocked me off my feet.

"Are you ok, Steph?" laughed Rosie.

"Yes thanks, just a bit tipsy," I replied, but thinking 'piss off' at the same time.

"Thought so, you look a bit flushed. You should pace yourself you know, don't want to be ill tomorrow," she said in a mock caring tone and I wanted to slap her but smiled through gritted teeth.

"I'm sure I'll be fine, Rosie," I replied as Mel appeared at my side and hooked her arm into mine in order to cross the road.

"Just ignore her," she whispered. "Don't let her spoil it, she's just jealous because you look so fabulous."

We giggled our way across to the other side of the street and into the doorway of the restaurant. The air was warm and smelled of garlic, the atmosphere was lively and there was a long table set for twelve against a wall with a painted mural that resembles the ceiling of the Sistine Chapel. At least I wasn't the only dark haired chunky bird in here tonight, there were a couple on the wall as well.

The waitress showed us to our table and after a little musical chairs we settled in our seats. Thankfully, I was on the end so had easy in and out access to the toilet and bar, with Mel opposite me. Rosie was to my right but was engrossed in saving the poor girl next to her.

Baskets of bread arrived and white ramekins filled with butter, as well as jugs of water with ice cubes floating on top. Menus were passed around and nit pickers shouted up about splitting the bill at the end, and that wasn't fair because so and so wasn't having a starter and anyway she was a vegetarian and the fillet steak was well over twenty quid if you got a sauce.

I rolled my eyes in Mel's direction over the top of the wine list and she laughed.

"Let's get pissed," I said, drinking the first and last glass of water that I'd have all night.

"I'll drink to that!" she said. "Are you sticking with white?"

"Yes, I think so. Don't want to get totally out of control," I said and hiccupped.

"Too late, then," laughed Mel and passed me the bread basket.

"Yup," I agreed and buttered a piece.

"So what's the latest?" she asked, lowering her voice and leaning in a little.

"Oh well…" I started, "I went to see my friend Lizzie, you know the lawyer…"

"What?" hissed Mel. "Steph, you know I'm on your side but you haven't really got any evidence that he is actually having an affair yet!"

"I know, I just wanted some advice," I said, breaking off the conversation briefly to ask the waitress for a bottle of house white. "In case things go that way, that's all."

"As long as that's all it was, I couldn't bear for you to break up your family because of a misunderstanding."

"I'm going to talk to him tomorrow night about it all and see what he says, Mia is at mum's," I said.

"Just make sure you don't go in all guns blazing, Steph. Sometimes two and two don't make four you know," Mel said. "Maybe there's a whole different explanation."

"Well it better be a bloody good explanation about why the dolly bird from the office is sending him text messages about meeting up and why a good shag is off the cards for me!"

"Shhhh!" Mel said, "You're pissed."

"Christ Mel, live a little!" I said and poured us both a large glass of wine. "Let's forget about all of that for tonight, I've got to face it tomorrow and I want a night off."

"Okay, you're right, let's change the subject." Mel raised her glass "Here's to a proper night off!"

"Cheers," I said and turned the conversation back to starters and mains.

Once the food had arrived and both wine and conversation were in full flow, it was easier to relax into enjoying myself. Some of the girls I hadn't met before turned out to be lovely, and we were all from such different backgrounds. There was a common thread that held us together, apart from being female and having the usual gripes about men, we were all mothers – apart from Rosie. Stories that were shared around the table were funny and heart-warming, and after suffering a subject that she couldn't really get involved in for long enough, Rosie commented that even on our night away from kids it was all about kids.

"Maybe you should get a life," she said and her words killed the conversation in that one sentence.

"I love my life actually," said Mel, who I'd always wished would stand up to Rosie.

"Whatever," Rosie said and rolled her eyes.

"Hey!" I butted in. "Don't speak to her like that."

"You can talk," she raised her voice so that not only our table could hear what was going on, but anyone else in a ten mile radius.

"Excuse me?" I matched her tone but not her volume, I had never been an angry drunk but she was sure pushing my buttons tonight. It was one thing making sweeping statements about being a mum, but picking on Mel was another. I'd watched her pulling people down for long enough and this was the last straw.

"Leave it, Steph," whispered Mel. "She's just jealous and bitter."

Forced conversations were breaking out around us to cover up embarrassment. I deliberately and metaphorically turned my back to Rosie and poured more wine for Mel and I.

"At least I'm not a doormat," Rosie said under her breath in my direction.

"What did you say?" I turned back to centre and looked in her direction.

"You heard," she sniggered.

"Say it again," I challenged her and Mel shook her head opposite me and looked anxious.

"I said," replied Rosie and then took a breath before she turned up the volume "At least I'm not a doormat." Another lull in the conversation occurred and as I sat with my mouth agape, a waitress approached the table and asked if everything was alright. Mel fluffed over things and asked for the dessert menu, but I wasn't going to let Rosie off with this.

"I have no idea what you mean," I said in a measured tone, even though I was heading for boiling point any minute now. I could have quite nicely delivered the wrath that I was hanging on to for Louisa, the failed romp and her sarcasm all in one hard slap.

"Well, I can easily enlighten you if you want me to." She matched my tone, the condescending bitch, and her question hung in the air like a bad smell.

I drained my wine glass and placed it firmly in front of me before forcing the widest and fakest smile I could muster up. "Please do!" I replied and sat back with my arms folded, waiting for her to hang herself with her own idiotic comments that no one would find interesting or believable.

"Well it's just my opinion," she started at a pitch that she knew would gain attention from those around us once again, "that if my husband was screwing some bird with huge tits that was ten years younger than me, and I was a fat, frumpy housewife of a nappy bag on legs, that I'd probably not fucking stand for it!"

Oh my God the public Drama Queen.

"Rosie!" Mel shouted as the restaurant manager marched over to our table and not so gently grabbed Rosie by the arm and asked her to leave.

"Don't you worry I'm going, I can't stand one more second with you sad bunch of washed up whingers." She made to stand up and stumbled, hissing at the manager to stop manhandling her. "If you want someone to grope, there she is!" she shrieked and pointed at me. "Even her own husband won't go the whole nine yards with her, she's desperate for a good shag!"

All eyes fell on me and I hung my head, allowing my hair to fall over my cheeks. Oh, My God. Even on my knees in the nightclub toilet I had probably had marginally more self-worth than I felt right now. I was beyond grateful that the chair I had chosen was facing away from the main restaurant. It must have been obvious to everyone by now that I was crying and as Mel pulled me to my feet and into the ladies', the mutterings from adjacent tables filled my ears.

I wanted to go home, slink into the spare room and hide forever. My whole life felt like a complete mess, even worse than that – it was now a public mess. Toddler group was somewhere I would never be going again, ever. I couldn't possibly face anyone again that had been witness to what had just happened, and I wasn't sure if I could face Damien when I got home either. He would see I'd been crying and want to know why, and I would have to spill my guts about the whole thing while I was pissed out of my bracket and feeling horrifically wounded.

"Steph, oh God, are you alright?" Mel asked me as she propped me up against the sink and went to dispense a handful of toilet roll. She wiped my face and asked me again, "Steph, are you ok?"

I didn't know what to say, I just shook my head and more tears came. Mel hugged me and I wept on her shoulder, until there were no more left and I'd stopped trembling.

"She's bipolar you know," Mel said and rubbed my back as I supported my weight on the sink and stared down the plug hole.

"She's a nasty bitch," I said.

"Wouldn't disagree with that one bit," agreed Mel. "She was well out of order there and she won't be welcome back to toddler group."

I couldn't help myself from laughing. I had often wondered how people in a crisis could find anything funny when life was kicking the shit out of them. Black humour I supposed.

"What's so funny?" Mel looked bemused.

"Barred from the bloody toddler group – I love it," I chuckled. "How will she ever live that down?"

"Glad to see you can still see the funny side," said Mel and chuckled too.

"I have to really, or I think I might crack up," I said.

"Might?" joked Mel and I smiled weakly.

"Thanks, friend," I said sarcastically.

"Anytime. Now are you going to come out and order a dessert?"

"Surprisingly, I have just lost my appetite," I said. "And it's probably best if I go home."

Mel looked disappointed but understanding and squeezed my arm. "Shall I get them to ring for a taxi for you?" she asked.

"Yes please, and could you get my handbag please, Mel? I don't want to have to explain to Damien why I look so dreadful if he's still up. I haven't got the energy for that tonight."

"Of course I will, I'll be right back."

Mel left me alone for a moment and I stared at my reflection. How could things have gone so badly wrong? Here I was, dressed to kill but feeling like death warmed up, after a humiliating slagging match with someone I hardly knew, and worried about going back home to the man I loved. The adrenalin that I had surging around my veins must have been counteracting some of the alcohol for the time being. I'd stopped feeling as giddy but I knew that in the morning I'd regret having the bottle and a half I'd managed to down in a couple of hours.

Mel returned with my handbag and I started to make up my face and fluff up my hair.

"The taxi will be here shortly, I've asked them to come and knock on the door so you don't have to go out there. They said if you wanted to he would pull up at the back of the restaurant and you could go through the kitchen," Mel said. "Everyone thinks she's a bloody outrage and they hope you are ok."

"Thanks Mel, you're a lovely friend," I said and hugged her.

"I feel awful, it was me that made you come tonight," she said.

"Don't you dare!" I said with my nose in my handbag, looking for perfume and polo mints. "None of this is your fault AT ALL and I insist that you have a great night and forget about the whole thing. I was always going to leave early, Mel. Please have fun with your friends and don't let that silly cow spoil it for you, or I'll be even more furious with her!"

There was a knock on the door and I took one last look at myself.

"Damien will never know," said Mel. "You look gorgeous, and who knows… if he is still awake then tonight could be your lucky night."

"We'll see." I said and she elbowed me and winked.

I waved a goodbye over my shoulder as I slipped through the kitchen door, and through the noise and commotion, to the fire exit at the back of the building. The waitress pressed down the horizontal metal bar and the cold rushed in, making me catch my breath again.

"Thank you," I said and stuffed some money into her hand. "That should cover my share and some extra for your kindness."

I held the handrail and made my way down the three stone steps towards the black cab with its engine purring. I opened the back door and stepped inside, relaxing into the back seat.

"Where to, Stephanie?" asked the driver in a voice that made my jaw drop.

As Jay turned in the driver's seat to look me up and down, I felt my heart pound in my chest.

Chapter 36

I was dressed up to the nines and pissed as a newt, sitting in the back seat of a taxi, fumbling with my seatbelt and totally tongue tied. Oh and my ex-husband was at the wheel. I opened the window a little, and tried to get some air. Who knows how long he could have been waiting but the car was so damn hot.

"I can't believe it's you," I said and tried to sound casual.

"Me neither, what are the chances of this happening?" he agreed and the indicator tick-tocked as he pulled onto the main street.

"A million to one I'm guessing," I said in what I hoped sounded neutral.

As he changed gear I noticed that there was no wedding ring, and then I felt cross with myself for even being remotely interested.

"Maybe fate has thrown us together tonight, Steph," the resonance of his voice started pulling into the past, and although the heartbreak had been unbearable, it wasn't that which I remembered in this moment. "What do you think?"

"I don't know if I believe in all of that really, Jay," I lied.

"Suit yourself, but I can't deny it that I am really glad I picked up this job." I could hear him smiling, and I smiled a little too. "What do you say we stop and have a coffee somewhere? There are loads of places still open. For old time's sake."

"I don't know Jay, I really should get back." I objected but the familiar smell of his aftershave was wafting towards me through his now open window and anchoring me back to a time when things were good.

"Back where?" he asked "You haven't even told me where you want dropping off yet."

"Oh, right," I said, but the truth was this felt anything but right, because in that moment I was fighting the urge to ask him to pull over and kiss me. What the hell was wrong with me? I had a lovely husband at home – who didn't want me of course. And what was one coffee? Maybe the universe had thrown us together this one last time to make sure that we had a chance to make our peace, to part on good terms and to finally close the chapter on us.

"You know I probably have got time for a coffee after all," I heard myself say, wondering if this really was something that I should be doing, but unable to stop regardless.

"Great," he said. "I know just the place."

A couple of miles and a little bit of small talk later, and we had arrived at a place in a back street called The Jazz Café. After parking, Jay came around and opened my door, leading the way past the doorman and up to the bar. I stood awkwardly, and began looking in my bag for my purse, to which Jay shook his head and said,

"This could be the last time I get to buy you a drink, Steph," so I relented.

The barman brought an ice bucket and two champagne flutes, and before I had time to object the cork was popped and Jay was passing me my glass.

"I thought you said coffee," I said as he took a step closer to me.

"I did, but I thought that coffee just wouldn't do on such a special occasion," he said, and he held my gaze. "Can't you feel it?"

"Feel what?" I asked, knowing full well what he meant and knowing even better that I should be on my way home. The energy between us was intense, our body language screamed out sexuality and I knew he was desperate to touch me. I sipped my champagne and slowly licked my lips.

"You know what?" he said and he let his eyes linger on my cleavage.

"Jay, this is madness. I should go," I said.

"Yes you should," he replied and stood stone still in my way. "But you won't."

He waited for a response but I had none to give, my head was starting to swim and my sense of judgement had sailed away the moment I got into his car. He reached for the bottle and topped up my glass.

"Shall we get a table?" he asked and I nodded.

There was so much to catch up on, so much to share, but neither of us wanted to delve into the present. Our thoughts and feelings were wrapped up in the memories of the past, and it was here that we found the most common ground. We talked our way through the whole bottle of champagne, and with each sip we seemed to get physically closer. My hand brushed against Jay's a couple of times to begin with, but after a while his hand was on my knee and I started to wish it was touching bare skin.

I wanted to kiss him. I could remember what it was like and I wanted it again, just one kiss.
That wasn't betrayal by any stretch of the imagination, and anyway I was in the middle of town, late at night in a place where no one knew me. One kiss was nothing, it was simply to check that my memory served me well. I knew that I could entice Jay to lean in and place his lips on mine. I subtly thrust out my cleavage and flicked my hair whilst looking up at him with smouldering eyes.

"Steph," he started to speak and I parted my lips slightly.

"Jay?" I almost whispered.

He slid one hand around my waist then he leaned in closer. As I closed my eyes and his lips touched mine, the memories of us being together, naked, flooded back and I surrendered to his advances. One kiss seemed to be lasting a long, long time.

Chapter 37

When I surfaced to breathe Jay pulled me back in, with one hand at the back of my neck and the other around my waist - I could have easily said that I had no choice but to comply. The truth was that lust was pounding through me, and combined with the alcohol I'd drunk, I felt red hot in more ways than one.

"I need some air," I said as his lips moved from mine and started to work their way across the plunging neckline of my dress.

"I need more of you," he said in a raspy, sexy voice that was so familiar.

"Jay, we can't, not here," I objected breathlessly. Although we were tucked into a corner and it was dark and late, we were still in public.

"So come with me," he said and stood up. I couldn't ignore the bulge in his trousers that was now at eye level and he raised his eyebrow when he saw me stare. He took my hand and dragged me to my feet, I swayed momentarily and he caught me, pulling my pelvis towards his.

"That's for you," he whispered and kissed my neck, then he led me through the crowded bar as the room danced in and out of focus around me and my stilettos suddenly felt like stilts. We passed the doorman who mumbled something to Jay about me having too much, and walked over the street.

"Where are we going?" I said.

"I'm taking you to heaven, Stephanie," Jay said seductively and I wasn't going to argue.

He keyed in a number and heavy glass doors opened into a foyer, where there were pigeon holes for mail and a lift. He groped my breasts as soon as the doors closed and stopped when they pinged open on the top floor. Jay turned the key to reveal a stylish bachelor pad, complete with a flat screen television and open plan kitchen diner. I slipped off my shoes and heard the sound of background music playing, songs from the past that he knew I liked. He led me by the hand into the bedroom and the long glass windows boasted a view of the town at night that was beautiful.

"What an amazing view," I said as the bedroom light dimmed to darkness and he stepped towards me, looking my silhouette up and down.

"I couldn't agree more," he said and tilted my chin with one hand so that his lips met mine, and with the other started to pull down the zip at the back of my dress.

Chapter 38

Light crept into the room as the sun peeped over the horizon, and I stirred a little. My head was still full of a dream where I was with Mia and I was pushing her back and forth in a swing at the park. She was laughing and I was laughing too and her red wellingtons were still wet from puddle jumping.

Mia.

I opened my eyes and took in my surroundings that merged all too quickly with flashbacks from the night before. The taxi, the bar, Jay. I saw my dress in a heap beside the long window, and my bra and panties draped over the back of a chair. The underwear I had bought for Damien, my husband who I had just cheated on with a bastard that I'd divorced called Jay.

I felt hot tears burn my cheeks as I thought of Mia and how I had cheated on her as well. I had no choice but to sit up abruptly as I felt vomit rise in the back of my throat, and I made a wholly undignified dash to the bathroom. I knelt on the floor, trembling and wishing that it was as easy to flush away the happenings of the night before as it was the puke and bile that I had heaved into the bowl.

I needed to get home, but I had no idea where I was. I remembered that the bar across the street was called The Jazz Café. If I could find my phone I could google the address. I carefully got to my feet and the room started to spin. I steadied myself using the hand basin and prayed that it would pass. My head was throbbing and I felt like I might pass out, I'd had some hangovers in my life but this was by far the worst. I thought back to how much I'd had to drink and the thought of it made me wretch again. This time I wasn't quick enough to move my hair and managed to spray some of it.

I had probably sunk to the lowest point in my life right now. I had lost my position on the moral high ground and done the most damaging and stupid thing that I possibly could have. God how I hated myself, but I still had to get home. I could make up something in the cab about staying at Mel's and my phone having no battery or not wanting to ring too late and wake Mia, or maybe my phone was lost or stolen, or maybe my drink had been spiked…

A hundred thoughts sped through my head at once but made no sense in the dull confusion that alcohol creates.

"Just get home," I said to myself and reached for a bath towel.

I opened the door as quietly as I could and tiptoed into the room to get my clothes. Wearing yesterday's underwear is an experience that I never want to repeat in my lifetime, and I struggled with the zip on the back of my dress for a good five minutes – but there was no way I was asking Jay for help. He had been snoring lightly when I'd gathered up my things, and if I had my way I would be more than happy to sneak away into the breaking dawn and never see him again.

I rummaged in my bag for a hair tie and a polo mint and my phone showed several missed calls all from home apart from one from Mel. I hugged it to my chest and closed my eyes, I couldn't believe how stupid I'd been. I gulped back my fear and dialled into voice mail, hearing at first Damien's voice saying that he was sure I was having a great time but would I be able to text him so he knew I was ok. Followed an hour later by him sounding a little concerned and saying I probably had no signal in the restaurant, but when I picked this up could I check in please. The next message sounded like he was pacing back and forth and said that he had spoken to the restaurant and they had closed an hour ago, the staff were about to leave and surely I hadn't gone on to a nightclub? The final message had only been left about half an hour ago. He sounded frantic with worry and on the verge of tears, saying that he'd spoken to Mel and woken her up and he was sorry but he couldn't help it - he was going to phone the police.

Panic filled my senses and I opened the bathroom door in order to bolt across the apartment and into the lift as fast as I could. Jay was standing at the breakfast bar, naked stirring a steaming mug of coffee.

"You're leaving so soon?" he said and the corners of his mouth seemed to curve into a sinister smile.

"Yes, I have to go. This has all been a terrible mistake, Jay, I should never have come here." I held my shoes in one hand and my handbag in the other.

"That's such a shame, I thought we could have done it all over again." He looked down at his manhood and then back at me squirming on the spot. "You were good last night Steph, the best ever. Dirtier than I ever remembered, you let me do things to you that I'd only ever dreamed of when we were married."

"Please stop," I said quietly and in disbelief, I had no fight left in me to shout.

"You were the whore I always wished for Steph. Don't be ashamed you were filthy and you loved it." He looked down at himself again. "Even the thought of it's making me hard again."

I shook my head and felt my cheeks burn with shame. I had no idea what I had or hadn't done. The last thing I could remember was him unzipping me and then fast forward to waking up. Whatever went on in between was unknown territory, and it might be a whole lot better if it stayed that way. I walked towards the door without looking back, and as I stood in the corridor waiting for the lift to arrive, I could have sworn I heard him laughing.

The joke is certainly on me this time, I thought, as I stepped inside and the doors closed behind me. *And it's the most unbelievably cruel joke ever.*

Chapter 39

I tipped the taxi driver generously and then made my way barefoot up the garden path. I wondered if any of the neighbours would see me taking the short walk of shame to my own front door, as I reached into my bag to find the house key. I hadn't turned it in the lock when the door flew open and Damien threw his arms around me.

"Thank God," he kept saying. "Thank God you are alright." He started to cry, probably through worry and exhaustion and I started to unravel.

"What happened to you? Where have you been?" he asked and all of the excuses I had thought of evaporated into thin air. I wanted to lie, not to get me out of the shit, but to save his feelings.

I'd been where he was right now, first with Jay and the actual affairs that he's indulged in, and then with Damien too – well at least I thought so. But no matter what he had done, to see someone you love looking so vulnerable, so frightened and exposed was beyond devastating.

"Steph, tell me – what's happened?" I sat on the sofa and he kneeled in front of me, almost begging for me to fix this shit cart of a situation and I wished with all of my heart that I could turn back time and stop myself from pressing the self- destruct button. Never mind tonight, it was all about to come out now. There was no way back that I could think of here and the only way through was to tell him everything, and watch the man I loved crumble before me.

I took a deep breath and my head thudded hard.

"Damien, can I take a shower first and then I'll tell you everything?" I asked tentatively.

He stood up and shook his head, then paradoxically mumbled, "Yes, yes of course."

I had only taken a few steps out of the room towards the staircase when I heard him stand up.

"I love you," he said stoically. "No matter what, I love you."

Chapter 40

I closed the bathroom door quietly and locked it behind me. I knew he wouldn't follow me, but I wanted to separate as much as I could from the outside world and scrub myself clean in case I contaminated anyone else.

The water ran hot and I stood and cried my heart out, knowing that things would never be the same again, and for so many reasons that this day could well mark the beginning of the end. I washed my body wishing that I could wash away the last twenty four hours of my life, and especially the emotional scars that I'd inflicted on myself by allowing Jay to use me in ways that I didn't want to imagine.

My hand glided over the top of my thighs and then briefly between my legs where I felt a tiny knot. I remembered. I'd started my period, and there was no way anyone or anything had been below my waist since I unwrapped that tampon. I cast my mind back to the very last thing that I could remember from the night before, and it was him unzipping my dress and it falling to the ground. Then there was my underwear folded over the chair, surely if he had ripped that off in the throes of passion it would have been strewn across the room?

My best guess was that I'd passed out and he'd put me to bed, but perhaps taken off my clothes for some reason? Although the thought was beyond terrible, it wasn't as terrible as the thought that I might have had full on rampant sex with him. Betrayal was betrayal, there was no getting away from it, but I'd far rather tell Damien that I was stupid enough to go back to his place and have a snog and leave it there.

By the time I crept downstairs in pyjamas, Damien was sitting at the kitchen table with two cups of tea. He looked like he hadn't slept in weeks, and maybe I was imagining it but there seemed to be more grey hairs than before around his temples. I sat down and cupped the steaming mug in both hands, waiting in the excruciating silence for one of us to speak.

"I love you," Damien spoke first, "and I know that things have been really hard for you, last weekend at the hotel, I need to explain..."

"I need to explain," I interrupted and knew that there was no way to hold back the tears. "I know about you and Louisa."

"What?" he said and looked at me in disbelief.

"There's no point hiding it anymore," I continued "I know that you two are together."

"Steph, no!" he objected, but of course he would, he didn't want to hurt me.

"Damien, it's ok. In some crazy kind of mixed up way, it's ok," I said, framing things up in a non-judgemental way, ready to tell him that in reality I was no better.

"That's a million miles from ok, believe me." He stood up and started to pace around the kitchen. "What the hell would make you think that?"

"Well the bedroom thing that happened at the hotel for a start," he shook his head and kept pacing. "And then the fact that you aren't in the office when you say you are, you're out somewhere secret together, aren't you?"

Damien stood still and looked at me. He ran his fingers through his hair and sat down to take my hand. Here it comes I thought, he's going to tell me that he is leaving us for her. I've seen that look before, the one that says I'm desperately sorry about what I'm about to say, but I have to say it anyway. The look that says your world is about to crash down around you and you'll take years to pick up the pieces - and even then some will always feel like they are missing, you'll never be whole again.

"Just say it, Damien," I pleaded. "Just tell me."

"Stephanie," he began with a tight hold of my hand, and his eyes cast down at the kitchen table. The words that followed made me pull away from him to clasp both of my hands over my mouth. I needed to contain the guttural scream that wanted to escape from my throat. If I had been standing I was certain that I would have fallen to my knees, not only because of the shock, but to pray to God that what I had just heard was nowhere near right.

"I've got testicular cancer. I've been going to hospital and Louisa's been driving me. She thinks I'm going for something to do with work, renting apartments to NHS staff on site and I told her that my car is due to trade in and I don't want the mileage any higher." He paused for breath and looked at me before continuing.

"I didn't want you to see my bollock swollen up like a bloody tennis ball, so I kept my pants on last weekend. I didn't want you to find out like this, I wanted to tell you once I knew what the prognosis was." He looked at me through frightened eyes that mirrored my own and waited for a response.

"I had no idea," I whispered as my hands fell into my lap and the world felt like it had stopped turning. "Damien, I had no idea."

"I didn't want you to have any idea," he looked at me through the eyes of love, "I didn't want to frighten you."

"But you must be terrified," I said.

"That's an understatement," he forced a laugh. "I'm shitting bricks."

"How long have you known?" I asked.

"I thought something was wrong a while ago, remember that night that Mia threw up on me?" he said, "I took a shower and I thought things felt different, but I did the usual man thing and ignored it. Obviously it didn't go away and gradually started to get a bit worse, so I thought I'd better go and see the doctor."

"I can't believe I didn't know that something was wrong," I said, feeling the crushing weight of a guilty conscience, as I thought about the conversation with Lizzie and even worse, last night with Jay.

"I didn't want you to know," he said bravely, as his love for me shone through brightly. How could I possibly have doubted him? I had given up on us at the first real hurdle in our marriage, and the irony was that it had been absolutely nothing compared to the mountain we faced now.

"What's going to happen?" I asked "They can fix it, right?" He pressed his lips together into a line and closed his eyes. He didn't want to say the words that were on the tip of his tongue, which meant that they were certainly not words I would want to hear. "Damien?" I asked and started to cry. Willing myself to hold it together, but not being able to I asked again through the tears "It's ok, isn't it?"

"I can't tell you that yet, Steph," he said after a long sigh.

"But what about chemo and radiation and stuff? What about operating and removing it?" I asked in panicked enthusiasm.

"Yes, there are certainly options and I am going back next week to talk them through," he said and looked at me. "But we don't know what we're up against yet."

"What do you mean?" I said cautiously now.

"I have to have a full body scan to check for secondaries." He delivered the news as softly as he could, but as the words hung in the air between us, I lurched to my feet and wretched in the sink.

Moments later, Damien was beside me holding my hair out of my face and rubbing my back. He let me get my breath back and handed me a glass of water and a tissue.

"Where were you Steph?" he asked and waited in the silence between us for the reply that he guessed was coming.

I remained at the sink with my back to him, I couldn't bear to look at him and I could hardly breathe. I took a couple of deep breaths and thought about lying to spare his feelings, but knew in truth that this would be mainly to spare my own. I couldn't take any more, but if I had any chance of saving us then I had to be honest, as painful as that was. I knew from my experience with Jay that lies catch up with you, and that they cause far more damage when they do.

"If it's any consolation, I totally understand," Damien's voice cut through the thick silence.

I closed my eyes tight and wished he would stop being nice about it, why couldn't he threaten to leave and tell me that we were over now and it was all my fault? At least then I could throw a whole load of crap about him not wanting me and being a cold bastard back at him.

"Steph, don't cry. I'm telling you that it's ok." His words sounded remarkably calm, but as I slowly turned around I saw before me a broken man, a man that I had broken.

"I can't believe that you'd say that." I had no right to be angry, but I could feel it welling up inside of me.

"What's done is done, Steph, and I'm not going to hold it against you. God knows what you were thinking after last weekend. I should have told you when we were away but I didn't have the heart to ruin it for you when you'd tried to make it so special."

"I can't believe you're being so nice to me," I said, skirting around the elephant in the room instead of just coming out and saying it.

"Why wouldn't I be nice to you, I love you and you're human," he said. "I don't need details, but I just need you to tell me that it's a one off and you'll never see him again." He looked at me searching for the truth and my anger turned to shame.

"Damien, I didn't sleep with him – I mean I slept with him, but that was all," I said looking at the floor.

Damien raised his hand for me to stop, "No details, just tell me that it's never going to happen again."

"Please, listen to me!" I fell to my knees in front of him on the cold, tiled floor. "I didn't have sex with anyone last night, I kissed him and he undressed me and I passed out," I cried. "Thank God I passed out." Damien nodded slowly, with his eyes closed tight - holding in emotion as best he could. "I know what you're thinking." I wiped the snot and tears from my face with the palms of my hands and then onto my pyjamas. "You're thinking that I'm an idiot, and that's what I am thinking, too."

"That's not what I'm thinking, Steph," he said, shaking his head.

"Well what then? What Damien? Please hate me, tell me I'm not good enough, tell me to go… anything!" I was raising my voice and crashed my fist down on the table top. Damien caught hold of my hand and dragged me to my feet. He spoke to me through gritted teeth and the fear that raged in his eyes.

"You could have been raped, Steph, you could have been murdered. You could have been drugged and dumped in a skip in a back lane and I would never have found you. Have you any idea what went through my head last night?" His words were loaded with pain and every one pierced my heart.

"We've got a kid, Steph, a baby who relies on us and you went missing and I've got bloody cancer!" His stooped over the table with both of his palms flat on the surface and hung his head.

His body started to shake with the sobs that wracked through him, the sound of which I will never forget. I threw my arms around his waist and cried too, holding him in his darkest hour - and as he turned around and I felt him envelop me in the sadness that we both shared, I thanked God for him. The man that saw past the human mistakes I'd made and still loved me regardless.

"I'm not saying I'm not devastated, of course I am. But I won't let this break us, Steph. I believe in you and I believe in us and I know that this is something that I can forgive you for in time," he said as we stood clinging on to each other, like the sole survivors in the aftermath of a natural disaster. I didn't say a word, I just held him tighter and breathed him in.

"God I love you," he said and kissed the top of my head. "We've got bigger things to worry about here, and I can promise you that I will find a way to cope and move on from this. I can see what drove you to do it and I played a part in that."

"No, no Damien. It was my fault, I got it all wrong and I didn't look past what was on the surface. I jumped to conclusions and I acted like a complete idiot."

"This isn't a time for us to be divided, it's a time for us to stand together and be strong, Steph," he said. "I need you beside me on this, if I've got any chance of getting through it then you have to be with me. You're my missing piece remember?"

"You still think that? After what I've done?" I sobbed.

"Always. For better or worse remember?" He held me at arm's length. "People mess up, Steph, and yes it hurts like hell to think of you with someone else, but it's some screwed up symptom of us being disconnected. I know when we're good, we are unstoppable, and I know we can get back there, somehow." He looked dreadful, and I felt worse than that.

"I can't believe that you are saying this," I said. "I don't deserve someone like you, Damien."

"Well let's just say that the last few months have given me some perspective on life," he replied. "You needed me and I wasn't there, and as much as it rips my heart out to admit it you turned to another man when I rejected you."

"But you did it to protect me."

"Yes, but you didn't know that. By not being honest with you in the first place I caused even more damage." Damien sighed and shook his head. "I need some time to process it all Steph, and I'm not up for any bedroom aerobics in the near future, so please don't think it's you."

"Of course not, I wouldn't expect that," I said feeling guilty for my reaction last weekend.

"I need to go to bed," he said. "I'm exhausted."

"Sorry," I muttered "Sorry for all of it."

"I'm sorry too, but it's how we move forward that matters. And as long as he was a random stranger that you're never going to see again I can work on getting past it." He started walking towards the door, but stopped and looked over his shoulder.

"And the fact that you didn't have sex with him does help," he added as his voice cracked with emotion. He turned his back on me and walked down the hallway, soon I heard his footsteps on the stairs.

Now was the one and only time I could tell him that it had been Jay, but I couldn't. For all kinds of reasons I couldn't. I followed him upstairs and stopped for a moment on the landing, listening to him crying in our bedroom. I silently sat on the top stair and let my own heart break too, waiting for what seemed like the longest time, for the moment when I heard the tears stop and his breathing deepen. I crawled into bed next to him and spooned into his back, feeling like both the luckiest and unluckiest girl in the world.

Chapter 41

Damien was still sleeping when Mia woke, I scooped her up and crept downstairs. My hangover was lifting a little – probably thanks to being sick and getting some sleep, and I even managed to have a slice of toast and a cup of tea.

We played with finger puppets and building blocks, then I walked her in her pushchair down to the corner shop to pick up milk. It felt like I was watching myself in a movie, an observer from the side lines of life – looking at my day as someone completely detached. I was going through the motions, changing nappies, singing nursery rhymes and drinking tea. This façade hid the dread that was shaking me to my core.

Maybe this is what it was like when you had a breakdown. Here but not here and scared to let yourself start crying again because you knew that you wouldn't stop. I had more energy than usual and found myself doing things that I usually professed to never having time to do, by lunchtime I had defrosted the freezer, dusted the skirting boards and washed all of the windows downstairs. My body felt like it was buzzing with adrenalin and caffeine.

I wanted to google Damien's condition, but I was terrified. There might be pictures and horrendous stories of surgery gone wrong and people not recovering. I knew enough about Law of Attraction to know that I needed to try to stay positive, to think about the outcome that I wanted to attract and to focus on seeing Damien fit and well in my mind's eye. All I could connect with was the image of him standing and weeping over the kitchen table, and me holding on to him in a gesture that was far too little and way too late. I found myself praying to God to help us, as I built a house with Mia's building blocks. I would have sold my soul to the highest bidder right now if they could have made this go away.

Mum and Dad called just after lunch to collect Mia. Thankfully they couldn't stay long and thankfully I kept a stiff upper lip. I waved them off from the garden gate and breathed a sigh of relief as they turned left at the end of the terrace and drove out of view. I scribbled a note on the pad next to the phone about going out for a couple of hours, there was someone I needed to see that would help me make sense of everything and I hoped that Sue wasn't booked back to back. I crossed the road and walked down about three doors to where the bus would stop, I couldn't take the chance that I was still over the limit. Shortly I was sitting on the top deck, watching the world go by and heading into town.

I didn't like to just presume it was ok to go up the stairs and camp in the little waiting room.
Instead I went next door and ordered a takeaway coffee, took a seat by the window and sent Sue a text. She had a cancellation in an hour's time, and I said that I'd take it. An hour is a long time with just your conscience for company. I stared out of the window and tried to guess details of the people's lives that were walking past and after a while came to the realization that in fact we perhaps never knew anyone really well at all. I wondered if Damien was awake yet, and how I was ever going to get through this. I'd seen fridge magnets and greeting cards with messages on about life only sending you what you

could handle, but right now it felt like my order had been horrendously mixed up with someone made of titanium.

"There you are!" I heard Sue's familiar voice and stood up. "I'm just going to get a cuppa, the kettle's on the blink up there," she said and hugged me. "What's up?" she said and took a step back. "What's happened, Stephanie?"

"I'm fine," I said, teetering on the edge of that emotional moment when you've been holding it altogether and someone asks you if you really are ok, the moment when the dam bursts and the tsunami starts. I was aware that my bottom lip was trembling and my vision was blurring with tears.

"You're so not fine!" Sue said softly and took my hand. "Let me get a drink and we'll work this out."

"I don't know if it can be worked out this time," I said.

"Well I am psychic and I think it can be," Sue replied confidently. "Do you want another coffee?"

I had started to tell Sue the tale on the way up the stairs, but she asked me to stop.

"Tell me later, or you're going to think that I'm making it up when I start reading the cards," she said. "It's happened so many times before that people spill their heart out to me and then they think that I'm a fraud when the cards fall that way too. I keep telling them, it's confirmation plain and simple, but it is better if you keep it in and I don't know yet."

We sat at the familiar table and Sue handed me the cards, asking me to shuffle and be open to receiving whatever was right for me to know right now. She zoned out and her eyelids fluttered slightly as she drew the top six cards and arranged them in two rows of two in front of me.

"I can tell you straightaway that this is a terrible time for you, Stephanie. You are being tested beyond belief and you feel like you have been through the mill in every possible way here, it's a wonder that you're still functioning." She looked at me and I nodded, then turned the first card.

There was a picture of a woman sitting in darkness with a blind fold on and her hands tied, with arrows and spears pointing her way. "Just as I thought, a psychic attack," said Sue.

"This card shows me that there is someone in your circle at the moment that really, really has got it in for you. This is someone that feels spurned, hard done to or generally dumped on by you and they are furious. This is a really nasty card, Stephanie. There is nothing I can do to dress it up and it's one that I fear coming out when I am reading because it scares people."

"I can see why," I said quietly, looking to Sue for guidance and help as to how I could cope.

"Yes, it's a very dark card and it brings with it a dark energy. It is often linked with jealousy and envy, and can be an indication for you to ramp up your protection and to exercise discernment when you are choosing who to spend time with. This card generally refers to someone that is clever and astute, sometimes manipulative, but they are not evolved in a spiritual way. This is the type of consciousness that would seek revenge and would seek to be deceitful in order to get what they want. It's come out first for you so it must be something that is happening now for you or is about to happen really soon." She looked at me and it was written all over my face that I knew full well who this person was.

"Feels like a masculine energy to me," she commented, and I am picking up the letter J. I shuddered. Although I knew this already, to hear her say it was chilling. Jay had brought me to my knees once, both metaphorically and literally, and I wouldn't let it happen again. Why on earth had I attracted him back into my life now? We were done and I had moved on, or at least that's what I thought I had believed before last night.

"This is a funny one, Stephanie," Sue said and tapped the card with her fingernail. "I want you to be really careful here, this man isn't done with you yet."

"What do you mean?" I asked, wide-eyed and afraid. I could feel an energy radiating from Sue that felt like fear, surely not. I was last night's conquest, and he put a spin on it for old time's sake, but I could have been anyone.

"I think he was looking for you," Sue said. "Not in the moment that he found you, but he had a very strong intention that your paths would cross again. Although he doesn't know about Law of Attraction, he works with it quite well. He wanted to find you to clear something up, to take something that he felt was his," she continued to channel the answers I was dreading but was compelled to hear. "He found you to bring you down, because that's what you tried to do to him."

"Sue, it's Jay, my ex-husband I know it," I said. "I was with him last night."

Sue didn't open her eyes, but I could see them flicker beneath her eyelids. "Ah yes, now that makes perfect sense," she said and I waited on the edge of my seat for her to elaborate. "I'm getting through that he thinks he's in for a pay out, some kind of backhander or belated settlement from you. He found out about the money that you won and he's going to try to get a case together to prove that you were still married when you bought the ticket. He thinks that he might have a claim against you."

"Oh God, Sue, really?"

"I'd say so, there's a vibe of entitlement coming off him really strongly," she said. "But how on earth did you end up with him last night?"

I told her in brief about the restaurant and the taxi, agreeing that there was no such thing as coincidence and that this was playing out for a reason.

"Well you don't need me to tell you that he's trouble, and if I were you I'd put him in the freezer."

"What do you mean?" I asked.

"It's reinforcing the intention that you want to freeze someone out of your life, and any influence that they may have over you. You write their name on a piece of paper and circle it three times, yellow is the most powerful colour. Then you place one hand on your heart and the other over them and you say "I bind you with light" three times. Then you fold them up and put them in the freezer for as long as you want. If you really want to make a big difference you can even use a food bag and fill it with water and then drop them in. As long as your intention is never to harm and only to contain their energy in a way that it isn't going to affect you anymore, then it's a really simple way of getting rid."

"I am so going to do that when I get home," I said.

"I keep finding people in between the peas and the fish fingers from years back that I've totally forgotten about!" Sue sniggered.

She turned the next card and there was a picture of a hand holding an apple and the message was about physical health and wellbeing. "This is about you looking after yourself more, and perhaps not just you either. There is a strong message in this card about what you eat and how it affects your body, whether that be weight gain or disease – it's asking you to have a really honest look at what you're putting in and how it affects you. I feel also that I need to encourage you to look at the energy in the food that you eat. As you are evolving more and more you need to make sure that you are nourishing yourself in the correct way."

"I think I have a pretty good diet," I said, a little defensively and thinking that I wanted to get onto the cards that were going to help Damien and save our marriage, never mind a bloody apple.

"Yes, I know you do, but if you did have a good diet and you were looking after yourself then this card wouldn't have come up for you," Sue paused. "That's your ego jumping in and trying to protect you, but the irony is that it's going to sabotage you even more. Remember lesson one."

"Be open to possibility," I said and sighed.

"That's exactly right," said Sue. "Now this card could be one of the most important ones that has ever been drawn for you, and you want to dismiss it. This is a lesson that could change everything for you. It could help you to heal and help to change your energy vibration so that you attract way more of what you want and less of what you don't. But it could well be out of sequence in this reading."

"What does that mean?" I asked.

"It means that you will come back to this one at the right time, and that time is as yet unwritten for you. In other words you have to be in the right place in your life to be able to work with it, and the universe will keep sending you signs and signals until you finally catch on."

"Ok then," I said, willing her to turn the next card.

"You're doing it now actually," said Sue.

"Doing what?" I asked.

"Being dismissive of this message, and I'm being asked to tell you again so there is no confusion – this is a key to resolving things, even though you think it's not."

I shrugged. "Noted."

The next card was one that I recognised, and I could remember that it was about working with lessons and knowing when they were coming up in your life.

"I've had this one before," I said to Sue.

"Yes, and it's coming up now because you haven't been working with your lessons effectively, Steph." She looked at me to see how I might react. "This card is coming out again for you because it's still relevant."

"Is that why everything is going wrong all of a sudden?" I asked.

"Yes and no, there is also the Shit Happens factor as I like to call it," said Sue. "By that I mean that we can Law of Attraction it and pixie and unicorn it up all we like, but sometimes it's going to hit the fan and all you can do is run for cover."

"I can't believe you're saying that!" I smirked. "Hasn't everything got some kind of lesson in it for us, or it's been brought in because we've attracted it?"

"In theory, Steph, yes." Sue put the card back in position in row one. "But in my experience of life, there are forces at work in the universe that throw us a cosmic spoke in our wheels every now and then and it's nothing to do with what we have been sending out there. I know that sounds like I don't believe in what I do, but that's not the case. What I'm saying is that there are anomalies if you like, or blips that don't make sense to our human mind, maybe there is some rhyme or reason to them but perhaps I am not evolved enough to see it yet." I sat back into my chair and sighed, this was all so confusing and perhaps I should have waited until a day when I could have taken it all in more easily.

"All I am saying is that sometimes stuff will come up as a lesson, or an experience to help you to grow and evolve, and you are going to attract a whole load of that in when you have started to walk the path of light. As I said before you are sending a message out to the universe from the outset saying that you want to evolve, and this is the way we do it on earth. You are also going to attract experiences through Law of Attraction, that match your thoughts, feelings and energy vibration, so you need to heal your wounds and be conscious in what you are thinking, as best you can in a human mind and ego. And thirdly – sometimes Shit Happens and we don't know why."

"Well that's a relief," I said. "So it's not all my fault?"

"That's not what I said and you know it!" Sue chuckled and the atmosphere lightened. "You need to go away after this and do some real soul searching. Be honest with yourself, Steph and see which of those three concepts applies to what is playing out for you. And whatever it is, be kind to yourself."

"But I have been such an idiot, Sue, really."

"There is a difference between taking responsibility for yourself and using your experience to evolve, and beating yourself up, Steph. When you are hard on yourself you start to feel less and less worthy, more and more stupid and think for a moment about what Law of Attraction would send you if that's what you were radiating?"

"Ok, I get it," I said, but wondering if I would ever be able to let myself off the hook.

"You need to step back from the human stuff that is playing out now and start to look past that. This is where you will see the lessons and the essence of what you are being asked to learn, it was meant to happen this way you know." Sue spoke kindly to me and her voice made me want to cry again.

"Really?" I asked.

"I think so. You aren't fully healed from you and Jay, and you need to go through this in order to see who he really is."

"You mean it's not done yet?"

"I can't say one way or another, but he is in your cards today and that means that his energy is still active in your vibration, but then again it was only last night and you are probably thinking about it over and over."

"So I'm sending energy to it and its growing?"

You are a Creator.

"Yes, you need to find a way to be able to close the chapter as soon as you can on it and move on. Remember forgiveness and compassion?"

"Yes."

"It's time that you applied that to yourself."

Sue turned the card at her fingertips and the writing said 'Miracle'.

"You're going to create a life that you love after all of this, and you're going to show others how to do the same. You're a teacher, Steph, a light that will shine bright for the world to see but in order to do that you have to go through the human trials and tribulations and make good from them. No one would take you seriously if you hadn't had to drag yourself through the mire at times. The universe needs you to be relatable, real and a bit battle scarred to help reach people and make them believe that they can do it too. A pedestal wouldn't suit you, and it wouldn't help you to connect with the people in the trenches that need you."

"I don't think that card is for me," I objected. "Everything else you've said makes complete sense, but that's not me."

"And that's why it is going to be perfect, because you aren't coming from a place of ego."

"I just want to get us through this, I don't have it in me to help anyone else." I said quietly.

"But you will have." Sue reached out her hand and took mine. "You're here to help so many people and you need to find a way to step into that greatness, Steph, and the universe is going to keep pushing you until you do."

"Soul Path. That's what all of this is about, Steph, it's about you going through these life lessons and experiences in order for you to find out why you are here and to share that with others. You weren't ready before, but after this you will be and you'll be ready to become who you were always meant to be."

"And what's that?" I asked, still stuck in the fear that my life was about to go monumentally tits up again, and trying to stop bloody thinking about it and sending it more energy.

Sue turned the next card, 'Betrayal'.

I smiled weakly.

"This is closely linked with Forgiveness and Compassion and also You Can't Fix Other People," Sue said tapping the card. "It's about knowing that everyone is doing their best and that when people do betray you, it is usually driven by fear in some way, shape or form. I can't dress it up, Steph, you'll be pretty upset about this one, it's going to be unexpected and it feels like it's going to hit you really hard."

"Will it be Damien?" I asked tentatively. "Is it me betraying him?"

"That is certainly a lesson for you, for both of you, yes, but this feels like someone actually betraying you in a big way. It also feels like it's going to come from nowhere and really pull the rug from under you." She paused. "There's going to be a moment when you feel like you have nothing left, Steph," Sue spoke in a serious tone.

"Yes," I agreed, apart from Mia I felt like my life as I knew it was slipping away and I was desperately trying to hold on and save it.

"You're not listening," Sue said. "I said there is *going* to be – it's not here yet."

I suddenly felt chilled to the bone and looked at her in disbelief.

"It's going to get worse?" I asked.

"I don't want to scare you," Sue continued and totally failed on that front, "but the energy that accompanies this card at the moment is one of you having to build from the foundations up."

"But I know that Sue, I know I need to," I said, feeling scared as she shook her head.

"I don't just mean with Damien, Steph, this feels like *everything* is going to be affected." She closed her eyes and her hands hovered above the card in question. "Ok, ok," she muttered to herself and opened her eyes. "You need to know that no one is going to die here, it's not *that* serious. Mia is going to be fine and you and Damien will get through this and be stronger than ever."

"Thank God!" I finally allowed myself to breathe.

"However, the universe is about to shake things up for you one last time, and it's going to take everything you've got to get through it, but you will." She flipped over the next card and thankfully smiled.

"Soul Path. That's what all of this is about, Steph, it's about you going through these life lessons and experiences in order for you to find out why you are here and to share that with others. You weren't ready before, but after this you will be and you'll be ready to become who you were always meant to be."

"And what's that?" I asked, still stuck in the fear that my life was about to go monumentally tits up again, and trying to stop bloody thinking about it and sending it more energy.

Sue took one final card off the top of the deck that I'd shuffled and turned it over. The picture showed a book and a quill, with scrolling words and stardust lighting up the pages.

"And there it is. The book you need to write about the lessons that you've lived, and you're living still. This is the way that you'll save yourself and then illuminate the way for others to do the same. It's your calling, and you can't escape it," Sue said. "The more you try to, the more you'll be pulled back to it."

"I'd forgotten all about it to be honest," I said.

"Of course you had, but the universe hasn't," Sue laughed. "And believe me, it won't.

I hadn't written anything down that Sue had told me, and as I looked at the cards on the table I started to slip into overwhelm.

"Take a picture," suggested Sue, "on your phone, and then you'll have a record."

I did as she said but there were aspects that I didn't want to remember. Sue reminded me that a reading was a snapshot in time, a visual of likely future possibilities, but that these could be changed with free will and intention. I wasn't to focus on the negative aspects of what had been said, but take them as a cosmic heads up of what could play out. I needed to know that I wasn't a victim, life was not happening to me but *responding* to me. That subtle difference would make all of the difference, even with a healthy side order of Shit Happens.

I promised to keep in touch and mentioned that Sue would be getting an invitation to Mia's naming day through the post, then I made my way down the steep staircase and back on to the busy street.

Stephanie's Journal ~ Lesson 19
Protect Yourself

Everything is energy, and when someone "sends" you negative or lower vibration energy in the form of gossip, malice, jealous or an intention for you to fail, this can have an actual effect on your life. A psychic attack is usually not something that is done deliberately, it is usually simply "bad feeling" that someone may have towards you for some reason. This can lower your vibration and manifest in your life as physical, emotional or psychological challenges, or actual experiences of things "going wrong". Use regular energetic protection and cord-cutting techniques and make sure that you do your best to be mindful of what you are sending out to others, as we know the law of attraction is at work.

"Fools take a knife and stab people in the back. The wise take a knife, cut the cord and free themselves from the fools." Unknown

Chapter 42

Damien was in the kitchen when I got home.

"Coffee?" he said and reached for another mug. "Is Mia with your mum?"

"Yes, she came to pick her up." It was impossible to relax into any kind of regular conversation, although we both wanted to. We verbally tiptoed around each other, Damien yawned and stretched.

"I don't know why I'm so tired, I slept like the dead," he said, quickly followed by, "Sorry."

"It's ok," I said. "It feels like nothing is safe to talk about."

"That's going to pass, with time we'll get back to where we were." He sat down at the table and dunked a biscuit.

"God, I hope so," I said and reached for his hand, remembering the sound of him crying himself to sleep.

"We will, it's just going to take time. We both want the same thing Steph, and that is a great start." He squeezed my hand back and although his mouth smiled, his eyes swam deep with the pain I knew he was drowning in.

"Thank you," I whispered. "Thank you for trying to forgive me, I know that you'll always bear the scars for what I've done and I hate myself for that."

"Scars fade Steph," he said and looked deep into my eyes as I felt my heart overflow with love for him. "Let me deal with this in my own way, I promise I'll be back."

I closed my eyes and he leaned forward to kiss my forehead, then pulled me in to hug me close.

That night we slept in the same bed, for the most part I was curled up into a ball with Damien's arms around me.

Although sleep came easily, my dreams were filled with images I recognized from the cards that had depicted my next round of learning and life experience. Their imprints were still in my mind when my eyes blinked open, and I carefully reached into the bedside cabinet and pulled out the notes I had made from two years ago. I wriggled free of Damien's protective hold and made my way into the study, where I could read the journal that I had diligently kept all those months ago.

There was a bundle of loose papers stuffed inside the front cover where I had written the last six lessons. One was on the back of a shopping list and one in tiny scrawl on a post-it note. I really should get them in order, especially if I had another six coming my way any moment now. Could I really bring all of this together into a book? And would people really want to read it? Seriously, I wasn't sure if I would want to read someone's sob story about everything going shits up and then coming good in the obligatory happy ending.

"If it does end that way…" I caught myself thinking. I had to believe it would or I might as well give up now, and that wasn't an option. Yes, things were looking pretty bad and I was shit scared, but there was no point in rolling over and giving up. I wasn't done yet, and although I felt broken I had to find a way to piece myself back together and it started here. I had to agree with Sue on one thing, if I could turn this around it would be a miracle. But miracles happen and who knows, perhaps it was my turn. I started to arrange the loose papers into chronological order from memory, and wrote the last six lessons in the journal.

I heard Damien stir and looked at the time. I'd been writing for nearly three hours and hardly noticed.

"Morning," he said as he padded past me and into the bathroom. "What's that you're doing?"

"Just thinking about the book idea still," I replied.

"You should do that," he said and turned on the shower.

"I think I will," I answered and wrote the next heading ready for the next lesson. The words 'Psychic Attack' seemed so sinister, and I was pleased to close the book on them. I made my way downstairs to put on the kettle for coffee and as it boiled I wrote Jay's name down in full and put him right at the back of the freezer.

Chapter 43

Mia was in good spirits when mum and dad brought her home, she had slept in the car and her hair fell in soft curls around her face. Damien played with her while I made tea, desperate to tell mum and dad about Damien but knowing that he might not want that.

"Are you ok, love?" Mum asked as I handed her a cup and saucer.

I paused for a moment for Damien to cut in, and he cleared his throat.

"We've had a bit of bad news to be honest," he said as mum screwed her face into a grimace and said I'd forgotten the sugar.

"Well?" she asked. "Spit it out will you?"

"I've got cancer," Damien said and Mum stopped stirring.

"Cancer?" she said in a disbelieving tone.

"Would you stop saying it please?" I snapped in her direction. "I hate that bloody word!"

"But, are you sure?" she looked from Damien to me and back again.

"Christ, Mum! Of course he's sure! It's not something you'd get wrong, you know!"

"Steph, it's fine." said Damien and reached for my hand.

"It's not fine, Damien. Cancer and fine don't ever belong in the same sentence."

I looked at him with tears in my eyes and he stood up. My parents sat awkwardly as he held me and I cried, then I heard Mum sniff and saw that she was crying too.

"Mum, I'm sorry." I knew that I shouldn't have lashed out at her.

"No need darling, no need," Mum dabbed her eyes with a tissue that she'd undoubtedly had pushed up her sleeve, and Dad shook his head.

"What are they going to do about it then?" he asked Damien.

"I'm not exactly sure yet. I've got to go back to hospital next week for a meeting with the consultant and they'll give me some treatment options then." Damien sat back down and shrugged. "I guess it's probably going to be chemo and maybe operating to get rid of it."

Mum was stirring another sugar into her tea and the spoon chinked against the bone china.

"That's bloody bad luck, son," Dad said. "You've never smoked as far as I know and you're not a drinker."

"Where exactly is it?" piped up Mum and I held my breath.

"Well it's somewhere easy to remove," Damien answered and waited for them to put two and two together. Mum's expression clearly stated that this wasn't going to be the case so he enlightened them further, as Dad visibly winced.

"Put it this way, you might want to call me Hitler when I get out of surgery."

"Keep us in the loop," said Mum as she fastened up her coat to leave. Dad shook Damien's hand and patted him on the shoulder at the same time, possibly the nearest to a hug he had ever given a bloke.

"Let us know if you need us," he said and Damien promised that he would, and in fact we would drop Mia off on the way to the consultant's appointment if that was alright. They drove away and I sighed with relief.

"God, that was exhausting," I said as I closed the door.

"People react differently to stuff, that's all," Damien said, and although I knew he was right I also knew that there was no way I could get my parents through this – I was struggling to stay afloat myself. "Your mum was asking me again about the christening when you went to the loo, you know."

"That's the last thing on my mind at the minute," I said. "I couldn't cope with seeing everyone and putting on the happy when it's not what I feel like."

"We'll have to get back to as near a normal life as we can." Damien was right. "No matter what happens, life goes on."

"Don't say that," I said. "It sounds like something someone would say on their deathbed."

"Touché," he said and forced a smile.

Chapter 44

"Are you sure you should be going in?" I asked Damien the next morning, when he emerged from the bedroom in a suit.

"I'm fine, really. If it's chemo it's going to knock me sideways so I need to make sure that everything is in order now. Apart from a swollen nut I'm fine." He picked up his briefcase and turned to kiss my cheek. "Actually have you got any paracetamol, I've got a headache coming on."

"Only Mia's Calpol for teething," I said. "But I'm sure it's just paracetamol in a liquid."

Damien took a large gulp straight from the bottle and gave me it back.

"I love you," I called as he walked out of the door.

"I love you too Steph, more than you know." And with that he was gone, and I was left thinking about the long day ahead and maybe I should see if Mel wanted to meet up.

I sent her a text - I owe you a latte and an explanation, soft play? She replied and arrangements were made, I had a ten minute ride in the car to decide how much I wanted to tell her.

Once Mia and George were camped in the ball pool, we claimed the table right beside them and I started talking. I covered in brief the happenings of last Saturday night, leaving out some of the gory details that I thought might make her pick George up and run a mile.

"I feel absolutely dreadful," I told her, as Mel sat opposite me with a look on her face like someone that had watched a full movie, only to be left with the most frustrating cliff-hanger.

"I can't believe it Steph, oh my God!" she said, missing the point that I had come dangerously close to breaking up my marriage. "What was it like, kissing another man?"

"Well I've kissed him before, you know, and a whole lot more besides," I said, getting frustrated that she was latching on to the wrong part of the story, but also finding it a little amusing that she was so interested.

"And how do you know you didn't do a whole lot more besides?" she raised an eyebrow and I could see that her face was getting flushed.

"Mel!" I said in a mock stern tone, then I leaned in and spoke quietly. "Maybe you should get something mail order in discreet packaging for yourself, you know the kind of thing that needs batteries?" We both laughed until I thought my pelvic floor might not take anymore, and as the giggles subsided she mentioned that Damien had called her.

"He was worried sick," she said. "He asked if you were sleeping on my sofa."

"Seriously, I feel terrible – I can only imagine what I would have been like if he'd done that to me," I said. "And the fact that he never would makes me hate myself even more."

"Have you told him what happened?" Mel asked, and I cast my eyes down to the table top.

"Yes, well no," I mumbled.

"Which is it, yes or no?" she said.

"Yes, I've told him everything that happened and didn't happen, but I haven't said it was Jay," I confessed.

"Well, perhaps it's a case of least said, soonest mended," Mel said. "There's no need to tell him in my opinion."

"Really?" I asked. "It's eating me away and I wish I'd said something at the time, but I couldn't."

"Well, whatever stopped you at the time was probably doing you a favour," Mel said and stooped down to wipe George's nose.

"Maybe," I half-heartedly agreed, "but if that's the case why does it feel like I've done the wrong thing?"

Mia broke my train of thought by starting to cry, and I stood up to make my way towards her, unable to shake the guilty feeling that hadn't left the edge of my conscience since the early hours of Sunday morning.

"You did the best you could Steph, and you can't really tell him now, anyway. You've got to try to move on if you can and do your best to forget about it."

"I suppose you're right," I said, "and when it comes down to it I missed the chance to tell him, and now it would create an absolute shit storm."

"Exactly," said Mel, pulling my pushchair out of the way as I swung Mia onto my hip and took her into the baby changing room.

Chapter 45

Robin sent all of her clients a text the night before an appointment, to remind them of their booking and her cancellation policy. For once I was relatively organized, I was dropping Mia off with Mum in the morning before my appointment, then meeting Damien for lunch and driving him to hospital.

"Everything ok?" he asked me when he saw me texting back.

"Yes, just sorting stuff out for the morning," I replied.

"But you're not picking me up until lunch time," Damien said in a suspicious tone.

"I'm going out before that, so Mia's with mum," I said a little defensively, and then I realised that he had every right to know my whereabouts. I had created the cracks in the trust that we had built, and it was up to me to help repair them. "Sorry, that came out wrong."

"It's ok, it's me Steph. I know that I can't police you, but it's early days and I can't help needing to know where you are and who you're with."

"Look," I said and showed him my phone. "It's a lady called Robin that I'm going to talk to about weight loss. I booked the appointment in a panic, after I thought that you couldn't bear to…"

"Ok, ok," he said and rubbed the heel of his hand on his forehead. "I'm just not having a great day."

"Are you worried about tomorrow?" I asked.

"Yes, there's that and work stuff, and I've still got that sodding headache."

"I wish you could take some time off Damien, even just a couple of weeks – if you were in a regular job they would have insisted," I said with a heavy heart.

"I know, and I will," he replied. "I just need to get things in order, and then once we're through this I'm going to see Ryan Sorby. He's been telling me for ages that I'm in a good position to talk about an exit strategy."

"You mean sell up?" I asked.

"Yes, I've got a plan to drop fees and gain a much bigger market share, especially in the rental market, and then have incremental price increases written into the agreement in the small print, so that we can scale up the income without any extra work. On paper it will look like the business is in really good shape to sell, then we get our money out and it's happy days."

"You have no idea how relieved I am to hear that," I said with conviction.

"I know you've wanted it for a while, and you're absolutely right. Especially if we can go out on a high like this we'll be talking a substantial pay out, and then if anything ever happened to me, I know that you and Mia are set."

"I mean that I want you around Damien, we're set financially anyway. I don't want you working yourself into the ground to generate more money for us when we are more than fine as it is."

"I know that, but I need to know that I'm doing something useful. Something constructive at the moment, and building up your future security feels that way to me."

"Our future security," I corrected him, worried that he had given up on recovering already.

"Yes, that's what I meant. But it all takes time and I need to get our ducks in a row, remember that we ploughed some of our own funds into the new branches and that we ring-fenced the rental properties that I had into a trust fund for Mia. I'm not saying that we're hard up Steph, I'm just being realistic here. A million quid is not as much as you think when you look at a lifetime of two of you earning and what that would add up to."

"Damien we're more than well off, if there's one thing we don't have to worry about, it's money," I said "We've got no mortgage, a thriving business and a big lump in the bank. Most people would love to be in our position."

"I'd swap them right now for my left testicle," he said soberly, and I cringed.

"Our money can buy us the best help there is for you though. It's not like you have to wait to be seen by a consultant or beg for a scan, and we certainly won't be subject to the postcode lottery when it comes to the best drugs."

"You're right, I'm sorry I need to go to bed." He stood up and kissed the top of my head. "And by the way, you don't need to go and see that woman tomorrow. To me you are perfect, and you always have been."

"Can I sleep in our bed?" I asked.

"I hoped you would," he replied and we made our way upstairs.

Chapter 46

Although I had come to see Robin about weight loss, the hour that we spent together rapidly evolved in the direction of relationships, sex life and then the inevitable emotional meltdown about Damien. This was interspersed with snippets from the night out that had resulted in me going back with Jay, the shame and the guilt of my alcohol-fuelled idiocy and the fact that I generally felt entirely broken.

Robin listened and nodded in all of the right places, and gently encouraged me when silence fell and I stared at my hands.

"I don't know what to do," I whispered and then looked at her through pleading eyes that said *Save Me*.

The hour we had together seemed to pass in a matter of minutes, and although I had no more of a plan or direction when I left than when I'd arrived, I did feel that the load had been lightened by being able to share. Robin handed me some books about weight loss and emotional healing, telling me that when the time was right I'd be able to focus on this. Other events had taken over and needed my time and energy, and that I may actually be surprised that even when I felt like I was not working on weight loss that in a roundabout way I was, whatever that meant.

By the time I got home, Damien was knotting his tie in front of the mirror in the hallway and Mia was gurgling in her highchair. He looked at the stack of books in my arms and rolled his eyes, theatrically.

"Does this mean I'm on bloody humus and carrot sticks then?"

I kissed his cheek. "No, not this week," I replied.

"Thank God for that!" He reached down for his case and when he turned to say goodbye I thought about how ironic his statement had sounded; if anything he looked a bit drawn and thinner. Hopefully, this was just stress and not… I couldn't finish the thought that screamed through my head as he announced that he would only be a couple of hours… I smiled in response as the word Cancer made me shudder.

True to his word, Damien wasn't long and we had time for coffee before we dropped Mia at Mum's and headed to the hospital.

"I've handed over the company finances to Lou this afternoon," he said blowing on the steaming mug in his hands.

"Oh?" I said, really just to buy myself a moment or two to gain some composure. *What was he thinking, for Christ's sake?*

"Yes, the accountants do the profit and loss and the VAT and such but I need someone on the ground that can keep an eye on fees that are coming in from solicitors as sales complete, and chase up rental payments. I've been trying to keep an eye on it all myself but it's nearly impossible at the moment and before I drop the ball – if you'll pardon the pun - I needed to hand it over to someone else."

"Right," I said, sitting beside him and opening a packet of custard creams. "Would Helen not have been able to do that?" I was trying not to sound panicked or defensive, both feelings were starting to bubble away inside of me and threatened to colour my tone of voice.

"She might have been able to," he said and dunked a biscuit, "but it's a more senior role really, and Lou is the manager."

"Right," I said again. Was it intuition or jealousy that felt like fingernails scraping down a blackboard inside my mind? "I'm sure you've thought it through, and you've always got Ryan to oversee things anyway."

"Yes, he's trained Lou on the chip and pin card thingy that lets you move money around. To be honest, Steph it's not that big a deal really, it's just time consuming and it takes up loads of my energy, and these days I haven't got so much to give."

I reached for his hand and smiled weakly. "We'll get through this Damien, I know it."

"Will we Steph?" I hated more than anything seeing him feeling weak and vulnerable, a side to this great man that he shared very rarely. What was a privilege, felt in that moment to be a heavy responsibility, and I didn't know if he was referring to the cancer, my one night stand or both.

I squeezed his hand three times. I. Love. You. He squeezed mine back and slid his arm across the table so that he could lay down his head and weep.

Chapter 47

The journey to Mum's was terrible, the traffic was dense and the mood was even worse. Saying sorry again was futile. Damien knew I was sorry and that's not what he needed right now, he needed me to be strong and stand beside him in his hour of need - not become all needy myself.

Throwing around more words meant nothing, promises now needed verbs in them and they needed time to cement together back into the foundation of trust that had been rocked so badly. Mia nodded in her car seat as we pulled on to the drive, and Mum came out to unclip her with a face that said she was feeling worried and helpless too, and had really no idea what to say.

Damien turned off the engine and walked around the back of the car to get the nappy bag from the boot. Mum gave him a kind of half hug, with awkward arm patting and a face that was trying not to burst into tears. Damien bent forwards and kissed Mia's chubby cheek, throwing an arm around Mum and telling her that it was ok to cry, but she was stoic. With Mia in her arms she jollied herself back up the drive, sniffing back her tears and waving a little hand in our direction.

"Say goodbye to Mummy and Daddy!" she said in a ridiculously cheerful voice, and I closed my eyes tightly in the passenger seat.

Don't cry.

But the weight of grief that belongs to someone you love soon breaks cracks in any dam of emotion that you try to build. Seeing my mother in pain, and Damien being brave, was almost impossible for me to witness, along with the knowledge that this was just the beginning and that things could get far worse. It's hard to be positive when you are driving to hospital so that your husband can have a full body scan that is looking for secondary tumours. That kind of fear can't be usurped by an affirmation, not in my experience anyway.

Damien got back in the driver's seat and we started the journey to the hospital, where we would spend the usual ten minutes looking for a parking space, rifling through pockets for change and trying to work out the twenty-four hour clock whilst estimating how long we might be. Normal stuff in the most abnormal situation. Damien tapping his finger on the steering wheel to a song he knew, and the indicators tick-tocking as I turned my face towards the passenger side window and said it looked like rain.

Looked like rain? Christ there was so much more I wanted to say right now, but I'd been reduced to that. Thankfully we didn't have to wait for long in the waiting room, although this was not a private hospital we had private cover, so we weren't in the medical equivalent of economy class. In fact, most of the appointments and even surgery could and would be carried out in a hospital not far away that had an entrance lobby rather like The Marriot. But the scanner was here, so here we were.

Damien's name was called and we were taken up a short flight of stairs and along a corridor, one wall was all glass and overlooked a square courtyard a few floors down, concrete grey with wrought iron seats for smokers.

Cancer sticks.

Damien had never smoked to my knowledge, in fact, he hadn't done anything at all to deserve this, or bloody well attract it. Why the hell would anyone attract an illness? Especially my lovely Damien - a man who always bought *The Big Issue* on a street corner, helped old people cross the road, recycled all of our cardboard and aluminium tins, and once risked life and limb taking a seagull to the vets that had become tangled in a fishing line. By the time he got there his arm was pecked to bits and he was covered in bird shit. Damien was a good human, a truly nice person and surely we had clocked up some good karma to go with that?

But he didn't look like the hero that rocked my baby to sleep some nights, and rubbed my feet when I was heavily pregnant. He had an air of bravado about him that only I could see beneath. I saw through his mask and recognized fear – not for the process, but for the outcome that would subsequently be discussed with an oncology consultant. I wanted to go to him and put my arms around him, tell him again and again that I loved him and scatter kisses all over his face. I wanted to lift the veil of vulnerability that I saw finely settle on his face, as he joked with the technician about his choice of music. No, he wasn't usually claustrophobic and actually he could quite fancy a nap anyway, so anything classical and relaxing would be just fine, thank you.

But just hurry up and pull me back from the ledge.

The door swung shut with the porthole window and warning stickers about radiation. And I was alone. I'd taken a novel with me, I found the page about a third of the way through with the slightly folded corner that marked my place and I started reading. I'd finished the page within a couple of minutes but had no idea what I'd read. I sighed and shut the book, closed my eyes and let the tears come. I started pleading in my mind, bargaining with a God that I was rapidly losing faith in. If there was such a thing as a miracle I was asking for one, no not asking but begging.

I wondered if I should find the hospital chapel, would my message get through clearer from there? Was it like a Wi-Fi hot spot for heaven? It was irrelevant, there was no way I wasn't going to be sitting here when Damien came through that swinging door.

Loneliness cloaked me for the following long moments, the silence was only broken once by two members of staff shuffling by in theatre greens. Time felt like it had expanded and slowed down, a never-ending numbness. I don't know how long had passed when I saw the door swing open and I saw Damien walk through. Although I wanted to play it cool, I strode towards him with my arms outstretched.

"Are you ok?" I asked him.

"I think so," he said running his fingers through his hair.

I linked my arm through his and we walked the length of the corridor and down the stairs retracing our steps back to the carpark.

"Steph," he said as I rummaged in my bag for keys. I looked up and his expression clearly said LISTEN. Listen now.

"Damien, what is it?" I asked as fear closed its long cold fingers around my throat and threatened to make my voice crack with raw emotion.

"I need to say this," he drew a breath and let it out slowly, trying to gain composure and managing slightly. "I love you."

"I love you too," I interrupted and quickly stepped towards him. I wrapped myself around him tightly and then his arms enclosed me too and I could feel his heartbeat next to my cheek. We embraced for a couple of deep breaths and then Damien's hold relaxed and I was left clinging to him like I might be shipwrecked. He spoke my name again and unlocked my arms from around his waist.

"I need you to hear this Steph," he said and I could tell that there were tears behind his words. "I love you, I truly, truly love you. And no matter what happens next I want you to know that you have been and always will be the love of my life. I've cherished every moment with you, you light up my life in ways that you might never understand, and you brought me Mia."

There was no holding back the tears once her name was mentioned for either of us, and we stood in a hospital car park crying and not wanting to say what we both feared the most. Today had been hard but tonight would be harder with the dark cloud of fear looming over us as we tried to sleep, wondering what the scan results would show.

"Can we leave Mia at your Mum's tonight?" Damien asked. "We're back here tomorrow, anyway."

"I'm sure that would be ok," I said. Actually, Mum had half hinted at that anyway and I could ring her from home.

"Thanks," he said and squeezed my hand. "It's just that it's so much to bear and I don't want her picking up on our feelings and being scared, Steph."

"I know," I agreed. "Me neither."

We drove home with me behind the wheel and Damien dosing on and off, the radio warbling out songs that I only half heard. We made our way up the stairs and sat in the pale lamplight of the bedroom, staring at the wallpaper we had put on just months before, and death in the face at the same time. I tentatively made my way around to Damien and stood between his knees, he leaned into me and I held him to my breast, stroking his hair and breathing him in.

Please God, let this be ok.

I unbuttoned his shirt and he slid out his arms. I folded back the duvet and gently rocked him onto the mattress, unfastening his belt and sliding his jeans to his ankles where I hooked my thumbs over the top of his socks and pulled them off at the same time. The light went out and I spooned myself into him, holding him as silent sobs wracked his body – my own heart breaking over and over again in the darkness that seemed to be a perfect metaphor for where our lives were tonight.

Chapter 48

The meeting with the consultant was at the private hospital where there was no issue with parking and a bean to cup coffee machine in reception. The girl on the desk checked us in and we sat on leather sofas in front of a flat screen television that was showing Sky News.

Mr Barrington arrived in person moments later and Damien stood up to shake his hand, which was then outstretched to me. We followed him in a state of nervous anxiety and fake bravado through a door and down a hallway, then into his nice office which was professional and tidy and also personalised with a couple of pictures that I took to be his family.

"Mr Anderson," he began as I held my breath, Damien's hand and Mr Barrington's gaze – all with everything clenched. "I have the result of your scan yesterday and it's good news and bad news really."

I exhaled slowly and felt a feeling of dread in me rise, as the look on his face turned to sympathy.

His tone was still professional, but softer. Like when you get dumped by a boyfriend, it is what it is and I know it's going to hurt you like a bastard, so I am going to say the thing you so don't want to hear in a way that might have less impact. Polish that turd until it's gleaming.

The only word that I really heard was secondary, and then after the initial feeling of being winded by a collision with a bus started to lift slightly, I heard the word brain. I was suddenly extremely hot and I wanted to flap my hands in front of my face to fan some air towards me so that I could breathe, never mind speak.

Mr Barrington was pulling out sheets of plastic that showed inside of Damien's head and he pointed out the "area" that he was talking about, and I asked him if he was sure that these were the right notes. Damien squeezed my hand and forced a weak smile in my direction as Mr Barrington silently slid a box of pastel coloured tissues towards the corner of the desk where I was sitting.

"I'm just saying that mistakes can be made, that's all. I'm not accusing anyone of being shoddy, but sometimes things get mixed up… I mean, look at what happened to that woman that lives in my parent's cul-de-sac, her notes got mixed up with someone else's because the woman that lived there before had the same last name as her and initial, and in the surgery someone had inputted C Lishman and she was Carole and the other woman was Celia and she ended up getting the wrong tablets for three months and wondered why on earth she felt so dizzy…" I looked at Damien and then back to Mr Barrington, who looked at each other in a knowing way that meant they were both going to have to pull hard on the side of the emotional safety net now. I was falling fast and although inevitable they may be able to help break my fall a little.

"I am pretty sure that these are the right notes, Mrs Anderson." His tone was kind and I thought about how hard it must be delivering this kind of news every day. "And the diagnosis seems to fit in with the headaches that you were describing." He looked at Damien who nodded in confirmation.

"You didn't tell me that!" I snapped, and felt hot tears on my cheeks.

"I didn't want to scare you anymore than you were, Steph," Damien said and I saw fear in his eyes that mirrored my own.

"I realise that this is a huge shock for you both," Mr Barrington pursed his lips together in a standard stoic line across his face and there was silence, apart from my sniffing.

It's more than a shock Mr B, it's the end of the world as I know it.

"Where do we go from here?" Damien asked one of the millions of questions that I wanted the answer to. The one that he voiced hung in the air between the three of us and I thought that he was asking about treatment, whilst I was thinking the very same thing about our lives.

"Well, treatment options would be an operation on the scrotum and the insertion of a prosthesis if you wanted that, and usually this is very straightforward. Have you any children?" he asked.

"Yes, one," Damien said quietly, we were both thinking the same thing.

We have a child that needs her father.

"Ok, it's not an easy discussion to have especially at such a sensitive time, but you may want to think about freezing your sperm if you think that you may want any more in the future." He continued to tell us that the brain tumour was likely to be a secondary and that it looked like it may be difficult to operate because of the location, but that he would like to suggest chemo, at the very least, and then discuss the case with a neurosurgeon.

We both nodded along for the next five minutes in a daze, asking a couple of questions here and there but taking in less and less. We'd heard what we could absorb, words like radiotherapy and lymph nodes filled my ears, but I didn't gain context or understanding of how they might fit in or what it meant.

Damien shook Mr Barrington's hand before we left, but I couldn't bring myself to. I know he was simply the messenger but I felt like the walking wounded and I couldn't engage anymore. I hung onto Damien's arm as we walked back to the car, I gulped in fresh air as soon as the glass doors swooshed open and the wind caught my hair.

Damien got into the driver's seat and I sat beside him. For a moment neither of us spoke, until he broke the silence.

"Let's go and pick Mia up and go for some ice cream," he said and patted my knee with his hand. "I want to do something normal with my wife and kid."

"I'm not sure the word normal will be used very often now," I replied.

"All the more reason to use it now then," said Damien and started the car.

Chapter 49

"Orchiectomy," said Damien that night in bed as he searched the good old world wide web for information that would perhaps empower him, but scare me shitless. "That's the fancy name for a bollockectomy by the way."

"Thanks for sharing," I said spooning mashed up vegetables into Mia's mouth and watching her spit it out.

"Just saying!" Damien was in good spirits, considering.

I, on the other hand, had hardly slept and felt that I was permanently just one step behind bursting into tears. I had heard people say on television programmes that it was sometimes harder for the partner that was not affected by an illness or a disease. At the time I had thought that ridiculous, but not now. Maybe it wasn't harder, just different. When someone you love is in pain or needs help your natural instinct is to step in and support them, when it's something like cancer, all you can do is prop them up emotionally, do the practical things and hope that the medics know their stuff.

"What shall we do today?" I tried to change the subject. We had a few days until Damien's surgery and then the chemo would start soon after. I wanted to make the most of the time we had together.

There was a chance that the brain tumour could be removed but we were waiting to hear another surgeon's opinion on this before things were made definite. Radiotherapy might be safer, depending on the precise location of the cancer cells.

Apparently there was a type of radiotherapy that sent beams from different angles and they all crossed over at the point of the tumour, giving a super high dose in exactly the right place and less damage to surrounding tissue.

"Well, I might have to go into the office this afternoon, just for an hour," said Damien rubbing his forehead with the heel of his hand.

"Is your headache back?" I interrupted him, I was a human symptom detector these days on high alert for changes or repetition that might mean things were getting worse.

"No, just thinking." He walked over to me and kissed the top of my head. I leaned into him and held back my emotions as best I could.

"Well, why don't we go out this morning and when Mia goes down for her nap you could go then?" I asked, a little more composed.

"Good idea, and then you can have a sleep too," he replied. "Unless we get back early, and then we can all have a sleep and I'll go in about four."

"Sounds like a plan." I stood up and wiped Mia's bib around her face. "Where do you think we should go?" I baby talked at her and she giggled.

"Let's take her to that farm where they let them hold the baby rabbits," Damien suggested.

"Mel took George there and one nearly gnawed his finger off," I replied. "Apparently it was a big fat ginger one."

"Well, let's be honest, you'd be pissed off if you were fat *and* ginger, now wouldn't you?" he said with a serious face that was hiding a smirk which set me away laughing too.

"Christ I know, that's God's sense of humour for sure - poor bastard."

For a moment we forgot what we were up against and laughed in the kitchen, with Mia looking at us and laughing too. "You are so lucky your mother's a brunette little lady!" Damien said and swung her out of her highchair.

"And beautiful," I chipped in.

"Oh God yes, I mean you should have seen the women I had before you came along… I don't want to say too much but the ugly stick had certainly been involved in some cases."

"Damien!" I shrieked. "You can't say that!" I was laughing hard and he shook his head.

"Why not? It's true Steph, and I still say that the woman that I met through that bloody awful internet dating thing really should have said in her profile that she had a prosthetic limb. She argued that people would judge her and not get to know the real person inside, but I can honestly say that when I had my hand on her knee and she couldn't feel it I was excruciatingly embarrassed. And then when she kept texting me and asking me why I didn't want to meet up again I had no idea what to bloody say."

"Stop!" I was crying with laughter.

"Had she been a looker like Heather Mills I might not have minded, but she was honestly nothing like her profile picture which was clearly airbrushed to death. I didn't know it was her for the first five minutes, I was standing at the bar like a moron looking around and then this bird in the corner who had been looking over at me on and off got her phone out and sent a text and my phone went bleep and I was forced to have a laugh about how funny that was."

"Oh God, how embarrassing," I laughed. "Could you not see her funny leg straightaway?"

"No, she was sitting down and wearing trousers. It's not the kind of thing I have a particularly keen eye for actually, not like your dad has with wigs."

"Mum told him off again for calling Joan over the road Joan-the-Syrup, obviously not to her face, but she's convinced it's going to slip out some time, probably around Christmas when the vicar has that mince pies and carols thing at the community centre. Dad always has too much sherry." I pulled the waistband at the back of Mia's pink leggings and peered down. "All clear on the nappy front."

"I love it that your parents do that," Damien chuckled.

"What, spot wigs?" I was stuffing a new packet of baby wipes into the large chequered bag.

"Yes of course that, but also that they call people their name and then a feature or their job or something," he said, "Like George the Taxi and Alan the Window."

"Yes, don't forget Ray the Paint and Bio-Dan." I slung the bag over my shoulder.

"Bio-Dan?" Damien asked as he handed Mia to me and started pulling on his jacket.

"Yes, that plumber that they had around to fit the new bathroom. Apparently he does that biomass heating, that's where it's from."

"Is that it? Sounded like a Superhero for a minute there. In my mind he's just gone from saving the world to having his hand up a u-bend."

"Nice bloke though, I met him a couple of times and he made me laugh. And Mum and Dad were grateful that he wasn't out saving the universe, or they would still have that horrible corner bath."

"Well, thank God for that. I was sick of hearing about it and soaking piles in some kind of Himalayan salt. They've ruined that for me when it comes to using that grinder thing you bought, all I can see is your Dad's arse when I'm twisting it."

"I didn't buy it actually, it was a present from Big Pat."

"Christ you're doing it now, just say Pat Parker!"

"You knew who I meant, though."

Damien shook his head and laughed again. "You can't do it with stuff that will upset people Steph, I mean you wouldn't say Claire the Calliper or Jimmy the built-up shoe would you?"

"Big Pat is not the same at that!"

"Might as well say Fat Pat and just get it over with."

"It's because she's tall Damien, not fat."

"She's not thin, Steph."

"She knows people call her Big Pat!"

Damien was howling with laughter and managed to say sarcastically, "Oh well, that's perfectly alright then."

As he held the door open for me to walk with Mia out to the car, who I was trying not to drop, I laughed too. "As long as she knows!"

"I saw her in Threadgolds fruit and veg shop last week, she must have been lost, they had no pies."

"You can't say that!" I snorted.

"I didn't say it - Gary did when she'd gone."

"And I bet Fiona gave him a telling off."

"Don't you mean Patsy?"
"Why does he call her that?" I asked.
"See it's not just my family that are strange." Damien laughed again and shook his head.

Chapter 50

The morning at the farm was a triumph. On and off I forgot that Damien was ill, and there were slivers of time where I didn't worry about his surgery, or him wasting away in the coming months. I hadn't realized how much I had missed the steady old pace of normal, the predictability and the small things that I had not been grateful for.

The human condition breeds this kind of complacency, and sometimes it takes a real rocking of our world to make us see what is really important to us, and that is the stuff that money can't buy. Like all of us, I thought I knew this. I liked fridge magnets and journals with inscriptions on them that told me to make the moments count in life and to live out loud. Inspirational quotes you'd call them, little reminders hand painted on shabby chic hearts and hung on kitchen walls. All lip service until now. If I could have bought my way out of this, heaven could have named its price.

I saw Mia touch Damien's face with her hand as he pointed to the animals, and in that moment fear crept in again. I felt swallowed up by darkness at the thought that he could die, and there was probably nothing I could do about it.

"Who's hungry?" asked Damien and delved into the picnic I had cobbled together. "I bet Big Pat would polish this off in a flash," he said and I found myself laughing again, and thinking it was most bizarre that in the face of the most adverse circumstances, I was sitting on a tartan rug and laughing about Big Pat.

I put Mia down for her nap as soon as we got home, and I was grateful to be able to get into bed myself and close my eyes. I expected to hear the door close as Damien left for work, but instead I heard his feet pad softly up the stairs and he climbed in beside me.

No words were spoken between us, and none were needed. I felt his lips nuzzle the back of my neck and his arms slide around my waist. He slipped his hands inside the tee shirt I was wearing and the touch of his skin on mine made me sigh softly. I folded my arms over his and drew him in closer. I felt him breathe me in and I knew without seeing his face that his eyes would be closed as his lips brushed the back of my neck again.

He stroked my belly gently with his thumb and I relaxed into him. Before long our breathing was in unison and I allowed sleep to softly take me into a dream where everything was perfect, because in that moment it really felt like it could be.

The date for Damien's operation came around within days. The cynical side of me wondered if the appointment was arranged because of urgency or because we were paying? I hoped it was because we were paying. The last time I had packed a bag for hospital it had been full of tiny clothes and excitement, this time it was full of men's pyjamas and dread. We'd had to go shopping for a dressing gown and slippers, Damien was used to walking around barefoot in his boxer shorts, probably like most men.

The drive to drop Mia off at Mum's was filled with forced joviality at first, and then as we got closer the radio filled the silence that had descended upon us. Inappropriately upbeat tunes created the backdrop to the heavy atmosphere, laced with trepidation and outcomes that neither of us wanted to mention, but both of us feared.

The surgery was bad enough, worse was the thought that this marked the beginning of 'treatment'. Damien would feel like he had had the shit kicked out of him for months and we would be walking on eggshells, hoping and praying that the radiotherapy and chemo were raging a war against the enemy cells that were multiplying in his brain. It's a terrifying feeling knowing that you have to go through something so horrendously hard, and that you have absolutely no choice at all. It felt like we were standing on the side of a massive dark precipice, with our life as we knew it hanging in such a fragile balance. Tenuous, breakable and unpredictable. And all the time trying to be optimistic for each other and for ourselves, but never truly being able to mask the fear that ate you up, ironically like a cancer itself.

I wanted someone to hold out their hand and bring me back from the ledge. It was a lonely place to be and although Damien was there with me, holding on for both of us was the only option some days, and the weight of this responsibility weighed heavy on my heart and soul. Supporting someone else when you are struggling to prop yourself up is not an easy feat to accomplish.

There were hopeful comments that things were likely to improve and statistics to support the efficacy of the treatment plan, and in moments of strength I bought into them and was grateful for modern medicine. The Law of Attraction, however, was doing a great job of matching me up to my worst nightmares. It seemed like every time I turned on the television or opened a magazine there was a story about someone's brave fight coming to an end. Sue had certainly been right that I wouldn't come out of the storm the same person that walked in, I just prayed that I wouldn't be walking out alone.

The car pulled onto Mum's drive and Damien patted my knee, a silent gesture of solidarity. Mia opened her eyes when the engine stopped and blinked into the afternoon sunlight, then rubbed her eyes and started to gurgle.

"She'll be hungry," I said as Mum opened the door and started walking down the drive.

"Where's that gorgeous baby?" she said melodically, more forced joviality here then. "Are you having a cup of tea before you hit the road?" No one wanted to mention the destination.

I looked at Damien and waited for him to respond. *Can you handle it? I'm not sure if I can.* He took hold of my hand and squeezed it.

"Yes, we've got time," he said and winked at me. I felt like such a fail. I was meant to be supporting him and here I was a bag of nerves.

Conversation was superficial and the elephant in the room (probably with only one testicle) wasn't mentioned until we were about to leave. I empathised with Mum and Dad when they struggled to find the words to say. Good luck didn't fit the bill and goodbye sounded, well, like goodbye.

Dad shook Damien's hand and said he would see him in a couple of days, an acknowledgement that he was away but also faith that he'd be coming back. Mum mumbled something about the food in these places and that she would make his favourite chicken casserole and bring it at the weekend. Building on that good old foundation of 'you're coming back' that Dad had started, along with a couple of rows of 'and you'll be feeling fine because you'll be hungry.'

"Right then," said Damien. I could feel that he didn't want to leave Mia, but he didn't want to prolong the agony any more than he had to. He kissed her forehead and then her chubby fingers and with tears in his eyes he told her that Daddy would see her in a couple of days. I placed a hand on his shoulder where he was probably feeling like he was carrying the weight of the world. We walked the few steps to the car in relative silence. Dad had taken Mia from Mum and he was waving her hand and baby talking. Mum was nowhere to be seen, but I knew that she would be somewhere crying and not wanting us or Mia to see her.

"Shall I drive?" I said as Damien clicked the central locking open.

"I'm ok," he said. "And you're going to have plenty of driving to do shortly."

"I don't mind being your driver," I said. "It's the least I can do."

"You might regret that after you've clocked up thousands of miles up and down to hospital for all of the chemo appointments." He tried to make light of the stark truth that we were both now facing. "And if you get a bloody speeding ticket you needn't think you're pinning it on me."

"As if!" I said with a forced chuckle, I'd done exactly that a few months ago.

"I'm going to be ok you know, Steph," he said and waited for me to respond.

"God, I hope so Damien," I replied and then in fear of the tears that I had been holding back overflowing again, I continued, "Who would put the bin out?"

He laughed and stole a sideways glance at me. "I should have shown you how to do it before today, maybe you could google it – you know, just in case the worst happens and I'm not back by Thursday."

"You've always been selfish," I said sarcastically, wondering how we could be joking about this and equally wondering how we would ever get through it if we didn't.

Before long we were pulling into a parking space and Damien was lifting the boot for his overnight bag, well two nights really. We walked into reception together and checked in, we were shown to his room and I fiddled around unpacking for a few moments, with my back to him. Damien put his hand on my shoulder and I turned around into his arms. He held me, and even though it felt like a long time as he combed his fingers through my hair and kissed the crown of my head, I wondered if it could ever have felt like long enough.

"I'm going to be ok," he whispered.

I closed my eyes tight and whispered, "Please God, please."

Damien walked me to the car and kissed me tenderly, after sweeping my hair behind my ear and lifting my chin. "I'll be back before you know it, the op only takes about an hour so I'll be back on the ward before lunchtime."

"Yes, I'll call as soon as I get up and then again mid-morning," I said, not wanting to go but knowing that I needed to. "I'm going to go and see Josie on the way home."

"Good. Why don't you stay with her tonight if she's got room?" he asked. "It might do you good to have a couple of glasses of wine and a catch up rather than being home alone and worrying."

"I thought I'd stay at Mum's actually," I replied. "It's closer to come back for you in case they let you out tomorrow afternoon."

"You make it sound like prison," Damien smiled. I looked at him and tears filled my eyes. "I'll be fine Steph, I promise." He pulled me in closer, into a bear hug this time and I guessed it was to stop me from seeing him crying too. "Now go, before the rush hour, and say hi to Josie from me. Make the most of having a few hours to yourself and I'll see you tomorrow."

"Ok," I replied, knowing that he didn't want me to see him feeling weak in that moment, this was a time when he had to shore up his faith and believe that everything was going to be alright, and I needed to believe that too. Time for me to metaphorically pull up my big girl's knickers and get the hell on with it.

"Right." He held me at arm's length "I love you."

"I love you Damien, I'll call you tonight."

"Make sure you do."

"I will," I said and stood on my tiptoes to kiss him one more time, then I turned to get into the driver's seat.

I couldn't look back at Damien once I had started to drive away, the tears flowed freely and I had a feeling that his might too once he got back to his room. Tomorrow was the beginning of the hardest thing we had been through together; it was cancer for Christ's sake. Not like he was in for a bloody hernia or ingrown toenail, this was the big C and it was beyond shittifying.

I drove to The Haven on autopilot, different scenarios drifted through my mind and opened doors to others as I changed lanes and stopped at traffic lights, aware of what was happening around me but only in a numb sort of way. The sound of the gravel beneath the wheels brought me back to the now as I pulled onto Josie's drive and remembered the day I'd met Damien here, hiding in the cupboard and looking like a drowned rat. I couldn't help but shake my head at my own idiocy, letting myself in and trespassing, but I was freezing and it was better than being soaked even more outside in the back garden.

And then there was our wedding day, where we surprised all of our guests with our windfall and shared with them what we thought would help them most in their lives, and a part of that was giving Josie this house so that she could continue her project to help women in crisis. I knocked on the big black wooden door using the brass knocker and thought about the way her face had looked when I'd handed her the key and she tried it in this very lock for the first time, then I heard her footsteps on the tiled hallway and the door opened.

"Stephanie!" she threw her arms around me and I hugged her back. "Sue, you'll never guess who's here…" she shouted back into the house.

"Sue's here?" I asked. "I can't believe it, I was thinking about calling her later."

"What do you mean you can't believe it?" laughed Josie. "Of all the people I know, you know how this stuff works better than anyone. Your timing is perfect, the kettle's just boiled and I am dying to hear all of your news and help you get organized with Mia's naming day."

I followed her into the kitchen where Sue stood up and hugged me. She still had her coat on.

"It's lovely to see you, but am I intruding?" I asked.

"Not at all, "said Josie. "You know you have an open invitation here Steph, we were just going to have a cuppa and a natter, the more the merrier as far as I'm concerned. Now do you want tea or coffee?"

Josie brought a tray with teapot, mugs and a milk jug to the large pine kitchen table and a packet of Hobnobs. "So what's new with you?" she said in my direction as she poured.

I have to say that I'd been holding it together until then, and doing so rather well, I felt. A good cry in the car had more or less set me up for facing Josie, but her caring tone started to unintentionally pick at my emotional resilience until I began to unravel a little.

Being in the company of friends that care about you seems to create a safe cocoon for you to fall apart, and fall apart I did. I spilled the whole story from Louisa through to chemotherapy, with a smattering of Jay and a prosthetic testicle thrown in for good measure. Both women nodded and gasped in the right places and Josie provided tissues and more tea.

"God, I am so sorry, I have completely hijacked your lovely afternoon cuppa and done nothing but whine," I said when I eventually felt myself running out of steam and story.

"Don't you dare apologize young lady!" said Sue in a tough love tone. "We're your friends and it's perfect that you came here today, part of the plan I would say, wouldn't you, Josie?"

"Yes, completely part of the plan. You were totally meant to come today so that we can support you. It's the universe showing you that you have people around you that can help," she agreed. "What a bloody horrible time you've been having, I wish you'd called me."

"Or me," said Sue.

"I guess I didn't want to burden you," I mumbled. "Both of you spend your days helping people in a crisis and I didn't want to add to that load."

"Steph, we are your friends," said Sue. "And either one of us would drop anything to help you, just like you would for us."

"She's right love, you would help us if you could – well, you did help us when you had the chance and we'll never forget that," said Josie, referring to the generous gifts I'd given to them both on my wedding day.

"You were both on my list, that's all," I said looking from one to the other. "It's what people do when they have fortune smile on them, they share it with people they love."

"And we love you, Steph, so let us in," said Sue.

"I just feel like I could lose everything here, I'm so scared," I said and lowered my eyes. "I know about the Law of Attraction and it scares me beyond belief that I've thought about what my life would be like if he died. I keep panicking and thinking that I'm going to draw it in."

"It's perfectly normal to be terrified, you're a human and this is big, big stuff to go through. I'd be more worried if you had your head buried in the sand and you weren't feeling it," said Sue.

"But by feeling it I am attracting it," I said. "And that's what scares me."

"There is some truth in that Steph, but there are two other things you need to consider. Don't forget the Shit Happens concept and also that it is your dominant vibration that the Law of Attraction is going to match up. As humans we all feel a range of emotions, but its practice with conscious thoughts, feelings and sending out the energy of what we want to create as consistently as we can that will draw in a match."

"So you mean it's the stuff we think about most, not just the stuff we think about?" I asked.

"In simple terms, yes," Sue agreed. "A repeated thought pattern has a more ingrained and learned energy than one you think less frequently, the signal is stronger if you like."

"So the universe tunes into it more easily?" I asked.

"Yes, I suppose so, but there are other things at play as well don't forget," she said. "I'm saying this because I want you to know that you are not creating Damien being sick Steph, and your fear of him getting worse is not going to manifest or attract in something detrimental."

"So this could be a shit happens scenario?" I said.

"It certainly could be, and if you start going into fear that you are manifesting a terrible outcome for yourself then your vibration will drop and you will attract more negative stuff in as a result."

"So what can I do, Sue? I'm struggling here." I puffed my cheeks out and sighed.

"You get back to basics, Steph. You look for ways to focus on what is good in your life and you send energy to that, you start to really practice deliberate gratitude. I don't mean just being grateful, I mean looking for things that you can thank the universe for and make it an active process. Remember that when you are doing this you are effectively saying that your life is full of goodness."

I nodded and she continued. "Be aware of your own thoughts and when you start to go into a negative spiral – stop yourself. Step back from it and breathe, create a space between those old thoughts and new ones and start to switch your thinking towards a better stream of consciousness."

"I don't want to sound defeatist, but that sounds so much easier than it is," I said.

"Remind me, what was lesson one again?" Sue asked with a twinkle in her eye.

"Ok, you got me. I'm being closed to the idea before I've even tried it." I smiled weakly.

"She's good!" Josie said laughing. "There's no fooling Psychic Sue!"

"I know everyone's secrets," Sue joked. "And believe me, some of them I'd rather not know!"

"I bet," said Josie and winked at me.

"So… supposing I was prepared to give this a go and be more open," I continued, "and I could let myself off the hook a bit and try to stop the negative thoughts by stepping back and changing my focus to a more positive thought, that would help me draw in a better outcome?"

"It would shift your vibration up a notch, and the more you did it the more you would shift, and that would help you to not only feel better, but you would be practising a vibration that would become more dominant. It will help you to draw in more of what you want and less of what you don't." Sue reached for another biscuit to dunk in her tea. "I know what you're thinking Steph, and it's perfectly normal and reasonable for someone in your situation to be thinking that, I would be the same."

"Can you tell me?" I asked and the question hung between us as Josie pulled out a chair and sat down too.

"I need you to remember that this isn't written in stone Steph, there is so much at work out there in the universe that we don't know about and you can pixie and unicorn and law of attraction it up all you like…"

"But shit still happens," I finished her sentence and she looked at me for a moment, then fluttered her eyelids closed and reached for my hand.

I looked at Josie who shrugged as Sue took two deep breaths then spoke in a measured tone.

"Ok, I'm getting a feeling of great physical weakness and emotional vulnerability when it comes to Damien. He is going to feel a lot worse than he's expecting and it's because of outside stress as well as his health issues..." Another deep breath. "He's worried about more than just his health, it's like he's trying to save himself business-wise as well, like he's under attack for some reason, he feels like he's drowning and it's going to pull you all under."

My instinct was to pull my hand away from her, but I'd asked for this and I knew at a deeper level that I had to hear it.

"I'm being told that this has to happen. There is no way around it, there is going to be one almighty shake up for you and a part of the reason is to help you to get onto your path." I wanted to butt in and ask her what the hell she meant by shake up. Please say that's what was happening now and not that there was going to be even more?

"You're right, you are meant to hear this," said Sue and I felt goosebumps cover my skin. "You were guided to come here today because it's going to get a bit bumpy for you, but you need to remember two things. The first thing is that I am getting a really clear message that things will certainly get better for you, a whole lot better and that's a fact. You have a calling to help many people and for that reason alone you are going to find that on the other side of this, that things will definitely get better, so you must have faith. Things have to fall apart sometimes in order to fall together again in a different way, a way that serves you and helps you to walk your path. And the second thing is that you're going to have to dig deep into all of the reserves you have and call on everything that you have learned in order to get through this, and there will be days that you feel like you can't, but know this…" Sue opened her eyes and looked right into mine. "You will," she paused. "And you'll have Damien by your side, I know it."

"So there's more coming?" I asked in a small voice.

"I can't lie to you, Steph, there's more. I don't know what exactly but it's going to be unexpected and will hit you both like a freight train, but I do know that it's nothing to do with Damien's health. That's going to be ok, in fact it's going to be something of a miracle."

"As long as that's the case, anything else I can cope with."

"Yes, but remember that it's easy to say that now and there will be days you don't feel that way coming up," Sue said.

"But we'll be here to help you," said Josie.

"Yes, of course we will. And it's not going to last that long really, that will be both helpful and unhelpful – you'll not have a great deal of time to process it all and you'll feel knocked off your feet, but the universe will push you out of the other side within a matter of months," said Sue.

"Chew me up and spit me out," I said.

"It's going to feel like that when it's happening love, but it's a means to an end. It's a reordering of things, a re-alignment, so keep thinking of it that way when the shit starts to hit the fan and know it's not forever."

"I can't believe I'm going through this again," I shook my head.

"It's the last big shake up." Sue sat back in her seat and smiled at me. "This is preparing you Steph, to be the extraordinary person that you came here to be."

"But I'm just me, Sue," I said quietly.

"You're a Lightworker, here to help many to wake up to living a more conscious life on earth. And you need to be accelerated through lifetimes of lessons in one incarnation to be able to help others to learn and live in a different way."

"I just want to get my own shit together really and help us get through this if it's all the same."

"You will, but the knowledge and experience that you are going to gain will be something that will help humanity on a global scale, and the lovely thing about you is that you are entirely unassuming and non-egotistical about the whole thing. You're real, Steph. You think about what to make for tea and that your bum looks big in your jeans. People need that, they are sick to death with airbrushed celebrities that haven't got a clue about real life. Humanity needs someone in the trenches reaching out a hand and saying that they have been through stuff too. It's your story that will make your teachings powerful and relatable."

"I've never even thought about teaching, I think I would hate that," I mumbled, not wanting to correct the universe of course.

"Lesson one, Steph, 'Be Open to Possibility'. It's not teaching as you are thinking, it's teaching people through a message, through your book. The universe is setting you up so that this is the fastest way for you to connect with the most people and make the biggest impact, helping the most people to change their lives, and helping to shift humanity up the consciousness scale at the same time. That's why you are here."

"Sue, I can't even begin to think about that at the moment, I hardly have the mental bandwidth to do a shopping list never mind write a book."

"The perfect time will never come, there will always be things going on that will fill in your days and your weeks and before you know it your life. But when you have a calling like this, there is no getting away from it. The universe will keep pushing and pushing you until you get to the point that you have no choice but to write it, so the sooner you get started the better. And anyway, it's more than half written already."

"Well, I've got notes I guess but it's hardly a book – it needs a proper tidy up and I really have no idea what I am doing."

"No one has any idea what they are doing when they first start out. I hope you're keeping notes on the lessons that you are learning now as well?" Sue asked.

"Yes, but they are a bit sketchy if I'm honest – I will have to go back through them and tidy them up, I have had other stuff going on." I cringed. "God I am just so full of excuses, it's never going to get done if I don't actually get on with it."

Sue laughed, "Phew, I think the penny has finally dropped Josie!"

"Alright, alright," I said as two of my best friends in the world had a giggle at my expense, but I didn't mind one bit. I felt a whole lot lighter and more positive for being with them today and I knew in my heart that Sue was right – about everything, but especially I hoped she was right about Damien.

Chapter 51

I left The Haven feeling hopeful and promising to come back soon. The drive to my parents' was only half an hour and Mum was delighted that I was staying overnight. The travel cot was in my bedroom as it happened, although she was apologetic for the fact that I might be up for a night feed – I assured her that I was more than happy with that, and with Damien being away I wanted more than anything to not feel alone.

I called Damien and he answered on the second ring, we talked about everything we could think of apart from his operation or treatment. Although neither were mentioned, the verbal skirting around the issue meant that there was plenty of opportunity for a Freudian slip and thankfully we both laughed when he said the newspaper he'd bought was full of bollocks.

"How are you feeling about tomorrow?" I asked in the conversational lull that followed.

"Well, obviously I'd rather be doing anything but having one of my knackers cut off – but I'm trying to look at it as a good thing. The start of me getting well again and all that, but to be honest I'm bricking it."

"Sue was there today," I said, "and she said you're going to be fine."

"Has she had a word with him upstairs on my behalf?" he asked.

"Yes I think it's all cleared with JC, Buddha and the Archangel Michael as well so you're all good. A couple of pixies and unicorns and a sprinkle of fairy dust, oh and she's going to dance around a fire naked tonight in her garden and do some chanting to the moon."

"She can skype me here you know," Damien said and waited for my response.

"Hey! That's my friend you are talking about!"

"But she's quite fit in a middle-aged psychic kind of a way Steph, I mean I know she comes across as being a bit straight-laced but I think the cardigans are a front for the woman that's desperate to get out and..."

"Stop it! You're terrible!" I snorted.

"You just tell her that I'm available to help her for the next full moon, or whenever she does this kind of weird shit – I'm in."

"I'll do no such thing, and you know fine well she doesn't do that sort of thing, I was just joking."

"But do you know that for sure Steph? I mean do you *really* know?"

I snorted again and he laughed too. "I want you to know as the modern metrosexual handsome bastard that I am, it's perfectly ok for you and your friends to do this kind of thing, as long as I can watch – and maybe video as well."

"Stop, I'm going to wet myself!" It felt good to be laughing, albeit in the face of adversity.

"There is something serious I wanted to ask you though Steph," Damien's tone changed and I could hear him taking a deep breath. I could feel butterflies in my stomach as nerves crept in from nowhere because of the sudden change in his attitude.

"What is it? You sound super serious," I asked, with everything clenched.

"It's nothing to be worried about, it's a good thing – I hope," he said, but I could feel that he was hesitant and couldn't work out why.

"Just say it, you've got me worried here."

"OK, well you know when we have Mia's naming day and you wanted the registrar to come and do a proper reading and make it all official for her rather than just a party?"

"Yes…" Where was this going and why did Damien suddenly sound so very emotional?

"Well I started thinking about it and the fact that everyone would be there that we loved, and all of our friends, and that we've had one hell of a year really… but hopefully by then I'll be pulling through this..."

"Stop waffling Damien, you're making me nervous, just spit it out!"

"Steph, I want to marry you again. Well, not marry you again, we're already married for God's sake, I want to renew our vows. So I guess I'm asking, in a roundabout and muddled up way with a whole lot of unnecessary buffoonery - will you marry me?"

I had to say something but emotion had a tight grip on my vocal cords and all I could manage was to sniff back my tears.

"Steph? We don't have to, it was just a thought," he said nervously.

"Yes," I managed to say. "Yes Damien, I want to marry you again." As I heard him chuckle down the line I could see him running his fingers through his hair in my mind's eye, the way he did when he was feeling a bit anxious.

"Thank Christ for that, or I'd have looked like a right knacker."

"Or a left one."

"Thanks Freud, you slippery bastard."

Chapter 52

I slept fitfully, which was annoying as Mia didn't stir until about six. I heard her babbling and it took me a moment to remember that I was not at home, and then the second thought was of Damien.
It was pointless ringing the ward until after the procedure, so I sent a good morning text and lifted Mia into bed with me.

The sun was shining through a gap in the curtains and the dust motes danced in a line across the room, as Mia stretched awake.

"We're going to see Daddy later," I whispered to her and snuggled her in close.

I sneaked down the stairs with her in my arms, and settled her on a play mat whilst I made coffee for me and tiny toast fingers for her. Damien would be in surgery by eight, and out by nine. I checked the time on the cooker clock, only two hours and fifty one minutes to wait for news. Of course it would feel like longer but mornings were busy, especially with a baby.

By the time Mia had eaten half of her breakfast and mashed the other half into her hair, and I'd almost managed to have a whole cup of coffee, Mum appeared in her dressing gown and started to potter around the kitchen. I wondered if I should tell her about renewing our vows, but for now it felt like a precious secret that I wanted to keep between Damien and me. Maybe we could even surprise everyone at the end of the naming ceremony and I could appear in a lovely dress and we could make our vows again, the vows I'd broken. Was that why he wanted to hear me say them again?

My phone pinged in my dressing gown pocket and a text message from Damien read that he hadn't slept very well and wanted to be home in his own bed. The breakfast looked good going past his room on the trolley but he was nil by mouth and pleased he was in first because he was starving. He was about to be prepped whatever that meant and might ask for a Brazilian or a Hollywood if they came near him with a razor, and that he would see me later.

I didn't know whether I felt relieved or more unsettled after hearing from him, but regardless, I had to have a shower and get dressed.

"Everything all right love?" asked Mum.

"Yes, just Damien saying he's going down soon to theatre," I said. "I'll jump in the shower."

"Ok darling, the clean towels are in the airing cupboard," she said and then followed on with, "have you thought about the next few weeks and how you'll manage, Steph? I can come and stay if you need me to."

"But what about Dad?" I asked, to be honest I hadn't thought too much about the next few weeks but I did know that there would be driving up and down to hospital for chemo and radiation treatments which meant me taking Mia, getting a babysitter or doing a circuit via my parent's house.

"Dad could come too, or he could drop me off and come home. We've talked about it and he's fine with either, we just think you're going to need some extra support. I could help you with the washing and cooking, and look after Mia when you have to taxi Damien to hospital. We could just pull up the slack a bit for you, love, it's what families are for."

"Oh Mum, I'd love that," I said. "Can I run it past Damien this afternoon and let you know please? I'm sure he'll be ok with it, but I'll just have to check."

"Of course, and whatever you both decide is fine by us. We can drive over early in the mornings if you don't want us there overnight, but if we did stay I could share the nightshift with you."

"I think the thought of a lie in a couple of days a week might just sway it," I replied and hugged her. "I love you, Mum."

"I love you too darling, just consider us at your disposal," she said and I felt so grateful for having her in my life.

I didn't take Mia into hospital, Damien said he would see her at home and he didn't want her sitting around waiting for the consultants to sign him off or for the pharmacy to dish out medication. He was in good spirits when I arrived, but a little groggy and sore, and he dozed on and off while his discharge notes were prepared and pharmacy sorted out something for the pain.

I watched him sleep and held his hand in mine, he smiled at me and I smiled back, and I said thank you to the universe for taking care of him. The journey home didn't happen until mid-afternoon, and although Damien was trying to be kind to me, I know he must have felt every bump in the road. Trying to avoid them made me more nervous and they started to magnetize the bloody car towards them.

"Just drive normally, Steph," he said with his eyes closed and fists clenched, how I wish I'd used the hospital transport that they'd offered.

Eventually we were home and mum had the heating on so high, opening the front door was like disembarking from a flight that's just touched down in Dubai in August. Damien walked gingerly into the front room and sat in the wingback chair that we usually kept in the dining room. Dad must have carried it through after we talked last night about the sofas being quite low down.

"How's things, son?" Dad asked.

"Oh, alright I think, there's a little horizontal cut a couple of inches below my belly button with a dressing on it and I feel like I'm certainly missing something.....it's painful and uncomfortable at the moment but hopefully that will pass soon," Damien said, trying to sound upbeat but I could tell that he was flagging.

"Do you want to go to bed and have a rest?" I asked "Or we could just tuck you up here and get the footstool if you like?"

"I don't mind, Steph," he said and reached for my hand. "I'm just glad to be home."

Chapter 53

Damien picked up over the next week, which was just as well as chemo and radiotherapy were starting soon. The results were back from the lab and thankfully it looked as if everything had been removed that needed to be, round one to us.

Damien went to the barbers and had his hair cut really short, like a burglar, Mum said.

"If it's going to come out anyway I might as well, it will be less of a shock to Mia," he said. That was something I had never thought about and I was grateful that he had.

The combination of treatment and the drive to and from hospital exhausted us both, especially Damien. Nausea and fatigue were two of the side-effects that hit him hard from the outset, and he was still trying to field phone calls from work and respond to emails when he could.

"I wish you could have some proper time to recover," I said one morning, as the tiny voice of Louisa on the end of the line made my hackles rise.

"Ok, ok that's fine. Yes." Damien ended the call and turned to me. "Steph, you know I have to do this, and you know I have a plan to be out as soon as possible. The numbers are looking good, I'm going to put a call in to Ryan to see when we can meet up to talk about me selling up and what we can expect."

"I know, I just want you to focus on getting well again Damien. All of the money in the world would make no difference if you weren't here."

"Steph, if I wasn't here you would be more than looked after – you'd have the business and Ryan would look after you, and the house is paid for."

"I don't even want to think about it," I said.

Damien's tone softened and the business edge was no longer evident in his voice when he spoke. "I know that, but thank God we're in a good position. I know I haven't got stacks of life insurance and critical illness and all that, but we've got the business to sell and after that we'll be sorted. The last thing you need when you are going through something like this is to be shitting yourself about money as well, that would be hellish. And anyway, my concern is not about me going – it's about me still bloody being here and us having enough!"

"Yes, I know you're right, I just hate talking about it."

"Don't worry about it, it's just numbers Steph. I'm going to be selling up regardless, but if the timing is right and the figures look good then we'll get a lot more. That's it in a nutshell, so there is nothing to worry about. You were right I should have done this before now, but you know I wanted to multiply our investment, and three to five years would have been ideal – but the market is taking a natural upturn anyway that we can take advantage of." He reached for me and put his arms around me. "And then my love, we're out."

"How long does Ryan think it's going to take to broker a sale? I can't think that these things happen overnight?" I asked.

"That's what I need to talk to him about and also how much we can look at selling for, the last time I spoke to him it was about gaining more market share in both house sales and lettings, but to go hard on the letting side if we could, to build up recurring income. We launched that profit accelerator thing for landlords on the back of it where we charge a lower monthly fee but they are tied in for a year, but that's really attractive to an investor because that's twelve months of recurring income per sign up."

I loved this side of Damien, he was shrewd and entrepreneurial and focused, and at every corner it was all about building something for his family. I knew that he would look after his friends as well if he managed to make a profit on the business that allowed for it, and the staff that had been loyal to him. He was good at business and generating money, but he was also a good custodian of that money and kind-hearted as well. He knew what a difference a Christmas bonus made to people, and even in the very early days when he first set up, when it was just him and Helen, she always got hers – even if he went without.

There was a good energy to his business, one of integrity and flow, and I wondered if he would attract someone that would operate in the same way as he had all of these years.

"Just don't overdo it, Damien," I said. "I know you thrive on this, but I want you here with us."

"I plan to be." He kissed me. "But I'd rather not be on the dole."

I laughed. "As if!"

Chapter 54

My life had soon changed into a different routine, one that revolved around hospital appointments, driving up and down the motorway and sitting in the coffee shop waiting for Damien. In between, family life continued as usual, but at a slower pace with afternoon naps and a lot more of Damien at home. Mia and him were far more closely knit, and the time that they spent together reflected in the fact that she wanted Damien as much as me now and he was loving being more hands-on. I knew that this time with us would spur him on further to sell the business, and as more time passed we started to ignore the odd call from the office and check his emails less. Apart from the hospital visits, some days it felt like he had taken a sabbatical, or retired early. I loved days like this, especially because there were moments that I completely forgot about him being ill.

Although our sex life had obviously taken a nose dive, the intimacy between us had never been more intense. The time that we spent together and the deep conversations that we shared were forging a bond that I'd craved, but never truly known. Lying in bed in each other's arms, skin on skin, with no expectation of intercourse was liberating in some way, and helped me so much to relax and enjoy the closeness in the moment. I realized now that I'd rushed the starters in order to get straight to the main course, and that there was an exquisite delight in kissing, stroking skin and holding someone close, knowing that there was no expectation of more. It was easier to carry this energy into the day, where our connection flourished into glances between us that said a thousand words, and fleeting kisses, his hand brushing mine or his arms around me and his hands in my hair, lighting up the most mundane household tasks.

This is what it felt like to be connected, and I never wanted it to end. The possibility had been there all along and I'd been swimming against the tide trying to make it happen, rather than allowing it to happen. The universe had sent me a gift in the most unusual packaging and I'd resisted unwrapping it for so long. I knew that when the moment was right, we'd connect again fully in the physical, and the funny thing was that I wasn't counting down the days this time. I was learning to love the whole of Damien and the whole of what we were together.

This was like falling in love again, but at a much deeper level. There was a disadvantage to this that I didn't see coming until the side-effects of Damien's treatment really started to affect him, and I found that I had little emotional resilience or armour to protect me against what was happening. There were days that I wished I could change places, even just for an hour to give him some relief. I knew that the drugs were likely to save him, but as they ravaged the cancer cells inside his body, they stole his energy and love of life at times. Let's just say that it's a very humbling experience to see someone that you love struggling and suffering so much, and knowing that the brave face they are showing the world is a mask that is fragile in every sense but painted on with a whole lot of courage.

Although side-effects couldn't really be predicted, and they were different for everyone, Damien's thankfully seemed to follow something of a cycle where he felt better in the morning than the evening, so at least he could plan around that. Some afternoons, as he slept with Mia, I reached into my bedside cabinet and pulled out my old journal, I had even started to take it to hospital and sat in the coffee shop highlighting sentences and scribbling down amendments. To an outsider it would probably look like a stack of nonsense and post-it notes, but to me it was finally starting to take shape. I had no idea if anyone would ultimately like it or find it helpful, but I knew that everything Sue had said to me so far had come to pass in one way or another, so I wasn't taking any chances.

The process of taking myself back in time and going through each lesson was at times uncomfortable. It was also full of lightbulb moments when I thought about the lessons one to twelve and how Sue had been exactly right when she said that they were layered into our lives on earth and that different aspects could play out at different times, and even alongside other lessons. I guess in the great cosmic scheme of things this was good revision.

I wondered if I needed to live the whole new twelve lessons that I had been given before the book would be complete? I'd just keep going and trust that once I got everything down I'd learned so far, that it was complete for now. I could always write the final lessons in after they had occurred, and quite honestly, I was hoping that I could skip the next one and move straight on to my Miracle, but I was guessing that might not be the case.

"Have you seen my laptop?" asked Damien, sitting in his pyjamas at the kitchen table. Mia was on his lap and slapping his now bald head with her palm and laughing.

"No, not for a few days," I said. "Didn't you take it to that meeting with Ryan?"

"Oh yes, I did. I must have left it in the office. I swung past on the way back to print out some of the sales figures we went through," he said. "I'll call in later for it."

"You're going in to work today?" I asked.

"Just for that, I'll only be an hour or so." Damien handed me Mia and headed upstairs for the shower.

"Ok, we'll wait for you!" I shouted along the hallway. "We've got a date to feed the ducks if you're up to it."

"I'd love that," he said and I knew that the subtext read - *If I can manage that.*

He came back around ten thirty, and I could see that he was tired when he forced a smile and said he'd come along but might not walk too far.

"I read that chemo can affect your memory, it must be happening to me because my laptop wasn't at work after all," Damien said as we pulled into the car park.

"It's probably just buried under a load of toys, or under the bed or something," I said, cutting the engine and clicking out of my seatbelt. "I'll ask Mum if she's tidied it into a cupboard or something when they come tomorrow, you know what she's like."

"Christ, is it tomorrow they're coming?" Damien asked.

"Yes, we've got to be away early the next day for hospital, your appointment is at quarter past nine."

"I'll look forward to the next instalment then," Damien said getting out of the passenger seat and opening the back door to lift Mia out.

"What are you on about?" I asked with my head in the boot, grabbing the foldaway pushchair.

"Alan the Window and Big Pat," he said. "Don't say you haven't heard the latest, Steph!"

"Oh God, is this a continuation of the Avon saga?" I said and rolled my eyes as I strapped Mia in. She had grabbed the bag of bread from Damien and was happily sucking on a crust already.

"I was only half listening to that," said Damien. "Why don't you tell me what you know and I'll tell you what I know."

"Well," I started, aware that I didn't want to walk too fast and noticing that there was a bench about fifty metres away if Damien needed it. "Mum got Big Pat's Avon order by mistake because it had been raining and the address on the bag was smudged, so instead of it going to number twenty- seven it went to thirty-seven, and even though mum hadn't ordered anything that campaign she couldn't help herself and had a peek."

"The nosy cow!" Damien laughed. "Actually I would have done exactly the same, especially if I knew it was Big Pat's order."

"Well, Mum got her eyes opened alright. There was some sensuous bath oil, a foot file, body lotion, and a size twenty-six leopard print thong from their big and beautiful range."

"Thanks for putting that into my head, Steph. All I'll see when I'm trying to go to sleep tonight is Big Pat huffing and puffing with a giant emery board trying to wear down her bloody hooves with her muff pelmet looking like it's suffocating an endangered species."

"You asked!" I laughed. "And so what if Big Pat's getting some, you see those documentaries on Channel Four about feeders and stuff, some guys like big girls."

"Yes but according to your mother some guy is actually Alan the Window."

"No way!" I said. "He would never go there!"

"According to your mother it all started with a cat flap, which he did reluctantly anyway, as it's such a small job and as you know he's Alan the Window, not Alan the bloody cat flap – that was your dad's input by the way…"

"I guessed."

"Anyway, people have seen a white van outside Big Pat's at lunchtime and the bedroom curtains were drawn, through the day! And now the Avon order, you have to admit, Steph, two and two make five."

I could hardly walk for laughing. "I can't believe the way they make things up, Alan is a really nice bloke and actually rather fit if you ask me. It must be all that physical work, I mean I haven't had a proper look but he does seem quite toned and the guy can practically run up a ladder."

"You fancy Alan the Window too! Well it looks like you're not his type, sorry to break the news but he's hooked up with the salad dodger over the road to your mother with the hard skin on her trotters."

"You can't say that! You don't know that it was his van!"

"Your mother does, and she knows everything," he said sarcastically and we sat on the bench and laughed.

"Do you really fancy Alan the Window?" he asked pulling my leg "Because I've heard that Ruth the Cupcake might be a bit bored with her second husband."

"That's why you've been asking about home delivery on the cheesecake, is it?"

"Look, why don't we just agree that we'll give each other one more chance and stick together?"

"Ok, but this is it mind."

"Yes, definitely it."

"I love you."

"Good. Do you want me to say it back?" I elbowed him in the ribs in fun. "Ok, I love you back."

And we sat and threw bread for the ducks while Mia ate her slice, and all was well in the world.

Chapter 55

Louisa called later in the day to tell Damien that she'd emailed him a holiday request yesterday and could he let her know please, it was a last minute deal and she wanted to book flights as soon as she could.

"Her timing could be better," Damien said. "But Helen can hold the fort, and the other sites have managers as well so it should be alright."

"It's only for two weeks," I said and handed him a cup of tea.

"I know, but I'd rather it was in a couple of months' time when I was back on form," he sighed. "I can't even find my bloody laptop to check my emails."

"Just do it on your phone or use mine," I said. "Damien, it's not worth stressing about. Schedule in a google hangout with the other branch managers and tell them to bloody well step up while she's away. You'll only need to have a shave and put a shirt on, they can't see your pyjama bottoms."

"You're right," he said and sat back in the armchair. "I guess if I did that then the only thing I would have to get involved in would be payroll, and Helen's done that a couple of times anyway."

"There you go then," I said, flicking the television on and feeling a bit unsettled. It was probably because Louisa had come into conversation and her name always had that effect on me, her actual presence even more so.

"Have you thought about when we might have Mia's naming day yet?" Damien asked as I scrolled through the planner for something to fill in an hour before bed.

"I haven't. To be honest, I wanted to see how you were getting on first," I said.

"I'm getting on fine, and I think it's going to be a good thing to have something to look forward to. And I can't wait for our surprise," he said, putting his cup down and pulling me onto his knee. We kissed, and my arms slipped around his neck. When we parted he looked at me and said, "There's nothing on television, shall we go to bed?" His eyes sparkled in a way that said we wouldn't be sleeping, and with no more words he took my hand and led me up the stairs, where we spent the next couple of hours between the sheets becoming reacquainted with each other's bodies, in a way that up until this moment in my life, I had only ever been able to imagine.

Chapter 56

"The good news is that the tumour has not grown," said Mr Barrington at our next appointment.

"But it's not shrinking either?" I asked the question for both of us as the consultant studied the most recent scan results on an illuminated whiteboard and looked at numbers on a printout that I took to be blood results.

"No," he replied. "But you said your headaches have stopped?" he asked Damien.

"Yes, I would say that I feel groggy and wiped out, but no more of those blinding, migraine type headaches."

Mr Barrington nodded and made a note of this. "That's a positive sign, and it's also early days. We never know how long someone is going to take to respond to treatment, all we can do is estimate based on what we have seen in the past. Hopefully, we will see some significant shrinkage of the area soon and this will continue to alleviate symptoms and give you a much better quality of life. If you do get any headaches, let us know but don't panic. This can be inflammation of the area due to the radiotherapy and not the tumour growing bigger."

"Will the tumour just disappear if we keep going?" I asked.

"The reason that we use radiotherapy is to shrink the tumour so that the symptoms are reduced for the patient, and in conjunction with chemotherapy we can sometimes see that. Sometimes the tumour shrinks right back and growth slows right down or stops altogether, and we have patients that have lived with a tumour for years. The best case scenario is that the chemotherapy starts its job and the radiotherapy follows suit, in a double pronged attack that will significantly reduce, slow down growth or eliminate the tumour altogether."

"I'll take that thanks," said Damien and squeezed my hand.

"I wish I could promise you that," said Mr Barrington. "Let's stay hopeful that this is the case and that you sail through the rest of your treatment. I want to stop the radiotherapy for now and keep on with the chemo, keep taking the steroids and anti-emetics, and the pain control as you need it. I want another MRI scan in about six weeks, with a follow-up appointment and we'll see what's going on then. Have you any questions?"

"I don't think so, do you?" Damien looked at me and I shook my head.

Do you believe in miracles, Dr Barrington?

"Please contact my secretary if you have any and I will arrange to phone you back, I'm sure you are looking forward to a break from travelling to hospital every day," he smiled conclusively, over and out.

"Well that was a bit of a non-event," said Damien as we walked back to the car.

"I know what you mean," I said.

"I guess we keep going then."

"I guess we do."

Chapter 57

Writing wasn't as hard as I thought it was going to be when I first started. It was finding the time to write that was the biggest challenge. My days seemed to naturally fill up with tasks, phone calls, distractions and more, from the moment Mia awoke to the moment I went to bed – there was no space in there for me to focus. Now that I had seriously started the process of writing my book, it felt in some ways like being pregnant again. I was growing something, creating something and nurturing it. It was getting nearer and nearer to the time when I would bring something that I had made out into the real world, and there was a real feeling of vulnerability in that. When I thought about other people actually reading what I was writing, the words dried up and I panicked. I wasn't a writer for God's sake, I was a girl at a kitchen table with a laptop and an idea, end of. People would sniff me out as being a fake, a mummy who is pretending to be a writer and possibly not even that good at it.

I made the decision that I had to write as if no one was ever going to read it. I really had to suspend the part of my personality that was happy to point out all of the reasons why I shouldn't be doing this, and remember that Sue said this would be important and that it needed to happen. She didn't say when it needed to happen, so maybe if I just finished it and put it back in my bedside cabinet that would be ok for now.

Once I had started properly though, I really couldn't stop. In the moments when I wasn't writing I was itching to. My time was so stretched that I didn't want to have to miss a day and read over what I had written the day before, I wanted to have it in my mind ready to go whenever Mia took a nap or Damien took her out for a walk around the block.

My book was taking up so much of my mental bandwidth I really had to make an effort to switch off from it and be present. Even when I did there was no real getting away from it, as ideas kept coming to me and I was forever scribbling notes here and there as reminders.

I guessed that I wouldn't be free from this feeling until I had finally finished, which wasn't a bad thing, it was highly motivational. I had even started to think cautiously about it being published. I had no idea of what this would entail or how the industry worked, so my starting point was google. Maybe I was being totally unrealistic. The more I read, the more I doubted myself and the more I thought that maybe, on this occasion Sue could be wrong. The websites I looked at talked about social media platforms, literary agents and polished first drafts; none of these boxes were ticked for me and I wasn't sure where on earth I would start.

Just get it done.

My intuition was to keep going and then come back to this once I was finished, otherwise the self-doubt that was being stirred up might stop me in my tracks. I had to trust that this was all going in the right direction and align with the outcome that I wanted, and right now that was a completed manuscript – the rest would unfold at the right time.

Chapter 58

"Why won't you let me read it?" asked Damien one afternoon. He had stretched himself awake and seen me tapping a pen on my teeth and deep in thought with my notebook on my lap.

"No, not yet," I said. "I need to finish it first."

"Ok, but I can't promise that I won't sneak a peek when you are not around," he said. "If you would even put that notebook down that is, I think you might need it surgically removed before long."

"I'm nearly finished, I just need to tidy up what I've done so far and wait for three more lessons," I said, absently doodling hearts on the cover.

"What if they don't happen in time?" he asked.

"I was thinking that," I said. "I also thought that maybe they won't happen at all, but Sue is usually right and she keeps telling me everything happens in perfect time."

"What are the three that you are waiting for? Just in case you miss them," he asked.

"I won't miss them!" I laughed. "The three I am waiting for are Integrity, Paradoxical Intent and Miracles."

"Stick me down for the Miracle if you don't mind."

"It's coming, I've placed the order."

"I bloody hope so I don't think I could take much more." He swung his legs out of the bed and sat on the edge, fully-clothed and bald as a coot.

"I'm sure we're on the up now," I said with conviction but not entirely feeling it yet.

Chapter 59

A month passed quickly, and by the time we were travelling back to hospital for Damien's most recent scan results I had more or less organized Mia's naming day, and finished the complete first draft of my book up to lesson twenty two. I was busy with lesson twenty three at the moment, and I had more or less put this down to Louisa and her making a play for Damien. I had made notes, but didn't want to get stuck in the energy of it, which unsettled me still. I knew that this was double-edged as well, and in fact I was jealous of her in some ways, trying to sort out my own feelings had become part of the lesson and I was struggling to get clarity. I had been trying to complete this chapter for a few days now and something just didn't feel right. I couldn't put my finger on it but I kept going over what I had typed and deleting sentences and paragraphs. It felt like I wasn't seeing something, and the more I thought I wasn't seeing it, the more muddled I became.

Thanks Law of Attraction.

Perhaps I had been distracted because of today's appointment.

"Should we get a children's entertainer?" I asked.

"What, generally?" said Damien.

"No silly, for the naming day!" I laughed.

"Ah right. Well how many kids will be there?" he asked.

I mentally counted through the guest list in my mind, which was more or less the same as our wedding apart from a couple or additions and subtractions due to new friends at toddler group and my cousin getting divorced.

"Five," I said. "And one new baby if you want Ryan and Jenny to come."

"Well if you think it's a good idea, but remember that I hate clowns."

"Six actually, I want to invite Gina and Taylor as well. They're from toddler group you don't know them."

"The more the merrier Steph, you are our social events secretary so you are in charge of the guest list. As long as it's all ok with Josie and you're happy, that's all I want."

"I think I will book an entertainer then. Josie said that we could use the conservatory for that if I wanted to. It's probably best to contain it a bit, Taylor and George are always full of it when they get together, boys are so different to girls, you know."

Damien was quiet, his reaction to being worried about today was to distance himself a little emotionally and lock down a bit, mine was to witter incessantly about something totally unrelated. I turned on the radio quietly and left him alone with his thoughts, trying to stop the fear that everything could go shits up from overwhelming me too much. I focused on the road ahead, the road that would take us towards a miracle or somewhere I would rather not contemplate.

Mr Barrington said that it was good news that there had still been no change. I was hoping that the universe had marked my miracle as dispatched and we were simply awaiting delivery. Although pleased that there was no bad news, we were both disheartened when we left. I did my best to lift Damien up, but it was a struggle when I felt the same way.

"It could be a whole lot worse," I said, with overemphasised yet faltering conviction, trying to convince myself of that as well as him.

"I know," said Damien and sighed. "I was really hoping that he would say it's shrinking and we'd be out of the woods soon. I'm sorry Steph, I feel as rough as a badger's arse this week, I know I should be thinking positive but it's hard when you're going through the mill like this and there's no good news."

"I know Damien, I know you're struggling." I slipped my hand into his and make a concerted effort not to cry. When the person that props you up needs you more than you need them, it's like walking an emotional high wire with no safety net. The last thing he needed to see right now was me falling to pieces, even though I felt I was.

"I sometimes wonder if it's worth it you know, all of these horrendous side-effects," he mumbled. "Especially when I've got my head down the toilet or I can't drag my sorry arse out of bed. I mean, if there's no result maybe I should just stop the chemo? At least I could enjoy what I have left."

I couldn't trust myself to speak for a moment or two so I squeezed his hand in response. There was a tidal wave of emotion welling up inside of me that was about to break drag me under, and I knew he would hear it in my voice. After we'd walked a little further and I'd had a second to think, we navigated the revolving door and out into the fresh air. At least it would have been the fresh air if there hadn't been so many people standing around and smoking.

"Let's sit down a moment," I said and made my way over to a bench with a small brass plaque screwed onto the back, in memory of Frank Carr. I took his hand in mine and spoke quietly and deliberately. "I understand that you feel like this Damien, and I'll support you in whatever you want to do. Just make sure that you think it through and get all of the facts, though."

"It's so subjective though, some stuff works for some people and not for others," he said, looking far into the distance and shaking his head slightly. "I want my life back, and I want to fucking keep it this time." He closed his eyes and a tear rolled down his cheek. "Sorry, I'm just done in Steph, I want to go home."

I stood up and told him to wait where he was, I'd bring the car round. This was simply an excuse for me to have time to unravel and then try to compose myself again. I was about ready to give up on the universe; after all it felt like it had given up on me.

Chapter 60

"Can I use your laptop please?" Damien asked later that evening. "I need to email Helen and ask her to do payroll when Lou's away."

"Where's yours?" I asked.

"I gave up looking for it in the end, it wasn't at work or in the boot of the car and to be honest I couldn't really be arsed," he said. "I'll get a new one shortly, it's no big deal."

"Leave it open when you're done, I want to look at caterers for the naming day," I said, sliding a cup of coffee on to the table beside him.

"Oh, speaking of food," Damien started "I'm going to go veggie."

"What? You?" I laughed.

"I know, it sounds ridiculous. But I was reading those books that you got from that woman you went to see, what was her name again?"

"Robin?" I said

"Yes, that's her. I couldn't sleep a few nights ago and I started dreaming about food and what you put into your body. One of them said that if you put dirty fuel into a car, the performance would suffer and that your body is no different."

"What's that got to do with being a vegetarian?" I asked "Surely you need protein, and I never buy cheap meat, Damien, or loads of processed food."

"That's what I thought as well, that you needed meat for protein, but apparently we can get what we need from a plant-based diet and it's loads healthier."

"I don't know, I'm old school when it comes to meat and two veg for dinner," I said cautiously.

"Me too, but the more I read about it, the more evidence there is to support it," he shrugged. "I've got nothing to lose."

"Ok then, we can give it a go," I agreed. "But you know I love my food, Damien. I can't survive on a lettuce leaf and carrot sticks."

"Me neither," he laughed. "I'll pick some recipes out and see what I can rustle up for dinner."

"You're going to cook?" I said with mock amazement.

"How do you think I managed before you came along?" he said. "And anyway, I like cooking, and now I have the time to do it."

"Ok, Jamie Oliver, knock yourself out," I said and chuckled to myself, but had to admit half an hour later the aromas that were floating out of the kitchen were mouth-watering to say the least.

"This is really good!" I said with a mouthful of courgette noodles.

"Don't sound so surprised!" said Damien. "I told you I could cook."

"Did you make this sauce from scratch as well?" I asked twirling long green strands on my fork.

"Yes, it's just tomato and some roasted vegetables with loads of garlic," he said "No vampires in our room tonight."

"You should watch out, I might get you to do the catering for the naming day if you carry on like this," I said gulping a mouthful of wine. "Aren't you having a glass?"

"I'm sticking to water for a while, I'm going to see if I can shrink that tumour myself," Damien said with more certainty in his tone than I'd heard in while.

Believe it and attract it in.

"Then count me in," I said "I'll eat what you do and that will make it easier for us both."

"Really?" he asked. "I have to warn you that this might just be the warm up, I've read some stuff online about full on veganism and how people have used it to reverse some really serious health conditions."

"Like cancer?" I asked, knowing that it must be the case or we wouldn't be having this discussion.

"Yes, like cancer. Some of the results are truly miraculous Steph, and like I said right now I have nothing at all to lose."

"Well maybe this is the miracle I ordered after all," I said, slurping the last of the food on my plate. "And if it tastes this good, I'm definitely in."

Stephanie's Journal ~ Lesson 20
Love Your Body

When you look after your physical body with good nutrition and enough water, you will have more health, energy and vitality, and your vibration will be higher. Eating a clean diet that is going to give your body what it needs to sustain health and wellbeing will ensure that you are less likely to become ill and more likely to recover if you do.

Food is energy, and so much of what we consume is made up from chemicals to colour, flavour and preserve. Our bodies are not designed for this, it's like putting the wrong fuel in a car so it cannot run properly. There is compelling evidence to show that a plant-based diet is the healthiest way to eat for wellness.

"Take care of your body, it's the only place you have to live in." Jim Rohn

Chapter 61

I still hadn't written the lesson about Miracles yet, or Soul Path, and my message to the world was still to be released. I had no idea what to say on any of the above. The one thing that I was waiting for wasn't showing up. I prayed to whoever was there - as a divine director. I hoped that it made no difference that I couldn't associate myself with a specific religion. I said affirmations in my mind day after day about Damien being healthy and well and full of vitality, and although there had been a change in his energy level and his mood, I wouldn't start to believe that there had been a positive change until I heard it from Mr Barrington. I wanted to believe, and I wanted to switch off the naysayer part of me that sometimes caught me off guard and contradicted my positivity.

I found myself getting angry with the human parts of me that couldn't let go of the fear, I knew that I was going to be wide open to drawing in a whole load of stuff that I didn't want – but I couldn't switch it off. I probably just needed some time, a good run of nothing going wrong. Six months of the tumour not growing and Damien's strength coming back, and then I could maybe allow myself to unwind a little, but just a little.

A combination of the nervous energy and eating so well meant that I was finally starting to lose weight. I must have dropped nearly two dress sizes since we started to clean up our diet, and I was experiencing other positive spin offs as well. I felt 'lighter', it was hard to describe, but just that, lighter. And I had more energy too, my skin and hair were in better condition and I was sleeping better.

It was wholly ironic that this was probably the worst time in my life and I was feeling so good physically. I had even thought about getting some exercise, I couldn't face going back to the local pool, thanks to Swimming Mummy, but there was a local power walking group that I might join. Walk It Off – sounds like a good idea to me.

Although I wasn't completely finished with the first draft until a Miracle showed up, I figured that I needed to find out about what might happen next. Since I had met Sue I'd had complete faith in what she's told me, and although I was keeping it entirely to myself my faith was waning. I didn't want it to, for the simple reason that she'd told me Damien would be alright. Everything had been right up until now, but the last two lessons were eluding me and I was frustrated on a personal level and also wanted to finish the book. With everything going on in my life I felt like I didn't have enough energy and emotional bandwidth as it was, never mind trying to finish a project that I had effectively started two years ago.

I supposed as well that a part of me was worried about the Betrayal and the big shake up in my life she'd mentioned. I did feel mangled and wrung out, and we had been through such a lot, but she'd said that it hadn't happened yet? She must have her psychic wires crossed, as far as I was concerned there was nothing else on the cards – literally or metaphorically that could rock our foundations now. Surely we were on the up, and the Betrayal card was probably something to do with me and the fact that I hadn't been entirely honest about the one nighter I'd had and who was involved. If I was going to say something about it the time had long passed, and how on earth could I backtrack now and tell Damien that it had been Jay? That was a secret that only two people would ever know and for bloody good reason, I needed to shift my attention to the fact that my Miracle was showing up any day now. I'd write what I could about Betrayal and not hang myself in the process.

I started to search the internet for information about publishers and agents, it seemed that there was so much onus put on having a marketing platform and a following that maybe I should give up before I started. I didn't have the first clue about Twitter or Instagram, and the thought of me having a YouTube channel was laughable. As for Facebook, I'd seen it on Mel's phone a couple of times but I had no desire to post pictures of what I was having for dinner or a quiz to find out which superhero I was.

And then there was the whole issue of submissions. Everyone wanted something different, writing a submission was going to be as time consuming as writing the book in the first place. I didn't know where to start with a synopsis, a blurb or a covering letter. Just when I thought I was finished, I had barely even started.

Damien came through the front door with Mia just as I was about to switch off.

"What's up?" he asked as he kissed my cheek.

"Nothing really, just the cold realization that I am absolutely deluded," I sighed.

"Aren't we all a bit though?" he said as he unzipped Mia's coat and pulled off her tiny shoes.

"Me more than most," I said in defeat.

He sat Mia in her highchair and gave her a biscuit, then took one for himself.

"I hope they are suitable for vegetarians, mind."

"They certainly are, and for those of us that are absolutely deluded as well." He passed me one and clicked on the kettle, looking over my shoulder and reading the screen in front of me.

"Ah," he said, knowingly. "So it's not going to be piss easy. I understand. You'd better quit now then."

I turned my head to look at him, my mouth agape. "You sarcastic bastard!" I said. "As far as I know you've never written a book!"

"And you'd be absolutely right," he replied. "But if I had put hours and hours into writing a book, I reckon it would be worth another few to get it out there."

I gave an indignant snort in his direction and said I'd have a coffee thanks if he was making one, the subtext being, You Are Such a Smart Arse. Damien knew me well enough to know that being called a quitter was a sure fire way of me keeping going. And he was right, what was the point in writing all of this stuff down if it was never going to be read by anyone? As I thought about that, I also thought that most of me would be quite happy with the current scenario. Getting out there into the big wide world with my little lessons could be a very scary experience. What if people thought my writing was rubbish? What if the lessons that I had been through were a big fat *So What* to everyone else? What if I got scathing reviews and became a literary laughing stock before I'd even managed to get of the writer's starting blocks?

"I could always help you." Damien's words stopped the pity party that was beginning in my head.

"No, no I'm fine thanks," I said automatically, and then regretted it.

"Well I might just do some research, and if I come up with anything I'll let you know." He knew that I was feeling overwhelmed. "And if you want anything printed off you can email it through to Helen," he ruffled my hair playfully, "if you don't quit that is."

Chapter 62

It took me about two weeks to prepare all of the things that agents and publishers ask for. Each was saved as a separate document and labelled, ready to attach to a standard query letter that I intended to personalize and adapt slightly depending on who I was pitching to. Damien had helped me with the marketing plan and included a social media strategy, which he was going to take care of - this was a fancy way of saying that my days of hiding from Facebook were over. Most of the people that I needed to contact accepted email submissions, which made life easier, but there were one or two that preferred hard copies.

"Do you think I should invite Helen to the naming day?" I asked Damien as I pulled on my coat.

"I don't mind either way," he said. "I guess if you did we would have to invite Louisa, and I know she's not your favourite."

"Well I've thought of that, and actually it's happening when she's on holiday."

"That's convenient."

"And that's sarcastic."

"Really?"

"Really. It just worked out that way."

"Whatever you say." He was smiling as he spoke. We'd talked about Louisa in the context of me being a bit jealous and feeling insecure about her, and Damien had made sure that he'd had better professional boundaries with her as a result. He had made a point of putting me first when we were in the same company, subtle yet evident shifts in the status quo had ensured that the message had been delivered loud and clear. Back Off Lady. She had been a good support business wise when Damien had been going through treatment, and the ad-hoc texting and phone calls had stopped once he stopped responding and arranged a twice weekly check-in call instead. Damien had explained that she was young and ambitious and really keen to impress him. At the same time it was her first senior role and she was inexperienced and didn't understand about how the relationship between him and her should work. I said she wanted to get into his pants. Not anymore he said, she knows I'm only half the man I used to be down there.

It was easier to talk about her, and a relief that she wasn't spending so much time with Damien, if there was an upside to him being ill it was that we had more of him at home. I would probably never like her, but I could tolerate her more. My intuition had been waving red flags in my face when it came to her initially, but perhaps this was not because I was under threat, perhaps I was just feeling a misalignment or a dissonance in her energy compared to mine. And it hadn't been deliberate that the naming day was happening when she was away, but I would certainly call it a relief.

"Right, I'm off. Is there anything you need from the office while I'm there?" I asked.

"Did you say your mum's coming over?"

"Yes, she'll be here in about half an hour."

"Great, I'll come with you and run over the final stuff I need Helen to take care of," said Damien

"Ok, I'll put the kettle on."

Chapter 63

Helen was on the phone when we arrived checking a postal address and sending out details for a detached property that needed some updating - estate agent speak for doer upper. She smiled as we walked in and kept talking in her professional voice, yes they were on the mailing list and yes she'd speak to the vendor for an appointment to view, but she also had a key so she could work something out that was convenient to everyone.

Damien and I made our way through to his small office and I checked the printer for paper before I sent the word document through. It was so much easier to edit and rewrite words on paper than on a screen, and I could keep them in my handbag to look at whenever I could grab ten minutes. Once I had reviewed the lessons and my miracle had arrived, I could flesh it out a bit. For now the notes I had made for the last lesson were hypothetical.

I turned to Damien with the naming day invitation in my hand and asked, "Should I have said that she could bring a guest?"

"Who, Helen?"

"Yes, who else?"

"Christ that's optimistic, Steph," he replied and chuckled.

"She's joined some kind of dating website I think, I was just wondering if it looks bad when I haven't said plus one?"

"Listen Steph, she's a nice girl but all she's got is that ugly bloody rescue cat. If you did write plus one she might have seen it as a piss-take."

"Oh, right," I said. "I didn't think of that."

"And if she's dating, then she could have brought anyone, and you don't want some kind of weirdo rocking up on the day do you? She's got a nice personality but she's an Ugly Betty."

"No, but that's a bit harsh Damien."

"It's you who believes in Law of Attraction," he said laughing.

"Stop it!" I said, laughing too

"She's got a lot on her plate," I said. She had told me some weeks ago about her elderly parents and the fact that her brother had emigrated so it was up to her to look after them.

"Steph, you don't need to tell me about her plate, it's obvious her plate's piled up full when you see the size of her backside," Damien said and I creased up laughing.

Neither of us heard footsteps across the shop floor and we both stopped laughing abruptly when the office door opened and Helen's face appeared.

"I'm putting the kettle on, do you want a cuppa in here?" she said as if she hadn't heard a thing, and I hoped that was the case.

"Yes please Helen," I said quickly.

"Me too, thanks," said Damien, immediately switching to poker face. The door closed and we looked at each other.

"Do you think she heard?" I whispered.

"God, I hope not. I was just having a laugh she's a great girl you know," he said.

"She might spit in our tea," I said.

Chapter 64

That night Damien showed me the Facebook page he had started for me. He explained that he'd set up a personal account as well, and that I could have privacy settings on here to stop random people looking at it. I said that would be good but doubted that I would ever get sucked into posting pictures of what I had made for tea.

"Right, here it is," he said and sat back from the screen.

"What do you think?" he asked tentatively. "I can change it if you want me to, but it's started getting likes already…"

"I love it!" I threw my arms around his neck. "I really love it, it's perfect!"

"Will you show me how it works?" I asked enthusiastically, pulling up a chair at the dining room table.

"It's so easy Steph, you'll get the hang of it in no time," he said and clicked the cursor into a box that said 'Status'. He typed a couple of lines and then clicked publish and ta-dah! The message was there for the world to see.

"I can show you how to make memes as well," Damien opened another tab and went to google. Before long he had chosen a stock free image, downloaded it and added on some scrolling text about being positive in life. He saved it and then uploaded it to the page and before my eyes people started sharing and commenting below it.

"That is really cool," I said

"And when you share from other pages people can see you," he explained typing in the text box and searching for something spiritual. Damien looked through the first few photos on the page and then commented underneath that he thought it was a powerful message and he was sharing. "There you go, now your page name will appear on their page and people will start to wonder who you are, and hopefully they will come and see your page. And who knows, this page might be grateful and share one of your posts later on."

"But it's got so many likes!" I gasped. "Hundreds of thousands in fact."

"That's going to be you one day Steph, I know it," he said and kissed my cheek. "Have a play around and let me know if you need help," he said and stood up to stretch.

"This is amazing" I said, watching the amount of likes start to creep up with each moment that passed.

"I know. And imagine how many of these people will want to buy your book," said Damien.

"This is the way I can reach and help so many," I said. "And never even have to leave home."

"I know, it's pretty darn perfect, and as you build it and help more people you will also be building something that will really impress an agent or a publisher. It's what they would call a win/win in business."

"Hey!" I said sarcastically. "Don't dumb it down on my account. I used to be out there before I had Mia remember?"

"Well I would suggest that you focus on building this and create something a couple of times a day to post on your page, share from other bigger pages that have your audience and generally get out there. I'll speak to someone I know that does websites and we'll get one knocked up so you can start a blog and a mailing list."

"It seems to be happening really fast." I said with a wobbly moment pending.

"It's the perfect time Steph, I am around and I can help you. And you've only got the final lesson to write, then we can even self-publish it if you've built your audience up enough."

"Won't that look a bit lame though?" I asked.

"Not according to what I've read," said Damien. "It's the smart thing to do as the landscape of publishing is changing."

"What's that supposed to mean?" I asked. "Landscape?"

"It's just jargon to say that the business isn't what it used to be. Don't know why I said it really. All I know is that self-publishing is actually dead easy and very well respected in actual fact. It's smart to be honest, especially if you have a platform that you can use to promote your stuff through."

"But I've sent out loads of pitches to agents and publishers so far," I said, "at least a hundred."

"That's fine, sometimes they like it that you've got some sales records and reviews and stuff according to some of the forums I've been asking questions in. It shows that your idea's got legs. I say build the platform, self-publish and keep pitching the big players. Go hard or go home, he said and did some kind of crazy finger snap thing that rappers do in music videos when they have their cap on back to front and they are grabbing their crotch.

"Are the forums you have been on American?"

"Erm, mainly."

"That figures," I smirked. "Well, thanks for that P Diddy, I'll get my head around it after hospital tomorrow."

"Oh God, yes I'd forgotten about that," Damien said and I saw worry settle on his face.

"How could you forget that? We were only there a couple of days ago when you had the scan."

"I know, I just zone it out I think. I've got loads more energy now I'm eating properly and I just keep forgetting I'm ill to be honest."

"That's a good thing according to Law of Attraction, if you keep sending out the belief that you are healthy you'll draw more of that in."

"It certainly feels like it at the moment," he said. "And long may that continue."

Chapter 65

We were only a week away from the naming day and my mother was in full-on organizing mode. Josie was great with her, she gave her free reign to visit The Haven to sort out a seating plan, flower arrangements and catering. There were no residents at the moment, and although that could change in a heartbeat, it was likely that Josie could accommodate some of the guests overnight both before and after the event.

No one knew that Damien and I had planned to renew our vows. We had talked about my dad walking me down the aisle again and decided that I'd ask him just before it happened so that he didn't get too nervous, or tell Mum, who would have done her best to keep it a secret but failed miserably. I also had a surprise for Damien, with all of the healthy eating we were doing, not only could I fit into my wedding dress, I'd had it taken in. I'd booked in for hair, nails and spray tan and I knew that on the day I was going to look fabulous. Shame Louisa wasn't going to make it after all.

I just prayed that there was no bad news. Maybe we'd been crazy organizing the big day when Damien wasn't out of the woods, but it had given us a positive focus and kept us going. We needed his check-up to be the same as the last one, where Mr Barrington sits back in his black leather seat and tells us that there is no change.

That's what I am asking for Universe. You have clearly forgotten my Miracle so this will do for now.

We took the familiar route to hospital and parked in the same bay as usual, making our way through to reception to be greeted by the same girl and wait in the same seats for the same consultant.

Same news please.

Before long we were in the same office with everything clenched.

Mr Barrington looked again at the notes and I thought that he might be squinting a little, looking more closely if you like. My heart started to race and Damien must have sensed the same, as he squeezed my hand.

NO, NO, NO!

The clock ticked away seconds that felt like a lifetime as we sat and waited.

He breathed in, he breathed out.

He looked again.

He looked once more at the black and white picture of Damien's brain and my feelings got the better of me and spilled over into words that trembled with fear.

"What do you see, Mr Barrington?"

He took another breath and shook his head, exhaling slowly.

"Can you bear with me one moment please I just want to check that this is the right scan result I'm looking at," he said and lifted the receiver on the telephone on his desk.

He read Damien's full name and date of birth along with his patient number to whoever was listening, and then asked if they had seen the scan. I looked at Damien and he shrugged, pulling his hand away from mine to wipe a sweaty palm on his jeans.

"That's what I thought, yes. Thank you for that." Mr Barrington looked at us both with terror written all over our faces, and the corners of his mouth turned upwards into a smile.

"I can tell you now that I have only ever seen this dramatic kind of shrinkage a couple of times in my career," he said.

Shrinkage, that's good.

"It seems like the tumour has almost disappeared."

Although we had been hoping and praying for this news for months, I couldn't take it in.

"What do you mean exactly?" I asked, thinking that I had missed something and feeling like I was watching a movie of my own life unfold and that this might actually be the happy ending.

"I mean, Mrs Anderson, that the treatment seems to have worked between this recent scan and the last one, and that the tumour has shrunk to a size that is hardly visible." He paused as Damien looked at me and my hands fluttered up to my face.

"So I'm nearly cured?" he asked.

"Cured is not a word I like to use, Mr Anderson. I don't want to take the wind out of your sails here because this is a truly amazing result, it's tiny but it's still there."

"But could it go altogether?" I asked.

"If you'd asked me earlier I would have said that it is super rare for that to happen, but I would also have said that this kind of result is super rare as well." He shook his head and smiled. "From time to time we see things that science can't explain. I could hypothesize about the radiotherapy dosage and the chemo cycles you've had, but in essence this is really rare to see. I don't know why or how there has been such a huge difference so quickly, but I want to get some more bloods done to check that they match up with what I'm seeing here," he said. "I don't want to get your hopes up just to dash them again, so forgive me if I don't commit entirely at this stage."

"I understand," said Damien, smiling at me and reaching for my hand. "Can I ask a question please?"

"Of course."

"Could this have anything to do with diet?" asked Damien, raising a point I hadn't even considered.

"It's hard to say really," Mr Barrington said. "I have read some studies where people claim to have recovered from debilitating conditions using food as therapy, but as a doctor I'm sceptical. There is no real hard evidence to show that there can be a definite measured change you see, it's all anecdotal. Have you changed the way that you eat?"

"Yes," said Damien "I read a couple of books about it and thought that really I had nothing to lose, so I gave it a go. To be honest I've been feeling fantastic since I started."

"Vegan?" Mr Barrington asked.

"Not quite, but certainly vegetarian. I'm not quite ready to go the whole hog if you'll excuse the pun, so I still have some milk and cheese but in small amounts at the weekends."

"There have been some small studies to show the effects of high dose antioxidants on cancer cells, and creating a less acidic environment in your body – of course cutting out meat and dairy and upping fruit and vegetables will do both of those things. Who knows how it's worked in combination with the chemotherapy and radiation, it's likely that we'll never know what happened here."

"Well I am hedging my bets and sticking to it," said Damien.

"I certainly would if I were you," Mr Barrington agreed. "It's obviously making you feel so much better, you have a great deal more energy and general wellness about you than most of the patients I see, it clearly suits you very well. In fact, it's not something the scientist in me likes to admit to but when you see something like this the only way to describe it is a miracle."

Stephanie's Journal ~ Lesson 21
Believe in Miracles

Miracles can only happen if you are open to them showing up. If you have a belief that they don't exist or they aren't coming your way any time soon, then that is the message that you are sending out to the universe, and you're well and truly blocking them in your life. Look for the miracles around you in your day to day life and send energy, attention and gratitude for them. There are far more than you think if you are open to seeing them. This will align you with the energy of miracles, help you to expect them in your own experience, and help you to attract them in.

"I am realistic, I expect miracles." Dr Wayne Dyer

Chapter 66

We drove home in a daze.

"He really said that, right?" I asked Damien for the umpteenth time.

"Yes, he really did," he replied, smiling widely.

"I can't believe it yet."

"I know."

"It's like any minute I'm going to wake up. I can't wait to tell Mum and Dad."

"Let's keep it for the weekend and make an announcement," Damien said. "Everyone will be there and we can tell them all at once."

"That is an excellent idea!" I said. "I hope I can keep it in until then."

"It's only a few more days," said Damien. "You can do it."

"Yes, and it will give us a few days to process it and start to believe it as well. You must have believed it on some level or you wouldn't have been able to draw it in for yourself."

"I suppose you're right. Those books you loaned from Robin just made sense, and they came at the perfect time."

"Yes, I feel loads better too and you're right, it's bound to make a massive difference when you put good stuff in your body."

"Christ, I honestly can't believe it." Damien laughed out loud. "I hoped that this would happen, I've read loads of stories on the internet about people who think that they've cured cancer with diet, and I hoped that I'd be able to say the same someday, but I was always scared that it might not work."

"I know you were, and we're not out of the woods yet," I said.

"Hey!" said Damien. "That good old Law of Attraction is listening!"

"You're right, and my miracle's arrived."

"Can't argue with that," said Damien, patting my knee. "And now you've got no excuse about writing the last chapter."

"You can read it now," I called to Damien who was cooking up something that smelled delicious in the kitchen.

"You're finished?" he called back.

"Yes, a first draft anyway. I know there'll be mistakes and typos, it will need a tidy up, but the good news is it's done."

"Well done, my love!" he said and appeared in the doorway with two glasses of red wine and a waft of garlic. "Let's raise a glass to your success as an author."

"And to your miracle recovery," I added as he kissed me and memories of the love we'd made last night echoed through my mind and body.

"Absolutely," said Damien. "We are on the up."

"Well, I haven't had a crowd of publishers beating a path to the door yet," I sighed. "Actually the book feels like a big fat *So What* after the news we got yesterday."

"Hey!" Damien said. "Stop that! You've worked really hard on this Steph, and it's going to help so many people out there. Don't you dare think for one moment that you've written this to keep in a bottom drawer. I've told you, self-publishing is the new way forward."

"Ok, I'll consider it," I said, sipping the wine and feeling hungry.

"Good," he chuckled. "Because I've found someone to edit it and format it as an ebook, so it could be for sale asap."

"Damien!" I yelled down the hallway after him.

"You're welcome!" he yelled back and I smiled to myself. The universe definitely wanted this book out there. Time to get over my fear and start walking the path my soul had intended me to.

Chapter 67

Everything was in place for Sunday, and the weather forecast was good. I had collected my wedding dress from the alterations lady and stashed it at The Haven, so I could do a quick change. Josie commented on how happy I was and asked a couple of leading questions, I was desperate to tell her the good news about Damien's scan result but somehow kept it in. I did tell her that our love life was well and truly back on track, and blushed a little as I thought of the physical connection we now had.

Jude, Asha and Sheila were all arriving at The Haven on Saturday. Facebook had been useful to contact them and have group chats about train times and taxis. I couldn't wait to see them and hear all their news, although we'd covered Jude's internet dating disaster, and Asha's new business idea already. Sheila had started to go to a yoga and meditation class and really found her spiritual side, which I was so pleased about – but wondered what the teacher had thought the first day when she had rocked up with tattoos on her knuckles, and probably had a smoke outside the community centre before class.

Our lives had changed and moved on since we had all been together, but that initial experience at Prospect House had forged unlikely friendships that I knew would never be broken. We'd supported each other at our most desperate, and the people that have helped you to take the first wobbly steps on your journey after life has kicked the shit out of you, are the people you want around you to celebrate when you get to your destination. And I certainly felt like I had arrived.

Things truly were perfect, I loved my life and I was starting to really believe that Damien's recovery was permanent. Each day that he looked healthier and stronger, each day that he didn't need to take a nap, each day that he didn't have a headache, was a day closer to me starting to relax and get used to the new version of normal. The one that we'd had before, but with a whole lot more gratitude now.

Thanks to Facebook I was starting to shore up some belief in my book, which was certainly good timing as the girl who was going to edit and format it had a cancellation and the process was underway. I was creating posters that people were sharing and commenting on that were based on the themes in the book, so I knew I was engaging with the people who would love it when it was released, which could be really soon. I had asked Damien to wait until after the naming day so that I could get my head around it better, but in truth I was really anxious about getting out there. My old fear of not being good enough came up every time I thought about it, and I started creating scenarios in my mind where people would leave me bad reviews and it would be an embarrassing flop, and that's never good when you believe in the Law of Attraction!

Maybe Robin would be able to help me with the fear, perhaps there was something she could do that would help me get out of my own way? I needed to give her the books back anyway so I would probably book back in with her.

With three days to go to Mia's naming day and us renewing our marriage vows, the registrar called to finalise the readings and such. Knowing what I did about Damien's recovery made me more emotional than usual, although we had agreed to have the standard vows read, we had also written personal letters to each other that we were keeping secret until the big day. It's a good job it was only three days away, there were a couple of times I'd nearly let the cat out of the bag and mentioned the scan results.

Mum had asked me a couple of times about Damien's recent hospital appointment, and I'd felt bad lying and saying that there was no change, but I knew that if she'd found out the truth she wouldn't be able to keep it to herself, and with a few days to go it didn't feel too mean. Actually now I came to think of it, when she had asked, it had been tagged on to the end of a conversation about Mia's dress, the caterers, the flower arrangements or the entertainer. She was in her element and didn't miss an opportunity to tell anyone and everyone that would listen about her granddaughter's christening. I had stopped correcting her, there was no point, and perhaps it was sign of maturity that I was finally learning to pick my battles.

After the registrar has ticked everything off her list I logged on to look at Facebook. People were commenting on the link about my book and saying that they were going to download it as soon as it was released! Damien had been right, a ready-made audience made so much sense. Now I just had to find the courage to get out there.

Louisa had sent me a friend request on Facebook – awkward. I was pretending that I hadn't seen it for now. I didn't want her getting any further into my life than she already was, and I certainly didn't want to be her friend in any capacity at all. I could say that I didn't make friends with people that Damien worked with, but I'd made friends with Helen, so that excuse wouldn't wash. I'd deal with it next week. I didn't want anything stealing the joy that I had about life at the moment, and especially not her, with her pouty profile picture and big knockers.

Saturday night came quickly and as Damien and I lay in the darkness of the bedroom, we talked about our plans for the next day. Jude, Shirley and Asha had all arrived safely at The Haven and it sounded like they were having a good old catch up with Josie. Matt was going to drive him and Lizzie, and stop for Hannah and her girlfriend, Sam, en-route. Taxis were booked, the caterers and the florists were all briefed and all was well. I could feel myself drifting off to sleep in Damien's arms, thanking the universe for my life and hoping that Mia would sleep through.

Sunday morning was bright, and I padded down to the kitchen early to make coffee and enjoy the silence. Mia gurgled gently on the baby monitor after five minutes, and I sighed with a smile. Being a mother was the most exhausting and rewarding job in the world, and I wouldn't change a moment. Today was the day that I officially thanked the universe for the greatest gift I'd ever received, and celebrate with family and friends.

I felt emotional as I picked Mia up and breathed in her baby scent, as she gurgled and patted my face with her tiny hands. Things could have been so different; we could have been facing a life on our own. I hoped that I could hold on to the gratitude that I felt, and that the human condition and day-to- day nonsense wouldn't eclipse it in my heart as time marched on.

"Morning!" said the man of the moment as he yawned his way into the bedroom in his boxer shorts and five o'clock shadow. "How are the two most beautiful girls in the world today?"

"We're fine thanks, Daddy, and your timing is perfect because one of us needs a nappy change," I said and passed him Mia.

"I get all the best jobs," joked Damien and carried her to the changing table.

"I'll have a shower," I said. "Can you give her some breakfast in her pyjamas, though? I don't want her dress on until the very last minute."

"Yes, boss!" he said in a sarcastic tone and then turned to baby talk to Mia about who was really in charge. I could hear her gurgling and giggling at him as he blew raspberries on her belly.

In a few hours' time we would be standing in front of the people that meant the most to us and sharing our love for each other again. But this time it would be after we'd survived the fight of our lives, not just survived - but won.

Chapter 68

Everyone was sitting around the big farmhouse kitchen table when we arrived at The Haven, with the remnants of what looked like a hearty breakfast laid before them.

Josie greeted us first and scooped Mia into her arms, who was still wearing pyjamas.

"Steph!" yelled Asha and jumped up to hug me. "It's so good to see you."

Jude followed suit and Shirley, who looked softer than I remembered and felt much less edgy. Josie made more coffee and Damien brought in the bags, comments were made about him looking well, which he did - the subtext was obvious and sympathetic – but then again they didn't know what we knew.

"How is he?" asked Jude, when Damien went out to move the car into the corner of the drive, announcing that it was staying here so he could have a drink later and we'd get a cab.

"Good," I answered, desperate to tell her, to tell all of them, my true blue friends who had supported me when the chips were monumentally down in my life. I didn't want to lie to them, and they would know soon enough anyway, so I hinted at the news. "Really, really good Jude. The prognosis is really, really good thanks."

"That's a bloody relief for you Steph," chipped in Sheila as Asha passed Jamal headphones for his iPad.

"God, what a thing to go through," she said, plugging his charger into the wall.

"Yes, it's not great, that's for sure," I said. "But honestly, we're on the up and it's all good now." I spoke conclusively to draw a line under the subject for now, just as Damien reappeared in the kitchen door and Josie handed him a coffee.

"Right, where do you want the bags?" he asked me and I turned to Josie.

"You can use my bedroom if you like?"

"Perfect thanks, the registrar is arriving about half past twelve for a one o'clock start." I looked at the clock on the kitchen wall. "So we've got loads of time."

"That's what it feels like now, love," chuckled Josie. "It's going to pass in a flash, remember your wedding day?"

I couldn't help looking at Damien and smiling. "Yes, I know what you mean. And once my mum gets here it's going to be panic stations." I laughed.

"I'll be around so don't worry about a thing," said Josie.

"We'll all be around," confirmed Jude. I had seen her in no-nonsense mode and had faith in her ability to handle anything.

"Yes, you go and get sorted," said Asha.

Shirley nodded. "We're on it."

"Like a car bonnet," said Asha and laughter broke out.

"Ok, we'll camp upstairs and start getting sorted out," I said, then caught a glimpse of a van pulling into the driveway. "Oh, here's the catering company."

"We'll handle it love," said Josie. "Go and get yourself sorted. Your guests will be arriving soon and it's up to you to meet and greet."

"Thanks," I said and took Mia from her. "See you all shortly!"

I made my way up the beautiful staircase and onto the landing with a large window that overlooked the drive and front garden. I remembered the first time I had set foot in this beautiful place and shook my head. I'd been soaking wet through, ready to pee my pants and nearly arrested for breaking and entering. Things had changed rapidly and for the better. Thank goodness I'd had the courage to stay on course with the lessons that brought me to my knees, but it was whilst I was on my knees that I could really clear out my foundations and build stronger than ever.

Damien looked handsome in his suit, the same one that he had worn for our wedding day, and my dress was hung on a hook on the back of the bedroom door, ready for a quick change. I adjusted Damien's tie as Mia gurgled at a cartoon on the small television, which thankfully had an integrated DVD player, so we were covered for about ten minutes before she got bored.

Damien leaned forward and kissed me. "Are you ok?" he asked.

"I think so," I said. "Nervous and excited at the same time."

"Same."

"This is the start of our fairytale," I said. "A happy ending and a new beginning all rolled into one. We are so blessed, Damien."

"Don't cry Steph," he said softly and pulled me closer. "It's going to be alright, exactly what you said, our happy ending and new beginning. Let's call it our happy beginning shall we?" He looked at me intensely and without words I knew what his heart was saying.

I love you, I forgive you, thank God I'm alive.

"I love that. Our happy beginning," I whispered. "And I love you."

"That's a relief!" he said sarcastically and the mood lightened. "Otherwise I'd have to find someone else who would stand in, and Jude wouldn't look very good in that frock you brought."

There was a sound of a car coming up the drive and I walked to the window. "It's my parents," I said, knowing that I would be happy to see them but also knowing that Mum had been building up to this since we first mentioned it.

"I have everything clenched," said Damien in fun.

Mum tottered out of the passenger side looking fabulous in her designer outfit and feathery fascinator, more mother of the bride than glamourous granny, so entirely and accidently fitting for the occasion. I could hear Josie greeting them and telling them to make themselves at home, and answering questions about the children's entertainer and the florist.

"Shall I put Mia's dress on and go down with her?" suggested Damien "That way your mum can parade her around a bit while she's all frilled up."

"Yes, that would be perfect, thank you. It would be good to arrive without baby sick on my shoulder, and mum's wearing cream anyway," I chuckled.

"I'll take one of those muslin squares," said Damien. "The ones your dad calls Muslims."

"It's ok, Asha's heard him before," I said. "Will you come back up and zip me up please?"

"Of course," he said, pulling Mia's pyjamas off and slipping on the gorgeous cream gown we'd chosen.

"Do you want to do something with her hair, Steph?" he said putting her chubby feet into tights and then adding the satin slippers with pink rose buds. I was sitting at Josie's dressing table with my make-up scattered across the top brushing on bronzer.

"Just wet it a bit at the back where it's sticking up and comb it through, it will curl up at the ends no matter what you do but you can at least tackle the bed head for today."

"Roger that." said Damien reaching for the soft white baby hairbrush that I'd packed.

"Right, be back in five," he made his way to the door. "Unless I get trapped by your mother."

"Put your mobile in your pocket, I'll ring you if you're not back soon," I said and off he went.

The naming ceremony was beautiful, and Mia was in good spirits. It was at the end of the service and after the registrar had completed the readings about children being blessings and family being our cornerstone, that Damien stood up to make our announcement. The registrar graciously took a seat and allowed Damien to take the floor. A couple of people turned and looked at me inquisitively, the last announcement that we had made like this had changed just about everyone's life in this room – but this one was our own personal victory.

"I just wanted to say a few words," he started and took a moment to look around the room and smile as his eyes met mine. "You all know that Steph and I have had a battle on our hands these last months, and that I have been really unwell." I could feel the energy in the room starting to change and I heard someone sniff.

"It has been the darkest time of our lives," he continued, "going through something like this forces you to consider things that none of us want to, and that, along with the incessant fear that your time is running out, is a weight that you feel crushing you more and more each day. It's beyond hard, thinking that your time might be cut short. But not for you. It was always, always about leaving the two people I loved most. The fear was fear for them, not me. I can take what life has to throw, but I couldn't bear the thought of what Steph and Mia would have to go through." He paused to compose himself and fight back tears that I knew would flow in any moment anyway.

"That ate me up more than any cancer could," he said into the room filled with love, respect and heartbreak for the journey we had recently been forced to walk.

"But I am here today as the bearer of good news," his tone changed and he became more upbeat. A murmur passed through the audience like a ripple and Damien smiled through his tears. "We found out only a few days ago that the tumour has shrunk so considerably in such a short space of time, that the consultant called it a miracle." He had hardly finished the sentence when I ran to him. Applause broke out all around us, whooping and high fives filled the air and I felt his arms holding me tight and his tears on my skin, whilst gratitude surged through every single part of me.

After nearly everyone had approached us to shake Damien's hand, high five him or hug him, and I'd had my fair share of it as well, I managed to find a lull in the conversation and get to Mum and Dad.

"Can I borrow you two for a minute please?" I asked.

"Darling, I could do with a drink after that. God it's fantastic news, it really is a miracle!" said Mum.

"Your mother's right love, the best news we could have wished for, we're over the moon for you both," said Dad.

Mum gave me a grilling on the way up the stairs to Josie's bedroom about why I hadn't told her days ago, but she soon got over it when I explained what was going to happen next.

"Mum, I need you to keep hold of Mia while Dad gives me away again!" I said. "Damien's telling everyone to take their seats again and to expect a surprise."

"Yes, yes of course I will Stephanie but you'll need to put some more make-up on as well. Quite honestly, darling, you look like you've been dragged through a hedge."

She was blunt, but actually right. Mia had tugged on my bun and wispy bits of hair were straggled onto my shoulders, and my tears had washed away most of my makeup.

"Mia go to Granny and I'll be back in a moment," I said and handed her over.

Five minutes later and Dad was zipping me up. "You look beautiful Stephanie, absolutely beautiful," he said as I linked his arm and made my way downstairs.

"Mum, don't cry!" I whispered to her in the entrance hall.

"It's my prerogative as mother of the bride!" she sniffed. "You look so beautiful darling, and you've even lost weight."

I chuckled and asked her to go inside the main doors that led to the vast living room where everyone was seated, and to give Damien a thumbs up. Dad turned to me as the sound of music filled the air, the same track that we had chosen last time.

"I am so proud of you," he said through glistening eyes, framed by feathered wrinkles and shining with the memories of my childhood.

"I love you, Dad," I said and walked through the door to gasps and then applause as I made my way towards the rest of my life, my happy beginning.

Chapter 69

"What a day!" said Damien in the back of the cab "I'm wiped out."

"Me too," I answered. "But I'm also starving."

"Could you swing by the Chinese please, mate?" said Damien to the driver who didn't mind, we were on the meter after all. Damien phoned our order in and we sat back in the darkness, all tipsy and loved up and talked about life in general.

"It was good of your mum to take Mia," said Damien. "We can have an actual Lie In."

"We're so rock and roll aren't we?" I laughed. "An ACTUAL Lie In."

The driver pulled into the bus stop outside the takeaway and Damien jumped out. A couple of minutes passed and he came back empty-handed. "It's bloody well rejected my card, have you got yours?" he said.

"Oh, yes it's in my purse in the suitcase."

"Great, I must have put the wrong pin number in. I suppose I am pissed!" he said as the driver opened the boot.

"It's Mia's birthday!" I shouted after him.

"Is it? Bloody hell do you think she'll know we forgot?"

"The pin number!" I laughed. "It's Mia's birthday, you can remember that, right?"

"Yes of course I can!" he said confidently, but I had my doubts. He appeared shortly with a carrier bag. "Well that was bloody well embarrassing. Turns out I don't know my own child's birthdate, after all."

"What happened?" I laughed at him and took back my card.

"I messed it up again but they took pity on me and it's on the slate," he said "I'll have to go to the cash point tomorrow and see if I can unlock our cards."

"You're just tipsy," I said. "Either that or the Visa system's down. It happened to me before in a supermarket and no one could pay."

"Someone managed to pay between my card and your card," Damien said. "It's just me being a moron, Ryan will sort it out for me tomorrow."

"It was nice seeing them today, his wife is lovely."

"Yes, they are nice people. We are lucky to have good friends." The taxi driver pulled onto our road and Damien handed him the last of the cash we had, which worked in his favour tip wise. We ate and then made our way up to bed, collapsing in a food coma and looking forward to sleeping past six in the morning with no night time feed to worry about.

"Morning," Damien said, as he slid his arm around my waist and curled his leg over mine.

"Is it?"

"It's nearly lunchtime."

"Already?" I asked, feeling Damien's arousal through his boxer shorts and hardening into the small of my back. He kissed the back of my neck and his hand wandered up towards my breasts, which responded to his touch, and I sighed softly. I was just about to roll onto my back and into his arms when the sound of the phone ringing stole the moment.

"It's probably your mum," he said, with his fingertips lingering on the waistband of my pyjama bottoms. We both listened as the answerphone kicked in.

"Damien, it's Ryan here. Sorry to bother you at home but something's come up and we need to talk urgently. Catch me on my mobile, you've got the number."

Damien pulled away from me as his mobile started to ring on the bedside, clearing his throat and sitting up he answered it, somewhat defensively.

"Hey Ryan, what's up?"

Although I couldn't clearly hear what Ryan was saying, I did manage to pick up the odd word here and there including fraud and hacked.

"Cleaned out?" Fucking cleaned out? Jesus Christ, Ryan! What the actual fuck are you guys doing about this? I thought your security was tighter than a duck's arse?" He was pacing now and running his fingers through his tufty hair that was growing back in shades of brown and grey.

"Fine, get here as soon as you can," he said and hung up, standing in front of me shaking his head in disbelief and shock written all over his face.

"The company bank account's been cleaned out," he said. "The whole lot, gone."

"How?" I said, and regretted it, his anger wasn't aimed at me but I was the only one there to take the hit.

"How do I fucking know? I don't know! Apparently Ryan doesn't know, some bastard better know because there was a whole load of money in there that's not in there now!" He paced again and threw open a drawer. Pulling on jeans and a t-shirt, and trying to contain his temper, he turned to me sitting upright in bed.

"Look, I'm sorry. I know that this isn't your fault, Steph. It's the bank's fuck up and they can sort it out. I need to go now, I'll call you."

And with that he walked out of the bedroom and slammed the door in temper.

Chapter 70

I sent Mum a text saying that I had a hangover and could she keep Mia until tea time, then I took a shower and phoned Lizzie. The legal system was her department, and fraud surely came under that heading.

"Hacked?" she asked me. "What do you mean by hacked exactly?"

"I don't know Lizzie, he went nuclear when the call came in and started shouting about being hacked and cleaned out, and that it was the bank's fault, a security breach or something."

"The bank will have some responsibility, but it's only up to a certain amount per account, I think," she said. "Let me look into it in terms of business banking. Are your current accounts with the same bank?"

"Yes, we did a switchover and Ryan handled everything a couple of years back."

"Did you have much in them?" she asked.

"We did in one account, the rainy day account we called it. That's where we kept most of it, we cashed in stuff that wasn't performing at the same time we did the switchover so that we could have all of our funds in one place. We were going to decide how much to tie up once Damien had sold the business."

"Well let's hope that hasn't been cleaned out as well, Steph."

"Oh, God," I started to cry. "Our cards were both refused last night when we went for food, Damien thought he'd entered the wrong pin number, he was pissed – we both were."

"Or lack of funds," Lizzie stated what I was thinking.

"Looks like it's more than just a rainy day, Steph. It may well have become torrential."

Ryan looked very concerned when I opened the door, I busied myself making coffee and heard Damien's raised voice from the kitchen.

"What do you mean an unknown account?" he shouted. "You've got a full bloody tech squad, get onto it and find our money."

I tentatively carried the tray through with three steaming cups, guessing that at least one of them would end up thrown against the wall if Damien didn't calm down.

"The tech guys are on it, they started looking into it straightaway but they have nothing conclusive yet," Ryan said, and I could tell he was extremely uncomfortable. Both he and I were braced for the response.

Don't shoot the messenger, Damien.

"For fuck's sake," Damien spat in Ryan's direction. "Look, I'm sorry, but you do know how much was at stake here?"

"Yes I do," said Ryan soberly.

"Of course you do, you're my bloody relationship manager, whatever that means."

I cast a sympathetic look in Ryan's direction and he sent one back. Just then his mobile rang and he took it from his inside pocket.

"Yes, yes, ok," he said. "Did you find anything else?"

He spoke for a couple of minutes while Damien paced and I alternated looking at him and then back at Ryan, whose body language gave nothing away. He hung up and spoke to Damien.

"It seems that the funds were transferred out on Saturday evening, into an overseas account."

"Where exactly?"

"We think it's South America, but that could be a holding account, it could be moved on again, and the trouble is that we have no quick access to information there because of time differences, language barriers and the fact that it's a different bank. Money can be moved instantly in this day and age when it's electronic, and by the time we crack an international fraud situation it's sometimes too late."

"Christ, Ryan! You're telling me it could be gone? But you insure people against this kind of thing, though?"

"Yes, we do to some extent but it depends on the circumstances." Ryan was trying to calm Damien down but his last comment was like a red flag to a bull.

"I'll tell you what the circumstances are," Damien started to speak quietly through gritted teeth, "I've been fucking robbed, and you need to sort it out."

"We'll have to involve the police," said Ryan.

"Good," replied Damien. "You do that."

Ryan stood up to leave. "I'll see myself out. Thanks for coffee Steph," he mumbled. "And for what it's worth you are the last people I would have ever wanted this to happen to."

Chapter 71

My fingers flew over the keyboard as I logged into Facebook and accepted the friend request that Louisa had sent days earlier. Her page loaded up with pictures of her all suntanned and bikini clad, hash tagging all over the place about beaches, booze and boys. There were a couple of photos of a luxurious hotel suite, a view of the pool from a balcony and then bingo. She'd used the Facebook check-inn app that stated her exact location, Peru.

I was making my way back downstairs to tell Damien that I'd solved the mystery when even more evidence presented itself.

"Inside job?" I heard him talking on the phone. I presumed it was to Ryan. "You've got to be kidding. Yes I'll meet you at the office with the police."

He turned to look at me, furious and vulnerable at the same time. I went to him and put my arms around him, feeling the weight of him lean into me and his head on my shoulder.

"How could anyone do this to me?" he said. "To us?"

And that's what it was all about. Losing the money would be a blow, but we could get that back. For Damien, to think that someone that he had helped and supported, taken care of and given a chance, to could rip him off so royally was the ultimate betrayal.

Betrayal – and there it is in all its glory.

"Who could have done it? I mean who's techy?" he thought out loud. "That kid in the high street branch that we took on, the gangly one that quit college, he's techy. I think he revamped the website."

"Damien, I think I know who did it."
"What about that old bastard Mark that I had to make redundant last year, the one with BO that was fiddling his expenses?" He was pacing again.
"Damien, I think I know…"
"Or that big lass that had a sickness record as long as your arm that got caught looking in someone's bag? She threatened with unfair dismissal until I said she could go quietly or we'd get the police in."
"It was Louisa!" I said, and waited.
"What?" he asked. "What did you say?"
"It was Louisa."
"But she's away on holiday."
"In Peru."
"Which is in South America."

"Ryan, listen I think I know who it was." Damien spoke on hands-free as we made our way to the office to meet the police. "Remember that girl that you met called Louisa? Well she's only in bloody Peru for her holidays and Facebooking herself in the lap of luxury paid for by yours truly."
"Great, we've caught her red-handed. I'll see you in five." After he hung up I suggested that we should call Helen and give her the heads up.
"We don't want to scare her, especially if the police arrive before us," I said to Damien, hoping she wasn't going to pass on the sickness bug that had stopped her from showing up at the weekend.
"Just text her," he said abruptly, and I did.
When we arrived moments later, the office was closed.

"Lazy bitch," Damien said under his breath as he got out and slammed the door.

"She's probably still ill," I said, stating the obvious but not wanting to upset him more.

"She could have bloody phoned in sick then and I could have been here. The phone will have been ringing off the hook. I'd like to protect some kind of income for us if I can." He opened the shutters and filled up the kettle, mumbling to himself as I perched on Helen's desk, next to Damien's laptop.

"I am obviously a hideous judge of character," he started to rant. "All I have ever done is help people and give them a chance, and they have ended up shitting all over me from a great height. Wait a minute, that's my bloody laptop!"

Ryan walked in the door followed by two police officers as Damien opened the lid and the screen lit up.

"Wait, Damien," said Ryan. "We might need the IT equipment to go to forensics."

"For God's sake Ryan, this is my laptop and it's been missing for months now."

"Even more reason that we take a look." A woman stepped forwards and introduced herself as Detective Inspector Jessica Wright. Her chubby colleague was Andrew Collings.

"Just what exactly are you implying?" said Damien, immediately on the defensive.

"I'm implying that if your laptop went missing and now it's back then it could have been used in the crime."

"That's great. So you're accusing me? Perfect. I've robbed my bloody self."

"No, Mr Anderson, we aren't saying that. We're saying that someone else could have used your laptop to send funds overseas." The plain-looking detective turned to Ryan. "You said on the phone something about a one-way ticket?"

"You didn't mention that to me!" snapped Damien.

"I had tech ring me in the car and tell me that there were two transactions on the business account. There was the large withdrawal that went overseas, and a payment to an airline that we've deduced was going in the same direction."

"It's got to be Louisa," I said with conviction. "She's been after you and the business since day one Damien. I told you she was bad news. She's been a calculated bitch and she's meant to take us down."

"Who is this Louisa?" asked DI Wright.

"She's a lying cow that Damien employed a few months ago, that he trained to do payroll and oversee all of the branches while he was off sick."

"So she had access to internet banking and the company account?" DI Wright turned to Damien for confirmation.

"Yes, yes she did." He shook his head. "God I am so stupid. I should have listened to you, Steph, when you said she was trouble."

"She's a con artist Damien, and she's probably very good at it. Don't beat yourself up, it's no good doing that we have to find a way through this," I said. "And I know where she is."

"Do you?" asked DI Wright, pulling out a notebook and pen.

"Yes, she's in Peru at a five-star hotel. She's been Facebooking for the last ten days about how fabulous her life is."

"Ten days?" interrupted Ryan.

"Yes."

"Well it's not her then, at least the flight wasn't her. That was booked on Saturday morning and left on Saturday night. It was in between the two that the funds were taken."

We all turned as the postman opened the door and handed me a stack of mail. On the top was a postcard, the picture was the London Eye and Tower Bridge, the postmark was Heathrow. My heart sank as I absently turned it over and saw two words and a kiss.

Ugly Betty x

Chapter 72

As the story unravelled, redundancies had to be made and branches had to close. If we'd had enough of our own money to bankroll the business for a while, we would have. But for now we had to rely on Mum and Dad to keep us going.

Damien hated letting people down and spent may sleepless nights talking about families and how he wanted to do more to help them. He knew it wasn't our fault, but it didn't make it any easier to swallow. He'd called an emergency staff meeting the day after we'd realised it was Helen that had used Damien's laptop to transfer the money out of our personal accounts and the business. The police came along and verified his story, and appealed for both discretion and further information.

Damien had saved the passwords for internet banking onto the device and when she'd logged on it had been easy. This had created a conflict of interest with the bank in terms of insurance. There was a duty of care from the customer and apparently we'd messed up by having the passwords saved and the laptop available. Damien had argued that the pin number that the bank phones you with when you create a new recipient was not secure enough. Helen must have been bricking it that they could have called his mobile, but luckily for her he had nominated his direct line as the primary contact number and she'd created the new payment as she was sitting at his desk.

Friends and family were supportive and some that we'd given money to offered it back. We said no for the moment. Ryan had managed to negotiate an overdraft on the company account on the strength of the rental properties the business managed. It was a case of starting from the ground up, but it was money coming in every month and Damien managed to keep his office open.

After a few months the betrayal didn't sting so much. I knew that the feeling of being tricked and stolen from would be with us for a long time, but the more distance we got from the actual event, the less consuming it was. Damien was working near normal hours again and actually enjoying going in each day. He had bought the business in the first place because he liked people and buildings, and as the business had grown, his job had morphed into management responsibilities and fire-fighting. He was far more relaxed when he came home now, far more like the Damien I'd first met. I knew that he was worried about money, and who wouldn't be? Ultimately things would be fine, Mia's financial future was safe because of the trust we'd created and we could borrow from that if we really had to. It was the month-to-month money at the moment that needed more flow. Damien was used to drawing a salary every month and then a dividend on top. We'd never had an extravagant lifestyle, but these days any purchases had to be very considered. Luckily, I had past experience that I could draw on and I started to list all of Mia's old baby clothes and toys on eBay which created money for grocery shopping and petrol.

I wished I could contribute more, but there was no way I could go and get any kind of proper job and pay for childcare. Even leaving her with Mum was a round trip that would cost petrol money, which would equate to nearly a day's work, and I didn't want to keep borrowing from my parents. We'd given them a lump sum in the first place to help them in their older age to have a more comfortable life, and I didn't want to take that back now, even though they would have given it freely. Even though things were tight, there was a feeling of teamwork, of solidarity and pulling together that felt good.

I needed something I could do from home to create an income for us, and not just eBay income. I needed something regular and substantial that would make a difference.

You've already got it, do what you are here to do.

I spent hours looking online at part-time opportunities with flexible hours, and realised I that the only ones I could seriously consider were an Avon lady or nightshift shelf stacker if I wanted to be with Mia through the day. Neither stirred my soul with passion and excitement, but I wasn't workshy and it would likely be temporary.

I started filling out online applications and sighed. What was I doing? Running from my destiny because of fear. My book had been formatted and was ready to be loaded up as an ebook. I was a couple of clicks of a mouse away from being an author and I was the only one standing in my way.

I'd managed to grow my Facebook page to several thousand. People were loving the content I was posting and more than likely they would love my book. We needed the income and I had a way of creating it, and I could stay at home. It was perfect – so why was I so scared?

"You can do this!" I said and before I had time to reconsider, I uploaded the cover and the interior file for ebook publication, telling myself that no one would even know it was there until I started to promote it. I was completely in control, but didn't feel it at all.

Stephanie's Journal ~ Lesson 22
Don't Stay a Victim

Being betrayed can bring up a whole raft of feelings - anger, resentment and pain to name a few. We might even go into questioning our own worthiness, and ask why this has happened to us. The way that other people behave often has nothing to do with us. Betrayal is driven fear, perceived physical and emotional needs and ego. It is marked by a lack of integrity and honestly, and people avoid this because they know it will bring pain or harm to others. They are scared of telling the truth to you and so they become a version of themselves that is not authentic and not aligned with who they really are.

This is their stuff, and although you may have attracted the experience as a lesson to share at this time, the way that you process and deal with the experience is what you need to focus on. Look at what you can learn and take from the situation. Work on moving forward and when you can face it applying some forgiveness. Change your story around what happened and check you are not getting sucked into the drama or getting stuck in victim mode. Know that anger and resentment can be detrimental to your well-being, do what you can to release it. What we send out, we attract - and that goes for us all. The universe has it covered so take what you need to and work on letting the rest go.

"Sometimes the person you would take a bullet for, ends up being the person behind the trigger." Taylor Swift

Chapter 73

I didn't tell Damien that I'd uploaded and effectively self-published my book, in fact I didn't tell anyone. I kept working on my Facebook page for a couple of hours a day, and when the title was live I took a deep breath and posted the link. I worked out that if I added the link retrospectively to a Facebook poster that had a lot of shares, that link would show up on every share. This meant that I needed to create posters that were engaging, funny, poignant and inspiring and share worthy – as well as juggling a baby, a husband and a house.

I did this religiously for four weeks, with the expectation that I'd be receiving a payment at the end of the month. After several days of watching my inbox I realised that the platforms I was using paid out two months after the sales had come through. I tried to forget about it and get on with my day-to-day stuff but I was bursting to tell someone.

One afternoon at soft play I was sitting with Mel and it slipped out. She'd bought the coffees (again) and I told her that soon I'd be reciprocating.

"It's just a coffee, Steph," she said. "We're friends and it's fine."

"I know, but I'm just saying that I'll be making some pocket money soon."

Ask me, ask me!

"Oh yes?" she asked and I feigned feeling compromised for a split second and then I spilt my guts.

"You know that book idea I told you about?" I said and Mel nodded. "Well I've done it!"

"What? You finished it?" she asked, sounding excited.

"Yes! And not only that, I've uploaded it for sale!" I smiled like a lunatic through clenched teeth.

"Seriously?" she said.

"Yes!" I squeaked.

"Oh my God!" said Mel and reached into her handbag for her phone. "I'm going to search for you, did you use your own name?"

"Of course I did, but listen Mel you're the only one that knows so far, apart from people on Facebook."

She belly-laughed at my naivety. "Oh right, well if it's just on Facebook, no one will know."

"I mean that I haven't told anyone in my real life," I defended myself. "Not even Damien."

"Why not, Steph? It's something to be super proud of, you should be shouting from the rooftops."

"There's nothing on your Facebook page about it." Mel was scrolling through my hideously boring personal timeline.

"I've built a proper page," I said, "where I'm promoting it."

"You dark horse! What's it called?" she asked, eager to start typing.

Moments later my page appeared on her phone.

"Nice," she said and kept searching. "Here we are. Wow Steph have you seen how many likes you've got?"

"Well I've been doing bits and bobs on there for a couple of hours a day so it's starting to pay off now."

"Pay off? You've got over thirty thousand followers! Steph, that's amazeballs!"

"I'm hoping that it translates into helping people and creating an income for me as well, but I have no idea how much I'm going to get or when because I'm a total tech fail."

"Well I'm not," said Mel, and clicked through the links on my Facebook page to the listing. "Ok so you're number sixteen in metaphysical and visionary category and number thirty two in spiritual guidance."

"How do you know that?" I gasped. I had no idea how many books were listed in those categories but my ranking sure sounded impressive.

"Here," Mel leaned in and showed me on her phone where the chart position was. "And here is your sales dashboard."

It looked just like a spreadsheet with different currencies and amounts listed in rows.

"But what does it mean?" I asked and Mel zoomed in and started to jot down numbers on the back of a napkin.

"It means that in three weeks' time you're going to get last months' sales, and that's going to be one thousand, four hundred and eighty three pounds."

"No way."

"Way!" Mel laughed.

"Oh My God!" I said and sat agape, before I joined her in fits of giggles.

"This is amazing!" said Mel. "I am super proud of you, and Damien will be too."

"I can't wait to tell him, he'll be so relieved that there's more money coming in."

"And make sure you tell him about the reviews as well." said Mel, still transfixed to the tiny screen. "You've got seventeen reviews so far and all are five-star, apart from one, which is a four. Steph, you have to read these, people are saying your book is changing their lives."

Mel handed me the phone and I looked through the list, swelling with pride and fighting back tears that the lessons I had shared with the world could possibly have made such a big impact on anyone's life, including my own.

Stephanie's Journal ~ Lesson 23
Walk the Path For You

As humans it is so easy to get fixated on the final destination that we forget about the journey of life. The value is in the journey; the challenges and the lessons that help us to evolve, even with the detours and dead ends.

Having a belief that everything is happening in your favour will help you to trust that the bumps in the road are a part of the plan.

Perhaps they are preparing you for something later. We all come to earth with a soul curriculum and plan, and sometimes, when the universe appears to be knocking you off your path, it's actually showing you a short cut that you haven't recognized yet.

"You are the universe expressing itself as a human for a little while." Eckhart Tolle

Chapter 74

I had everything planned and when Damien came home there was a vegetable lasagne in the oven, a lovely bottle of wine breathing on the kitchen counter and Mia nodding off in my arms after her bedtime bottle. I was going to wait until after we'd eaten to tell him, it was no good trying to talk when he was hungry.

He carried Mia upstairs as I served up and we sat in front of the television on low volume, small talking about the day and feeding our faces.

"Damien," I started after we'd both cleared our plates. "I have some exciting news."

"Oh?" he asked, flicking through the planner to see what we could watch.

"Yes, super exciting actually. I've got some wine open so we can have a toast." I took the plates into the kitchen and reappeared with two large glasses of Cabernet Sauvignon. He looked at me expectantly and I explained that I'd known he was worried about money, and that I knew it would be totally short term and I had faith in him building the business back up again, but I loved it that he was less stressed and more available at home…

"Spit it out, Steph!" he laughed and took a gulp of his wine.

"Oh God, I don't know how to say it really." I squirmed in my seat and gulped back some wine too.

"Well?" he asked and raised his eyebrows.

"Well," I took a deep breath. "I listed my book for sale like you said, and it's started to sell!"

"That's great!" he said, and grinned from ear to ear. "I knew you could do it! I am so proud of you for getting over your fears and getting out there, even if it doesn't make much money Steph, that's fine, I just love it that you've done it." He raised his glass and so did I. As they chinked together in celebration I spoke again.

"The thing is that it is making money, my first month's royalties are one thousand, four hundred and eighty three pounds." I waited for a reaction.

"Bloody hell, Steph, that's brilliant!" he said "Are you sure?"

"Yes, Mel showed me how to look at my sales reports today," I said. "And that's just for the ebook downloads as well. There are people asking on my Facebook page for paperback copies as well and I don't think it's that hard to get them done either. There's this thing called print on demand and you don't even have to have any stock."

"I don't want to say that I don't believe it, because I have always had faith in you, but I seriously don't believe it!" He laughed and so did I.

"I know!"

"This could be the start of something really amazing, like really, really amazing Steph, I have such a feeling about it."

"Me too, it feels so good to be contributing to us financially and helping other people as well. That was always my intention, as you know. Some of the reviews say that it's life changing, I honestly can't believe they're talking about my book."

"Believe it my love, your time has come," Damien said, leaning forward and kissing me with gusto. "Maybe the universe was conspiring to make us skint so that you'd finally get out there."

Before we went to sleep we talked in the dark about marketing, distribution and a sequel, all ideas that made me feel totally out of my depth and ridiculously excited at the same time.

"Who knows, we might even be able to make a million?" I said.

"And why not? That would be amazing, and I have every faith in you," he sighed and kissed the back of my neck. "Actually the police called me today, speaking of millions."

"Oh?"

"Yes, they'd had a tip off that Helen was coming back into the country and she was arrested on the tarmac at Heathrow."

I braced myself for the barrage of anger that Damien must have been feeling towards her.

"They wanted to know if we wanted to press charges."

"Right," I said, then cautiously. "What did you tell them?"

"I said no," he sighed.

"I don't get it?" I asked.

"They told me what she'd been through Steph, and I couldn't make things worse for her. I know what she did was wrong and it's been financially horrendous for us, but when they told me her story, I honestly didn't have the heart to kick her when she's down, no matter what she's taken from us."

He took a deep breath and continued. "Apparently she'd been suckered into an online scam where men from Africa and South America groom vulnerable women from the UK and then rip them off. She'd been talking to him for a few months and he'd seemed really plausible, the police assured me that they are professionals and they look for middle-aged, plain-looking women who don't have a marital status on their Facebook profile."

"Oh God, that's awful," I said.

"Really awful, Steph. He'd been sending her pictures and writing her poetry and all kinds to reel her in. Telling her he was falling in love with her and that he needed to meet her and be with her, he'd skyped her but told her that she couldn't skype him because it was from an internet café and he could only afford to go once a week… it goes on and on and she got further and further in. She started to send him some of her wages, but he spun her more and more lies, saying that his life was in danger if he didn't get out of the country and that he needed to go into hiding. He said that he would travel to stay with a friend and then onwards to buy them a house and he would wait for her."

"I feel sick Damien. I think I know where this is going."

"The police showed me some of the emails with attachments from alleged estate agents that were going to rent them a house to begin with until they knew which neighbourhood they wanted to settle in, and it had to be near a nursery for the children they would have. They said that in one email she had admitted that she was a virgin, and he'd made all kinds of promises to her about treating her with respect and love and that they were soul mates. They said it's like rain in the desert for women like Helen, they feel loved for the first time and they just can't help themselves."

"And then they go in for the kill," I said.

"Then they start to ask for the big bucks and turn the volume right up on the manipulation, she was desperate Steph. He promised her the earth and when she transferred the funds to him he promised that he would meet her from the plane, and they'd book into a hotel for their first night together and then fly out in the morning to start their life together."

"So what happened?" I was almost frightened to ask.

"She arrived in Mexico City late at night expecting to be swept away by Prince Charming, instead she found herself waiting for four hours frantically messaging a Facebook account that was suddenly unresponsive until eventually she was blocked. By which time she had no battery on her phone, and she was tired and hungry. Apparently she flagged down a cab which cost her most of the currency she had taken and stayed at a nearby hotel. The rest of her time there was pretty horrendous to be honest, she ran out of money quickly and had some time on the streets where she was beaten up."

"Oh God, Damien, that's terrible." Lovely quiet Helen wouldn't have stood a chance out there, it sounded like the price of love had been a whole lot more than the money we lost. We had made fun of her lonely life, and even worse than that – she'd heard.

"I know, I know," he said and I could tell that he was trying to reconcile his feelings and have compassion for her, but he was still angry and perhaps feeling guilty just as I was.

"How did she get back?" I asked.

"Someone said she should go to the British Consulate and tell them what had happened, so she did and they contacted her parents who wired her some money for the airfare home and for food and clothes."

"The poor girl," I said.

"Yes, literally."

"She's certainly paid her penance."

"You know what, I think she has," said Damien. "And I feel sorry for her. Don't get me wrong I'm still peeved, but I know in time I'll get over that. My life is full of things that money can't buy Steph, and hers was empty – she chased after what we've got."

"We are so blessed Damien, and we'll be ok money wise as well."

"Yes, I think we will be." I felt him lie back down and relax a little. "To be honest it's a lot less stress to be back in the branch, I didn't realise how much I'd missed it."

"And I love having you less stressed and home at a proper time, so does Mia."

"And I love it that you've taken the plunge with your book and it's doing well."

"We've got nothing to complain about really, Steph, and everything to be grateful for. It was only a few weeks ago that I was thinking about my funeral and now I've got the odds stacked in my favour again. I'm the luckiest man alive. I might not forgive Helen straightaway, but I'm working on it.

You have to look past what someone's done to appreciate their motive or intention, and hers was never to do anything other than find love. I've got that in bucketfuls and I wouldn't change that for any amount of money."

"I love you," I said. "And I love that you can have some compassion for Helen, I'm working on that too."

"The money is long gone now, Steph, and I refuse to drag the resentment round for any longer than I have to. It's not going to change a thing apart from robbing me of joy in the now with my beautiful wife and child."

"When did you get so wise?" I asked.

"I downloaded your book while you were washing up and started to read it."

"You'd better leave a five-star review," I joked.

"I certainly will, it's changed my life already."

He drifted off to sleep far more easily than before, and I said another silent thank you to a universe that was helping us both grow in amazing ways.

Chapter 75

Life was good, and I was living in The Flow.

Damien's business was building nicely and his latest scan showed no trace of the tumour at all. My book was doing well and I was looking at ways to get distribution into shops, to go more mainstream and to help more people. Mia was adorable and changing every day. Moments were precious and for the most part we managed to remember that, and stay as present as we could. We made the little things count, we were in gratitude and we were in love with life and each other. I felt like another cycle was complete, and the Happy Beginning that I'd manifested was working out perfectly.

When the first consignment arrived of my paperback copies, I posted one to Jude, Asha and Sheila. I posted one through Josie's letterbox and made my way to Sue.

"I love it!" she said, flicking through the pages and stroking the cover. "It's got a great energy about it Steph, it's going to help so many people and truly be the making of you."

"Do you still believe that?" I asked. "I mean the sales are coming in every month and it's like having a wage, Sue, I love it. It means that I can be at home with Mia and spend time growing my Facebook page, which in turn reaches more people and sells more books."

"That's just the start for you," Sue said. "I think you're building a foundation here that a big publisher will find very attractive one day in the future."

"I hope so, that would mean that I could reach a whole new audience."

"It would mean that you would be stepping up to play your part in the consciousness shift, which is why you came," she said. "And the universe will reward you for that. You've come such a long way, Stephanie, it's been a pleasure to see you blossom."

"How long do you think it will be? Until I get a big break?" I asked.

"I can't say exactly, but it doesn't feel like far away," Sue replied.

"Is there anything I need to do?"

"Stay aligned and take inspired action as usual, be present and create the feeling that this has already happened in the now time."

"Right."

"But make sure that you have a strong belief that this is happening perfectly for you and your family and your book, an all-encompassing belief that it's all unfolding in a way that serves you best for your highest good. That way you won't be scared of it when it comes in. You do have a tendency to push things away when they start to show up because you go into fear."

"Ok, I'll work on that," I said.

"Good," Sue replied. "And there will be more lessons, so look out for them and keep moving forwards. I can't tell you what they are just now, but I do know that the first one will be about being in your truth, integrity, something on those lines, but that's all I'm being told."

"Thank you," I hugged her tight. "I'll come back for a full reading soon."

"Well, you know where I am," smiled Sue. "And thanks for this," she held the book close to her chest. "Thank you on behalf of me and the universe, it is much needed."

Chapter 76

Out of the blue one afternoon, the phone rang while I was cooking dinner, and the number was withheld. When I said hello there was a slight delay on the line, and then the friendly voice of an American lady who introduced herself as Madeline from the Madeline Kent Literary Agency. She told me that she'd read my book and all of my reviews, and that she had watched my Facebook page with interest.

It wouldn't put her off that I was self-published at all, in fact it showed initiative, hard work and the fact that the book had legs. As long as I owned all of the rights and I had no skeletons in my cupboard (now was the time to tell her - her reputation was priceless), then perhaps I'd like to consider working together.

"I must have emailed her ages ago, before we self-published the book," I explained to Damien.

"How does it work?" he asked.

"She's an agent, so she is working on my behalf. She goes out and gets the deal and gets a cut of it."

"Right, but what if it's a shitty deal?"

"Then I don't have to take it."

"Ok, and I'm guessing that they chase the big bucks so they can make more as well."

"Exactly. And she's made a lot of authors a lot of money."

"Well, you should go for it."

"There's only so much I can do with Facebook. If I want to really get out there and help more people, I need distribution, and that's really hard on your own."

"You should definitely get the contracts sent over and we'll look through them."

"This could be it!" I was cautiously excited.

"I seriously hope so, for you Steph, I would love that."

The day that Madeline called me to tell me that a publisher was interested in making me an offer I was in the supermarket pushing Mia around in the trolley and looking for baby wipes. The mobile signal wasn't very good and her voice cut in and out against a background of piped music and the bleeping from the till.

"Hi, Madeline, yes I'm great thanks." I covered one ear and paused by the shampoo, trying not to shout like a moron.

After the initial small talk she cut to the chase and started talking about an offer she had received on my behalf. My heart skipped a beat when I heard the words hundred thousand. I could hardly speak for the lump in my throat. I swallowed hard and blinked back tears.

"You have no idea what the money would do for us right now, Madeline. I am so, so grateful to you." In my mind I was joining up dots on how I'd tell Damien and how the pressure would be off until his business was booming again, I was truly elated. "One hundred thousand dollars would save us at the moment."

"Stephanie, are you ok? Honey I didn't say one hundred, I must have broken up – I said five hundred thousand."

Stephanie's Journal ~ Lesson 24
Your Message to the World

No one is here by accident. Think about it, years ago there was one sperm that made it against all the odds, to conceive one egg in exactly the right moment and biological conditions. You made it! And your soul chose to be here at this exact time. You are precious and you have something to share with the world.

This might be through your occupation, your parenting, the friendships you have and the life you live. And always, always shining your light and being yourself. The message that you have may be one of hope, of survival or of guiding others. It may need to be shouted out to the world in a big way, or whispered to someone's soul when they need it most, but regardless of that it is needed.

Your soul is here to find out who you are, and how you can contribute. Your message is important and it's time to make your voice heard in whatever way feels right to you.

"Your life is your message to the world, make sure it's inspiring." Unknown

Chapter 77

I doubted if things could get any better for us.

I was eventually starting to believe that I might deserve the life that I'd manifested. The time lapse between doubts creeping in was getting longer and longer. I know I am still a work in progress, and accepting that makes me human. It's laughable to look back and think that I had measured my worth based on the car I drove, the stuff I had and the job I held down. I'm sad to think that my self-worth was so practically non-existent that I believed spending money I didn't have, to impress people I didn't really like, was necessary to feel good enough.

Family, friends, health and love are where it's at, and I know that now. The rest is necessary nonsense that we have to go through in order to live a life as part of the human race. But it's not a race, it's a journey and there is great value in that if we will stop and look. My abundance only started to appear when I was able to work on my own stuff. If I had insisted on hanging on to the old story, the drama and the old ways then nothing would have changed. If I have any message to share above the lessons that you have read, it's that you are worthy of that as well.

I am managing to balance my book signings and appearances around my family life. Right now, I can hear Damien laughing with Mia in the garden as I write this, it's a summer's day and he is filling up an inflatable paddling pool with warm water for her to splash around in.

I know that there will be more lessons to come, and I hope that some might be easier than the ones I've already

been through – regardless though, I have a belief that they will be the right ones that I need to grow and evolve.
This is also my wish for you.

Before I shut down my laptop I double checked that Facebook posts were scheduled for the next twenty four hours and a red message flag caught my attention. Probably someone letting me know that they had read my book and loved it. I always made time to respond, even if it was just one line so that people felt valued. I opened the message and my heart sank down to my flip flops.

"I see that things seem to be turning out just fine for you and I wanted to share some photographs that I kept as a reminder of our night together, I think your fans would love them! If you want to ensure that these are kept private then maybe we should talk sooner rather than later."

If embarrassment could kill I'd have dropped down dead.

There I was lying on Jay's bed in all kinds of compromising positions that left not much at all to the imagination. I had blacked out, but the pictures told a very different version of events due to the blindfold he'd used along with other accessories I can't even bear to mention. Even though my eyes were covered, it was clearly me in the shot. It was heartbreakingly ironic that the wedding band Damien had commissioned to be inset with diamonds glinted on my finger.

For better or worse, and I guessed that things might be about to get a whole lot worse.

Summary of Twelve Lessons Later

Ready to connect with Kate?

Visit her website: www.kate-spencer.com

Also available:

The
Twelve
Lessons
Journal

By Kate Spencer

Not just a self-help book, and not just an inspirational diary.

Both.

Because you are living a spiritual life in real life.

Because you need space to write your everyday stuff, and factor in retrogrades and manifesting with the moon.

Because you need to know how to use the Twelve Lessons principles to create positive change in a real-life way.

Because you need to be organized (with a sprinkling of woo-woo).

A modern day spiritual manifesto, journal and diary all in one ~ infused with love, inspiration, support and encouragement to help you to create your best year yet.

Lightning Source UK Ltd.
Milton Keynes UK
UKOW04n1433201015

261003UK00003B/62/P